FAREWELL
GREAT KING

JILL PATON WALSH

FAREWELL
GREAT KING

COWARD, McCANN & GEOGHEGAN, INC.
NEW YORK

FOR TONY

CHARACTERS

ADEIMANTOS – Corinthian commander
ADMETOS – King of the Molossians
AESCHYLUS – Athenian dramatist
ALKMEON – an Athenian politician of the Alkmeonid family
AMEINIAS – an Athenian captain
ARISTAGORAS – the Milesian leader of the Ionian revolt
ARISTEIDES – Athenian democrat
ARISTOGEITON – tyrannicide
ARTAPHERNES – Persian satrap of Sardis
ARTAXERXES – Great King (464-424 BC), son of Xerxes
ARTEMISIA – Queen of Caria, an admiral in the Persian fleet

DARIUS – Great King (521-486 BC), father of Xerxes
DAMARATOS – Spartan King (c. 510-491 BC)
DATIS – a Mede, commander of the first Persian expedition against
   Athens

EPIKRATES – an adherent of Themistokles
EURYBIADES – Spartan commander of the Greek fleet

GELON – tyrant of Syracuse (485-478 BC)

HARMODIOS – tyrannicide
HIERON – tyrant of Syracuse (478-467 BC)
HIPPARCHOS – brother of Hippias
HIPPIAS – tyrant of Athens (527-510 BC)

Characters

ISAGORAS – Athenian oligarch, opponent of Kleisthenes

KALLIMACHOS – Athenian polemarch at the Battle of Marathon
KIMON – Athenian politician and general, son of Miltiades
KLEINIAS – an Athenian captain of the Alkmeonid family
KLEISTHENES – Athenian democratic reformer, an Alkmeonid
KLEOMENES – Spartan King (c. 519-487 BC)

LATYCHIDAS – Spartan King (c. 491-469 BC)
LEONIDAS – Spartan King (c. 487-480 BC)
LYKOS – a fictional character, friend of Themistokles

MARDONIOS – Persian commander at the Battle of Plataia
MEGAKLES – Athenian politician, an Alkmeonid
MILTIADES – an Athenian, tyrant of the Chersonese and general at the Battle of Marathon
MNESIPHILOS – an Athenian sage

PAUSANIAS – Spartan commander, nephew of Leonidas
PEISISTRATOS – tyrant of Athens (d. 527 BC)
PERICLES – son of Xanthippos, later famous as Athenian democratic statesman
PHRYNICHOS – Athenian dramatist

SIKINNOS – Persian slave of Themistokles
SOLON – Athenian lawgiver (archon 594/3 BC)
SOPHOCLES – Athenian dramatist

THEMISTOKLES – Athenian democratic statesman (c. 527-461 BC)
TIMOLEON – brother of Themistokles (real name unknown)

XANTHIPPOS – Athenian democrat, married into Alkmeonid family
XERXES – Great King (485-465 BC)

FAREWELL
GREAT KING

THE LETTER FROM THEMISTOKLES, LORD OF MAGNESIA IN THE SATRAPY OF YAUNA, TO ARTAXERXES THE KING, THE GREAT KING, THE ACHAEMENID, TRANSCRIBED INTO CUNEIFORM UPON TABLETS OF CLAY BY GUBARU THE SCRIBE; AND GUBARU MADE FOR EACH TABLET A TITLE, ACCORDING TO THE USAGE OF THE ARCHIVES OF THE KING AT SUSA. THE WORK FAITHFULLY COMPLETED ON THE TWENTY-EIGHTH DAY OF MARKHESHWAN IN THE SIXTH YEAR OF ARTAXERXES THE KING.

S A Y to Artaxerxes, the King, thus saith your servant Themistokles: Greetings, Great King, King of Kings, Lord of the East and West, King of the Lands, King of Anshan, King of Parsa, most favoured son of Ahura Mazda the All-High, Bringer of the New Year in the halls of Persepolis – three times I kiss the ground before you.

With this letter the messenger will bring you the news of my death. Your anger will be great to hear how I have deserted you, great and terrible. You will not read what I have to say. And yet, it may be, later, when your anger has cooled, Lord Artaxerxes, perhaps as you make a gift to some other man, you will ponder about it. 'To Themistokles the Athenian', you will say to yourself, 'I gave three cities, and land, and power, and a fine house, and vineyards. For five years I smiled upon him, and he flourished greatly, yet in the end the service he had promised me he denied me, preferring death.'

Do not hold back your hand from giving to that other man, Great King, whoever he may be; doubtless he will repay you better than I have done. But when you have dismissed him, then perhaps you will call for this letter, and a scribe to read it to you; you will learn, if it pleases you to learn it, why I have chosen to die.

I could say, 'Because I cannot perform what I rashly promised you; I cannot raise my hand against my native city. Therefore, Great King, tomorrow, going to perform the accustomed sacrifice, I shall drink the blood of the bull, and quench my thirst for death.'

And that would be answer enough for any Greek. But to a

Persian, who serves a great state, rather than a city, and is bound in honour to his King – that King who brings good order and justice to all who bow beneath his equal yoke, and whose rule would have kept peace between us for ever; to a Persian this answer is a Delphic answer, or no answer at all.

Still, it is all the answer I would give you, Great King, in return for three cities, and a governorship, and the wine and oil and gold I have received from you. You see how grudgingly, ungratefully, a Greek will serve a king. But because of other things, for other reasons, I will make you a better answer. One evening at Susa, for example, when I told you a sad tale of my broken drinking-cup, and you gave me from your own table a fluted goblet, propped on the back of a crouching golden lion. Or that day in Persepolis, when walking with me, you took my hand in yours, as though I had been your brother, and we talked of the gods of your country, and of mine, and of what the truth might be, as a Greek talks with his friends. Or the last time I attended you, in Sardis, nearer home, and we poured wine, and sat together, watching the setting sun.

When you gave me refuge, Great King, it was as a king you acted, in that you thought you could make use of me; and as a man you acted, in that my courage and cleverness pleased you. The King is doubtless angry with me for ever, for evading my obligations, failing to obey his orders; but the man was always magnanimous, and may yet wish to understand me. Because you have been my friend as well as my King, I will make you a better answer. This day, the last day I shall live, shall be for writing to you. I will make the best account I can of what I have been; the clearest defence I can of what I have done.

I am Themistokles, son of Neokles, of the deme Phrearros, of the tribe Leontis. I am an Athenian first, and anything else I am as well comes a long way after that. I dare say if you ever asked any of your father's commanders about my homeland they spoke slightingly of it; and it is true that the lands you have given me here are more fertile, and nearly as large as the whole of the lands the Athenians have ever owned, and to any eyes but mine, perhaps, more beautiful. Still, I have only to say to you, as you love your lands so I love mine ... you will understand me. You told me once a tale of Cyrus, who wanted to live still hardily in the barren hills, and not go down to the rich plains he had conquered, in case they corrupted his soldiers with sunny ease. Well, Attica, too, is harsh land, not fertile, where men break their backs hoeing a stony soil. It breeds proud men. I sleep softly and wake in comfort every day now, and yet like your Cyrus I still love the land that made me great. He wrote only, 'I, Cyrus, the King' upon his tomb; I have seen it. I would write, 'I, Themistokles, the Athenian' on mine, if I did not scorn to borrow another man's phrases, however fine. And I suppose, now I come to think of it, that someone will get my dust home to Attica, and so I will have to be buried in an unmarked place, and there will be no grand words written for me at all. For all that, and whatever harsh names they call me, there was never a time when I was not a good Athenian.

I remember a lesson at school once, when it was very hot, and we had learned and recited our Homer for the day, and been to the Palaestra for exercise, and returned tired to the master's house through the dusty streets, and instead of handing out wax tablets for writing he let us sit under the fig tree in the courtyard of his house and debate amongst ourselves. Each boy who spoke had to stand, as if he were addressing the assembly; it was a lesson still, in its way. The subject he gave us to talk on was 'What is the greatest good fortune the gods can bestow on a man?' I was a new pupil then, and I said nothing at first, but sat and listened, and enjoyed the shade of the fig tree, and wondered if any of the fruit was ripe enough to fall into my lap and, if it did, whether I could suck it without being seen.

Draco was saying that wealth was the best thing the gods could give; wide fields good enough to grow wheat, and a grove of old olives, wool and linen to wear, and horses, and a hoplite's armour made of the finest bronze, wrought like the shield of Achilles in Homer. The schoolmaster said these things were good, but there were men who had them all and found them not enough.

Diophon said that health was a better thing. It made a man take pleasure in every movement of his body, every step he took, and if he worked and trained hard it could bring the glory of a laurel crown at the Pythian Games, or at Olympia. Diophon was strong, and a good athlete; he hoped to gain a crown for running in the games that year. He was to lose his race, but to win a crown in the pentathlon three years later; but the master told him that such things were young men's pleasures, for a man who had won the crown had many years still to live in which he would lose the suppleness and strength of his finest years. Diophon was silent, and I knew why, for I had been to his house, and seen upon the wall a long row of vases of sacred oil which his father had won in the Panathenaic Games, for this event and for that; and his father had got his lovely vases still, but was grey now and walked with a slight stoop.

Archilochus said power was the great thing; could not a tyrant help himself to anything he lacked? The master was angry, and reminded us that tyrants might die violent deaths; and besides, he said, how could one call a man blessed by the gods who did evil while he lived?

Then Mychos said beauty might be the greatest luck. He looked sideways under his lashes at Diophon as he spoke, although Diophon did not look at him, either then or on any other occasion as far as I know. The master raised his eyes to look at his tree, and arranged his features to conceal the slight trace of emotion that had crossed them; then he advanced the same objection that he had raised to Diophon, that the gift in question was always much shorter than life, unless some misfortune cut off that life too soon.

Aeschylus said he would for himself prefer a power that could be used without force; the gift of a golden tongue, to move men and persuade them, to honour the god Dionysos in the theatre perhaps, or bring about a unanimous vote in the assembly. That certainly was a power I would have liked for myself too. The master smiled at Aeschylus, and said, 'My boy, if the little ode I found scarcely erased on your writing-tablet the other day is anything to go by, it may be you have the very gift you prize; go and make an offering in the shrine of the muses, and ask Apollo to make you fortunate.'

After that a silence fell, for it was awesome to think that Aeschylus, sitting among us, might have his heart's desire; then suddenly I said, 'I think you are all wrong!' getting to my feet in a graceless scramble as I spoke. The master looked surprised. I dare say he had not expected any of the smallest boys to speak.

'Well, Themistokles,' he said. 'Come on, let us hear it, since you know better than us all. Teach us; what is the greatest good luck the gods can bestow?'

'To be born an Athenian!' said I. Without realising it I had spread my arms wide as I said it, as if to embrace us all. Everyone laughed, and clicked their fingers at me; the master smiled deeply, and said:

'That is a good answer. There is truth in it.' And Diophon said joyfully, 'Tremendous! The greatest good luck the gods can give is something we all here have!' so that Mychos scowled at me, for having won a moment of Diophon's attention. But my moment of glory was brief, because another boy rose and spoke.

'Better than to be an Athenian,' he said, 'is to be a just man in any city.' He was a tall, lean boy, tanned golden brown, with a narrow face, and gently hollowed cheeks. He wore only a black woollen cloak, next to his skin, leaving his arms and chest bared to the sun. The master said to him:

'You have answered rightly. You have spoken the wisest words today.' And then he dismissed us to go home, and the debate was closed. And this boy was Aristeides, the son of Lysimachos, whom all his life the Athenians called 'Aristeides the Just'. I have loved him, and hated him, and struggled against him all my life, and at the end he is in Athens, at home, and I am here, with the gifts of the Persians all around me, and a little phial of poison hidden behind the wine krater on the shelf, and yet I must tell you that it is true that he is just, and has never in his whole life done anything of which he need be ashamed. You, Lord Artaxerxes, will hardly have heard of his proverbial justice; but you might have heard of him nevertheless, for he was the Athenian commander at the battle of Plataia – he who dealt with the Thebans while the Spartans hacked up the Persian immortals, and killed Mardonios, your father's general.

The next day I fell in with him as we walked to the Palaestra, and said, 'But of all cities in which it is good to be a just man, it is best to be a just man in Athens!' Then he laughed, and said, 'You are like a dog, Themistokles, that gets its teeth into something, and won't let go!' In the Palaestra he gave my cloak a sudden tug, pulling it from me and leaving me naked, and then cast off his own, and threw it in a bundle with mine upon the bench, and crying 'Race!' he tore away for the finishing-post, with me running in the dust thrown up from his heels.

The boys in my cities here exercise Persian fashion, on horse-back, or at archery, with all their clothes on their backs, and wash themselves afterwards in private, I suppose. It strikes me as I think of it that you cannot know each other as the Greeks know their friends, every inch, seeing them naked daily. I wonder if this is why you are always more formal than we, in visiting, in talk, in respect for those above you? I even saw two lads the other day, walking by the river, their arms about one another's shoulders, over their cloaks, and I thought how muffled their touch was, by all that wool. Well, I know what you think of Greek ways in matters such as that ... but I was going to say how a man's body and mind are after all the same animal; a man can be known through his body. We would both judge the spirit of a horse by looking at muscle, you and I.

Aristeides was lean, but taut, not loose-limbed as a fine runner often is. When exercise has made us sweaty and dusty from head to foot, we rub oil on our skin, and scrape ourselves clean with a strigil, as I once told you. Nobody can reach his own back; friends help each other. When I poured oil into the hollow between Aristeides' shoulders the golden pool lingered for an instant, because he was leaning forwards, sitting on the bench, hands on knees. Then it divided, softening in the warmth of his body, and of the sunlight, a rivulet flowing sideways across each flat shoulder-blade, and a torrent down the hollow of his spine. I caught the running gold with outspread hands, rubbing upwards, and sideways, damming it from running off him to drip wasted into the dust, watching the trickle that had found a channel between his thin ribs and was flowing round to his chest, sliding my hands over him, with the surplus oil pushing up between my fingers, until he shone like polished marble, and moved contentedly, arching his back slightly under my hands.

'You have used too much, Themistokles,' he said.

'From my own alabastron,' I said. Then I took up the strigil, and scooped off the surplus oil, bumping down the rounded protrusions of his spine, outwards across his shoulders, leaning over him to scrape down his arms.

'Your turn,' he said, and tackled my wide, flat, muscular back energetically, till the skin tingled, and then glowed in the supple oil. He had his cloak on in moments, and was ready to go; he waited for me.

'You have the body of a wrestler,' he said. 'Is that to be your chosen path to glory?'

'No!' I said, sharply. 'All that pure-minded striving after laurels! A rich man's game, for those who have nothing to do.'

'Nothing to do?' he said laughingly. 'Have you seen how they train?'

'There are better things to do,' I said.

'The names of the victors in the games are inscribed in marble for ever,' he said, with mock grandeur.

'I'll make my mark on something better than a block of stone!' I said.

'You've a sharp tongue,' he answered. 'In a contest of wits you'd leave me standing, as surely as I'd outrun you in a race.

But I wasn't debating, I was asking. You, Themistokles, you won't learn your Homer, or else you won't recite it. You won't learn to sing; anyone can see how you hate to be made to play the lyre; you fall asleep when we read a poem longer than a skolion; and it isn't to be wrestling either, it seems. You'll be a terrible rough nut of a man for the head of a priestly family, however they've come down in the world. What is it that you want? Tell me, what do you expect to do with yourself?' That's why I liked Aristeides; he talked about important things. There was much to talk about when we were young.

We always differed in talk. Nothing remarkable about that, especially in Athens, where men will talk nonsense on purpose, just to keep an argument going – a practice which horrifies my Persian friends, for it seems to them close to lying. But Aristeides and I were in a very similar situation when we were young, and might have seen things from a similar viewpoint. We were both nobly born, both one day to be the head of a family, for he was the only son, and I was the eldest. And both of us would inherit too little money to shed glory easily on our future. Even when we were boys, the prospect of duties and scant means to discharge them weighed on us both, and, as always, in talking of it we differed.

He thought it was possible to be poor, and yet a great man. Poverty seemed to him no disgrace; only a man's own conduct could disgrace him. But I thought how it would disable a man in action, limit his path in life. I wanted to give bribes, to give lavish parties, never to be outshone. I didn't mention the bribes to Aristeides. I had some gossip from home a little while ago, according to which Kallias was accused in the law courts of letting his famous relative, Aristeides, go threadbare in the streets, while he himself wallowed in preposterous wealth. It made the court so hostile that it damaged Kallias' cause, till he brought Aristeides into court and called him to witness that he had often been offered money, and had steadfastly refused every penny Kallias had ever offered him. It probably isn't true, of course; but imagine the character of a man about whom people spread stories like that! As for me, I take all I can get – bribes too, on occasion, when I have been offered them by those who deserved to win the case anyway. And perhaps you will think my three cities, my Persian titles also, which I have taken eagerly, and for which I now will not repay you, fit in with that only too well. I can't deny it. But, however heavily he has dipped into his pockets for me, however much he calls me greedy and dishonest, I am in debt to no Athenian; all debts were paid when I won the city its freedom.

Freedom. I know the Persian word for it. But, knowing the word, I still find it impossible to explain to a Persian what it means to a Hellene. I have tried many times, many times, at other men's tables, and at my own, when the lamps have burned low and the wine kraters are light and nearly empty, and friendship and hospitality have loosened men's tongues, warmed their hearts to accept me. Over and over again some Persian friend or neighbour has said to me, 'Come, Themistokles, explain. Tell us what made them fight with such passion. Is it so bad to be a subject of the King's?' How can I answer?

'I find it very comfortable to be where I am,' I would say. 'But, as to freedom, I can no more tell you about it than I can tell you the taste of a wine you have never drunk.' .

'Ah, well, if you mean they were *drunk* when they fought us,' says that dandy Tissaphernes, 'I'll drink to us finding them sober next time!'

During one such conversation, I remember as I write, I caught the eye of a little Lydian slave-boy of mine, who was pouring the wine. It struck me he could tell them what I was talking about if it ever occurred to them to ask him, or anyone like him. I must remember to tell my wife before tomorrow that he is to be freed when I die. And now once more, for your ears, Lord Artaxerxes, I will construe a meaning for freedom, force it out of Persian words. You will never conquer the Hellenes if you do not understand it, because you will not understand what they are likely to do next. You will make the mistakes your father and grandfather made, or others like them. Darius, your grandfather brought Hippias with him to Greece, so that we all knew what tyranny we faced again if we should lose. That hardened us at Marathon. Your father thought we would not unite against him. These were misjudgements. And, since I will not be here to guide you, you must do the thinking yourself.

I remember being told that the archives of your palace at Susa contain tablets piled upon tablets of reports about the Greeks; and that these tablets tell over and over the tale of our quarrels and wars among ourselves, the tale of the enmity between one city and another, and the verdict that save for a few festivals and gods in common we were not one people at all, but so divided that our cities, each puny on its own, could be conquered one by one. Your spies did not observe how supremely important to us are the things we do together, because these things are done in honour of our gods. They could not have seen the feasting and singing, and the joy in the prowess of the athletes which unites us when the games are held, at the Isthmus, or at Olympia, or for the Pythian Apollo at Delphi, when the Greeks come from every part of Hellas, and from further away still, to compete, and honour the gods. These things weave bonds between us. It was in a grove of trees at green Olympia, for instance, in a crowd that had gathered round a young boy from Kythera, playing the flute like a god, that I first met Pausanias, a leader of the Spartans, who was my friend; a brave man, now dead. The manner of his dying haunts me, so that often I wake, dreaming of his death, and tremble under the covers of my rich bed, comparing his fate with mine. Then I will pace out into the moonlit garden of my house, and the wine I call for will taste sour when they bring it, no matter how good the vintage.

Your spies did not tell you, either, that we speak the same language, and all read the same books of Homer, and have a scornful word *barbaroi* for the whole world elsewhere that do not. Still, it is not surprising if they were less struck by these things than by our long and bitter fighting among ourselves. Yet they would have informed you better if they had also written why we fought. Greek cities fight for their independence, fight to be free of one another, to remain separate, so that each may choose its own laws, rule itself, be its own place. And the Greek cities fought against the Persians for their independence, to remain free, so that each city might remain the place it was. Thus it was the same desire that divided us when the Great King seemed far away, and that united us when he overshadowed us. There has never been a greater threat to the freedom of Athens than the might of Persia; but there are many smaller threats, from nearer home. And when the greater danger is averted one must look to the lesser ones, for it is possible for a strong man to fight off an armed warrior, and then fall prey to the bite of a scorpion.

Sparta is the scorpion in Hellas. Sparta, where every detail of the citizens' lives is rigorously detailed by law; Sparta, whose land of Lakedaimon is tilled by a whole population of slaves, called helots, crushed into wretchedness. Sparta, whose matchless military power is always at the service of petty oligarchs, always ready to strangle freedom in a neighbouring city.

At Athens, on the other hand, the love of freedom has grown

stronger roots than anywhere else in Hellas, because in Athens
not only does the city maintain its freedom against its enemies
among the other Hellenes, but also the laws of the Athenians have
been shaped so that within the city men are independent of one
another, equal before the law, each playing a part in the assembly,
however lowly; each man serving the city, be he rich or poor. At
Athens men do not fear oddity, do not dislike a neighbour whose
way of life is unlike theirs, but live as free men. They do not
need savage laws, and years of military drill, as the Spartans do,
who live such iron lives that the Persian Immortals in training
for battle would groan under it; at Athens men are united by love
of their city, and can afford to differ in lesser things, each man
being free fearlessly to be himself, and to enjoy other men for
what they are. How different, for example, am I from Aristeides;
most men in Athens prefer him, admire him; and yet how lucky
for the Athenians that they could also give power to me!

Such glory as the gods have given Athens would be bound to
have enemies, and enemies it has always had. In my time those
enemies have been chiefly two – the Great King, and the Spartans –
and my counsel to the Athenians, as long as they would hear me,
was always that they must fight both; both at once if need be.
Freedom such as ours was not easily won. It took years of struggle
to win; and the men who won it have been ready to stand and
fight against the whole might of your empire, Great King, rather
than lose it. How often have I said all this to some Persian friend;
how hard it seems for them to understand it; yet you might
understand it, Lord Artaxerxes. For in all your wide realm, and
wealthy satrapies, there is not one man, not even one, who has
as much freedom as the poorest citizen of Athens, saving only
yourself.

During the whole of my boyhood this freedom was slowly being
won. Looking back, I suppose the first step was the killing of Hipparchos, a brother of Hippias, who was then our tyrant. One can still
find old men who say that the tyrants' rule was not so bad while
both brothers were alive, though they kept the laws of Solon only
in form, a mere outward show. They had inherited the city, like a
chattel or a slave, from their father Peisistratos, who died the year
I was born, and there were always men around to say that his
had been an age of gold. My father, indeed, shaking his braided
hair at the times he lived in, said as much. Peisistratos had brought
prosperity to the city, welcomed any foreigner who knew a trade,
ruled well and wisely, so that I am ashamed to say that in his

time men do not seem to have missed their freedom, or the rights guaranteed them by the laws Solon made. They lived contentedly, Great King, as your subjects do – a good argument for your belief in the value of order. But his sons were different. They ruled as their father had done only for a short while; then they began to go rotten. So my father says; I can't remember.

The first public event I can remember was the uproar over the killing of Hipparchos. He was struck down in the market place, during the marshalling of the Panathenaic procession by two brothers, Harmodios and Aristogeiton, who suddenly drew swords from under branches of myrtle, and hacked him down before anyone could stop them. They probably meant to get Hippias too, but he escaped them. I didn't see it; I and my whole family were still in our house, preparing to join in the procession – purifying the threshold, blessing the myrtle boughs we were to carry, crowning the herms with garlands. The news went through the city like fire, and soon friends were hammering on our door, and there was shouting and running in the streets.

At first we assumed that it had been an attempt to rid the city of tyranny, which had failed, since Hippias was still alive, but the news was scarcely abroad before it was followed by scandalous rumours. Hipparchos had forced one of the murderers' sisters; he had seduced one, none knew which, from loving the other, and so on, each story more outrageous than the one before. The guards cut down Harmodios at once, and the procession of the Goddess broke up in disorder; men fled to their houses, or to warn their friends, and then the streets of the city fell into an unusual hush, with nobody putting a nose out of doors.

I remember lying sleepless on my bed that night, my heart racing with excitement, and then jumping up as there came a knocking on our door. It was Phokas, a friend of my father's, come to tell us the news. And I remember it well, because after the knock, and the thud of the door closing, and the scrape of the bolts being drawn, there was a murmur of voices, pitched low so that strain as I might I could hear nothing. And then suddenly my father's voice was raised, calling, 'Themistokles!' Astonished, and eager, I leapt up, clutched my cloak around me, and ran down to the courtyard of the house, passing my mother, standing in the door of her room as I went.

'My son is fourteen this year. He shall hear this too, if you will Phokas,' said my father, as I reached his side. And Phokas said, in what words I have forgotten, that Hippias had put Aristogeiton to the torture, to make him say who had plotted with him; and Aristogeiton had named, one by one, nearly all the cronies of the tyrants, and one by one Hippias had sent armed men to put to death those whom Aristogeiton had named, so that by evening he had scarcely a friend left; and then Aristogeiton, dying at last under the knives, had said there were none left whose lives he wished to take, except Hippias himself. Now Aristogeiton was dead, and twenty men with him, murdered without trial. 'But had all Hippias' friends really been plotting against him?' I asked, mystified.

'They were Aristogeiton's revenge,' said Phokas.

'Be that as it may,' said my father, 'it is not the dead but the living we shall have to fear.' And he was right, for from that time onwards Hippias suspected everyone, and shed blood every day, and there was nobody in the city who could stop him.

The city was quiet the next day. The streets were unusually empty. At first both I and my father stayed at home; he sat on his favourite chair, turning and turning in his hands a painted krater which had been made for him by Exekias, long ago. He loved this cup, and it had a story behind it. My father as a young man had given a slave his freedom because of the beauty with which he had painted a vase; and Exekias had come to hear of it. Exekias was the finest painter of that time, who made the black-figure ware which is old-fashioned now, though my father always preferred it. When he heard of my father's fine gesture he had made the krater as a gift for him. That morning my father looked at it, and I chattered on, unable to curb my tongue, babbling away about the city, and about Hippias, and what would happen now.

I can see my father even now, in my mind's eye, stroking with one hand the linen folds of his garment, for he wore the older kind of dress, winding his hair in long braids round his head, and fixing it with a golden clasp made like a butterfly; and he always had linen under his woollen cloak. At first he answered me when I spoke. It seemed there had been signs of trouble coming, illegal things which the tyrants had done, and the tyrant's murdered brother had been proud, overstepping his rights. If the tales told now about what Hipparchos had done to anger Harmodios and Aristogeiton were all true, said my father, that would not surprise him. There had been trouble coming. And he added that this was a bad time for the city to be divided.

'Why, father?' said I.

'What do you learn at school, boy?' he said sharply.

'Oh, nonsense about playing the lyre, and running in the games, sir.'

'Humph,' he said. 'And you're not interested?' I shook my head. It seemed to me my father was noticing me for the first time – at last!

'Do you know about the Chersonese?' he asked.

'No, sir,' I said.

'It commands the Hellespont,' he said. 'Peisistratos secured it in his time, by sending a troublesome young man called Miltiades out there. He has made himself tyrant there; while he holds it the corn from the far shores of the Euxine Sea will always reach us; without the corn, Athens would go very hungry. But now the Great King has crossed into Europe, and is marching upon the Scythians. Miltiades is campaigning with him; we must hope he can hold his own, and keep on the right side of Darius.'

Rare as it was for my father to talk seriously with me, I hardly listened. I came out with, 'Father, did they do right?'

'Who?' he said, frowning.

'Harmodios and. . . .'

'Get off with you to school!' said my father sharply. 'And leave me in peace.'

So I summoned my pedagogue, and went, gladly enough. I wanted to hear what Aristeides would say about it all. I left my father still sitting, still grim-faced, turning and turning the freedom cup in his thin, pale hands.

The schoolmaster's house was only a few streets away. My pedagogue walked ahead of me, carrying my writing-tablets. We saw no one, and when we knocked at the schoolmaster's door it was a long time before a slave came and admitted us. The court-yard was empty. All the other boys had been kept at home. I almost snarled with frustration. I wanted to talk! I glanced at my pedagogue, wondering if he would agree to take me to Aristeides' house. I didn't think he would. I sat down under the fig tree, and then jumped up again at once, and pacing up and down, talking to myself, began to play all the parts in the trial of Harmodios and Aristogeiton, impeaching them for murder in pursuit of private revenge, and then defending them, raising my voice as I got carried away, and imagined myself strutting on the rostrum, addressing the assembled people, and the archons.

'Even if it be true,' I told the fig tree, 'that it was to avenge some insult, to punish some intolerable affront, that these two men shed blood, yet that does not remove their right to be considered as liberators of the city; for it is the essential nature of tyrants to abuse their power, to shower insults on their fellow citizens; therefore, he who reacts against those insults acts against tyranny also, and should be honoured as a liberator. Nor is an insult to any Athenian', I told my pedagogue, 'merely a private matter. If a citizen has been wronged, and can find no redress, that is a public matter, that concerns, or should concern us all.' I put great heart into the uttering of these sentiments; I knew this part of the argument would have to be good to stand up to Aristeides, for I felt sure he would think nothing could be said for those who killed in open streets, let alone those who defiled the procession in honour of Athena, by the shedding of blood. 'Athena herself', I cried, as this thought occurred to me, 'will not frown on them. For there is a great difference between the cowardly killing of the weak by the strong, and the acts of those who kill in pursuit of a cause for which they are themselves prepared to die.'

And at this point I realised that the schoolmaster was standing in the deep shadow of his doorway, listening to every word I said. I broke off, and a fierce blush burned my cheeks. He looked at me with an expression that combined mirth with deep gravity. 'At least there will be nothing petty about you, my boy,' he said. Coming up to me he laid a hand on my shoulder. 'You are going to be a great man, one way or the other, either for good or evil.'

Then, swelling with pride, I smiled up at him, thinking he wasn't such an old fool after all.

'Well, Themistokles,' he said, looking round. 'It seems you are my only pupil today. And we are not going through the streets to the gymnasium this morning. So let us learn whatever you like best. What shall it be? The lyre?'

I grimaced. He smiled. 'The flute then?' I hung my head. 'Shall we read Homer together?' He was mocking me. 'Is there nothing you want to learn, Themistokles? Are you quite insensible to beauty?'

I was angry at being mocked, but I found my tongue, 'I like, well, *public* things,' I said. 'The beauty of the temples or the stele on the graves of great men in the Kerameikos – that sort of thing.'

'Oh,' he said. 'No poetry?'

'I like Hesiod better than Homer,' I offered, aghast at my own heresy.

'An odd taste, certainly. Why?'

'He writes about justice. I like other things better still.'

'I see,' said the master. 'Well, take the lyre, and sing to me something you like better.' He sat down to hear me. I struck four false notes before I found the right one to start off with, and with each false note the master's face contorted as though he had been struck. I got launched at last, into a lyric of Solon's:

'I gave the commons their sufficient meed
Of strength, nor let them lack, nor yet exceed.
Those who were mighty and magnificent,
I bade them have their due, and be content.
My strong shield guarded both sides equally,
And gave to neither unjust victory.'

Great words; even my harsh singing-voice was steadied by them. For a long while we neither of us said anything. The master seemed to have fallen into some deep thoughts, from which I hesitated to recall him. At last he said, 'There is much of the day still left. What would you like to learn, boy?'

'I would like to learn how affairs are conducted in cities other than ours,' I said, after thinking a moment. Judging by his eyebrows, I had surprised him again, though I was only showing my natural bent. Years later, if ever someone handed me the lyre at a feast, I would say, 'I can't fiddle; but I can lead a city to greatness.'

'I will teach you the laws of Lykurgos, by which the Spartans are governed,' the master said, 'if they would interest you.'

'Greatly,' I said, sitting down at once, cross-legged and pulling out my writing-tablet to make notes of it. But just then there were sounds from the door, of another pupil arriving. The master looked up.

'Good day to you, Aristeides,' he said. 'I am glad I have more than one pupil, even today, who is not afraid to walk the streets.'

'The others will be back tomorrow, sir,' said Aristeides, 'when their fathers see that there is no disorder or danger in the city.'

'Is there not indeed?' said the master.

'None of a kind to trouble boys going to school,' said Aristeides quietly.

'Themistokles has chosen the lesson for today,' said the master. 'And it is to be the laws of Lakedaimon. Will you learn of them?'

'Gladly,' said Aristeides, sitting at my side. So I talked with him that day, after all, since our ways home lay together as far as my door, and it turned out I had misjudged him, for he thought that even tyrannicide might be justified, if it removed injustice that could not be peacefully remedied.

27

'For no man's rights,' he said, solemnly, 'not even his right to life, is more important than the good of the city.' But at this our pedagogues, whose job it was, after all, to bring us safely to and fro, became alarmed, and shushed us, and told us to keep our talk off the streets.

Someone spoke to my father that day, the pedagogue, or perhaps even the schoolmaster, for something alarmed him on my account, and packing the whole family into a waggon, he rushed us out of the city, to spend some time on our farm. I suppose with Hippias hacking his way through the citizenry it was too much for him to have a son who talked politics in the streets. Aristeides' father evidently thought the same; they, too, left the city for the country.

Our lands lay to the south-east, at Sounion, nearly the last farm in Attica, where Attica meets the sea. There is a high cliff there, a craggy height, crowned with a temple to Poseidon which gleams white above the trees. When we were at our farm I could slip away, and walk there, and watch the ships crossing the endless sea. At Sounion when the sun is high the land looks black against the light, and the sea is silver, sparkling with points of light which are daggers to the eyes, so that one blinks, and frowns to look at it. Only the pathways of the fast-moving currents flatten the sea; smooth ribbons in the shining dance of light showing where danger lies. The temple on the cliff-top is a good viewpoint, but I preferred my own, the branch of a tree lower down, for sitting astride it, wind-rocked, I could see more clearly the sights below.

Coming round Sounion into home waters the helmsman would pour a libation to Poseidon, and I could see his hand go up, raising the krater to pour. If the winds were unfavourable and the ship was under oar, she would put into the beach at Sounion and her important passengers would disembark, because they could make better speed to the city by the road along the coast. That made bustle, as the ship was beached and floated again, and voices would rise to me where I perched, watching, sharp as the cries of birds. But if the winds were favourable the ships came by like birds in flight, sails spread, the white spume surging under the black curved prows. Often I would stay there, looking, till the harshness went out of the light, and the columns of the temple glowed orange and pink, and the island of Helena to the eastwards had faded to a violet shadow in an azure haze. Doubtless it was here that I learned to think of the sea as the true country of the Athenians; for the land ends here, sharply, but the shimmering plains of the water go on and on, till their margins dissolve in the sky.

So we went to be quiet in the country, and not be seen. At first I was happy enough; I could take the dogs out, carrying a spear, and go hunting in the hills; or stride across the fragrant scrubby tufts of thyme which cling to the rocky bones of the land where it rises to Sounion; or watch the slaves working the farm, and listen to the earthy talk of our neighbours, plain honest men, who think as much of the weather as of what may be afoot in the city. There are figs and vines to tend, and the red-brown soil to keep hoed and ploughed, and groves of green olives, from which in harvest times the riches come pattering down like rain; and now and then a festival to keep, with everyone assembled, laughing, and wearing his best, the whistling flute, heads garlanded in the sun, and the sleek-flanked oxen led to the sacrifice. Then roast meat, and wine, the twang of the lyre, someone singing to Apollo late into the night, and a simple dance, in the cool evening air; I could break my heart, now, to be home again, only to think of it!

But then, of course, I was bored, and longing for the city after only a week. Aristeides came once to see me, riding a fine proud horse. My father let me ride, too, and together we trotted through the olive groves and on to the sea, Aristeides not wishing to look at it as long as I would have done. My father bade him to supper with us, and entertained him as he would have entertained his father, and among other things Aristeides asked about Kleisthenes, and where his lands lay, for surely they were in our direction? My father declared his allegiance; the lands of the Alkmeonids lay next to ours, and stretched all along the coast; my father was Kleisthenes' loyal man.

'Speak that word softly, sir,' said Aristeides.

'What do you mean?' I blurted out, astonished.

'My father sent me here today,' said Aristeides, 'only to say to you, if you are with Kleisthenes, don't speak of it.'

'Something has happened,' said my father, grim-faced; and I, reeling with the sick disappointment that Aristeides had not, after all, come because he wanted to ride with me, hardly heard him answer, 'Not yet, sir.'

But soon afterwards we heard that Kleisthenes had fled the city, and then later that he was at Delphi. He was a man whom my father admired more than any other Athenian living; his banishment affected him deeply. I was growing up, yet he would not talk of it to me, and seemed to wish that I would take an interest in nothing but the farms, or perhaps also in going trading with a ship. I grew bored and troublesome, and my father at last, in exasperation, promised we should return to Athens in the autumn.

Before that, as it happened, I found something to amuse me. Mnesiphilos came. He was a near neighbour, a grizzled, tough-looking man, who farmed the other side of the hill from us. He came riding a donkey up to the house like a slave on an errand, sweating, and grunting as he slipped to the ground, greeting my father with due ceremony, but somehow as if he thought the ceremony was a matter for irony; I had never met a man like him.

He had come to talk with my father about the spring on the hillside which watered both our farms; it was running nearly dry that year, and Mnesiphilos wanted to dig out a deeper course for it, and wanted my father to share the cost. They talked, sitting in the shade, sipping wine. Mnesiphilos stared round him, his eyes licking over every detail of our house – cracked whitewash on the walls, thatch patched all over, brand-new olive-press standing in the courtyard, unstained as yet by a single harvest. He stared, too, at me; especially at me. When the work on the spring was all arranged between them, Mnesiphilos, looking at me, said to my father, 'Is that boy good at anything?'

'Talk, only,' said my father.

'Hmph,' said Mnesiphilos. 'Well, there isn't enough of that in the country. He doesn't take after you, then, Neokles?' My father, too, looked at me. 'He's more like his mother, in some ways. She, too, has a golden tongue.'

'And that's what seduced you into marrying an alien?' My father frowned and did not answer. 'Well, I'd like to see what harm the son can do. Send him to me for an hour in the evenings, when he's done his share on the farm, Neokles.'

'He has a teacher in the city,' said my father.

'Oh, a teacher. . . . I don't mean to *teach* him,' said Mnesiphilos, snorting. 'Just talk to him. I won't charge for it.'

'And I'd have some peace while he was gone,' said my father. 'My thanks to you, neighbour.'

Every evening then, up the dry track across the crest of our hill, sand prickling in my sandals, scrambling over thyme that shed a faint dry fragrance as I trod, down the other side to Mnesiphilos' house, trim, and well kept, standing in a garden of herbs and full of slaves, padding bare-footed and silent, bringing tapers, wine and bowls of figs and honey-cakes. At first I thought he must be richer than us, as indeed he was, though by less than I'd have guessed at. But the difference in his house was more than that. He had no wife, no children, no jugs or vases well made or finely painted, no lyre or flute anywhere, no hanging or curtain, nothing to please eye or ear. Only the pleasures of the body were attended to in his house, and those with delicate obsession; those and talk.

Such talk! I'd never heard the like before. The schoolmaster in the city talked about laws as though they were architecture – great structures, holding the balance, taking the strain this way and that, but static, fixed. To Mnesiphilos there wasn't anything grand or noble about them; they could change, and indeed they would. 'The laws aren't strong, boy,' he would say. 'They reflect well enough where power lay when they were made. When power shifts, they are like straws before the wind.'

'Not our laws,' I said. 'Not Solon's.' But Mnesiphilos didn't admire Solon, or not in a way I could recognise.

'Solon did the best he could at the time,' he said. 'Better than most men could.' But, he taught me, Solon's balance of power had been swept away by the tyrants. The tyrants, too, could be swept away.

'Where's the power to do that?' I asked.

'In the people,' he said. 'Listen. You see these slaves of mine? Do you know how many there are? Thirty on this farm. And there's only you and I to give them orders. Why do they obey? They could kill us both and escape if they would agree together first.'

'They'd be caught and punished,' I said.

'We are three miles from the sea. There are ships pulled up all along the shore. Most of them have homes across the sea, and at least two among them can steer a vessel.' I stared at him, round-eyed. 'I'll tell you why we're safe,' he said. 'They are slaves; mean-minded. Bondage has crushed their spirits. They won't agree together, because they are too busy squabbling about who will smooth my couch tonight, or who will have the chance to carry goods to market, and pocket a small profit for himself. They won't stir; not even if we gave orders for every one of them to be flogged. But if they did ... they are thirty to two.'

'What are you trying to say to me, sir?' I said, puzzled, flicking my fingers at the slave-boy to bring some more wine.

'All gods together, strike!' he cried. 'The only excuse for a

31

face as ugly as yours, boy, is that it has a mind behind it; do you tell me you're an idiot as well?'

I hung my head. Sooner or later I was always nonplussed. Sometimes he would bundle me out of the house, swearing at me vilely, and send me home, and I would never catch up with what he had been getting at; sometimes he launched into a great tirade which I could follow if I tried hard enough. That night he got launched. As slaves to master, so citizens to tyrant; nothing happens without the tacit consent of the people. 'Oh yes,' he said bitterly, 'a free man is murdered, or tortured, and the people consent, because they do not refuse to suffer it. They do not rise. They do not demand their ancient rights. Now, I used to think a spot of tyranny would do Athens no harm at all; Peisistratos would smash up the aristocracy, I thought, and give *hoi polloi* a chance; then the *hoi polloi* would get rid of him. But it seems every man of spirit has been crushed, and we are left with a limp mob who won't unite and stand up for themselves. If they did....'

'More powerful than all the aristocrats,' I said. 'Stronger than any tyrant would be the man who could lead the people!'

'Yes,' said Mnesiphilos, 'though like anyone else who rides unbroken horses he'd have his neck broken sooner or later. You admire Solon. Well, he wasn't a god, you know, and he didn't command an army. The people were ground down till they demanded change, and Solon gave it to them; gave as little as he possibly could, so that it was enough to keep them meek under their masters. The strength of his law was that everyone consented to it; for a while. You can change anything if most of the people agree. It will be tried again; soon, I think.'

I imagined myself as another Solon. I, Themistokles, addressing the assembly, smashing my enemies with the voice of the whole people; but when he said it would be tried again soon I had to admit that he couldn't possibly mean me.

'Who will try it?' I asked.

'Several might. There's Kleisthenes.'

'He's been exiled,' I said. 'My father grieves over that. And his family don't have many friends among the other families that count for much.'

'So he may seek friends among those who count for little.'

'He's still in exile.'

'Oh, he's not here, I grant you. But where is he? Rotting in some obscure backwater?'

'He's at Delphi, so I've heard,' I said.

'Well, *think*, boy. He's rich. He's at Delphi. They say he's rebuilding the temples there, pouring out gifts to the god. I wouldn't be entirely surprised if the god repaid him.' I gaped. 'Suppose the god told the Corinthians, or better still the Spartans, to see to it that Kleisthenes came home?'

His blasphemy appalled me. I thought Apollo himself would blast him, in a great flash of golden anger. The very thought of bribing the gods seemed to rock the floor under my feet. He acknowledged what he saw on my face with a twisted contemptuous smile. 'You're a fool, boy,' he said. 'Why should I trouble with a fool? Not only a fool, but a vain one. You see yourself doing great things, don't you, Themistokles? Ambition struts in your every step. Well, maybe, maybe. But you won't do as you are. You'll have to learn to use things for whatever ends they'll serve. You mustn't rely on a strong speaking-voice, and the wit to string a speech together; it's actions that make men famous, not words. Unless, of course, you want to be a *poet*. For the moment you bore me. Come back when you've changed something, made your mark somewhere, and I'll talk to you then. Go home.'

And seething with anger I set off in the darkness, stumbling after a slave who carried a torch before me; and my father, seeing my burning face and uneven steps as I crossed the courtyard to bed, blamed his neighbour for giving the boy strong wine. Strong wine indeed, indeed!

My father took me with him on our last morning before returning to Athens. We had to look at everything on the farm, see that all was in order till we came again, talk to each overseer, make him feel we trusted but were watching him; we had to talk to the slave who wanted to marry, and to the old one who could not work after this year, for even a slave works better for a considerate master, but little by little my father turned his steps from the expected circuit, until we were walking by the shore. There is a narrow fringe of sloping beach there, then a strip of rushes, then a salt pan, striped white and sparkling like untooled marble in the sun. The sea was like the curly flange of a green glass bottle I had out of Egypt. Beached above the sand, in the green border between sand and salt pan, lay the hulks of two ships, like bones, bleached nearly white. Only the ribs and thwarts remained.

'Themistokles,' said my father, 'a man has a duty to the city, and to his tribe. Most men do that duty gladly, and seek no more of it. But you, I am told, have ambitions of a grander sort.' I did not answer. 'You have a great energy,' he continued. 'Use it in private life.'

'As you have done?' I asked insolently.

'Look at these ships,' he said. 'That is how great men are treated when the people have no more use for them.'

I looked at his land-locked hulks. Sea gorse and thrift grew round them, and they lay abandoned, as he said, by those whom they had served, like you and me, Pausanias my friend, like you and me. But when I raised my eyes to them, I saw also, far out to sea, a penteconter in full sail, flying on the bright water.

When we got back to Athens, I set myself to change something, to take up Mnesiphilos' challenge. I wanted my father to take me from school, and send me to Mnesiphilos instead. And there was a thing that needed changing, and that was the question of the gymnasia. I, like every other half-Athenian in the city no matter what rank he occupied, had to register at the Kynosarges outside the walls for exercise. The place was dedicated to Herakles who was only half a god. It was not that it was an inferior place; it was a well-found building, with cool fountains, in a green and shady grove, more pleasant really than the one within the city, that was restricted to those of unmixed descent. But Aristeides, Athenian to the last drop of his pure blood, ran and played at the other one, and with him the sons of every important family, boys whom I wanted as my friends; and I could not go, except with the schoolmaster, to the boys' palaestra there. Closed to me, too, were the glances of the older men who came and watched the boys at exercise, laying bets on who would win the prizes at the next important games, choosing, sometimes lovers, but more often a boy to play father to, to take around and introduce to the life of the city. There were watchers at the Kynosarges too, but they were less important men.

I determined to change all this. One morning I stood waiting in a side street till Aristeides and his friends came by. Then I seemed just to happen to meet them. I, like them, carried a little bottle of oil, and a woollen mantle to put on after exercise. So we walked on together, talking. Naturally, I had chosen a morning when Aristeides was in good company. A Philaid boy was there, and Aeschylus, and Xanthippos, and two brothers from a branch of the Gephyraian family. With a little cunning I had us talking as we went of the trade brought to the city by the metics;

that is, the resident aliens. Then we were standing in the portals of the gymnasium, and suddenly I held back, face darkened.

'Come on, Themistokles!' said someone who didn't know me well enough to see the situation. 'I'll have a reason from you for that last remark of yours, or I'll throw you for it!'

'I can't come in here,' I said.

'Who'll notice, in this crowd?' said Xanthippos.

'I'm not going to creep in sideways, like a cur!' I cried, and now that everyone was embarrassed I looked straight at Aristeides. He must do this for me unasked. If I start saying how unfair it is he will see the justice of my words, but he will hesitate; if he feels it himself, nothing will stop him.

'What nonsense!' he said. 'Of course Themistokles will not creep. We'll all go with him instead.' At once they were delighted, laughing out loud. 'There isn't actually a rule excluding *us* from Kynosarges, is there, Themistokles?' They felt generous, and daring, and anyway the Kynosarges is a handsome building that they had never before been inside. In a minute we were striding off together, me leading, and loud talk ringing round me, through the city gate. We were of an age to be impudent about rules made by our elders.

What a flurry we caused at Kynosarges! Astonished boys staring, whispered the grand names to each other, and the men murmuring, 'Who did they come with? Ah, Themistokles!' I gave a handful of silver to the attendant, and hissed at him, 'Quickly, have wine and honey cakes ready, and rose petals in the washing-basins!' He gaped at me. 'Do you want to serve metics all your life, you fool,' I insisted. 'Or aren't these customers good enough for you?' He ran.

There was suddenly a hush. My friends had stripped; they were standing apart, ready, and the others were staring, overawed, ready to be resentful. I hastened towards them.

'Isodoros will give you a good bout of wrestling, Xanthippos,' I said, naming, of course, the best wrestler at Kynosarges. I took him by the arm, and led him forwards to meet Xanthippos, whispering to him as I did so, 'Not too hard; not today!' Now who could run against Aristeides? Kimakles, perhaps? So I got things going, and as soon as we ran and wrestled the stiffness disappeared, and everyone laughed together, especially when wine was brought round, and a little metic boy whose voice is like outpoured silver agreed to sing for us. At last we dressed and went home, talking on the way.

'They are good fellows down there,' said Xanthippos. 'I had a job to throw my opponent.'

'The water is far sweeter,' said Aristeides.

'It comes straight from a nearby spring, and doesn't have to be brought in a conduit,' I said.

'Think what we've been washing in all this time,' said the Philaid boy, 'and that cunning fox Themistokles keeping it all to himself and saying nothing about it!'

In a few days men at the city gymnasium were asking one another where everyone had gone; then one by one the older men came down, each looking for his favourite athlete to watch. The clients list of the Kynosarges was starry with the names of fine families, and then the city gymnasium, for fear of losing its primacy altogether, was taking all comers, and no questions asked. Any day I liked to go out, I could see two boys walking together or running together, who would not have known each other a mere two weeks ago; and all over the city fathers were aghast to learn who their sons' latest acquaintance was.

As for me, I gloated, I basked in glory. One day in the agora, buying herbs for my mother, I met Mnesiphilos.

'They tell me,' he said, 'that just anybody exercises anywhere now, and both gymnasia have registered all sorts of people. I hear that the older men object very strongly, but it has all gone too far to be stopped.'

'Will you talk to me now, Mnesiphilos?' I asked.

'Hmph,' he said. 'Yes, I rather think I will.'

It was lucky indeed for me that I got back into favour with Mnesiphilos just then, for without him I should never have understood the storm of events that was about to break over us. My youth and my father's strong dislike of talking politics conspired to keep me ignorant; Mnesiphilos could inform me. And after the affair of the Kynosarges he never again called me a fool.

Looking back on that first achievement of mine, I am astonished that ever I got away with it. But Athens then was not herself; the whole city groaned under Hippias, and since all sorts of men suffered equally under tyranny perhaps men were readier than they usually are to sink their differences. Certainly nobody would have chosen that moment to pick a fight with another group of citizens; not even over so fundamental a matter as the descent of the boys one's own sons mixed with. Perhaps it strikes you as surprising that an Athenian should care much not to have any other Greek blood in his veins; but the wish of the Athenians not to give privileges or power to any but Athenians is the same impulse that makes the Great King so often give satrapies to his kith and kin; understandable, if not always wise.

Anyway, as I was saying, the city groaned. Bands of horsemen from Thessaly, armed to the teeth, and hired archers from Scythia, who could kill a man at a great distance, on a swift hiss of the air, roamed through the streets. No one else was allowed to carry arms, and the streets hummed with the rumour of brutalities; of a tanner killed on the spot for carrying a scraping-knife, and suchlike.

One morning, soon after I was reconciled with Mnesiphilos, he came looking for me, and found me in the barber's shop, trimmed, and gossiping, waiting for Aristeides, who was having his new beard clipped. Mnesiphilos told us to come and see something, and off we went, the three of us together. Soon we found ourselves walking out of the city, on the road to Phaleron. We were curious, and kept asking what there was to see, but Mnesiphilos wouldn't say. He was seething with inner excitement, and walking so fast we had to trot to keep up with him. Unlike him, to say the least. Phaleron is a lovely curved shallow bay with a gently sloping beach, facing the open sea to the south-west, and at that time the Athenians drew up their ships there, and used the place as a harbour, much as the Spartans still use the Lakonian Gulf at Gytheon. It was a good place to idle in; much coming and going, and ships to look at, and boxes of fish, and a smell of tar from the little driftwood fires lit on the sand by the workers who scraped and caulked the ships, but it seemed we weren't going there that day; instead we began to climb Mounychia, a steep little hill overlooking the bay. Long before we reached the top we could see what it was we had come to see.

There were workers and slaves on the hilltop, marking out the ground plan of some building – a large one. On either side of the pathway to the top a couple of archers stood, slouching, careless, but commanding the approach. We didn't go near them; instead we withdrew a little and sat on the hillside out of their view.

'Now, what do you think is happening here, Themistokles?' said Mnesiphilos at last.

'Hippias is building a fort,' I said.

'Ah, but *why* is he?'

I reflected. From where we sat, we could see on one side the wide sweep of Phaleron Bay, and the two small deep pools, sheltered by the hill beneath us on the other, at the place called

Peiraieus. In one of these pools a barge lay, carrying stone from a quarry somewhere along the coast. 'Hippias is fortifying the hill so that our ships will be safe,' I said. 'There should be a good harbour down there, out of the storm, and well protected from this hill.'

Mnesiphilos laughed. 'And what say you, Aristeides?'

'Hippias is building himself a stronghold, with an escape to the sea,' he answered.

'I think he is,' said Mnesiphilos. 'And is that a sign of strength, or of weakness, do you think?'

We did not answer, for just the question had convinced us. His excitement caught me too. 'What is going to happen?' I asked. I admired him inordinately at that time, for he seemed almost to have second sight.

'I'll tell you within walls,' he said. 'I'm off home now. Will you come too, Aristeides, son of Lysimachos?'

So we found ourselves sitting in his dining-room, eating figs, and listening. He said there were more and more men exiled from every noble family in Athens; it had reached the point where the exiles could make up an army. Not all had suffered at Hippias' hands; there were many whom his father Peisistratos had seen fit to get rid of. And most of them were the old guard; men of good birth, proud and conservative, who would turn back the wheel to before Solon if they could. But among them now was Kleisthenes the Alkmeonid; and he was more likely to get help from other cities. Together, they might even be a match for the horsemen from Thessaly. But, he added, he had heard news a day ago. He thought the aristocrats wouldn't wait for Kleisthenes, but would try and make a come-back without him. 'They hate him too much it seems,' he finished.

'Have they a chance, without other help?' asked Aristeides.

'Not a hope!' said Mnesiphilos, gleefully.

His tone shocked Aristeides into tight-lipped silence, but he seemed not to notice that. 'You see, Themistokles,' he went on, 'when we get rid of Hippias, the fun will be just beginning. There'll be a dog-fight over what sort of city there's to be, and where the power will lie. Now if those oligarchic young idiots get themselves cut to pieces first, there'll be fewer of them to deal with when Kleisthenes comes home.'

I walked with Aristeides to his door, later. He said, 'Themistokles, you should not talk with such an evil man.'

'Evil?' I cried, astonished.

'The men he calls idiots, and on whom he wishes defeat, are noble Athenians, wrongfully exiled, and fighting for their rights,' he said, gravely. 'That is an evil viewpoint.'

'Rights or no rights it will be better for us if they lose,' I said, 'for the reasons which he gave.'

'He has corrupted you already,' said Aristeides, 'with his slick talking.' He fixed on me a steady stare of his uncomfortable grey eyes, and held it, until I looked away.

'Evil viewpoint, nonsense!' I said angrily. 'Mnesiphilos has sense. He sees what is likely to happen, that is all.' Aristeides turned away into his doorway. I can see now just the gesture with which he left me, pulling his black cloak a little more closely round him, with sorrow, or anger, in his lean set face. It is late to weep over Aristeides now, and yet it pricks me still to think of that long cool stare, and silent parting.

Everyone in Athens, it seemed to me, was to weep the battle of the aristocrats when it came. They marched into Attica, and encamped on the slopes of Mount Parnes, and Hippias led out his foreign troops from the city, and slew them, at a place called Leipsydrion. Most of the dead were both well born and young; the heirs of all the great families, like a swathe of ripe corn, cut down at a stroke. The streets were full of the wailing of women, and fathers who looked ten years older overnight; and Hippias' victory celebrations insulted the grief of those who mourned the dead. There's a song made for them that can still bring tears to Athenian eyes: 'Ah, Leipsydrion, thou hast betrayed them, these thy comrades....' Any tears I have wept at it are not for the dead, for whom I care nothing at all, but because it's a plangent tune, and it was over that battle that Aristeides and I first deeply disagreed.

It was when the temple Kleisthenes was building at Delphi was very nearly finished that the god started to nag the Spartans. Whatever they sent to ask the oracle, the same reply came back: 'Set Athens free.' In the streets of Athens, and in the market and the barbers' shops it was even being said that they had asked the oracle where they should run a drain from the privies in their barracks (being worried about offending the river gods) and the god had answered, 'Set Athens free!' They're a devout lot, the Lakedaimonians. I, from that time onwards, and bearing in mind what Mnesiphilos had said, was a good deal less devout about the oracle; though why should Apollo not wish to see Athens free?

The Spartans have two kings at a time; and at that time one of them was Kleomenes, a brilliant and able man, who would have liked to force cities beyond the Isthmus to accept alliance with Sparta. In the oracle he saw his chance to set up a nice, orderly, pro-Spartan oligarchy in Athens. He had with him Isagoras, a noble and reactionary Athenian exile, whom some people said had fought at Leipsydrion and survived it; though if he had he kept very quiet about it. He might have done; he turned out to have a talent for dishonourable survival. At first Kleomenes launched a small expedition in ships, which was easily repelled, and then he prepared to march into Attica with a full force of hoplites. At that stage, Kleisthenes joined him. Hippias drew up his hired cavalry on the plains of Eleusis, to meet the oncoming invasion.

The news ran round the streets, and I went running to Mnesiphilos' house, bursting to know what he would have to say over an alliance of Kleisthenes and the Spartans; but Mnesiphilos frowned when he saw me, and said, 'Go home, boy. Go home.'

'Are you tongue-tied for once?' I asked him.

'The eldest son of Neokles should be at home today,' he answered. Then an inkling of what he might mean penetrated my excitement, and I went.

My father had collapsed when walking in the agora the evening before, and had been carried home in a litter. He said it was nothing, a passing fit of faintness; and, truth to tell, I had forgotten about it, and not even asked the slaves before leaving in the morning how he had passed the night. When Mnesiphilos sent me home, I returned to find he was dying. He had some swift fever upon him that the doctors could do nothing with. So the Spartans marched, the city hummed with rumour; Hippias was defeated before Eleusis, and his mercenaries deserted, and fled helter skelter through the Kithairon passes and home to Thessaly; retreating upon the city, where his bad deeds caught up with him, and no man would be his friend, Hippias holed himself up on the Acropolis, and built barricades there. But I knew nothing of any of this. I sat indoors, on a stool beside my father's bed, while my mother sat on the other side. Daylight came and went in the room, and my father too came and went, saying sometimes more, sometimes less fantastic things, talking to my mother about a time before me, in terms I did not understand. We dipped a cloth in water, and laid it across his forehead, and watched the feverish heat of his burning brow dry it again; again, again. Just once in many days he spoke sense to me, and my mother had to shake me awake to hear it, because I had fallen asleep where I sat. He told me to look after her, and my brother; and he told me of all my friends the son of Lysimachos was the one to trust: *'Don't ever quarrel with him, boy'*. Then he slept. And woke again, muttering nonsense. Watching, with all his household, my mother and I, and my brother, still only a child, and all his slaves, a change came over me. The feared and hated death became slowly, as he suffered, a longed-for thing; a desirable harbour.

It happened that I had had a little sleep, and towards evening I sent my mother away, and with her the red-eyed and wearied slave-women, saying I would watch alone for a little. The evening deepened. A rectangle of smoky violet glowed softly in the window opening. I went and looked out, and saw above the rooftops the Acropolis, tinted lilac against the opalescent sky. The rows of columns round the great temple Peisistratos built, that topped the rocky hill, reminded me of the spikes on a diadem; as though the tyrant, forbearing to crown himself, had crowned instead the high place of the city. Peisistratos crowned her in white marble; but every evening the gods crown Athens in purple. And at that moment, Hippias was up there somewhere, doubtless still cunning, and afraid.

My father stirred, and I took water to him. The room was nearly dark; I trimmed and lit the lamp myself, not wanting to call a slave. It shed a flickering golden light on my father's wasted face, and an odour of the olive press from the farm; a smoky fragrance of olives and cypress wood from the new press. Suddenly noises from below; someone entering the house. Footsteps rapidly mounting the stairs; a man at the door, who does not hesitate for an instant, but walks straight in, stoops over the pallet, and lifts my father's limp damp hand in both his own. Friends and servants came with him, and stood grouped round the door.

The newcomer was a forceful man, grey-haired, well built, he said, 'Neokles, my friend, dear friend'. Then my father opened his eyes. To the man leaning over him he said in an astonishing voice, as steady and strong as his living voice, 'Kleisthenes, my dear fellow, how good to see you again.' Then his lids closed once more. For a long while, or so it seemed, the room was stilled on those words; I stared at the famous grey head, gilded with flickering light from the little lamp, and wondered at the vistas of unknown things about my father that suddenly opened up.

41

My father's voice broke the stillness, and this time it had faded out again, to a difficult whisper. 'The boy is my son Themistokles,' he said.

Kleisthenes looked at me, briefly but sharply. 'I'll remember him, old friend,' he said, quietly. My father did not answer. He did not move or speak again. Kleisthenes stood upright. He beckoned me to the door of the room.

'Tell your mother, if she needs any help or advice, I am home,' he said, and left the house. Dazed, I said to one of his company, 'I didn't know he had come back.' The man turned, half-way down the stairs and said, 'We have only been here since noon. He came at once, as soon as he heard that Neokles was dying.' I remember how my heart lifted. If Kleisthenes felt like this over father, what might he not do for me? Might he not give me the foothold I needed, to become a powerful man? Then I looked towards my father, not dead yet, not quite yet, and I already thinking how to flout his wishes for me, and going to lay my head at the foot of his pallet I wept.

Once, Great King, when all the wrongs done to me were new-made wounds, I remembered my father's words about the ships upon the shore, and in bitterness said he was right, and wished that I had heeded him. But in truth, at the end, he was wrong. If I had not become a great man, the Athens my father loved, and all Hellas besides, would now be enslaved, under a more terrible tyrant than Hippias. I speak of you, Lord Artaxerxes. Of you, my friend and master, Great King.

My father died at dawn. And when later in the day I went out into the streets, to buy myrtle and spices and bid his friends to the funeral, I learned at once from all sides that Hippias was even at that moment leaving the city under escort. The Spartans had captured his wife and children, trying to escape to the sea, and to save them he had come down from the Acropolis, and agreed to whatever terms they asked of him. They were seeing him out of Attica. For my father we had a fine white marble stele made. It shows him sitting at a table, with the freedom cup in his hands. Your father's barbarians threw it down, and chipped the corners, the first time they sacked Attica; but I set it up again.

For two years after the death of my father I was enrolled as an ephebe, undergoing military training. The Athenians, Great King, do not employ paid professional soldiers; they might too easily desert, at a time of crisis, as Hippias' cavalry deserted him. Instead every citizen is trained to carry arms, living the life of a soldier for two years, from their eighteenth to their twentieth birthday. Aristeides and I were enrolled in different divisions, being from different districts. It's a good life in its way, though without much work for the mind to do. First there is a festival, at which one's hair is cut short; then much parading through the streets, visiting one shrine after another, wearing the short cloak and short tunic of a soldier, drawing the envious eyes of boys and the bright glances of women. I don't know how many times I wandered into the agora to read my own name on the list of ephebes posted there.

I was trained by a tough, low-born bastard called Phrixos who worked us nearly to death. One of the first things he did for us was to take us out of the city, to the slopes at the foot of Lyka-bettos, where the Spartans who had come with Kleisthenes were encamped. They had set up their tents in rows, and dug a neat ditch round them, and made a large mess-room, by constructing a thatch roof on timber uprights; and there they were, little-Sparta in Attica. Outside each tent stood a pole with numbers on it, and the names of the men who slept there. Phrixos marched us up through a wide road between lines of tents, and as we came a contingent of Spartans marched off across our path, all perfectly in step, their own footfalls drums enough for them; and Phrixos, looking at his raw bunch of falterers, yelled at us, 'that's how you ought to march, you blasted ... Athenians!' The Spartans laughed. They were burnt brown from the weather, tough faces, looking as resilient to onslaught as the exposed crags of stone upon the hills. They were quiet, except for their mirth at us pink boys; and they were all alike engaged upon the same task – cleaning weapons.

One of their officers saw us, and offered Phrixos a dish of wine. He went into the mess hall, and left us standing to attention in the hot sun. Then there was a trumpet call. In a whirl of cloaks and a clatter of hastily seized weapons the Spartans tore away up the slope to the top end of the camp, and fell into line there. Their officer was going to impress Phrixos by drilling them. So we stood on the edge of their encampment for more than an hour, watching the phalanx of men on the hill above us, flashing with points of dazzle in the sun, wheeling, marching, moving crabwise, dividing, reforming, all in blocks as though a hundred of them were one animal, a centipede trained to the trumpet. Then it was over, and they marched back in double file, coming past us without turning their heads, and one saw they were after all human; sweat on their bronzed temples ran down in streams, and darkened the leather chin-straps of their helmets. 'Oh, for a sweet Athenian girl this night!' murmured one, without turning his head, as he passed us.

Suddenly yelling at us, Phrixos made us stand to salute while they marched past us; then he addressed us. He told us they were bloody marvellous, paragons of battle, iron men, half-way to being gods, compared to a rabble of half-trained Athenians, who all wanted to be consulted by their commanders before a simple order was given. ... On and on he went, haranguing us unpatriotically till we cringed under his insults and the amused, contemptuous glances of the men around us.

Phrixos was a bastard, all right, though after a year's serving under him one conceded a reluctant respect. When he had finished with me I was bronzed, tough and muscular; my body, that had always been stocky, had filled out with muscle, my shoulders were wider than ever. I could march all day without dropping, without needing to drink. I could ride a horse in tight circles, or over a mountainside if need be. I had learned not to argue with commands, though I still knew what I thought of my commanders. I had learned to live outside the city, to live hard and work hard. I hated every minute of it.

My second year as an ephebe I spent on garrison duty at Phyle, on the north slope of Parnes, facing the frontier with Thebes. It is a desolate sort of place; mountainous, isolated, holding a road, along which travellers come, especially men from the north, trading in slaves and horses, but wherever they come from they don't want to stop at Phyle. Oh, the boredom of it! Still, there were compensations. I had time to read. I had some books written by Ionian men that interested me; Mnesiphilos sent them, with letters about the goings-on in the city. I was the only man in my troop who got letters, and that made me a butt for jokes. Not too much joking, though; I was as strong as a horse.

I made friends among my troop, especially a man called Lykos. He was my inferior in every respect, but not so much inferior that he could not see my merits and like to listen to me. As the best conversation I could get consisted of instructing Lykos, I did it willingly enough. In return, he could sing well. He had a light touch on the lyre, and a vague, expressionless, handsome face, and a clear sweet voice, not loud. Also he could remember more lyrics than I'd have thought possible, though he liked the words of

Simonides best of all, better even than Sappho. Near Phyle there was a grove of Pan, with a spring of clear sacred water. The people of the place honour it, being simple folk, shepherds and goatherds, mainly, the natural followers of the oldest gods. There, when we were free, we would go and sit, and hear Lykos singing, and he would often win us from an admiring onlooker a simple gift; a basket of figs, or a bowl of goat's milk to pass round and share between us. The place was haunted other than by the nymphs, for a girl wandered there; a mad girl with a lovely face, and un-combed hair garlanded with flowers, who yearned towards Lykos, without shame in her witlessness, coming to try to twine him in her arms when he sang. The girl was sacred to Pan we were told.

At this long distance I can remember next to nothing about duty at Phyle, except the lie of the land there, for which I had even then a strategic eye; and Lykos. I saw Lykos drown at Arte-mision, in the second battle, his body sucked under in the strong wake of the ship, his fine face glazed in the green race of smooth water amid the foam. About Lykos at Phyle two things have lodged in my mind. First that I had to tell him about the Plataians.

We were to exercise with them for a day. 'Who the Hades are the Plataians that we should drill with them?' he asked. I told him. They were our allies, wished on us long ago by Kleomenes the true Spartan, who never wished Athens well. The Plataians were distinct from their neighbours, being the only survivors of a people before the Boiotians, and Thebes had threatened them. They had asked for help from the Spartans, and the Spartans had told them that they were too far away for Spartan help to save them, and advised them to ask the Athenians instead. Hippias had taken them under our wing, for we lost no love on the Thebans, governed by as nasty a hive of oligarchs as you'll find anywhere in Hellas, and a good bit too powerful to make a comfortable neighbour, and, as you will know, Great King, ready to make common cause with an invading enemy against braver and more noble cities than their own.

'I'm all for doing down the Thebans,' said Lykos. 'But for heavens' sake, Themistokles, what good to us are the Plataians?' That's a question to which time gave an unexpected answer; I remember Lykos for it.

I remember him also for a punishment he suffered. He got him-self flogged and shackled in irons for a day and a night, for having fought another man of the troop, and with his bare hands having broken two of the man's ribs, and his nose, and his jaw, so that the victim was lucky to survive it, and wouldn't smirk in a mirror again as long as he lived. I went to see Lykos under punishment, hanging up in wrist irons from a tree, and I smuggled a little water-bottle under my cloak. The guards were sleepy, and I managed to let him sip from it without being seen.

'Why in Hades did you do that, Lykos?' I whispered, leaning over him, so that the drop of my cloak would hide the forbidden water bottle.

'He touched the mad girl,' said Lykos, in a dry, grating voice.

'I didn't know *you* fancied *her*,' I said, startled. 'I thought that was a one-sided affair!'

A wince slowly creased his stiffened face. 'I have a sister ... like her,' he said.

Think of it, Great King. I gazed at Lykos' weal-marked flanks with awe. There is a level at which all men are passionate, at which even a fool acts like a god. I taught Lykos about the Plataians, and he taught me respect for ordinary men; even the plainest of them may take fire, as lightning flashes from a humdrum grey sky. He was my friend, because of that, until he was drowned. I wonder what happened to his sister then? Did she haunt a shrine, in all weathers, at the mercy of the piety of men?

All this time I was dependent on Mnesiphilos' letters to keep me abreast of events in the city. His letters made grim reading. Kleisthenes had promised to remember me; so I hoped for advancement through him. I thought, as everyone else did, that power in the city would always continue to be in the gift of a few great men; Kleisthenes would dole out something to me. Just so, Great King, do men rise in Persia, and in the satrapies. But in the battle for influence Kleisthenes was getting the worst of it. All the aristocratic families, other than his own Alkmeonids, were sinking their differences, intent on keeping him out. Kleisthenes had already been archon, so he couldn't stand for the archonship again, but he was pressing the claims of his kinsman, Alkmeon. But Skamandrios was elected; and then Lysagoras, and then Isagoras, the Spartan lackey. To do myself justice, it wasn't only for my own sake I was downcast at what was happening. Right to my bones, I didn't like the kind of thing the eupatrid lordlings were doing. They were busy launching a purge of the voting-lists, striking out everyone who was not affiliated to one of the ancient priestly brotherhoods called phratries. It was a clever move. In the countryside of Attica, where the phratries are strongest, the noblemen also are strong. They own the lands, they are the priests of the local cults, they dominate the lowly men, and could control their votes in the assembly; and votes were going to matter again, now that the tyrants had gone. But the city was full of men who were independent. Solon had ruled that any man who knew a trade could find work in Athens, and be a citizen. Many useful men had come. Nobody had questioned their right to citizenship before, but most of them had not bothered to get adopted by a phratry, and they couldn't be bullied as easily as small-holders. They owned their own workshops, were self-supporting and self-respecting. Striking them off the lists would leave power where it had lain before the tyranny, before Solon – with the owners of wide lands.

My family's farm was small. Yet I, too, was a nobleman. I don't know why from the first I allied myself with the city commoners. It gives me pause, Lord Artaxerxes, to think how my whole life was shaped by an allegiance of which I do not know the origin. Does any man know the very root of his ways of thought? Perhaps it was because I always loved to walk through the trading-streets, watching the potters at work, and the leather workers, and the silver smiths. Perhaps it was a love of well-made things, which I learned from my father, for nearly all the lovely things in Athens were made by metics – Solon's new citizens. Like the freedom cup, made by Exekias. More likely it was because the traders and mariners came from this class of men – the sailors whose ships coming past Sounion had reminded me of birds in flight. More likely still it was my own half-breed standing, making me conscious of how narrow the exclusiveness of the oligarchs could be. For whatever reason, the endless news of disfranchise-ment in the city angered me at my duty in remote Phyle.

In the last few weeks of my time as an ephebe, Kleisthenes suddenly proposed in the assembly that all free Athenians should be placed on the citizen lists at once, with no more fussing over the old rules. Joyful crowds started to throng the streets in support of it; all those who had lost their rights, and many more who feared loss of status, and, to do the people justice, a certain number whose own rights were not in question, but who did not like to see their neighbours pushed around. By a stroke of good for-tune my troop was brought back from Phyle, and set on guard duty outside the Bouleuterion, where the Council were in session preparing the agenda to put to the assembly of the people. Of course, outside the Bouleuterion the crowds were thickest, and loudest too, but they weren't really disorderly – all we had to do was to stand by the doors, swords unsheathed, and watch them. I call it good fortune that brought me there, because I hated to be out of the city when anything of moment was happening: just as I hate it still; I hate it now. Even now, while the day warms the garden beyond my shady colonnade, and bleaches the distances into a pale grey-green, and I sit in my cool inner room, and write my last letter. Well, I am not your prisoner, Great King; I could always have gone home, always, any time I had been willing to face my accusers.

There I was in the middle of it. Isagoras wouldn't put Kleisthenes' proposal to the assembly; instead he said that the Alkmeonids all ought to be banished; they were still under an ancient curse. And he sent messages in haste to his friends in Sparta. It really looked as if we might have open fighting in the streets. But Kleisthenes went. He did not try to address the assembly; he took all his family and followers, and went. Men felt deserted. The crowds dispersed, and a sullen quiet hung over the city. A small contingent of Spartans came, led by Kleomenes himself. Small, but well armed, and this time they camped within the city, billeted in a district of rich houses, filling Isagoras' fine garden with rows of tents. Isagoras thought the trouble was over. He started to wear a cloak of purple, and walk around with a pair of Spartans trailing two steps behind him, just as Kleomenes did. Kleomenes strutted around the streets, looking at Athens as though he was thinking of buying it, and a whisper went round that Isagoras' wife was the main attraction of the place. What a spectacle! A King of Sparta, no less, patrolling the streets of our city, all to make sure that some honest potter or hard-working shipwright doesn't get a vote! Everything was quiet; they mistook it, those two, for calm; it was the heavy hush before thunder. We ephebes were released from our training on time, and went to enroll as citizens. Lucky for me that in my mixed inheritance it was my mother, not my father, who was the metic.

The banishment of the Alkmeonids was proclaimed and pinned up in public places, and still there was quiet. Then young bluebloods from Isagoras' supporters went out to the Kerameikos, marching down the sacred way, taking Spartan soldiers with them; and coming to the place of graves they smashed and threw down the memorials to Alkmeonid dead. Then they dug up the graves, and shovelled the bones into a cart, to be trundled across Attica, and thrown into a ditch beyond the boundary stone. Then they came back through the city, with the stench of corpses on their impious hands, and still, still, there was quiet.

The thunder broke when Isagoras, with a troop of Spartans, went down to a meeting of the Council, and proclaimed that the Council was dissolved, and would be replaced by three hundred men, named by him, in his capacity as archon. Now at that time the Council were four hundred men, chosen by lot, according to the laws of Solon; that is, they were just ordinary men, elected from their farms or workshops, or grand estates, by mere chance, or by the gods if you believe it so. And they met outside their chamber, the Bouleuterion, which is on the south-east corner of the agora, where the market is held every day. So a large crowd had gathered within minutes of Isagoras standing up to speak. A large crowd, and I myself among them.

I was standing far back, and could not hear the words that were spoken. There was an interchange going on between the president of the Council, and Isagoras. The crowd on the agora, massed at Isagoras' back, began to mutter angrily as the news of what his proclamation contained filtered back through them; but for a while it wasn't clear what was going to happen. At last the president stopped talking to Isagoras. He sat down. He sat in the marble chair from which he presided over the Council, the councillors moved little by little closer together, and stood facing Isagoras and his Spartans.

As soon as the president sat down, we could see that the incredible had happened. The Council was refusing to go! The crowd cheered them, noisily, and stamped rhythmically on the ground chanting Solon, Solon, Solon! From all the streets leading to the agora, men came pouring at a run. The councillors looked very frightened. They huddled together like sheep in a rainstorm, but they stood their ground. The president for that famous session, which had met only to pass the usual day's business in the usual way, was a nobody, a nobody in particular, a salt merchant living near Phaleron, a respectable man, willing enough to serve a year on the Council, but without ambition. Oh, but he too, when something kindled fire in him, acted like a god! He sat in his chair, and banged his staff on the ground, as though he actually proposed to call the meeting to order and get on with the day's work! At this point the Spartans drew their swords.

A hush fell over us all. There was a long silence, like an indrawn breath; and almost the whole body of the people stood so still that we could hear faintly, far away above us the sound of the silver gong in the temple of Athene on the Acropolis, marking the time of prayer. On the grape-basket on the fruit stall beside me, the flies buzzed audibly. Then a voice, ringing like the voice of an actor in the theatre, cried an order. Some few of the Spartans turned round to face the crowd; the others, levelling their swords in front of them, moved slowly up the slope towards the councillors.

A multiple, ugly low growling rose from the crowd. The Spartans continued to press the four hundred slowly up the slope. The president held his gilded staff like a spear, as though to ward off blows. His men edged backwards, little by little. A voice from behind me in the crowd inquired, 'Athenians, shall we see our council murdered before our eyes?' From all parts of the crowd at once, a roar followed, and the whole mass of us rioted, shrieking, and rushed upon the Spartans. The few men who had turned to face the crowd and hold us back were overwhelmed instantly, checking the onrush for only a bare second. Then the crowd had swept through the Spartan platoon and trampled them down; the rush carried them right to the doors of the Bouleuterion, where men leapt and danced on the steps, and embraced the councillors.

The Spartans, separated from each other in the mob, were being kicked, and manhandled, and stripped of armour and weapons, and even of the last garments they had on; and somewhere in that boiling mass was Isagoras, or so I thought. I hoped he was getting torn limb from limb. Suddenly we saw him, dashing out of a side door of the Bouleuterion, into which he had somehow wriggled when the crowd broke. He was running for his life towards the reinforcing platoon of Spartans who had appeared at the south-east corner of the agora. Howling like dogs we chased after him. He shot into the massed rank of the new Spartan troop, and disappeared from sight.

They didn't even try to hold their ground; they began to back up, behind their levelled spears, immediately, and the whole crowd pressed after them. Everyone was shouting something different round me; it was a rhythmic yell: 'Pigs, pigs pigs pigs, Lakedaimonian *pigs*!' When they reached the foot of the path up to the Acropolis, they broke formation, and ran. We grabbed a few of them, and at least one man was dragged down and trampled to death before my eyes; most of them got to the top, and barricaded the path. There was a pause. The great crowd came to a halt. Looking upwards, and remembering Hippias holding out there, we could see the fun was over, for the moment.

The Spartans were not the only ones to underestimate the

Athenian crowd. I thought, 'If someone doesn't *do* something, they'll all go home. Who might come, and give orders? All the great men of one persuasion are up there behind the barricades, and Kleisthenes has gone, with all his friends, and we are without leaders. But it seemed we didn't need them. Someone, a mere voice louder than the others, cried, 'Spread out! Cut them off from the other path!' And the crowd began to run round the foot of the Acropolis, flowing through the streets like floodwater, and breaking off in groups to hold this place or the other, without needing to be told. I, too, ran. I found friends, slaves, a barber, a bath-attendant, anyone whose name I knew, and said to them, 'Go to the men holding such and such a street, and ask them where they live, so that you can go and fetch their arms to them.' And people went at once to obey me. Not from any authority of mine; for all over the city men were following any sensible suggestion, no matter who it came from. Xanthippos suddenly appeared beside me, as I grabbed someone's arm, and began the request again.

'What are you doing, Themistokles?' he asked.

'Asking men to bring arms to their fellows in the streets,' I said. 'Good,' he answered. He was staggering under a great armful of rusty swords. 'I got these from an armourer's shop,' he said. 'Help me to take them to the men up there, facing the pigs' barricade.' I took half his load. We scrambled up the path, pushing our way through the throng, till we reached the group of men who were nearest the enemy. We handed out our scruffy gifts. Most of the men there were old soldiers, greybeards, our seniors, but they thanked us respectfully; we had shown presence of mind. 'We shall need water next,' someone said to me.

'I and my friends will see that you get it,' I offered.

Then we were running down the hill, back to the agora. I jumped on a stall-holder's barrow, and cried out, 'To me! to me! I need fifty helpers, for the good of the city!' A sea of upturned faces gathered round me. 'Go round the houses,' I told them. 'Bang on the doors, call for the lady of the house. Tell all the women to bring food and water; tell them not to look for their own men-folk, but to trust their sisters for that; tell them to take food and water to the nearest group of citizens they can find, for we shall be watching all this night.'

'Some this way, some that!' cried an answering voice. Xanthippos was pushing people off, making sure some went in each direction. I left him to it, and went running to see what was happening round the walls.

The walls were swarming with men. Each gate was held by a crowd, all spy-points on the circuit were occupied. Not that the Spartans could bring up an army to the rescue before many days; but that news might not easily reach them, for the crowds at the gates were greeting people coming in, and scrutinising people going out. Men came to and fro, carrying weapons and water-bottles. Men who only yesterday would never have trusted a neighbour with an obol were giving the name of their house to any stranger; armour worth a year's work was taken from the walls of a house by a poor man and carried to its owner as though no one had ever heard of theft. Women walked through the streets offering water or wine to men unknown to them, as though they had never heard of shame; the Spartans might be able to walk across a hill like one great beetle in their phalanx, but we too can act as one; we too!

Sometime that afternoon I went home to my mother and my brother. My mother was in great distress, wringing her hands, saying a man had come who told her to go out and offer food to strangers.

'Mother,' I said, stooping to kiss her cheek (I do not remember an earlier day on which I had to stoop down to her) 'go and do so; you will be proud to tell your grandchildren about it one day.' To Timoleon, my brother, who was only a lad, I said, 'Take all the male slaves in the house, Timoleon, and carry oil through the streets, offering to fill men's lamps against the dusk. Oh, Timoleon,' I called him back, for with a joyful face he was already running on his errand, 'do not fail to tell any man who takes your oil that it comes from the household of the sons of Neokles.'

'Must I be back by dark?' he asked, his face flushed with excitement.

'Stay till the oil gives out,' I told him. My mother made a gesture of dismay. 'Only the Spartans will come to any harm in the streets of Athens tonight,' I told her.

After the sudden dusk, when stillness spreads over the city under the wing of darkness, I thought again that a time had come when men might one by one go home. I ate a little, and then went out. And every street, like a golden necklace, was twinkling with lines and clusters of lights; each watching man had lit a lamp beside him, that the Spartans might see that he was there. Torches burned in the agora, and by the city gates. Exultation lifted my tiredness away. I walked on and on. All through the city the streets were full of sleeping men; they lay against the walls of the houses, armed, with loosened fingers still curved around their sword hilts. Who will dare stir this hornet's nest?

At dawn we could see the Spartans; faces looking over the crags, and over the barricades. Doubtless they could see us, too. Even before first light the gates were opened for men pouring in from the countryside, well-armed men, coming to play their part. Those who had watched all night could stagger home to their beds, leaving newcomers holding every possible line of descent from the citadel, every corner in the streets. The countrymen had brought food; the stall-holders in the agora had set up their wares again, and were knocking down the price of things to men in arms. The women were out again, bringing bread and wine; it really might have been a public feast-day rather than a siege. The sun burned higher and higher in the sky, and men reminded each other that there was no water on the Acropolis, and no store-house either. In joyful indignation we rehearsed to each other our outrage at the gross attack on our ancient rights; not even Hippias had attacked the Council. Drunk with euphoria men even brought lyres and flutes into the streets, and sang to each other where they sat. The streets rang with music and laughter; could they hear us, up there? 'Sing louder! They'll have dry throats up there; let them hear us!' said someone, as I passed by. Another voice struck up, loudly, with a familiar song: 'Pallas Athene shields us with her arm!' His friends chime in with him.

Again at the second dusk lights were lit all over the city, to burn all night. I put on my father's armour, and going up the path nearest the Acropolis I found a sleeping man and, shaking him gently, told him to go home and leave his place to me. So I sat, leaning against a wall, and looked at the stars for a long while. A little way off a sleepy man was playing the lyre, softly, slowly, and then more slowly, till at last the notes stammered into silence.

When the moon had set there was a sudden noise above us; a tramping of feet. They were trying to break out. All round me men leapt to their feet, shouting, and banging their shields with their sword hilts to rouse others. We linked arms, and stood in a chain, ready to meet an onrush coming down on us in the dark. Men came running up behind us, and formed another rank, and we could hear the alarm being cried from street to street down through the city. But all that came was the scampering, shuffling noise as the sally party changed its mind, and scuttled to safety again. We shouted jibes into the night.

I turned to the man whose arm was linked in mine, about to

say something as we released our hold on each other. It was Aristeides, helmeted, his face full of shadow in the angled light of a lamp.

'Why, Themistokles,' he said, smiling. 'You are proved right, I think.'

'In what way, out of many possible?' I asked him.

'Was it not you,' he said, laughing, 'who claimed that the greatest good fortune possible was to be an Athenian?'

'You don't like all my sayings,' I said, resentfully.

'No,' he said, 'I don't. But few men are always right, Themistokles.'

I smiled at him. But the slight chill between us remained.

At dawn the next morning, a scruffy unshaven delegation, bearing a branch of olive, came down to negotiate. They wanted to find somebody with whom they could talk privately, but they were told that the only lawful authority in the city was the Council, or the Assembly. The Council would hear them, in full session, sitting in public. So people flocked to the agora, and this time I made sure I was near the Council dais, and able to hear what was said.

They brought messages from Isagoras. He said he would not, after all, dissolve the Council, if the people would return to their homes, and restore peace in the streets.

The Council president retorted that Isagoras had not the power to dissolve the Council. Let him not bargain with them over that.

Then the delegation said Isagoras was the lawfully elected archon. In the name of the archon, therefore, the Council must order the people to go home, and cease to molest him, and his guests. This had answer enough in an enraged roar from the massed listeners in the agora.

At last they asked for water and food to be brought up to them.

'Do you think we will make you comfortable, while help comes from Lakedaimon?' said the president. 'We are not fools. Since the first hour you fled away from us, we have watched every road, every pathway out of Attica. If a message has slipped through concerning your plight, and reached the Spartans, it was a cunning messenger who brought it. It will be many days before help comes to you, and you shall have neither water nor food from us.'

We could see the despair this brought them to; they drooped visibly.

'These are the terms we will make with you,' said the president, in a loud voice, carrying over their heads to the people beyond. 'The Spartans and their King may depart, if they lay down their weapons first. We will escort them out of Attica. Isagoras the archon, and all the Athenians who are with you, must surrender themselves to judgement by the people.'

The leader of the Spartans raised his head. 'You will regret this, Athenians!' he cried. 'You will bring upon yourselves the vengeance of armies! A wise man would think twice before he made enemies of the Spartans!'

'We have not made the Spartans our enemies,' said the president. 'They have made themselves the enemies of our liberty. But we are of one mind to defend it, against anyone.' Then the people cheered him. We roared and stamped and waved our arms. The little group of Spartans stood close together. Still their leader found courage to cry above the uproar, 'We cannot hand over our friends to massacre!'

The president raised his staff for silence, and hushed the crowd a little. 'They will not lose so much as a hair from their heads till they have had a fair trial,' he said. And the people agreed. I wouldn't have given much for their chances if the people had set hands on them, but nobody would want to hang another scandal round the neck of liberty, like the one which still haunted Kleisthenes. One of his ancestors, more than a century before, had killed off the supporters of an earlier tyrant without trial, and only a few weeks back Isagoras was still getting the Alkmeonids banished for it. When we had seen the bedraggled delegates off the scene, the Council announced that they had prepared a resolution to put to the Assembly at noon, to rescind the ban on the Alkmeonids, and invite Kleisthenes to return. He was already in the city; as soon as the proposal was voted, he appeared in person to thank the citizens, and to be carried round the city shoulder high by joyful young kinsmen. Kleomenes meanwhile accepted our terms. He couldn't do anything else.

I have seen many extraordinary sights, in a long life, Great King; but never anything to beat the sight of the Spartans filing down from the Acropolis, misery eaten into their faces, throwing their arms onto a great clanking bronze pile at the foot of the path, their eyes turned longingly towards the fountain that trickled nearby. They were obviously afraid we would mishandle them, but although the people turned out to see them go they were marched away with nothing worse than jeers thrown at them,

55

each man between two Athenians. Kleomenes himself came nearly last, holding his head high, unhelmeted though he was. They were hustled out of the city, and along the road to Eleusis, and got over the frontier just before darkness fell. The Athenians who had taken their part were thrown into prison. But Isagoras himself, the arch-traitor, was not among them; Kleomenes had smuggled him out, somehow. Soon it was being said he had been bundled up in a basket of soiled linen; the vengeance of the city was frustrated, and issued out as a stream of lewd jokes. Even my mother got to hear of them. And a bawdy trader in the agora, whose usual stock was gear for horse-riding, started selling his linen trusses as 'Isagoras' headbands'.

And that, Great King, is how the Athenian people won their freedom, in spite of the Spartans. I, a young man, who till then had always lived under tyranny, was filled with passion and ambition by the days I have described to you. I saw the city like some splendid fiery horse who goes lame and sickens, is a jade without spirit if it is beaten and made to carry burdens, but who would gallop all day and all night for a rider who let it run free. No power that rests on fear and force of arms can compare with the power given freely by the citizens, and I would have refused the throne of the Medes and Persians if I could have had the archonship of the Athenians instead; for what I craved (in those far-off days) was not power for the pleasure and use of power, but power for the glory of being chosen, being chosen by the men of my own city.

All in good time. I was twenty in the archonship of Isagoras, which fell in the year of the sixty-eighth games at Olympia. The man who could ride the city was Kleisthenes, and over us all the impending vengeance of the Spartans hung like storm-clouds over harvest fields.

The assembly voted Kleisthenes' bill to make a citizen out of every adult in Athens without delay; and a feast was held to purify the Acropolis and give men a chance to celebrate. But it was one thing to vote the bill, and another to make it work. There would have been trouble and great bitterness had we forced the family cults to accept new members. Instead, Kleisthenes worked out a new system altogether. In place of the four ancient tribes, he made ten new ones; we called them after heroes of Attica in legend, submitting a list to Delphi for the final choice of the Oracle. Every man in Attica belonged to one of the new tribes, depending on which deme, or locality, he lived in. To be a citizen, one had only to belong to a deme. Thus everyone, no matter who his parents were, could register as a citizen. All citizens could vote in the Assembly, and the Council was enlarged to five hundred, so that ten tribes could be equally represented in it. Kleisthenes was a clever man, an architect of the laws; he did not just divide the land into ten areas. Had he done that, all the new voters, whose support he counted on as his and his family's for ever, would have been in the same tribe – the city one – and always outnumbered by the other nine. Instead he made every tribe, roughly equal in numbers, out of three parts; one from the city demes, one from the inland demes, one from the coastal demes. Democracy is so unfamiliar to you, Lord Artaxerxes, that you may not realise at once what differences this made; indeed, many of the Athenians who voted for it did not fully realise. But, however powerful a local lordling might be, from now on for ever, he could never control more than one-third of the votes in his tribe; the other two-thirds came from other parts of Attica. Anyway, many men found themselves owning land in demes belonging to several different tribes, but they could only vote in one. And in each of the ten tribes, one-third of the members were city-dwellers – the traders, and sailors, and artisans – who would never again be subordinate to the will of the farmers, and who owed their new power to Kleisthenes. The city was thus made powerful, and the chances of a return to oligarchy were smashed for ever, unless it came from outside, from Isagoras, restored by the Spartans. Henceforward a man would be registered in the deme of his father, even if the family had sold off their land and moved elsewhere; and so as time went on the local interests would grow weaker, and one part of Attica would have no means of quarrelling with another.

Having dealt with oligarchy in this way, Kleisthenes also moved a bill to make a return to tyranny impossible; he passed in the Assembly a law that made it possible to banish a man from Attica for ten years without taking away his property or his right to return when ten years were past. In this way, Kleisthenes told us, we would always be able to get rid of a man whose power had grown too great for the safety of the city, even though he had committed no crime. The Assembly, happy to entrench its liberties, passed by large majorities everything Kleisthenes laid before it. There was a moderate rejoicing, clouded by the knowledge that the spring would come, and with it Kleomenes and his Spartans, eager for revenge.

As soon as the enfranchisement of new voters had been put to the Assembly, Kleisthenes moved that we send an embassy to Persia to seek alliance with the Great King, that he might protect us against the Spartans. This, too, the people agreed to; but Kleisthenes did not explain the terms the King was likely to exact before he would agree to help us. Not many Athenians knew much about the east; I think they thought the King was the master just of a great city, like Sparta. Nevertheless, Kleisthenes had miscalculated, Great King. He had expected, I think, simply to add the people to the Alkmeonid following, and for this purpose had freed them from the need to follow anybody at all. He had expected to lean upon the Persian King, but he had forgotten how many of his new men were those who had fled out of Ionian cities, escaping from the Great King's rule.

As for me, I had admired Kleisthenes, I had been ready to fight in his support. Still I thought him a great man, was glad at the changes he made. But when he sent envoys to Persia I parted company from him; I knew he cared not for freedom, but only for power for himself. If he had cared for Athens he would not have been ready to sell her into the Lion's maw. From that moment onwards, I did not expect to rise as Kleisthenes' man, but by my own efforts. For Kleisthenes had made an opportunity, a great one, for a man who was both democratic and against the King. Who else would the mariners, and the traders, and exiled Ionians follow? This business also affected my friends, divided our paths a little. Aristeides, passionate for the rights of the people, could not see Persia as a danger – could see no further than Sparta. Xanthippos followed Kleisthenes, and could see no wrong in him.

Be that as it may, the envoys were sent to Sardis. They arrived, Great King, when Artaphernes, son of Hystaspes, was the satrap there; and on hearing their request he asked them for earth and water, as Kleisthenes must have known he would, and they gave them, as I am sure they had been told to do. But in Athens the Assembly met every day voting the very liberties that our envoys, bowing before the satrap, were even then giving away; and long before they returned time had caught up with them, and the friendship of the Lions of Persia was too late.

For in the spring the Lakedaimonians came up the Isthmus, marching with all their allies into Attica. And at the same time the Boiotians, with the Theban dogs at the head of them, and the

Chalkidians, putting across the channel from Euboia, moved down on us from the north and the north-east. The Spartans were burning crops and cutting olives and defiling the temples at Eleusis, and we raised every man in Attica who could carry arms and marched out to meet them. We were drawn up in battle order at dawn, standing in long lines across the approaches between the forests of Parnes, and the high ground called Aigaleos. We were on a long slope there, and we could see the enemy on the plains beneath us. The morning light shining on the plain of Eleusis and on the bay shimmered green and blue in our eyes. And all across the plain the Lakedaimonians and their allies glittered in ranks of bronze. We were outnumbered many times over; four times – five? We had time to count, to stare, to tremble. Lykos, and I, and the others who had trained with us were lined up with Phrixos in charge of us again, and all, I imagine, as I did, thanking him instead of hating him for the iron training he had given us.

All through a long hot morning we stood there in the sun, sweating like pigs and passing the water-bottles from hand to hand. We stared at them. What were they doing down there? To our right the Corinthians were drawn up; we could see the dolphins flying on their pennants. They were firm allies of the Spartans, but had also been friends of ours in the past. We could see the twin tents of the Spartan Kings, with a shining standard on the door-pole of each one, a little way behind their lines to our left. And we could see a great deal of coming and going, with horsemen riding to and fro, and small detachments of men, escorting the captains, perhaps, moving here and there. The sun burned over our heads, and each man stood in his own shrunken shadow, and still they didn't move. Our own generals began to confer. Should we force a battle, by moving down the slope?

Then, thinned by distance, we heard the trumpets calling. The Corinthians began to move. Why did they move, when the others stood their ground? And before our disbelieving eyes the whole force of the Corinthians wheeled and marched away. We cheered them, and watched them until they were only a cloud of dust, dimly discernible in the mists of the horizon, towards Megara. And now, one by one, contingent by contingent, they all drew off, even one of the Spartan Kings striking his tent and retreating; and last Kleomenes went too, melting away in the sun.

Later we knew that the Corinthians, when they heard what Kleomenes' goal was, and why he had called them to arms, re-fused to fight, and then the other king of the Spartans, Damaratos,

– that very Damaratos, Great King, who is now a courtier of
yours – took up their argument, and the other allies followed him.
The Spartans were never again to allow both their kings to go
on one expedition. As for us, we marched away, taking a route
across country, to meet the Chalkidians in the east. When we were
half-way to meet them our general suddenly turned us about, and
we went for the Boiotians instead. They were not expecting us, and
were in marching lines, trailing over a wide stretch of the country,
going to aid the Chalkidians. It was too late for them to form
up in battle order; only their cavalry managed to group itself in
time. A well-drilled phalanx of hoplites can easily upset cavalry –
pricking the horses with their spears, and keeping out of reach of
the riders' swords. We broke them, and they fled, riding out of
Attica with their whips on their horses' necks, each man saving
himself. Their foot soldiers were left to our mercy. When we were
sick of killing there were seven hundred left as prisoners.

By now it was some three hours until dusk, and the Chalkidians
hadn't waited for us, but had taken to their ships, and gone home
across the water. But the Eretrians, who had been bullied by Chalkis
for many years, had drawn up along our coast a flotilla of ships
and barges, and they sent messages, offering to convey us across,
and to bring water and food for the troops. Our generals came
before us and said, 'Athenians, shall we go after the Chalkidians
this very day?' Who would have his neighbour hear him say no
to such a question, no matter how tired he might be. So off
we went. And the gods, or our good opportunity, favoured us, for
the Chalkidians never suspected we might follow them at once.
They were just disembarked, clustered round their shipways, and
the Eretrians brought us round a small hill that concealed us from
sight till the last minute, giving us time to make our line of battle
before we came down on them. They broke and ran almost at
once, and then one party of us marched into the strong places
of their city and held them till dawn, and the others caught and
fettered prisoners.

So when night fell on the day of battles the Athenians were in
Chalkis. And in Thebes there was weeping, and in Sparta shame.
We had seen out of Attica three armies, and there was no state
in Hellas that would readily broach us again.

Our victories made a new dawn for us. We held our prisoners
to ransom, for two hundred drachmas a man; most of them were
in irons a long time. When they were all bought free, we hung
up the fetters that had bound them on a wall on the Acropolis,

facing the doors of the temple of Athene; when I was last in Athens they were there still, hanging in molten lumps, on a wall scorched and blackened by Persian fire. With a tithe of the ransom money we had four bronze horses made and set up outside the temple, with a boasting inscription beneath them. Those are gone, Great King, and doubtless some satrap of yours knows where, taken in plunder; the base and the inscription remain. They were fine beasts, with stamping hooves and flaring nostrils.

From Chalkis also we took a wide swathe of land, green land and fertile, where the proud men of that city had pastured horses. We divided it into farms, and offered it free to the poorer men of Attica. And, so deeply had Kleisthenes' new liberties moved the hearts of the Athenians, that we could not find settlers enough to fill the new land, till Alkmeon intervened. Alkmeon was Kleisthenes' kinsman, and had been elected archon when Isagoras' term ran out – though Isagoras himself, you recall, had run out somewhat before that. Alkmeon proposed to let takers of land in Chalkis retain their rights and duties as citizens. Those who took land on these terms were called cleruchs; they were not very different from farmers in the remote parts of Attica itself, coming into the city to the Assembly only when some danger threatened or some change in the price of corn or oil was rumoured.

And so it happened, Great King, that when the envoys from Artaphernes returned to us, bringing an alliance with the King, they came too late, when the danger against which we had needed you had been dispelled by ourselves alone. When it was known that the envoys had given earth and water, and made the land a province of the King, a vote was moved in the Assembly to put them to death as traitors. Kleisthenes did not move to save them; so great was the feeling of the people after their victories that he would have failed, and perhaps encompassed his own condemnation. Naturally the envoys protested that they had been given authority to do what they had done; but everyone knew that the earth and water had not been authorised by the Assembly, so our unfortunate messengers were thrown into the execution pit.

Kleisthenes himself escaped condemnation, or even rebuke; he was still honoured in the city. But he knew, and we knew, that he had bred a horse he could not ride. The city was not his to control; Athens would not be his. We were not going to follow him, Great King, into the jaws of the Lion. As I said, Kleisthenes had miscalculated and forgotten that many of the new citizens had come to us out of Ionia, where the yoke of the King was even then rubbing shoulders sore. He was an old man by then, and he died just before his reforms were completed in the Assembly. He was a great man; and, though he would have made us Persians, yet at home he made us free. Without the changes he made, that gave power to the ordinary man, I would not have been able to do what I did; and so in the end we would not have been saved from being Persians. Was he then a friend or an enemy to the Kings? Or which am I?

About the time of Kleisthenes' death, I remember, I first heard that infuriating song, which honours Harmodios and Aristogeiton, those two ineffective men, as responsible for freeing the city from tyrants. Even in the new dawn, the Athenians praised the undeserving, and forgot their true benefactors. I did so myself. For I must admit that the song was sung often enough under my roof; I was trying to entice great men to gather at my house, and so was paying good singers, like Epikles of Hermione, to sing and play at my dinner table.... 'A myrtle bough my sword shall wear....' One can't deny it's a good tune. Sung in a fine house, too; for about then I sold off the farm at Sounion, keeping the tumble-down house there out of sentiment, and at the same time sold my father's little house in the city, and with the money I had built a fine house in the best district, and brought my mother and my brother there. I ignored my mother's distress at this change in family life. To my brother I made some explanation. I was to be a new Athenian under the rules of Kleisthenes. I did not need land to be somebody, and I wasn't 'Son of Neokles' only, but Themistokles from the deme Phrearros, in the tribe Leontis. I pleased Mnesiphilos, when I sold the farm, by having the crier list among its advantages that it had a good neighbour.

And in the new dawn I, like all the others, turned my back on Kleisthenes. I didn't go to his death-bed, as he had come to my father's. And all because he had had dealings with the King! Artaxerxes, my friend, did you once doubt that the gods have a sense of irony?

In the years that followed I set myself to gain a following among the people; to detach from the Alkmeonids – they have hated me for it – all those who were disenchanted because they were against a Persian alliance. I took up the life of a citizen. I went assiduously to the Assembly, I walked the streets, and sat in the barbers' shops, and talked to men of all kinds. I got a reputation for never forgetting a face, or the name that went with it; I had to work hard at that. A poor and humble man, Great King, can be made your friend for life because you remember him when he expected to be forgotten. And no man, however humble, is of no account in a city where all men have votes in the Assembly. I noticed that Aristeides was making a name for himself as an arbitrator of disputes; doubtless he knew the laws as well as many another, but it was for remarkable fairness, and the refusal to take bribes, that he was becoming known. I thought that was a good line to have, and I began to seek the same sort of reputation myself. I never exactly got it; but I have sharp wits. I could get people out of tangles, and suggest solutions that neither had thought of and that would satisfy both. I should explain that plain men in Athens will often go to some citizen of standing with their troubles, trying to avoid the expense and notoriety of the public law-courts.

I did not cease to seek Aristeides' company; there had been a disagreement between us, but I wouldn't let it go; I would have worried at it like a dog with a bone, talked it over and over till we could have agreed; would have, if ever I could have got near him. But in those days he was going around with a young dandy called Stesilaos, a man from Keos, who had the loveliest face and limbs that ever were born in Hellas, and the wits of a singing bird. So I couldn't find Aristeides alone. Stesilaos was not unfriendly, nor indeed was Aristeides, but as soon as we started to talk Stesilaos would chip in with some frivolous or ill-informed remark, to which Aristeides would listen with grave attention as though it had come from me. Infuriated, I would stop trying to discuss things with him and, being no good at light elegant chatter, would take myself off. Still I kept trying to find Aristeides alone, and he never was. Stesilaos put a slack, calm look on Aristeides' face, like the look of a man after wine, and made him laugh, suddenly creasing his lean cheeks and solemn mouth with mirth. Surely he hardly ever laughed before? I asked myself, angry.

Then, late on a summer evening, as I was making my way homewards through the streets, I came upon Aristeides, who had just seen Stesilaos to his door and was on his own way home. We fell into step together without a word, and walked slowly the length of the street together in silence. Then he said, 'What have you done today, Themistokles?'

'I have exercised, won a bout at throwing the discus, walked, talked, settled a shipmaster's quarrel with a merchant, been to the

Assembly, listened to gossip about what Kleomenes is plotting in Sparta, drunk wine with a friend, and now go to my bed,' I answered. 'And you, Aristeides?'

'Oh, much the same,' he said. 'What's all this about the discus, Themistokles? You never used to care for all that.'

'Not for winning, and having odes written for me!' I said, laughing. The sheer pleasure of talking with him sensibly again warmed me so that I could have embraced him. 'But the trainer tells me it will strengthen my arms and shoulders.' He roared with laughter, staggering as he walked with mirth. 'But my dear fellow, you're nearly square already!' Then he flung an arm round my shoulders, and said, 'You're like a plough ox, already! Whatever has got into you?'

'Truth to tell, Aristeides,' I said, 'I came back from Sounion last week with a shipmaster who let me try a turn with the steering-oar. I am glad to say I got the hang of it well enough and didn't let go till Phaleron, but I ached more cruelly the day after than any day since I first carried a shield.'

At this we had reached my door, but I took his arm as he slipped it from my shoulder and said, 'Come in and drink a little wine with me before you go. You'll sleep better for it.' He hesitated, then he came.

He had not been into my new house till then. He raised his eyebrows at the width of the portico.

'This is splendid,' he said.

'It has a cool garden,' I said. 'Come and see.'

'In the dark?' he said.

'The moon's rising,' I answered. It had lifted just high enough to pour silver over my fig tree and onto the surface of my little pool, and we wandered across and sat on the marble bench I had had built beside it. A slave-boy, drowsy and slow, brought wine and a drinking-cup. 'Not that one,' I said. 'Bring the one that hangs on the wall beside my bed. And have a care with it.'

So the boy brought the freedom cup, and I mixed wine for Aristeides. When he had drunk a little, I risked, 'I have wanted a chance to talk with you, and missed it.'

'What do you want to talk about, Themistokles?' he asked, with an edge of wariness in his voice that surprised me.

'This and that,' I said. 'Mostly of what you well may know about the happenings in Sparta.' His careful face relaxed at once.

'You knew I had been sent with the others, to spy?'

'I knew.'

'Well, Kleomenes has dropped Isagoras. He has assembled all the allies of Sparta to ask them to help him restore Hippias.'

'Perhaps Isagoras has come to smell of dirty linen,' I said, raising a smile on his face. 'Was Hippias there?'

'Oh yes, robed like a Persian, flowing from head to foot in purple and gold, and carrying scrolls of oracles around with him everywhere. I'd forgotten he would be old. He's an old man now.'

'And is it true, as I hear, that the Corinthians again refused to help him against us?'

'Just so. They would not; and then Damaratos, the other Spartan King, opposed it too, as he did before. There's no love lost between Kleomenes and him, and they share the power.'

'The threat melts away again,' I said. 'Though we cannot always be depending upon the Corinthians. I have been wondering why the Corinthians do as they have done. I think it must be that they approve Sparta in the Peloponnese, but would feel too much hemmed in if her power ran on beyond, and surrounded them.'

'Why must they have a selfish and calculating motive, Themistokles?' he asked. 'Why not the one they gave?'

'Under fine words people always do have mean motives,' I said, but seeing the distaste on his face, since he turned into the moonlight just in time, I hastened over it, and said, 'What was the reason they gave?'

'Sosikles, their delegate, got up and said, "The heavens in future will be beneath us, and the earth above, since the Spartans wish to put down free government, and set up tyrannies in the cities." Then he reminded them forcibly that they made sure enough of their own freedom, and told them that the Corinthians themselves could remember the ways of tyrants only too well. He gave some blood-curdling illustrations; I had no idea what the tyrants at Corinth had been up to! Anyway, we had guessed already that he would speak in some such sense, for he had agreed to hide the three of us Athenian observers among his attendants, so that we could witness what was said.'

'Perhaps, then, Damaratos will crush the danger from Kleomenes,' I said.

'Yes, I think he will. Though I would feel easier if I thought he did it from love of us, or liberty, rather than from pure dislike of Kleomenes.'

The boy came, and hung a lamp from a branch of the tree over our heads. A golden, smoky flame leapt and glimmered darkly in the deeps of the pool.

65

'Aristeides, what do you think we ought to do?' I said. 'What steps should we take to protect ourselves?'

'From the Spartans?'

'From them; and from the Persians.'

'The Persians? Shall we need protection against them too?'

'Yes, sooner or later. Sooner, perhaps, since we have outraged the King by executing the men who gave him earth and water.'

'That's a bad prospect,' he said.

'Yes. I think we should take to the sea.'

'The sea?' he said, astonished. 'Oh no, Themistokles, we'd be like a rabble of Phoenicians. We should stay what we are, since that has served well so far.'

'Do you draw no lesson, then, from our day of battles?' I asked him.

'That our hoplites are as good as any.'

'With the Spartans we did not have to try that,' I reminded him. 'No, I mean, without the ships the Eretrians brought us we could not have followed the Chalkidians. We should have had ships of our own!'

'The Eretrian ones did well enough,' he said, smiling.

'But another time ... and we could have been stopped had the Chalkidians had ships to oppose us.'

'There's no telling just what may be needed another time,' he said. 'But we shall need our good phalanx of hoplites, whatever happens.'

'Listen,' I said, overeager as always. 'We can never match Spartan power on land, never outnumber her army, or drill our free citizens as she drills hers. We can't win that game. But we could easily outbid her for power on the sea. We could have more ships, we could hold the waters, and harry their coasts if need be, or help the Ionians against the King....'

'A war can't be fought with just ships,' he said. 'The enemy would simply march into Attica, and seize the city, and that would be the end of it.'

'Let them have the city then,' I said. 'We would....' But he was laughing at me.

'Oh, my old bull-dog!' he was saying. 'Do you *never* let go, however absurd your bone?'

'Beat you at Kottabos!' I said. We were down to the dregs of the wine.

We floated a little dish in the water, and tried to sink it by tossing into it the slops from the krater of wine. Neither of us could hit in the dark. We laughed, and poured more wine to have more dregs to try again. The flying drops splashed in the pool. 'Your pool will smell of stale wine in the morning,' said Aristeides. 'Like an unwashed jar!'

'A memento of a friend,' I retorted, trying again, and going wildly awry. We sat silent for a moment, watching the surface of the pool smooth itself after the splashing, flatten, and darken, and contain, instead of fragments and rings of gold, only a single, still, amber image of the hanging lamp.

'Stesilaos could do it,' said Aristeides. 'With a single graceful sweep of his arm.'

I turned away, and drew my cloak over my shoulder, as though I had felt the cold of the evening air.

'Themistokles, when Stesilaos is with us, you are easily wounded,' said Aristeides, with an unfamiliar softness in his voice. With that softness in his voice he drew my eyes to his, as if I had lost the power to choose where I turned them. Warmth flooded my limbs and tingled on my skin, as though I had been sitting in the noonday sun, instead of under the stars.

'Dear friend,' Aristeides was saying, 'do not be so. I make no move to draw him away from your company, though I easily could. I will not grudge you his attention, so you do not grudge him me.'

'Grudge *him*, to *you*?' I cried. He would not have astonished me more had he suddenly struck me. 'You're welcome! Do you think I care a handful of straw for that, that fool – that empty vase, that ... that....' I stammered into silence, appalled at myself. He thought I had been seeking his company because of the other; but now ... I should have guarded my tongue.

He shook his head. 'I had hoped we might understand one another,' he said. 'I thought you would be generous enough.' He thought I was simply jealous.

'By the gods, I swear to you, Aristeides, son of Lysimachos,' I said to him, 'that I'll never interrupt your love-chat again, though I die for it!' The wild oath tore out of me like a cry.

'Themistokles!' he said, taking a fold of my cloak in his hands, and holding me to look at him, 'I can't understand you. I can't think what I've said to wound you, for I meant only to be generous towards you.'

He can't think what he said! Well, it wasn't for quick wits he was famous. 'Get you gone, and good night to you, Aristeides,' I said. 'I'll trouble you with my earnest talk no more.'

'It grieves me to the heart,' he said, 'that you should suffer enough to bring yourself to this state of mind. Come, friend, a boy can have more than one companion. Come tomorrow, and run and wrestle with me, and ... him.'

Gods! He still thought I was after his boy. I was trembling from head to foot, and he still holding my cloak, gazed at me with frank, puzzled, innocent eyes. At last I managed to lay my hand over his, cool, smooth, fluted with slender bones, to slip my fingers under his, and straighten them, and so release his hold upon my cloak. For a long extended moment while I had his hand in mine, it seemed to me that I was going to grasp him with the other hand also, and lay my head against his shoulder, and weep; and then the rage against him that was half my grief mastered me – he with his chill disapproval, his icy rectitude, his lapses into stupidity, he, he, scorning me, and seeking instead a sculptor's model, an empty-eyed mask, for company! As for his pity, it choked me! I thrust his hand away.

Then suddenly the gentleness in him snapped. He stood, still facing me, and said, 'And how are the aqueducts running, Themistokles? I am told that since you have been elected to see to them they run with silver!'

'I have been fining those who knock holes in the public supply conduits,' I said. 'And those who let water run to waste, that was needed by others, perhaps. The money I have raised will be used to pay for a statue, at one of the public water-fountains.'

He looked a little abashed, I think. But he only said, 'So. Good-night, Themistokles.'

That night I tossed on my bed, and railed against him, and ground the knuckles of my clenched fists against the head-posts and turned, and still lay sleepless. And in the grey light of the dawn at last, I knew that I wanted nothing in the world as much as I wanted the good opinion of that one man; and that I would never have it; because he was what he was, and I ... it was true, I knew it, though nobody else did, that the statue would not cost me all the money I raised from my office. Great King, the shadow of the column in the window silently rotates across the floor; I shall be writing late into the night. And then another grey dawn will come up on a wakeful night; and as for what I wept for, so long ago, I have lived without it, and will die without it still.

I went to Tempsa, in Italy, to fetch copper for the smelting of bronze for my statue. I had reasons for going myself; chiefly I

68

wished to become knowledgeable about the handling of a ship. I had found quickly in talk with sailing men and their cronies at Phaleron that I knew nothing and less than nothing about the open sea. I thought, if I wished to lead this class of men, I should not seem a fool in talking to them. So I went for the copper myself. It was useful to me; I talked with men of the west enough to learn how power lies there, to make friends, and we weathered a storm or two, and I learned the names and places of a scatter of useful stars. Later I was to remember the forests, and stand up and say that I had seen them with my own eyes. . . .

Coming home we skirted the coasts of the Argolid, and then set course to make a wide arc round Aigina to the east since, being an ally of Thebes, she was hostile now. When we sighted Sounion – a tiny white glitter in the misty haze of the landfall – we turned north-west, for home. And, although it was shining day, there was a cloud in the line of the land ahead of us; just one, a white one, lying low. Then, as we drew near, we could see that it was smirched with black, and the smell of burning drifted faintly, but unmistakably acrid, across the water to us. With cries of alarm the crew ran down the sail, and the ship drifted, rocking, on the water. I ordered them to take up their oars, and hugging the coast, cautiously, we came up to Phaleron like a fox slinking home. Every ship that had been beached there was burning, or rather, by the time we got there, smouldering. Little tongues of flame still licked up and down long slicks of molten tar, making a boat-shaped margin to the heaps of wood ash. All the slipways on the shore had also been fired, and my ship, gliding shining and salty from the water, grinding to a halt with her prow ploughing into the sand, looked like Odysseus among the shades in Hades.

The Aiginetans had been and gone. And as I hastened towards the city, on foot, eager to get there and hear what had been happening, I met the block of hoplites marching down to the rescue, two hours too late, and found myself bringing news instead of getting it, for nobody in the city knew any more than I. Most of the Athenians regarded the raid as of little consequence, save to those who had lost property; it seemed to them like any other brief attack on our frontiers. I rose in the Assembly, however, and told them that, whether they had noticed it or not, we lived by trade as much as by farming now; and for trade the loss of the ships was not like the loss of a harvest, but like the loss of seed corn. I suggested that the city should pay for the damaged ships out of public funds, and should complete the fort at Mounychia, begun by Hippias, and keep a garrison there. This speech had no effect on the Assembly; they listened, it's true, to my enlarged, powerful voice, resonant with space; but they voted against me. That speech marked me out as the leader, the natural spokesman, of the trading citizens.

My statue was made and cast in the year after I laid down the office of keeper of aqueducts. It was set up at the public fountain in the agora; a slim and graceful girl, one arm raised to balance a water-jar on her shoulders, her head slightly leaning to one side, because of the jar, and a soft smile on her face. The smile was usual for statues made in those days. She charmed me; and she did not cost much − not nearly as much as I expected on the understanding that the sculptor was not asked to account for the weight of metal he had used. I understood him perfectly. Still, the profit cost me a flinching thought of Aristeides, and so I paid extra, a little, to have green and white enamel used for eyes for her; and then she was bewitching. Underneath, I recorded my tenure of office, and the date. Some people complained of my pride and self-importance in this. I was gratified, for it showed I was rising in consequence enough to arouse jealousy.

I think, until the time of which I am telling you now, Great King, I had wanted power only to glorify myself. Greek boys are bred to compete with each other, to race and run and fight, and the greatest prize that can be won is a crown of laurel that fades within a day, or a jar of oil that cannot be sold, or an ode on a beautiful young man's victory, wrung from an old man's heart. It is only for glory that such things can be desired; they are not, after all, like the wide lands and herds of horses which reward the endeavours of those subjects of Persia who please their King. I was never made to be an athlete; power in the city was the race I had chosen to run in, and until the year I was twenty-eight I had no better ambition than to wear some public office, like a laurel crown.

That changed. I came to burn with desire to be mighty in Athens for reasons which are like the reasons you gave me once for the necessity of kings, Lord Artaxerxes: that government might be good, that the right decisions might be swiftly made.

It was the events in Ionia which changed me in this way. It was the spectacle of Athens nearly helpless, and throwing away what force she had through incompetence. In the first place we should have rebuilt the ships that the Aiginetans had burned −

and more. When I urged this in the Assembly, I was answered that there was no guaranteeing that the Aiginetans would not burn them again; and the Athenians were so short-sighted, they were prepared to let matters remain like that. Then Aristagoras of Miletos came to us, asking for help. He told the Assembly a pitiful tale of the sufferings of his people under the rule of the Kings.

Looking back now, I wonder how much of it was true; not all of what he told us, I think, now that I, too, have lived under Persian rule. Of course, your grandfather Darius was a cunning and capable man, and after the revolt he made changes, so that many grievances of that far-off time had been removed long before I came here to see for myself. True or untrue, however, he told us a tale of wrongs to make our blood burn with anger for our kinsmen; out of our ancient history we think of the Ionian Greeks as that – more nearly related to us than ever the Spartans were or will be, or the Thebans, or any mainland Greeks. We were ignorant of the ways of the Kings; had he told us that the Medes and the Persians supped the blood of the Ionians for wine, we would have believed him. And as well as the wrongs of the Ionians he laid before us an inspiring view of their courage, their willingness to join forces and fight, not saying that their only hope lay in winning help from us. At the same time as he spoke to us news was coming in to Phaleron on every ship, telling of the whole of Ionia ablaze with the fires of revolt. The news from Sparta was slower in coming, it seemed.

Living as a Persian has changed my viewpoint on Aristagoras' claims. Yet I do not doubt he was justified. The whole matter is not without interest; and because I propose to refuse your assistance in taking the Greeks for your own there is no reason for me to grudge you my more immediate usefulness as your educator and adviser on Greek affairs. The Ionian revolt seems to me to illustrate the virtues and the weakness of Persian rule. I have no doubt that all of the atrocities of which Aristagoras told us were the doing of the Ionians' own tyrants, and no doing of the King or his satraps at all. The Kings are benevolent, and tolerant of the ways of different peoples; and this had led you to support the tyrants of Ionia, because you do not tamper with local ways of government, and there were tyrants in the cities when first you took them for your own. But a tyrant's son is usually a worse master than his father was, and as time went on the rest of the Greeks overthrew tyrannies. Only in Ionia they remained, because of your might behind them. Thus it was the very liberality of your rule that led to its being after a while intolerable. Once it was intolerable, Great King, there was bound to be trouble, because there were no ways of getting change peacefully. Your rule when once established is inflexible, and remote, and those who complain are in danger of their lives. Sooner or later, therefore, men plot sedition. This is what happened in Ionia. Make what you will of this diagnosis.

Aristagoras was a good orator; he stood up before our Assembly, and moved us like the wind among leaves. The Athenians wept for him, admired him, and threw themselves into his struggle with all the strength they had; they gave him twenty ships. We had no more to send. On one of the twenty I served as shipmaster. Long before we set sail we heard that Aristagoras had been first to the Spartans. They had refused him. A tale was going round that he had brought with him a map drawn on bronze made by Hekataios, the Ionian scholar, which showed all the cities of Ionia, and the land of the Great King, and Kleomenes had asked him how many days' march it was from Susa to the Ionian coast, along the road shown on the map. Aristagoras had answered, three months. Then the Spartans had told him to be gone from their city by nightfall. We felt very grand and brave to be lunging in where the Spartans drew back out of fear (well, some would call it sense) and all with our twenty ships.

Something could have been done with them, all the same. I could have made them tell in the struggle. But Melanthios was the general in charge, and since the Eretrians had sent five ships he had Evalkidas the Eretrian as his second in command. I thought Melanthios was a fool at the time, and I spent a lot of the angriest days of my life, grinding my teeth in frustration or telling all the other young men around just what I thought Melanthios ought to do, and why, and just why what he was doing was wrong, and why it would lead to disaster. As it happened I was also laying the foundations of a reputation for military insight, when all my predictions came true enough to break our hearts.

We should never have left the coast. Any fool should have seen that, even without Hekataios to tell him. I imagine Melanthios was after some quick results, to quieten opposition at home. Since I had sailed with the ships to Miletos, I didn't know about what was happening at home. I wasn't there to witness the first unedifying example of the Assembly's habit of changing its mind overnight. No sooner had the expedition left than voices were raised to point out how dangerous it was to provoke the King again. He might possibly have overlooked the earth-and-water débâcle, since after all it was our own messengers we had killed, not his, but if we meddled in Ionia he would certainly remember it ... and so on. Of course, all of us who had been loudest in urging the people to help the Ionians were gone, and so the feeling of the citizens veered round with nothing to steady it. Melanthios had despatches from home; I think he was panicked by the very knowledge that he couldn't afford to get into difficulties.

When first I heard of the change of feeling in the city I was dumbfounded by the blatant stupidity of my fellow citizens. It seemed to me as clear as daylight that Athens had no choice but to fight the King. We had a choice whether to fight on Ionian soil or on our own; but no choice otherwise. It all seems less surprising now that I have seen Athens for nearly twenty years refusing to see that she must fight the Spartans, sooner or later must fight them. You know, Lord Artaxerxes, that I was right; the Kings have rolled their power across the world, like a great wave, and have taken everything, except where they have been stopped by force. And the wave when broken draws back, and gathers force to strike again. Twice in my lifetime we have defeated you, and now at the time of my death you are dreaming of conquest again. I shall not see it.

Be that as it may, I was telling you how I was certain that, had I held Melanthios' command, all would have turned out well and, had I been in the city, the Assembly could have been kept seeing sense. From the time Melanthios left the ships, and marched upon inland Sardis, I knew that I had to win power in Athens, for the sake of Athens herself, as well as for my own.

Artaphernes the satrap acted swiftly, and well. He didn't wait for help to come toiling up to him from far-off places along that famous three-month road; he struck at Miletos with all the forces he had to hand. Then some bright fool on our side thought it would answer if we played the same game, and hit at his head-quarters in Sardis. So we brought our ships north to Koresos, the port of Ephesos; and Aristagoras, who stayed at Miletos himself, sent every man he could raise to join us. Our commanders took Ephesian guides and marched inland to take Artaphernes at Sardis by surprise. And I – well I was left behind, put in charge of the ships, as a punishment for having too glibly uttered my opinions to my commanding officers. I was then in a junior position, and I never was much good at taking orders.

Off they all went, marching away in the sun up the river valley, and over the mountain; and I was left with one or two bored hoplites and a rabble of jovial oarsmen and the company of whatever Ephesians I could meet. The ships rode at anchor in blue water, sheltered from storm, and needing no attention from me. I walked round Ephesos, a fine city with a lovely prospect. From the gentle hill it stands on, one can look out towards the sea; there is a theatre in the hillside, with a long receding plain, and the shimmering basin of the distant harbour behind the scaena; there are some handsome temples. The citizens are mostly traders, good enough fellows to drink with, very like their kind at Athens, though perhaps with even readier ideas on their tongues. They all seemed to know about the theories of this famous man or that, and taught each other what to think the world was made of, all fire, or all ice, as though the price of bread depended on it. I imagine the theories I heard were garbled, otherwise the Ionian lovers of wisdom hardly deserve their reputations.

I could not long be diverted by such company, for I was in a wrought-up state of mind. Every time I looked at the ships lying idle on the open pathways of the sea, I ground my teeth. I do believe they are the worse for it to this day! Not a city in the revolt that could not be reached and supplied by sea; and the land so mountainous and the defiles so narrow through the mountains that the gods might have made the land to hamper infantry and favour ambushes. But the Athenians are slow to see such things about their own land, let alone one they come new to. One day I took a horse and a local man to guide me, and went riding inland, being tired of looking at the sea, with its grudging reminders of neglected possibilities. We rode through some steep mountainous lands, very like home, and at last we could see down from a height into a green flat valley with a silver ribbon of river twisting and winding along it. Had I ridden a few yards further, I must have seen the city of Magnesia; placed on gently rising ground, on the nearer slopes, looking over the wide valley-floor where the river turns southwards for the sea. This city where I now sit and write.

'Where's that?' I asked my guide.

'The valley of the River Maeander, sir,' he said.

'This is a goodly country, by the look of it,' I said, 'yet on the mountains here fewer flowers grow than in Attica.'

'Here are flowers, sir,' he said, pointing to the side of the hill above the track we had come along. We turned our horses for home. Idly as I rode I looked around me. I thought of the hill above the house at Sounion, with poppy and vetch, and iris and orchid, and hundreds of others breaking out upon it in spring.

'I see only dog-daisy in as great abundance as at home,' I said, 'and asphodel, which we call the flower of the dead.' For indeed that pallid column of ghostly pink bloomed everywhere, around, as it does still.

When we returned to the city we were greeted with the news of the capture of Sardis. Sardis was in our hands, and in flames. The news threw Ephesos into frantic rejoicing; there was a night or two of feasting in which mine was the only voice raised asking if Sardis could be held. What was the use of Sardis, if we could not hold it; even Sardis standing, let alone Sardis burnt down?

The Persians besieging Miletos started back for Sardis at once, and all the reinforcements that Artaphernes had asked for began to come in to him, and we were lucky indeed that our army, falling back on Ephesos, reached it safely at all, since they could easily have been cut off. But they got back with an immense army chasing on their heels. I don't need to tell you what happened next; on the plains below Ephesos we were cut to pieces; our lines collapsed under the great weight of the Persian charge, and after that it was more a massacre than a battle. I have no doubt that Artaphernes the satrap wrote a splendid account of his victory for the archives of the King, and Persian princes in their cradles were soothed asleep with talk of it. I took a flesh wound in the arm, trying to cut my way through to Evalkidas the Eretrian, when he was surrounded, Melanthios having forgiven my indiscretions enough to give me that dangerous commission. I didn't make it; Evalkidas was killed. He was a loss not only to the Eretrians but to all Hellas, for he had won the pentathlon at the Isthmus, and been celebrated by the poet Simonides. Of course, he had bungled his command – but death's a hard punishment.

When night fell the victorious Persians drew off, and we found that our Ionian allies could think of nothing more, save of making home to their own several cities. Melanthios was of the same mind, and we began to embark by torchlight. There was a tent on the shore, where a doctor was putting on salves to keep new wounds free of the salt spray from the sea; I stood there, holding my arm out in the light from a driftwood fire to have the wound dressed. On the other side of the fire stood Melanthios, leaning on his spear, wincing while the doctor pulled fragments of broken sword-blade from his thigh. He looked up at me.

'Well, you're the young man who knew this was going to happen,' he said, dryly. 'Tell me, how could it have been avoided?'

I wasn't sure he wanted an answer, and I hesitated. Then I realised he needed something to take his mind off the doctor's probing fingers. 'We should have persuaded the Ionians to make walls to keep their cities from attack from the land,' I said, 'and then we should have held the sea. No harm could have come to them, or to us.'

'Ah,' he said, relaxing as the dressing went over his wound. 'Well, another time, I would know one could do worse than to listen to Themistokles.'

'There won't be another time for you,' I said. He heard me, but he turned away as though he had not.

So we embarked in the darkness, losing another man by drowning in the process, and sailed for home at daybreak. Melanthios had done more than lose a battle; he had lost the support of the citizens for fighting any battles at all. They turned a deaf ear to Aristagoras' pleas for help after that.

I thought we had achieved worse than nothing; but the Ionians seem to have been cheered by discovering that Sardis was flammable; the revolt spread, and they fought bravely for four years. Yet, by all accounts, even that morale-raising firing of Sardis had been an accident spread on an unlucky wind. That was an accident that would cost Athens dear. I remember coming home, on the run up the coast from Sounion to Phaleron, standing in the prow of my ship, watching the ram plough through the water, its war-paint unscratched. You have to stand there to feel the speed and power of a ship. There are always men around who want to use ships like tiny islands, and fight infantry battles on the decks; but I always knew that the ship herself is the weapon, beautiful and deadly as the finest steel, and swifter than the finest horses.

'Athens! Athens!' cried the men behind me, I raised my eyes, and saw the distant sparkle of light on her crowned and lovely height, and wondered grimly how long it would be before the fire at Sardis came home.

回回回

The state of feeling in the city was deplorable, and it was clear to me at once that, if I did not win power quickly now, Athens would ruin herself. Every further request for help to the Ionians met with refusal; yet Athens let her own hope of safety rest on the efforts of the men she would not help, and still supposed she need not fight herself. In fact we had just three years to cower behind that fragile shield, and most of the citizens, like mice in the path of the reaper, went on building nests, farming, trading, talking in the market place, all unconcerned, seeing no further than the ends of their noses. But I spent those years well, growing in the city, gathering support. There were, after all, men of sense and honour left in Athens who agreed with me. I campaigned ceaselessly, and without success to get help sent to the Ionians; but the wind of opinion was blowing the other way. The Athenians were afraid of the King, and wished to make peace. In the year of the seventieth Olympiad they even elected Hipparchos as archon. Hipparchos had been a general under Peisistratos, and his sister was married to Hippias, that old vulture, who was still living in exile at Sigeion, in the lands of the King, intriguing to come home. Your grandfather, Great King, had given him much what you have given me, in return for the same expectations. But Hipparchos was a decent man, who had done nothing to help democracy and would do nothing to harm it either; clearly his advantage in the eyes of the people was that he might intervene and appease the King. So little did they understand the magnitude of the danger!

In the archonship of Hipparchos, I submitted to my mother's anxious badgering and took a wife. I married a girl of my mother's choosing, Archippe, daughter of Lysander from the deme Alopeke. Mnesiphilos fixed it up for me, standing in for my father. We had a fine bride-feast in her father's house in the country, and Aristeides was a guest there, for his family were neighbours of hers. Lykos came from his farm to be my parachos – the bridegroom's companion. He talked idly of our days at Phyle, a little diffidently, as if I overawed him now. He had not lost his touch on the lyre, though, and he played sweetly outside our chamber door, far into the night, when we had with laughing and singing at last unveiled the girl and brought her home. Outside the door Lykos playing softly; inside my wife weeping more softly still, and I, never having spoken to a girl in all my life, watching her, confounded. Her tears didn't last long; she made me a good and trustworthy wife, taking all the trouble of running the house from me, selling her weaving at a profit, honouring my mother while my mother still lived, bearing sons. I never talked to her save of domestic affairs; indeed she bored me. Only now, after years of knowing Persian women, who live and talk like men, does it occur to me that she might have been anything else. I find myself wondering what she was like behind that placid, oval face, wondering even what she thought of me. At the time I saw only that her presence, minding the house, and directing the slaves, gave me as much as an hour longer each day to go out and about, and that she made things pleasant to come back to. She loved the garden especially, and grew tender plants there.

I gained ground, little by little. Seamen did not think of Persia as far away; the traders knew we must fight in the end to hold the corn route through the Hellespont; there were many in the city who had come from Ionia, and could see and understand the actions of the King. But it was a slow business, gaining inch by inch on the willing makers of peace, and the frightened, and the tattered adherents of ancient ways of thought. And all the while battles raged in Ionia and cities were crushed, and men died, and the great wave rolled on and on, gathering strength as it came.

At Aeschylus' house one night – Aeschylus the poet whom I was at school with – I found myself sharing a couch with a dark-haired, taciturn man whom I did not know. I had arrived late, and was not introduced to him before we went to eat. Together we dipped hands in the bowls, and drank wine ladled from the same krater. It was not a cheerful party, for the news had just reached us of the fall of Miletos; garbled accounts, clear only in that surely now was the end. Suddenly the man beside me began to talk, in a low and dry voice. 'If only men could foresee disaster before it comes upon them ... but that's a rare gift.'

'It isn't so very difficult to foresee disaster now,' I said.

'You perhaps don't quite grasp what I mean,' he answered. 'I don't mean it's hard for a sensible man to see trouble coming ... I mean, if only people could *see* it; see what it will be like. Men aren't moved to act by the ideas in their heads, Themistokles, but by lurching feelings in their guts. Now, if the Athenians were now at Miletos, to see the yoke laid upon women, smell the blood of slaughter, and watch the young boys castrated, there'd be a sufficient sickness in their guts to put some fight into them. That's what I meant.'

'Ah,' I said, 'pity it can't be done, then.'

'As it is,' he went on, 'the fall of Troy, or the murder of Agamemnon, will always be more real to them; for they have seen that presented in the theatre.' With that, abruptly he rose to go. 'And you, my friend,' he said to me, as he put on his cloak, 'and I, and some few others, are condemned to the pains of Cassandra.'

'Who was that?' I asked Aeschylus, as soon as he had gone.

'The two most famous of my friends, and they do not know each other!' exclaimed Aeschylus. 'That was Phrynichos, the dramatist.'

'I'll know him next time I meet him,' said I.

As well as working in Athens, I was keeping an eye on Kleomenes of Sparta. We had relied on Damaratos, his fellow king, to keep a check on his power; and he had lost so much face in his dealings with us that he seemed of less account for a while. But, while all eyes were bent on the events in Ionia, Sparta and Argos had quarrelled, and fought at Sepeia, with Kleomenes in command of the Spartan army. He had won a victory of shattering force; he had smashed the Argives, killing so many of their well-born sons that a government of humble men moved into empty offices. For a long while there would be nobody to dispute with Sparta her power in the Peloponnese, and nobody to dispute with Kleomenes his power in Sparta. I saw this with concern, though as it turned out there was nothing to worry us about it; for in the next scene of the action Damaratos was to be the enemy, and Kleomenes the friend.

As darkness and defeat rolled over Ionian cities, a feeling of shame and unease spread in Athens. It seemed to me that all the great families were united in wanting peace at any cost. Did they remember how comfortably incumbent holders of power had continued under Persian rule in Ionia? But the people knew they had betrayed their kinsmen's need. And with each defeat across the water it became clearer that our turn would be next, and that the refusal to fight had brought not peace but a nearer danger. This feeling brought power to me. Other men, in the glory of their family names, might hold the votes of the countryside, but a third of the votes in every tribe were the votes of the city-dwellers and most of those now belonged to me. I got sneered at for troubling about the price of tar for caulking, about the safety of the seas from piracy, about the defence of the ships at Phaleron; the lordly and the proud talked instead about horses, and hoplite gear. 'Themistokles the trader,' they called me, and spread tales about my birth, smears on my mother's breeding. But Athens was full of men who were really traders, and really of common birth; and each sneer made them love me better. And, besides all this, I was right.

An attempt was made to ruin me on the eve of my final success, for I had enemies enough. The incoming archon, Adeimantos, chose me as choregos to sponsor a play for the dramatic competition at the Dionysia, a festival we hold in spring of each year. The choregoi are chosen from among the wealthiest citizens, and they must choose a dramatist and supply the whole cost of the play. It was a clever attack to choose me; to trap me in the guise of doing me an honour. The sting lay in the fact that I was not rich. Should I mount a niggardly production I would annoy the people, who like splendour in public life and castigate their great men if they fail to provide it. Should I plead poverty and seek to evade the duty, I would have to humiliate myself before the whole city, and would doubtless acquire a name for meanness which would stick with me for the rest of my life. The third prong of the hook was that, if I accepted the duty and tried to discharge it, I would bankrupt myself and sink out of sight under a load of debt and poverty. Even as I squirmed in this trap I admired its ingenuity.

But, as it happened, it was not quite as bad as it might have been. I had enough money hoarded away. I had a good sum in fines paid by foulers and filchers of water, all that had not gone to pay for the statue of the water-girl. Naturally enough my enemies did not know about that; but I resented being forced to spend it. Much though I honour the god Dionysos, I had had some more serious – or rather more practical – uses for it in mind. Then I suddenly saw how to turn the situation to good use. I searched out Phrynichos.

I found him walking in the colonnade of the Temple of Athene on the Acropolis. In the striped light and shade we sauntered together.

'Good day, Themistokles,' he saluted me.

'I am to be a choregos,' I said. 'Will you be my dramatist?'

'You honour me,' he said after a short pause. 'Are we to work for something very simple and austere?'

'No,' I said, 'I can find the money to do the thing reasonably well.'

'Ah,' he said, 'that's interesting. I'm glad to hear it.' We turned about, and began to walk back along the columns. 'Of course,' he said, 'I don't mean to say I wouldn't be willing to do something on the cheap.'

'I'm not asking to put limits on the expense, my dear Phrynichos,' I said, halting, and catching his eye. 'But I want to choose the subject.'

'That's different,' he said at once. 'A man can't undertake to make plays out of stuff that doesn't interest him.'

'Oh, I think you'll take well enough to my subject,' I said, smiling a little. 'It's to be "The Sack of Miletos".' I saw the immediate, answering glint in his eye. But he said, 'That could be dangerous.'

'I have misjudged you,' I said. 'I must look elsewhere.'

'You are quick to call a man a coward,' said he, putting a hand on my arm to detain me, 'but I ask you this, son of Neokles. If there's trouble, shall the risk be shared, as the work of production is?'

'All risks shared, as far as we can contrive,' I said.

'Then I'm your man,' he said, smiling stiffly. He always smiled as though it might crack his cheeks.

I was busy then, finding and engaging good actors, fine scene-painters, women to stitch costumes, a mask-maker, a prompter, and so on, not least a whole chorus of handsome boys, and a trainer to teach them their parts. I summoned Lykos to listen to flute- and lyre-players, and choose out the best for me, since his ear was better than mine, and I coaxed help out of a good number of other friends.

While we were busily engaged on it all, in a flurry of excitement, Miltiades came home. He escaped by the skin of his teeth, leaving the Chersonese when the Phoenicians in the service of the King had brought their fleet even as far as Tenedos, seeking to crush him as the last unpunished conspirator in the defeated Ionian revolt. Of the five ships he fled in, they chased and captured one, and that one carried his eldest son Metiochos; he joined Hippias as a subject of the King. Darius gave him a Persian wife, and lands, and he has been my friend these last few years, though his Greek is halting now, and his memory of the city faint and distant.

Miltiades' homecoming certainly caused a stir. His family, the Philaids, were enemies of old of the Alkmeonids, and they accordingly set about plotting against him the moment he landed. Those who still feared tyranny were fluttered by his friendship with Hippias; those who still foolishly hoped for peace with Persia were alarmed to find in their midst the man who had robbed the King of the islands of Lemnos and Imbros ... indeed hardly a citizen talked about anything but Miltiades for a month. I was busy with my play, but I spared the time to meditate about Miltiades. I thought we could afford him. Those who feared him had not yet realised, I thought, how completely the city could now destroy any man who threatened it; the power of the demos lay coiled, like a sleeping snake, as yet unused. Ah, well – I myself did not realise that the truth might apply also to me!

For the performance of Phrynichos' play, I took the seat reserved for the choregos, in the front row, among the priests and archons. The choregos' chair was well round the curve at the side of the stage arena, and as I seated myself, resplendent in a cloak of white and gold, which my wife had made for the occasion, I saw with satisfaction that I commanded a very good view of the audience of banked-up citizens. It was them I intended to watch, not the actors. I felt that slight tautness in the belly, and flow of spittle in the mouth that a man feels when he is about to address the Assembly. First came Phrynichos' chorus, announcing themselves as the citizens of Miletos, men, women and children. A buzz of voices rose from the tiered seats behind me, but the play was sacred to the god, and as soon as the actors began to speak the Athenians hushed, and listened. They listened, and soon the women began to weep, and I looked with gloating satisfaction. The actor playing Aristagoras cried from the dais,

'Do not despair, my friends!
Remember our sister city,
Shining Athens, lover of freedom;
Late her help comes, ah late,
But now, surely now,
At our time of utmost need,
She will speed to aid us!'

Men groaned aloud and covered their faces in the borders of their cloaks, and I rejoiced.

Now there followed a splendidly contrived dialogue; the leader of the chorus, requested by Aristagoras, climbed up upon the scaena behind the stage, and looked out as though scanning the horizon for ships. Below him Aristagoras looked up, beseechingly.

'How many ships? How many ships draw near?
Thirty? No, that would dare too much;
Twenty would presume too far.
But ten, ten, even ten might turn the tide.
How many ships draw near?'
'... None, my lord, none.'

When the last word of the play had been spoken, there came our master-stroke. On marched a second chorus, as numerous as the first, and splendidly costumed as Persian soldiers, with reckless disregard for expense. Indeed, I was rather disappointed the next time I saw Persian infantry, for they were not as glorious as my painted ones. They came stepping to the notes of a flute and the tap of a muffled drum, they yoked and bound the first chorus, and dragged them off the stage in silence; not a word or a sound, until the last actor off the stage turned suddenly and, raising her fettered arms to the audience, uttered a loud lamenting cry, and was dragged away.

Some few of the Athenians rose, and went stumbling out of the theatre. But most sat weeping in their places till long after Phrynichos and I had left. He and I went up the Acropolis together, to offer gifts in thanks. To Athene honey, to Dionysos wine and a laurel crown. Then as we came down we met Aristeides going up.

'You have blasphemed the god, Themistokles!' he said, genuinely, I think, horrified. He reminded me of an earlier myself that had been appalled to hear talk of bribing the Delphic Oracle. 'What is wrong with our play, Aristeides?' I asked him ironically.

'There has never before been a subject not drawn from the past,' he said, 'as you know well.'

'So,' I said. 'And how far in the past does a play have to be, to be suitable? One year? Two? Two hundred? Is not the god himself, then, of the present?'

'It is not that,' he said, angrily, 'that blasphemes the god; it is that you make use of him!' And he hastened on, not wanting a reply. 'If even the god can serve Themistokles' ends,' I said to his retreating back, 'well and good.' And I went on down the path, to feast and drink with the actors till late into the night.

We had stirred up a hornets' nest. The city was infuriated. They put Phrynichos on trial before the king-archon, for impiety in choosing a contemporary subject, and fined him a thousand drachmae, 'for reminding the people of troubles that touched them nearly'. They added an injunction that his play was never to be performed again. I hadn't an obol left, and the fine had to be paid. Phrynichos offered to raise it himself, but I knew it would ruin him.

I contrived something. I posted men of my following all round the streets of the city, carrying begging-bowls, and placards: 'A thousand drachmae – the price of telling the truth in Athens.' I myself asked in the Assembly whether those who did not wish the fate of Miletos to be known and understood in Athens were planning a similar fate for Athens herself. The mood of the city shifted; when the bowls were brought in and the money counted, at the end of the day, we had raised a great sum; and mostly in small coin, the contributions of the common men. I announced that the money so generously given came just short of a thousand.

and that I would contribute the rest. We went with a group of friends, Phrynichos and I, carrying the money ostentatiously through the streets, in linen sacks, to pay the fine, and standing around in the public eye while the treasurers counted the immense quantity of small silver. But, as a matter of fact, we had raised more than a thousand, and the surplus slipped into my coffer, to go a small way towards replacing the money I had laid out as choregos, to be kept for some future need.

Meanwhile the elections came round. Miltiades was chosen as the general of his tribe; a natural enough result. And I was chosen, by a huge majority, as chief archon. I, the trader, the champion of truth-telling in the city! I had at last got my hands on some substantial power. I triumphed.

Once elected, the officers of the state must submit to a dokimasia, an examination by the Council, to make sure that they are qualified under the law for the honours they have won. Mine was the first, since my office was the first in importance; mine took a matter of minutes; but for Miltiades, the dokimasia promised to be more than an empty formality. In fact, it was to last all day.

It began with the usual questions, quickly asked and answered. Who is your father? His deme? Who is your paternal grandfather? Who is your mother? Have you an ancestral Apollo, and a household Zeus? Where is your family tomb? Do you honour your parents? Do you pay your taxes? Have you done military service? Then a series of witnesses are called to swear that these questions have been truthfully answered. And then, 'Has anyone anything to say against this man?'

For me there had been the usual silence, quickly broken by the words of acceptance from the examiner. When Miltiades' turn came, suddenly Xanthippos was on his feet, crying 'Yes! I have!'

Xanthippos, the same who had come with Aristeides and the others to the Kynosarges long ago, had married a niece of Kleisthenes, and allied himself with the Alkmeonid faction for a time. He accused Miltiades of tyranny. That was not too hard a case to make out. Miltiades, as he said, had been sent to the Chersonese by Hippias, and under his protection. Once there he had ruled as tyrant. Meanwhile, his family in Athens had thrown their political weight against the lovers of freedom at home. (This last was ridiculous. In the absence of Miltiades the Philaids had counted for little, and what Xanthippos meant was that they had opposed the Alkmeonids – a private quarrel, nothing to do with freedom. Indeed, I have always held this against the ancient families, that they pursue their own feuds and friendships, as though political questions and the welfare of the common men were just so many horses to ride. It has been an advantage to me to be an outsider.)

'At Athens there is now a law against tyranny!' Xanthippos proclaimed. 'This man is unsuitable for office here.' And after him another speaker rose to tell us how Miltiades had helped King Darius against the Scythians, made himself an ally of the King. And then there was Aristeides, making a sombre speech on the evils of tyranny, and the wrongs committed by Hippias. Since he said not a word that was unjust to Miltiades, it was only half to the point; however, it was a good speech, made with feeling, and carrying weight among the listeners. The attack went on and on. Speaker after speaker rose, and badgered him. Miltiades answered the accusations as best he could; but he was ill at ease, rattled even. I thought grimly that he showed only too clearly in his manner that he was unused to open opposition.

Sitting in the chair of the archon-elect, I watched it all. I thought best to leave it to run its course, until a good number of people might have begun to feel that it had all gone far enough, or too far. Then at last I asked the president of the Council for permission to speak. There was a hush. It reminded me of the hush, the indrawn breath of my companions, when I had raised my sword once to kill off a dog wounded in the boar hunt. As soon as the blow falls, men breathe again. Now there was that eager silence, lusting after the sight of the death-dealing blow; and Miltiades, proud man, stood facing me, waiting.

'Son of Kimon,' I said to him, evenly. 'How did your father die?'

The question surprised him. 'He was murdered,' he said.

'Do you know who killed him?' I asked. This time he took the cue. 'I do not know who struck the blow,' he said, 'but it was at the time when Hippias was tyrant at Athens.' An answering murmur ran around the Council. I decided to labour the point. 'What manner of man was your father?'

'He was famous; having thrice won the chariot race at Olympia.'

'Were his killers brought to justice?'

'No effort was made to find them,' he said. He was suspicious, expecting me to trap him any minute, but he was beginning to play to my questions, to make the best of them.

'When you asked for justice, Hippias sent you out of the city, to the Chersonese; is it not so?'

'Yes.'

85

'And when Darius came, to cross the water, and fight the Scythians, you were his ally?'

'For a while. But as soon as he had departed, and we Greeks were left, holding the bridge by which he had crossed over, I proposed that we should destroy it, and so consign him to the mercy of the barbarians.' He paused, but I said nothing and he went on, 'For this reason, on his return, Darius drove me out of the Chersonese, and I went as an exile to Thrace.'

'How did you come to return?'

'My subjects, the Dolonkoi, sent messages, begging me to return to them.'

'Those very people whom you have been accused of tyrannising?'

'The same.' It was really shameful how well the old fox and I could put on a show. I didn't believe a word of it, but it was all having its effect.

'The cities of Ionia were then in revolt against the King,' I said. 'What part did you play?'

'I recaptured Lemnos and Imbros from the Persians, and offered them to Athens,' he said. 'There are now Athenians settled there.'

'Miltiades, son of Kimon,' I said, coming at last to the heart of the matter. 'Are you any friend of the King's?'

'I am not!' he said loudly.

'Have you fought against Persian infantry in the field?'

'I have.'

'Do you understand their tactics?'

'I believe so.' I had finished with him now.

'Athenians,' I said, addressing the whole Council, 'we are examining this man because he has been chosen as a general. We don't have to consider his qualifications to be tyrant, since we haven't a vacancy of that kind to fill!'

They laughed; it was put to the vote, and Miltiades was accepted, and by a good majority, though a number of votes were nevertheless cast against him. His supporters carried him out of the Council shoulder high, and all over Athens it was talked of as his triumph, but I thought any triumph about it was really mine. I knew well enough that he would be a great man in Athens now; but I thought I could unmake him when I needed to as easily as I had made him.

As it happened, I had acquired an ally. It certainly wasn't from gratitude; Miltiades was lordly and thought of me as a low-born upstart. He found it hard to come to terms with the kind of

Athens Kleisthenes had made, and he loathed me, and everything
I stood for. But he was a first-rate general. He understood strategy;
he understood the military importance of ships – that obvious
fact which was so unclear to the traditional man of Attica – like
Aristeides, for example. So, as it happened, all through my year
of office I had no sooner put a major proposal before the Assembly
than up stood Miltiades, pat on cue, to agree with me in spite of
himself.

I had support enough to do what I wanted, but not so much
that Miltiades made no difference. I used my power to good effect.
I persuaded the Athenians at last to fortify the Peiraieus and begin
there the building of a city which is now stronger than Athens
herself. There is a hilly promontory called Mounychia, and behind
is a bay, well sheltered from storms and of deep water. In the
curves of the coastline are three basins; Karinthos, Mounychia, and
Zea. Under my guidance we built on the hill of Mounychia, using
the foundations laid out by Hippias, a strong-walled bastion; and
on the opposite shore another, so that they faced each other
across the narrow entrance to the bays. No sooner was this
work in hand than the ships, the traders and fishing-boats, and
all the tackle and little shacks that went with them, were brought
round from Phaleron by their owners, and the same disorderly
shore scene began to grow at Peiraieus. I had to risk a brief but
fierce hostility from these people, my staunchest supporters, in
order to clear it all away again. We laid out streets, marking the
land so that there would be wide roadways round the shore; we
made spaces for sheds and warehouses, but also for houses for
the citizens, a market place, a garden and a temple. People thought
I had gone mad; but it costs very little to drive in stakes, and mark
out land for dreams, so I was not opposed. And when the job
was done my people were well contented. There would be no
more jostle and squalor round the shore, but a well-run seaport.

When the marking was done, and leaving nearly as much land
again within the circuit, I marked out a line of walls, to defend
Peiraieus from the landward side. With this there began to be
opposition. The farmers told me in the Assembly that if the city
didn't throw walls round their farms they didn't see why they
should vote money to wall in the ships. 'In my time,' I replied,
'the Lakedaimonians have stood in armed ranks at Eleusis. The
Aiginetans have burned ships on the shore. As to the relative importance of ships and farms; why, when the farms of Attica produce
enough wheat to feed us, and we do not need to trade with the

Euxine shores to buy our bread – why, then we shall indeed be wise to leave the ships undefended and throw walls round every farm.'

But, argue as I might, I could not get the citizens to vote money for the walls. I had to save my fire for getting slipways, and they were expensive, for they had to be cut out of solid rock, every one of them wide and long enough to take a trireme, though at that time many of the city's ships were still only penteconters. I was not allowed money for as many as I would have liked. Behind the slipways ran a wide road, to make access to the ships easy, and at one end of the road we built a tall shed for hanging gear. Along the landward side of the road the craftsmen of the shore built shops and workrooms, where they could make and sell oars and ropes and a hundred other useful things. Lastly we made a jetty, so that the embarkation of men could be swift and easy.

I worked hard at it all my year as archon. With so many plots of land to sell, and workmen to employ, and goods to purchase, I could have made money; true, I pocketed a little. But less, far less, than I might have. It wasn't just because gifts to the archons were unconstitutional, and there was a high likelihood of being caught out; but the works at Peiraieus were near to my heart, and I would not let work go to any but the best artisans, no matter what I was offered. Sometimes, though, the man I had decided to choose anyway happened to offer me a bribe. That was different. Well, who was harmed by it?

When I laid down my archonship at the end of the year, the Peiraieus was humming with life; houses were springing up there, and workshops, and chandlers and provision merchants, and wine-shops and inns to serve the seafarers. The city had just voted money to pave the roadway between it and the city. I regarded it all with such satisfaction and delight, such a pride in the new safety of the ships, that I could not be more than briefly irritated by the complaints against me, of which the most serious was that the Peiraieus was two miles further from the city than the shore at Phaleron. It is certainly a disadvantage of democracy, Great King, that one has to contend with the loudly expressed opinions of idiots.

After my year as archon, with every other living ex-archon, I joined the Areopagus. There's more glory in that than power; but also my tribe elected me a general. The generalships can be held year after year, and they carry with them a seat on the Council which draws up the agenda for the Assembly, so I was well pleased with my place there. And as soon as I had ceased to be archon, and it was no longer illegal to make me gifts, I received a gift which was dear to me on two counts at once; it was a house in the Peiraieus, on the slope of Mounychia, overlooking the three harbours; and it had been given by a group of wealthy traders. They told me that, when it became known for whom the house had been bought, it had been furnished and filled with gifts by many of their fellow craftsmen, less wealthy than themselves, but not less friends of mine. It was a good house; I always felt befriended there, and at peace – always until the last night I was there. From the house I took my sons out walking, and showed them the ships, and taught them about seafaring. It was there that I slept, or wakened rather, the last night that I spent in Attica.

The light of the day is flushed with warmth now; a pink and orange fire infuses it, and it loses strength, so that the shadows blur at the edges, and creepingly spread. Evening comes; and, after evening, darkness, and I shall need lamps. I have much more to tell; some of it will be of use to you; and if the words of friendship you have spoken to me were not all fool's fire, all that I write will interest you. Was it not you yourself, rebuking me, who said that to see a man whole meant not (as I had said) to see him mind and body, but meant rather to see his whole course, from boyhood to the grave? I must hasten the tale a little, for even if I write all through the night the time is short for the task. I must write faster, or I shall become the only man who has ever gone down to death before his life was finished!

That year, the year after I was archon, comes back to me as clearly as though it were born on some whiff of remembered fragrance, or the notes of a tune heard in the past; it had an evening glow to it. I feel now that the stars here are brighter, the garden more fragrant, the tinkling fountain more musical than ever before, and all because I am leaving them. It was just the same then. Each ship brought news of the stir along the Ionian coast as the King prepared to do battle. We heard that Artaphernes had come down the coast to be the commander, bringing with him Datis the Mede – he who had won the great sea-battle at Lade that led to the sack of Miletos, and finished the Ionian revolt. We heard news of the number of soldiers, and rumours of cavalry, though we could not think how they would come. And all the while the sun shone in Athens, and the festivals of the gods were kept in due order, and life had the unnatural sweetness of things one is soon to lose. I walked in the city, and kept noticing things

– those young boys, laughing together, that grave old man in deep talk, all the marble girls and boys on the Acropolis, or at home the cool shade of the loom-room, smelling of wool dust from the beating of the shuttles, and full of soft women's-talk, and the babble of my infant sons. Oil on the skin, wine on the tongue, round honey cakes baked as offerings, the shade of trees, the salt smell and sparkle of water, and the tarry heat reaching my skin from the sun-baked sides of the ships – everything that seemed to me to belong to being Athenian stabbed me to the heart with fear.

Then Datis sent envoys to the Greeks, and asked us for earth and water. The men of the islands gave it, bringing stepping-stones for the enemy nearly to our shore. The Thebans, those noble people, gave it, relishing no doubt the thought of trampling over us in the Persian entourage. The Aiginetans gave it. With that we were in mortal danger, for they commanded our shores and they had twice our number of ships and more. But at Athens I persuaded the Assembly to put your envoys to death, Great King, using as an excuse that they had outraged piety by delivering their evil message in Greek, the language of our gods. Privately I had a better reason than that, of course. I feared the faction among the Athenians that were ready to make peace; I hoped that if we murdered the envoys we would make peace impossible. For a whole day of debate their lives and ours hung in the balance, as the Assembly debated what to do; there were voices enough to tell us to submit. Other voices reminded us that Hippias was with the King's generals; if we submitted, we would have to take him back as tyrant over us. Many of us could remember very well what Hippias had been like. At last, in a misty dusk the vote was taken, to kill the envoys at dawn. That done, there was no going back. And the following day we learned that the same thing had been done at Sparta. 'At least we shall not stand alone,' men said to each other.

So then we complained to the Spartans about the Aiginetans, saying that their allies had imperilled us by giving tokens to the King, and by their conduct made themselves traitors to Hellas. I feared we would get a brutal answer, since Kleomenes was still king there, and remembered, no doubt, his stay on the Acropolis. But I had misjudged him; he knew a serious threat when he saw one; he could overlook old alliances, like Sparta's with Aigina, and see very well who was enemy, who friend, in a crisis. He marched and sailed to Aigina, and demanded hostages. They rubbed his nose in past disasters, saying they would not give them unless both Spartan kings demanded; and Damaratos would not, so Kleomenes got rid of him, digging up some scandal about his birth, and claiming he was not legitimate; it must have taken a good deal of doing, and soon stories about oracle-bribing were ringing round Hellas again. Still, Kleomenes did manage it, and got himself a more obliging co-ruler, in a man called Latychidas. Then he returned to Aigina, took hostages, and delivered them at once into our hands. Thus prepared, we waited for fate.

We heard of Datis bringing his ships across the Aegean; at Delos, our messages said, he had offered incense and barbarian gold; and it was true he was bringing cavalry, he had had horse transports built specially for his great fleet. Those ships of his made me sick at heart. My fellow generals calculated endlessly his superiority in numbers of infantry, in cavalry and in the deadly power of archers; I, tossing sleepless on my bed, thought of his ships; and of Attica in the embrace of the sea, her headlands and promontories, her bays and beaches, like the unprotected legs and arms of the hoplites, offering themselves to the blows of the enemy. Since we did not know where in all the miles of coastline the enemy would descend, we could make no move to protect ourselves. The Assembly drew up marching-orders, told every man of fighting age to have his weapons ready, and his water-flask and a pouch of food. What more could we do?

I imagine, Lord Artaxerxes, that having plans now for a conquest of Hellas you have brought out of the archives at Susa the accounts of earlier expeditions that were written and stored for the King. If they are not before you as you read, they are, I am sure, fresh in your mind. You know that the Persians went first to Eretria, and that we did nothing to help the Eretrians, though they were our allies. Well, a little better than nothing, perhaps, for we sent messages to our settlers in Chalkis, ordering them to go to the aid of Eretria. Those settlers numbered four thousand. Do you think that a puny number, Lord of the Lands? But Athens herself in the time of her greatest need could put only ten thousand in the field. As a matter of fact the men from Chalkis did not fight at Eretria, for the Eretrians having decided to defend their city walls had no food or water or living-space to spare in their crowded stronghold and so sent our reinforcements away. We managed to take them off from Euboia, with our fleet, though Datis should have prevented it had he been alert enough. We had only fifty ships at that time, and most of them only penteconters.

The fate of Eretria

In the year that I spent in Susa, learning to speak your language, my King, I grew tired of the close walls of that great city, and rode out one day towards the black wells in Kissian country, of which I had heard, and which I was curious to see. In the heat of that golden land I stopped in a village, and asked a little girl, playing by the well there, to bring a vessel, and draw me some water. I spoke in limping Persian, and she seemed to have difficulty understanding me. I asked again, with gestures, miming a man raising a cup to his lips, and tilting his head to drink. Then she ran away, calling out to her mother in the purest Greek, ringing like music in my astonished ears.

A woman brought me a cup, and gave me water. 'I thank you, lady,' I said to her gravely, in Greek. The watching children scattered, calling, and soon the street filled with folk coming from their houses to stare at me. The oldest man, wearing a ring of office, said to me, 'Who are you, coming from a far country?'

'I am Themistokles, the Athenian,' I said. 'Who are you?'

'We are the Eretrians,' he said. 'And when we were taken from our homes, Themistokles, you did not come.'

'We could not,' I told him, but my voice shook a little. 'Come let us talk, old man, and I will tell you about it.'

He brought me into his house, and men gathered round to hear me. 'It was because we had not enough ships,' I said, 'that we could not come to your aid. Had we left Attica, Datis could have landed his army anywhere on our coasts – at Athens itself even – and we could not have got back in time, as we did from Marathon. We ought to have had more ships ourselves, and ourselves been able to move swiftly.' They stared at me. 'As soon as the gods gave me the opportunity,' I said to their blank faces, 'I made sure the Athenians had ships enough for all needs.'

The old man raised his red-rimmed eyes to look at me. 'Nobody here has set eyes on a ship these twenty years,' he said. 'The children do not know what they are.'

I was deeply moved, racked as I was with homesickness and bitterness myself. I began to weep, openly.

'Darius the Great King, wept when he saw us led before him in chains,' the old man went on. 'He forgot the anger in which he had meant to kill us all, and showed mercy, and gave us this dry place to live in. But some of us can remember the sea.'

I could bear no more; I took my tears and my shame away from them. I did not try to tell them how I had raged and grieved over our helplessness to help them; though I had indeed. Rage though we might, we simply had not ships enough.

Even when the news of the fall of Eretria reached us in Athens, the waiting and waiting was not over. The Persians rested when they had led away their captives. Each day of waiting increased our fear, our sense of doom. I am ashamed to say it, but there were men in the city who would have welcomed Hippias with tears of joy, if he would have turned away the rage of the King. There were also a more contemptible sort, who thought that under Persia they might get positions of power that the people would never vote to them freely. These men, whoever they were, could not allow their treason to show too soon – the loyal mob might hammer them to death – yet they had to act before Persian victory became certain; they had to help it along in some way, or lose their share of the carrion.

We fidgeted, like athletes at the starting-post, loyal and disloyal alike. Then soon after daybreak one morning there was smoke on Mount Pentelicos, sighted in the city. Trumpets called men to take food and march. And one beacon answered another, all across Attica. The smoke meant Datis had landed on the plains of Marathon; and the signal had been ready because of Kallimachos, our commander-in-chief, who had guessed that's where the landing would come, though the rest of us thought it would be Phaleron. Kallimachos remembered that Hippias had landed at Marathon when he was a boy, coming with his father Peisistratos, and successfully entering Athens; whereas Hippias himself had fought off a landing at Phaleron, when the Spartans tried it. Hippias was with Datis, and Kallimachos proved right. Old men, they understood each other.

We marched out, as fast as we could, having first despatched a runner to Sparta. We went by the coast road, which is longer but easier to march by, and since it is the only one for cavalry it was the road we expected the Persians to take. We detached one tribe, the Antiochids, to go by the hill road and hold it should the Persians be coming that way instead. But we met them on neither road; they were not in a hurry. Perhaps they thought we would take refuge in the city, and defend the walls, like the Eretrians. That was hardly an encouraging example. Anyway, when we got there, the Persians were still disembarking, their ships drawn into the shelter of the Kynosoura promontory, and some detachments already landed, visible marching southwards between the marsh and the sea. We occupied the mouth of a valley debouching into the plain, beneath the village of Marathon, where the hill-track from Athens came out. The Antiochids, with Aristeides their chosen general, came up behind us almost at once. Eight deep, our usual formation, we could draw up our line stretching from side to side of the valley, and have steeps on either flank, and positioned there we cut off the hill-road, and commanded the flank of the coast road, thus holding all ways to Athens. Except, of course, the sea. There we waited, and watched.

Kallimachos called a council of war. We were saddled with a most ridiculous system of command. He was in charge, and I think the citizens chose well. He was elderly, but still vigorous in body and mind, and he had fought against Chalkis and Thebes long ago, and had a well-stocked memory. Under him were the generals, one for each tribe; and we were supposed, under the polemarch, to take a day each, turn by turn, as second in command. I can imagine what you, Lord Artaxerxes, would think of generalship by committee; and you would be right. The system was supposed, of course, to ensure that no one general got too powerful.

Kallimachos had pitched his tent in a place called the precinct of Herakles, sacred to that god. He assembled us there, and gravely asked for our advice. As it happened it was Aristeides' day for precedence, and we all waited for him to speak. We were a curious lot for fate to depend on: the polemarch and the general of Pandionis, both grey-beards, grand old men; Miltiades; and then a motley collection of younger men, among them Aristeides and myself. I hoped fervently that the battle would come on the morrow, my day, both for the glory, and for the good hope that would offer of getting the tactics right. But even as I sat there, hoping, Aristeides began to speak.

'Kallimachos,' he said, 'there are many here present who have never till now commanded men in war; and more depends on success or failure now, I think, than ever before in the history of our city. Today is my day of precedence, but I make it over freely to Miltiades, in the hope that my brother generals will do likewise. For he is the one among us best fitted to advise the polemarch, on any day.'

There was a silence then, while we thought it over. Undoubtedly he was right. But I waited for the others to agree, not realising that, since my day came next, they were all waiting for me.

At last, 'Do I have your support, Themistokles?' Miltiades asked me.

'If you didn't have my support, Miltiades,' I said, 'you would

94

not have the generalship of Oineis. As for my days, you may have them, for as long as you need them.' He winced slightly at my arrogance, but he was eager enough to accept. The others all agreed with us.

'Athene be thanked,' said Kallimachos, 'for a gift of wisdom to us all. Now let us hear what Miltiades advises us to do.'

'For the moment we should wait,' he said. 'The runner Philippides needs at least two days to reach Sparta; only the gods can tell how swiftly they can come to us here. We have very little chance without them; we are too heavily outnumbered.'

'What if they move towards Athens?' I asked him.

'We outflank them along the good road,' said Kallimachos.

'I meant, if they move off by sea.'

'If they try to move by sea, we must fight them at once,' said Miltiades, 'whatever the odds are. In the meanwhile, we must hold this position, day and night. We must bivouac where we are.'

They did not move away by sea. They brought their immense host up into position, facing us across the road to Athens between us and the shore. We commanded a downwards slope towards them, but they outnumbered us so greatly that their lines were nearly twice as long as ours. They drew up in battle order, with the terrible battalions of the immortals, Persians and Sakans to a man, in the centre, and great massed hordes of archers and light-armed auxiliaries on the wings. And then they stood their ground and waited. By night the plains were starry with their campfires, by day the green plain glittered with their bronze and steel.

'I do not know why they wait,' said Kallimachos. 'What are they waiting for?'

'They don't like to attack us in position, perhaps,' said Aristeides.

'Yet if they start to embark they know we must move down on them,' said Miltiades. 'What keeps them from going, unless they are waiting for something?'

'If they are waiting for something, I can hazard a guess what it is,' I said darkly, 'and I pray god it does not come.'

To the men, especially the young men, burning to race downhill and fight, we generals said constantly, dozens of times a day, every day, 'we must wait for the Spartans. We must wait.'

On the evening of the second day, ringing down the valley behind us, we heard the tramp of armed men, and the squeal of the martial flute. We ran out of our tents to see, thinking in a leap of hope that some miracle had brought the Spartans already to our aid. Of course, it was not them. Instead it was the men of Plataia, that small city. (Whatever use to us are the Plataians? Lykos said laughing, once.) They had brought all they had, every man, every boy, a thousand in all. Their general, Arimnestos, presented himself to Kallimachos. 'We come, as we are pledged to come,' he said, 'and here we are.' Kallimachos directed him to the left wing of our line; they marched along our ranks to reach their position. And I swear, Great King, that we wept to see them come; our puny allies, throwing themselves into danger, when they might easily have stayed safe at home. They relieved our loneliness, our sense of standing unsupported, deserted, alone among the Hellenes, meeting the threat to all. It was just as well we had something to cheer us up before the answer came from the Spartans. They were keeping the feast, they said, of the Karneian moon; and while the moon waxed they were forbidden to march in war; as soon as the moon passed its fullness, they would come.

I have often wondered about that. Naturally, an Athenian can't help wondering if the phases of the moon would have worried the Spartans if the Persian army had been marching upon Lakedaimon, instead of upon her rival. But it is true they are very pious; and they marshalled their men on the very borders of Lakonia, and stood ready, peering at the sky, to move the instant the full moon began to fade. Perhaps the truth is that they were divided again, some wanting to come, some others wanting not to. I'm sure Kleomenes wanted to come; why otherwise would he have coerced the Aiginetans into peace with us? But he always had enemies in Sparta, and they had got their teeth into evidence that he had bribed the Oracle. Anyway, come they did not, though we knew the day of their coming, and of course they were bound to be too late, for Datis too knew when they would come; such matters can't be kept secret. We waited, knowing almost surely he would move before they came; he waited, as long as he could for something, whatever it was. The moon shone on our midnight encampments, her pallor making us both alike seem like a ghost army, men of asphodel. And when it came at last we were still waiting alone, we and the Plataians. To this day, Great King, when an Athenian raises the wine cup and calls a blessing on his city, 'Good luck, good harvests, and happiness to the Athenians,' he says, 'and to the Plataians!'

On the fifth day of the vigil, Datis moved, or, to be exact, on the fourth night. It was the night of the Karneian full moon; he knew the Spartans would march at dawn. The first we heard of it was a wolf call, ringing among the trees which grew scattered thinly on the plain below our lines, screening the centre. A few sentries went down, looking for the beast, and found instead two Ionians, with faces blackened with charcoal, who were crouched down in the shadow of a broken branch.

'The cavalry are at this moment being embarked!' they said. 'Tell your generals.' Then they melted into the night. You might notice, Lord Artaxerxes, that the affection for the Ionians that brought the Athenians to Sardis, and first caused them to anger the King, is not one-sided; in expeditions to Hellas, I warn you, the Ionians will never make trustworthy allies of the Persians.

In the light of that triumphant moon, Kallimachos called a council. 'The Medes have embarked their cavalry,' he told us. 'They will take them round to land at Phaleron, and so we must now fight them, at daybreak, like it or no.'

Then we all listened to Miltiades. 'The main danger comes from the archers,' he said. 'They can kill dozens before they are within a spear's reach. So we must close with them at a run; the faster we come the shorter the time of their advantage. The Persians charge very bravely – we must exploit that.'

He was a great man, Miltiades; one of the few I have ever met whose thinking was not chained by knowing the way things have been done before. He reversed the usual order of battle; we were to be thin in the centre, and double deep on the wings. The centre was merely to 'show a line' among the scattered trees, and was expected to give way, as soon as the enemy attacked it. Somehow we had to get into formation, with thin centre, and heavily grouped wings, quickly enough to take the Persians by surprise, and all at a run, to defeat their archery. Miltiades suggested we should draw up two columns, side by side, in line down the valley. Then we should run; the leaders of the two tribes at the head of the columns should turn outwards, and run to left and right, until they were opposite the ends of the Persian lines, and then run to close with the enemy. The rest of the column would run after them, and this would lead naturally, with the impetus of the downhill run, to a crescent-shaped front, thin in the middle, massing at the wings. He drew up a marching order for this manoeuvre: on the right, the polemarch, with his tribe, Aiantis, in the place of honour; followed by Erectheis, Aigeis, Pandionis, Leontis; on the left the Plataians, followed by Akamantis, Oineis, Kekropis, Hippothontis, Antiochis. The two in the rearguard, who would form the weak centre, therefore, and face the Persian Immortals, were

Antiochis, commanded by Aristeides, and Leontis, commanded by me.

'You two,' said Miltiades, 'I can rely on you two to understand me fully. If you keep running, and turn to face the Persians only when they are upon you, you may even find a gap has already opened up in the middle, that they will pour through. Don't try to hold out more than a few minutes; move sideways, that will keep your losses down as far as possible. And, when they have crashed through, we will be behind them, I trust. You understand, generals, that the wings must deliver their attack *inwards* when it comes – in a converging direction.'

'Has everything necessary been said?' asked Kallimachos. 'Let us now propitiate the gods.' It was still dark. Only the faintest bleaching of the eastern skyline was yet visible, and all the stars were bright. Kallimachos went to the altar of Herakles, and sacrificed a young kid to the gods; but to Athene more than the rest, since she was our own. 'Victory, and safety for thy own dear city, goddess,' he said, arms raised. 'And we promise you in sacrifice a fair young kid like this one for every one of the Persian dead.'

I turned to Aristeides. 'Farewell, dear friend,' I said. He looked surprised, whether it was at my farewell, or at my speaking to him with affection, I cannot tell. He looked at me, and decided to forget what he had against me. He reached out, and grasped my arm. 'May the gods make this unnecessary!' he said. Then we went to instruct our captains, and form up the columns.

He and I both conducted ourselves with great distinction that day. What was asked of our tribes was not easy; nevertheless, we performed it. We showed a line in the centre, and for a few terrible moments withstood the full weight of the Persian charge. The breathless running downhill, and the shouting, were quickly followed for us by nightmare chaos. I have been told that when the Persians, looking uphill in the grey first light, saw us running towards them they said to each other, 'These men are mad!' I wonder how long they thought so. All the while they charged us, I suppose; splendid in their massed ranks, their leather and bronze. All the while as they fell upon my people, and killed them, and rushed over and through our line, and poured onwards, inland up into the narrowing valley that led nowhere, and got steeper with every step. Then suddenly the battle was behind them; they were facing the wrong way, their leaders were in the rear, they were cut off and surrounded. In the centre, Great King, having trapped them, we killed the Persians almost to a man; the wings, which had been put to flight by our wings, before they wheeled and fell upon the centre, largely got away towards the ships. There seemed to be an age of hacking down the trapped and disordered Persians, and then suddenly it was over, and we hurtled off in pursuit of the rest. They crowded the narrow path between the shore and the marsh, and fell to be smothered in the quagmire. Their ships ran onto the beaches, trying to take men off, and we fought them, calling for fire to set them alight. In the skirmishing at the ships we lost Kallimachos, fighting like a man half his age; and Aeschylus lost a brother there, whose hand was hacked off as he grasped the stempost of a ship.

And then the noise died away. Open water lay between the beach, and the last escaping ship. A straggling line of men, who must have fled in very good time, could be seen beyond the marsh, stumbling towards the few ships still beached at Kynosoura. The loudest voice was that of men gasping for breath and the waves upon the shore. As we leaned on our swords, or on the shoulders of the nearest man to us, half-choking with triumph and fatigue, like runners at the finishing-post, half-laughing as the blood frenzy left us, suddenly someone cried out, and pointed back. There were daggers of light flashing on the slope of Pentelicos, beyond the plain, towards Athens. A signal, flashed from a shield in the early sun. That was what Datis had been waiting for; someone in Athens was ready for him now.

The trumpets called us into line again; we walked stepping over the strewn bodies, the lizard-like bodies of the dead, scaly with plates of bronze. The captains began a roll call. And the tally of our dead was one hundred and ninety-two. Of that number fifty-three were from Aristeides' tribe, but he was not one of them; and forty-five were from mine. As for the dead Persians they seemed countless in the mid-morning sunlight on the plain, but in fact there were six thousand four hundred, to be paid for to the goddess, according to Kallimachos' oath; and they outnumbered all the kids in Attica.

Miltiades, lifted to shoulder height by two of his comrades, raised his voice, and spoke to us. 'Athenians, here is a day's work well begun. But before first light this morning, the Persians had embarked their cavalry; and they still have a fleet of ships. They hope to take Athens while we are away. You all saw the signal made to them behind our backs – perhaps they have helpers ready. We must be home before those ships can come. Shall we march?' So leaving Aristeides and his tribe, since they were badly cut up, hardly a man unscathed, to guard the bodies of the dead, we jostled into column again, and marched away to Athens.

When we left the plain of Marathon the morning light had been low enough to strike flashes off a shield on the mountains. We marched through the heat of the day, driven by fear that our victory might be snatched from us. Early in the evening, when the light first softens, and the shadows blurr a little, we came up to the walls of the city, and our outriders learned that all was still well there. Whoever had signalled to Datis had not shown his hand openly. Miltiades took us then towards the sea, out through the gardens round the walls to the Kynosarges, where I used to run and wrestle long ago. The Kynosarges was dedicated to Herakles, as the place had been where we camped at Marathon. In front of its walls we drew up in fighting order, and then stood, drooping with fatigue, facing the shore. We saw the Persians coming, like black birds on the silver roadsteads of the sea, their haste slowed by distance. There were hundreds of them. Weariness veiled our eyes, as we watched them. They drew near, near inshore. They surely could see us too, across their road to the city, a dark line of men, prickling with ready spears. Behind us our city rose, wearing her evening apparel of lilac light and shade. They saw us across their way, and they turned their ships and sailed away. As for us, many of us lay down and slept in our places in the line, unable to move another step.

I don't remember a better awakening than on the morrow of Marathon, when I opened my eyes to find myself, cold, stiff, aching in every joint, lying wrapped in a dew-soaked cloak on the hard stony ground of home; and free.

I rose, and jerky with stiffness began to walk home. Half-way I met a boy, with joy on his face, coming with a friend to 'see the army'. I gave him a drachma, and asked him to carry my armour home for me. As I stood, unbuckling the cruelly heavy bronze, he called for his friend to help him, and the two of them, stretching eager hands for their burden, both begged to carry my sword. 'You'll carry a sword soon enough, lads,' I said, smiling.

'If you gave me your sword to carry, sir,' said the first lad, 'I could tell my own children one day, that I was an armour-bearer after Marathon!' At that, I gave it to him.

'To whose house shall we carry these?' they asked me.

'Themistokles' house.'

'Themistokles? He's a general!' they cried. 'Are you him? Really? Oh, what was the fighting like, Themistokles?'

'Hard enough to make a man tired,' I said, though indeed I could have leapt around, and shouted, just as they were doing. 'Off with you now, or I'll ask your names, and inquire whether your parents knew you were out by yourselves so early!' They looked chastened, and began to walk soberly towards the city, weighed down by their armfuls of leather and bronze. I went to Kynosarges, and bathed there, along with many others who had slept out, as I had; and the bath attendant, a man bent with age, brought rose petals to float in the basin he filled for me.

'What's all that for?' I asked him. 'Do I look as if I'm on my way to meet a young boy?'

'Don't you remember, Themistokles?' he said, 'It's what you told me to do, once, if the customers were good enough for me!'

'Why, yes,' I said, 'I remember. Well, I'd say I deserved them today; bring me some oil now, will you?' So I rubbed a little looseness into my limbs, and went home to my wife, who had feared I was dead till the little boys brought my armour in.

'Come, wife,' I said to her, 'put on your cloak, and gather the children. Today we will all go together to offer honey and wine to the gods.'

That morning the streets were full of other families, on the same errand; Athenians crowned with flowers, with their wives and children around them, climbing the Acropolis, and crowding the temples and altars. Phrynichos was there, with his grandchildren, and poor, red-eyed Aeschylus, making offerings for his brother at the altar of the dead, and Miltiades with a pretty daughter and a slim young son, and Aristeides with his boys, and indeed all of us, and all glowing as though we'd drunk wine. I don't doubt a good many of us had!

At midday the Spartans arrived, two thousand, in good order, marching up the road from Eleusis. It was then three days from the full moon; certainly they had marched like Trojans, doing their best to catch up with their piety. We generals received them, still crowned with flowers, offering them food and wine, and saying with thinly veiled glee, 'We thank you, but we got on very well without you!'

Their generals wanted to see the battlefield, so we took horses, and rode across the hills, and showed them around, with Miltiades explaining his tactics all the way. Aristeides' men were still at their posts, guarding the slain; they had gathered the bodies of the Greeks together, and covered them, ready for the flames, and made lists of names and tribes. The Spartans walked among the Persian dead; they praised us, then they left for home. They had been generous in their way, if you forgive them their moonstruck religion, but I was delighted to see them go. As things turned out it had been a good thing they had not come in time; that way we owed them nothing.

Later at Marathon we burned the dead. Your people we threw into a ditch, ours we laid all together, and piled a mound over their ashes. On the mound we raised tablets of marble, bearing their names. With the gold and jewels plundered from the Persian dead we built a treasury at Delphi – a place of safe-keeping for Athenian offerings to the god. It was a little house of white marble with a porch of two columns – like a small temple – and before it we set up a row of statues. To Olympia we sent twenty bronze helmets, with an inscription engraved upon them: 'Taken by the Athenians from the Medes.' For an epitaph on the dead we held a competition, which to Aeschylus' bitter disappointment was won by Simonides, although he had once been Hippias' friend. We gave orders that the head of Athene on all our silver coins was to be crowned henceforwards with laurel, and a waning moon was put on the obverse side, to remember the Spartans by! That left only Kallimachos' rash promise of a kid for each enemy slain. Being unable to pay it, we promised the goddess to offer five hundred a year instead and besought her to accept them; they are being sacrificed still, Great King.

So gradually the excitement died away and Athens resumed her normal ways. There was a difference, though; the people had gained confidence. The men who had stood alone against the majesty of the King would no longer be humble, respectful of their betters, diffident in taking what Kleisthenes had given them. Miltiades didn't realise that, I think; but, of course, his glory shone so brightly, he was so much the greatest man in Athens, that there were many things he mightn't have seen lurking in the shadows he cast behind him. Worse luck for him. He put on the agony a bit, swaggering around in purple robes, with a mob of young men at his heels. That reminded people of the past, but still he could do nothing wrong in their eyes.

He put his prisoners up for sale, on a market day in the agora, with their armour going too, in separate lots. I hadn't taken prisoners myself, for it hadn't been that kind of battle in the centre, where I had been fighting, but I rather wanted a Persian of my own, so I went and bought one. I must have a good eye for a slave, for I picked out a man of high rank, and good education. He had been roughly treated, and beaten, for Miltiades had hired out his captives to the silver mines while he waited for a good time to sell them. When the slave came to me he was frightened. But he spoke quite passable Greek, having lived in Karia for some years; I made him a tutor and pedagogue to my children. He was called Sikinnos – a name which I daresay got into Persian despatches later. And so abject is a man rendered by slavery that, merely because I didn't flog him, he loved me and would have done anything for me.

At the height of his triumph, Miltiades approached the Assembly with a request. He had let it be known he was about something important, and the Assembly was packed solid. Miltiades stood at the rostrum, and asked for seventy ships, and men, and money. He asked to have full command. 'I would rather not say in public, Athenians,' he said, 'what country I propose to attack; I don't think it good policy to inform an enemy that you are setting out against him!' He was smiling, and the people laughed. 'I can say, however,' he went on, 'that it's a rich place; I promise you won't be out of pocket.' At this the listeners cheered him. 'Furthermore,' he said, 'in case anyone is interested in any further justification, what I do will be for the good of Athens. Athenians, give me your trust. Give me your votes!' And, as easily as that, he got them. We voted him seventy ships, which was absolutely all we had, and the gods help us if the Aiginetans caused trouble again – with, of course, men and money, everything he wanted and not a question asked. Off he went, with all our ships, to his unknown destination.

He worried me. It did not look easy now, as I once thought it would be, to get rid of him when I pleased. And his power was immense – the people would do anything for him. They were never to trust me like that. If he came back victorious, there would be no room in Athens for anyone but him. He had enemies, of course; the Alkmeonids hated him with a pure flame of hatred that made one almost suspect they would really have preferred Hippias – poor sick old Hippias, who died in the ships going back to Ionia. All over the city men were saying that it was the Alkmeonid faction who had shown the shield signal to Datis on the morning of Marathon. The men who did that whoever they were, had not shown themselves openly, there were only guesses about it. Mere guesses, very persistent ones, were enough to discredit the Alkmeonids – after all, had not Kleisthenes sent earth and water to the King? Thus Miltiades' strongest enemies were in disgrace, and powerless to influence or balance opinion in the Assembly.

Mnesiphilos talked to me about it one day, when I met him on the road to Peiraieus. I hadn't seen him in years, and I didn't recognise him at first, an old fat man on a shambling donkey, going so slowly that I was fast overtaking him on foot. As I passed him, I glanced at him, and saw something familiar in his bloated face. Gods, I had thought the man dead long since!

'Mnesiphilos!' I said to him. 'Where have you been hiding your-self?'

'Hmph,' he said. 'So it's true what I hear that the great Themis-tokles never forgets a face.'

'Never yours, man!' I said, noticing how much he had aged – the sharp eyes sunk in their sockets, and dimmed, the rosy face coarsened and roughened. 'Come, tell me what to think about the latest scandal in the city.'

'I don't go into the city much, nowadays,' he said.

'How do you spend your time, sir?'

'Oh, on my farm, you know. My farm takes a good deal of my time. Neighbours aren't what they were, but the olives are good this year. Right weather for them.'

'I'm going to Peiraieus,' I said. 'Are you coming that way too?'

'Quiet down there with the ships away,' he said.

'I have a house there, you know. On the very spot, or near enough, where we sat together that morning, and I told you what a good harbour could be made there!'

'Oh, yes, you've done well,' he said. 'You've certainly done well. Always knew you would. Remember telling your father so.' I thought he was well into his dotage, and found nothing more to say to him.

'Well, what d'you think of Miltiades the mighty, then?' he said suddenly. 'Where's he gone, then? D'you know what I think? Paros. That's where.'

'Why Paros?' I asked, giving him now my full attention.

'Because he had a score to settle with Lysagoras the Parian – the one that shopped him to the King when he talked of breaking the bridge down. The ship the Parians sent with Datis will give him his excuse.'

'If Miltiades thinks the islands ought to see a show of Athenian strength, and the ones which helped Datis should be punished,' I said, 'well, I agree with that.'

'But it isn't your doing, is it, boy, so whatever comes of it you won't get credit for it, though you agree with him till you're blue in the face. But there, I'm an old man, and all you youngsters seem delighted, and don't see anything to worry about!'

'By the gods, Mnesiphilos,' I told him, 'Miltiades' glory keeps me awake at night!'

'Ah,' he said. 'Yes, you've got more sense than many, I'll give you that. Remember telling your father so.' And off he shambled, taking the coast-road to somewhere, raising his puffy hand in a brief gesture of farewell.

Miltiades' absence in search of further glory at least meant he couldn't be elected archon that year; in my worst dreams I imagined him coming home just in time to be made chief archon, but the Parians were capable men; they detained him. He had collected indemnities from several surrounding islands, for help unwillingly given to Datis, and from the Parians he was asking a hundred talents, which would have made the ship they sent to Marathon a costly one indeed. However, they closed the gates of their city against him, and held out long enough to allow us to elect Aristeides as archon.

I supported Aristeides, quietly, without making a show of it. He was just about the only man who had a position in the hearts of the people which might possibly allow him to limit Miltiades' power. And his inflexible sense of right conduct, irritating though it was to me, was a good safeguard to liberty; nobody would tamper with the freedom of the citizens during Aristeides' archonship.

Looking back, I don't think Miltiades would have got the archonship; so my concern was for nothing. The people hadn't beaten off the Persians in order to be tyrannised by Miltiades, or anyone else. For the city has its own counterbalance to ambition; the rise of any member of one of the great families instantly brings the hatred and jealousy of the others into play; they throw the weight of their factions into scheming to destroy the rival, and at the same time the people can easily come to feel that enough is enough. If they have given too much power they begin to fear tyranny. So it is that the higher a man rises in Athens the greater the danger he is in.

And not only did Miltiades not come back in time for the summer elections, he did not come back successful. He injured himself, jumping from a temple wall, it was said, in some madcap midnight assignation with a priestess, who had some kind of pull in the negotiations with the Parians. He broke his right thigh-bone jumping from the wall of her temple, and was lucky to get back to his own lines alive at all. Whatever plot he had been hatching came to nothing; the Parians said they would negotiate, but then they saw smoke over on the island of Mykonos and thought it was the Persians coming to their aid. It was nothing of the sort, of course; it was a forest fire; but it gave them heart to chase away Miltiades. So he came home without his hundred talents, and, indeed, without money to pay his soldiers. A sombre little crowd gathered at the jetty in Peiraieus to watch him come ashore. He came with an arm around the shoulders of each of two friends, hopping between them, swinging his injured leg, which was bound up to the end of an oar.

Athens was in uproar. There is no man on earth more resentful than an unpaid soldier; and the Assembly, reluctantly, and with much bitterness, had to vote money to pay off the men. It cost the city fifty talents, and not a penny had been brought in, for Miltiades had spent already the money he had raised from smaller islands, more easily browbeaten.

Xanthippos brought him to trial. Xanthippos still acting as the mouthpiece of the Alkmeonids. Xanthippos accused him of deceiving the people, and chose to make the case against him before the Assembly. I was satisfied with that. Let the Alkmeonids get rid of Miltiades for me; after him it would be not their day that dawned but mine. However, I thought it possible that Miltiades might succeed in swaying the Assembly, so I prepared a speech against him, and went ready to deliver it. Others, I was sure, and the viper-tongued Xanthippos among them, would tell everyone about Miltiades' personal feud with Lysagoras the Parian, and we would hear again every detail of the antityrant rigmarole that had been brought against him before. So I intended to cross-examine him again, this time about his knowledge of strategy at sea. I was all ready to ask him how he imagined the city was going to defend herself against Aigina when all her ships were at Paros.

It was a cool day, with great phalanxes of grey clouds marshalled above the city; the Assembly was packed, Xanthippos stood ready, the judge was seated, and Miltiades had not yet arrived. A herald called for him. Then there came a hush in the buzz of excited voices. A little party of Philaids came in, and in the midst of them Miltiades, carried on a stretcher. They set him down on the ground in front of the rostrum, and as the feet of the pallet met the solid pavement, and it jerked a little, the man on it started with pain, pain that bared his teeth, and arched his back, though he uttered not a sound. Miltiades was not going to sway the Assembly when he spoke; he was not going to say a word in his own defence; Miltiades was dying. He even smelt of death; those who sat around me, downwind of him, were discomforted by the foul smell of gangrened flesh. Standing before the people, Xanthippos asked for a sentence of death.

I had put aside the idea of speaking against Miltiades the moment I saw him. And now my gorge rose. Xanthippos' clear voice, ringing with 'he deserves to die!' and the repeatedly wafted stench in my nostrils – ugh! I could think only that we were like carrion birds, flocking greedily round the fallen. Miltiades' friends defended him. They said he had done good service to the city at Marathon. Xanthippos wasn't fool enough to deny that – he stuck to the main point; Miltiades would not tell the people where he was going; he promised to make a profit, actually he lost lives, gained nothing, and made a financial loss. Deplorable. But, of course, however different it all sounds, what he was really on trial for was being a possible tyrant; just like last time. For being an enemy of the Alkmeonids, just like last time. Once more, Aristeides made a speech about the danger to freedom – this time the danger to freedom of giving too much power to one general. I sat through that freedom speech of his on so many occasions that I know it nearly by heart. And all the while Miltiades lay there, silent. Did he hear what we had to say about him? I don't think he did; I think he was too far gone. But beside him, standing at the head of the pallet, among his friends, standing facing us across his father's body, all day stood Kimon, Miltiades' son. When he was not stooping to comfort his father he stood bolt upright, head held high. I stared at him. I suppose he was about sixteen – tall, slender, handsome like his father, under a crop of shaggy curls, stonefaced, contemptuous, I thought (and who could blame him?) of those whom he confronted. Kimon's opinions are deplorable, Lord Artaxerxes. He likes the Spartans; it is because of him we haven't fought them, because of him, and his spite, and his reactionary ideas that I am here now; but one has to admit that what the Assembly did to him that day is no way to make a man a democrat.

The Assembly found Miltiades guilty. Then Xanthippos asked for the death penalty, and Miltiades' friends proposed instead that he should be fined. Some bright wit, sitting far back among the men of small consequence, called out, 'Athenians, if you want to *execute* Miltiades, you'll have to be quick about it!' And the

Athenians voted to fine him fifty talents – the sum his expedition had cost. The fine, of course, was the heavier punishment, since his death was exacted anyway, by the gods; the fine stripped him of property and ruined his son. As for me, I didn't change my mind far enough to speak in Miltiades' defence. After all, I did want to be rid of him.

Leaving the court, among the other Areopagites, I met the chief archon and his party. I was angry, at the unseemliness of what had been done, I think, and not from foreknowledge.

'What does the just man of Athens think of today's affair?' I asked Aristeides, bitterly.

'My friend Themistokles knows very well that the archon cannot prevent a case being brought to trial,' he said evenly. (So he had tried?) 'But the trial was a fair one. And I'd have thought you'd have approved, Themistokles. Aren't you glad to see the back of him?'

'There must have been a less disgusting way of going about it,' I said.

'Yes,' he said. 'I agree. I was for using Kleisthenes' law of ostracism, if Xanthippos hadn't forestalled me.'

'He, and the gods!' I said.

And that was the manner, Great King, in which the Athenians rewarded the victor of Marathon – doubtless he would have preferred to suffer the punishment of Datis the Mede.

Miltiades died three days later. The city seized his house and everything he possessed, and sold it in an attempt to recover their fifty talents, and after that had been done the larger part of it was still owing. The body had to be buried at the expense of his friends. Kimon, and Elpinike, his half-sister, were turned out onto the streets, without an obol between them. I suppose they had help from some of the Philaids; anyway, they bought a tiny house, in a poor district of the city, and lived there very quietly. Since Kimon hadn't found a husband for Elpinike, or set her up in her own house, they were pursued by scurrilous rumours that they were infatuated with each other, and slept together, as though the fact that the boy couldn't pay for one decent house, let alone two, and couldn't raise a dowry were much the least likely reason. One way and another, although the girl was pretty, the talk, one imagined, would ruin her chance of marriage for good. My wife told me that the women of the city could talk of nothing else, and I gathered the poor wretches gave colour to the scandal by being visibly and pathetically devoted to each other. Such misfortune touches even a hardbitten man; and, after all, I had sons of my own, but Kimon sent back the gifts I sent them, with a letter of proud refusal. My wife found ways of sending things anonymously that didn't come back.

While the children of Miltiades were being spat on in Athens, the Spartans were employed in murdering Kleomenes, and mutilating his dead body hideously with the knife. Before Marathon, Kleomenes had saved us, taking hostages from Aigina. But Aigina, like her of Doric race, was an ancient friend of Sparta, and the Aiginetans complained bitterly at being sacrificed for us, Sparta's rival. To get his way over hostages Kleomenes had thrown out his fellow king, Damaratos, and bribed the Oracle to do it – all in a good cause, but scandalous. A king in Sparta doesn't have a free hand; he's not a king like you, my Lord Artaxerxes; as well as sharing power with a king of the other royal house, he has a body of officials called ephors, who watch what he's up to and check him if they think fit. Kleomenes had forced the whole body of the Spartans out of their natural allegiance, not, I am sure, out of affection for Athens, but because he could judge what kind of enemy the Persian king would be. Now the whole pack of his enemies fell upon him, and Sparta was too hot for him. He went to Arkadia, a place of high mountains, and tribes of hill folk, not organised in cities. They are fine soldiers, but will follow only a man, not a cause. He started to enroll them as his private followers. The ephors were alarmed, and summoned him home. When he went, they threw him into prison, allegedly for striking fellow Spartans in the face; and in prison, they say, he went mad and hacked himself up with a dinner knife, starting at the heels, and not dying till he reached his stomach. That's the official story. And such is the chance of inheritance that he, that cunning, devious, brilliant and dangerous man, was succeeded by Leonidas – a man as straight as a spear shaft, and as stupid.

As soon as Kleomenes' death was known, we had trouble with Aigina. The Spartans sent Latychidas, whom Kleomenes had installed in Damaratos' place, to demand the return of the hostages held in Athens. We refused to return them; they were well fed and comfortable, confined on the Acropolis. Then the Aiginetans raided Sounion while we were holding a festival there, the festival that launches the sacred ship on its voyage to Apollo at Delos, the holy isle. On board the ship were members of just about every important Athenian family, and a chorus of beautiful boys, who were going to sing and dance at the Delian shrine. Among the boys was Phrasikles, my brother's son. So now they had pawns of ours to balance ours of theirs, so they were free to make trouble again. The Aiginetans, Great King, are what the Spartans would be like if they all turned into traders – what a thought! They are Dorian with a haughty aristocracy and brutal gods. They are vengeful, vicious and mean-minded, and their only topic of conversation is the price of corn. But nobody could deny their courage in battle. They do not, like the Spartans, keep helots – that is a whole population in slavery – but they treated their common folk abominably, and in that fact we saw their weakness.

There was a man called Nikodromos who had lived in Attica as an exile for some time, as a punishment for having 'stirred up trouble among the people of Aigina'. In Athenian Greek that means 'having championed the cause of the poor and the oppressed'. He was a man after my own heart, and I suggested to the Assembly that we should back him. The college of generals got together, and we made a plan for putting Nikodromos and his small band ashore in the coast of Aigina, and then, while he raised a rebellion, and held the old town, we would attack by sea. The first part of this plan was easy. We put our party ashore on a lonely beach, on a night so calm and still and starlit that the dripping water from the lifting oars glinted silver and tinkled, it seemed, loudly and clearly enough to wake the whole island. Then we stood out to sea again. So far so good.

But I was uneasy. The second part of the plan would be the difficult part, for the Aiginetan fleet outnumbered ours, and while they had a good number of triremes we had mainly penteconters. I voiced my unease so loudly that at last I was sent to Corinth to beg them to lend us ships.

The plan miscarried. The lords of Aigina got wind of what we were up to, and asked the Argives for help. The Argives were a pitiful remnant of that once-proud city, since Kleomenes had smashed them at Sepeia, and having spilt most of their blue blood they were a kind of democracy; but though they refused, officially, the request for help, volunteers poured in, young athletes, young princes, eager to fight the friends of democracy and prove that their blood ran pure. Their leader was Eurybates, who had won the pentathlon at the Isthmus. Meanwhile, I was at Corinth, asking for ships.

It's a fine city, Corinth. It lies on a gentle slope, overlooking the calm waters of its perfect, sheltered harbours, with the snows of Parnassos distinctly visible beyond. Behind it towers a grey precipitous mountain, with a temple on top. The city bustles with trade and travellers. The Corinthians were, and are, our friends, but unfortunately they have a law, as allies of the Lakedaimonians, which forbids them to supply warships to any city which is not in the alliance. Still, they were rivals in trade with Aigina, and eager for an opportunity to injure her. My embassy was kindly treated, but detained in endless talk. Then at last we found a way round their law, and they sold us twenty ships, for five drachmas each; since their law didn't prevent them from *selling* ships. Five drachmas, Great King, is about the price of a mixing-jar in the market at Athens – a derisory sum for a ship. Naturally we were to return the ships and accept our money back later! They even arranged that all twenty ships should be lying on the eastern shore of the Isthmus, so that we could be on our way with them as soon as possible; but in fact we came too late. The whole affair was a shambles.

We routed the Aiginetan ships – I think it was the surprise of our superiority in numbers, for our tactics were crude in the extreme. We simply sailed towards them, and rammed any we caught. So we got ashore, only to find that Nikodromos had been defeated the day before, and had escaped with a few men by sea, while his supporters had been massacred. While we were masters of the town we were even shown the Temple of Demeter, with a man's severed hands clasped upon the ring of the doorhandle. He had run for sanctuary, and they had not been able to drag him away. The door was defiled with blood. We prayed that Demeter might take note, and went on our way. The next day there was a bloody but inconclusive infantry engagement, and the day after that Eurybates the Argive, who behaved as though he thought he had been written by Homer, challenged us to send men against him in single combat. He killed three men, and was killed himself by the fourth – Sophanes of Dekeleia. And while we were all standing round like the crowd in an epic poem the Aiginetans surprised our ships, capturing four of them. I and my fellow generals, summoned in haste, watched miserably from a promontory. The Aiginetans were fine seamen; one had only to watch them to see we hadn't a chance till we had trained our men better. So we withdrew, before our losses became too serious, and for the moment contented ourselves with settling Nikodromos at Sounion, and letting him loose like a pirate on Aiginetan shipping.

It did not escape me that it might have been a very different tale had we had ships enough in time.

It was after the Aiginetan affair that I become really worried about my prospects of holding on to power in the city. Naturally, my prestige had slipped a bit, through presiding over an unsuccessful skirmish. A man could be elected archon only once in his life, and each year, therefore, someone else was elected to an office that I myself could never hold again. In this situation my opinions, my policies, above all my urgent demand that the city should build more ships, had no chance of gaining acceptance, for the archon was very powerful during his one short year, and the archon was always a man of status and note. But whereas the community of hoplites, of farmers, could expect to have their interests well served by any one of a dozen men of family, there was only one man who served the interests of seamen and traders, and the humble artisans, and that was me. In the interests of democracy, therefore, I had to get a firmer grip on power. Well, I've never been slow to think of expedients, and after the fracas on Aigina I thought of a brilliant one. I began to recommend that we should alter the law of Kleisthenes, so that instead of being elected, archons were chosen by lot from a short list of five hundred, elected by the demes. Now the advantage of this proposal was that it was calculated to appeal to a lot of people. Even to my own following I could hardly say, 'I want to stay in power, give me more of it!' but I could easily say that choosing the archons by lot was a more democratic procedure; I could point out that it would break the monopoly of great families in leading the state. To the pious, on the other hand, the use of the lot is attractive, because it replaces the wisdom of men, and substitutes the will of the gods. Should we not let Athene guide us? Does she not watch over our city at every turn? More cunning still, the idea would appeal strongly to many of the wealthy, undistinguished hoplite and cavalry class of men, small farmers and the like, who would usually have opposed me, and supported the aristocrats, because of course, though they could never hope to be elected archon, yet theirs were the names that would appear constantly on the short list. Thus under my system they might well hope to be archons – to have public events dated for years to come by having their names tacked onto them – 'it was in the archonship of so-and-so . . .'; or go down to history as the polemarch in a battle; or join the revered ranks of the Areopagites. In short, they might hope to win the most glorious prizes the city had to offer. It was sure to tempt them. They aren't exactly modest, those typical Athenians; it wouldn't occur to them that merely the fact that it was going to be possible for them to be archons would rub the gilding off the archonship. It proved to be remarkably easy to raise a surge of enthusiasm for the idea.

But, although I was the cleverest man in Athens, I was not the only one who had his political wits about him, and my enemies could see what I was getting at. If ordinary men were to be archons, and chief archons, then the archon would cease to be important. Power would shift to those who did hold office as a result of direct election – to the generals, in fact. Unlike archons, generals could be re-elected every year, and I, Themistokles, was safe in a generalship. There was yet another twist to all this. Having been archon I was also an Areopagite, and I knew very well that the leaders in that body – that grey-bearded hive of reactionaries – were the newcomers, those who having most recently triumphed in elections, and fresh from wielding power, were the most knowledgeable, the most able to feel the pulse of the city. In the Areopagus, therefore, I was influential, but in danger of being superseded by younger men, new arrivals. I would scotch that danger for good, if the newcomers were to be nonentities, non-elected. In the long run, the Areopagus, which always stood ready to oppose change, unthinkingly, like a man who has a nervous twitch, would die away, its power would be sapped. In the long run – meanwhile it would serve my purpose.

I struck pure panic into the hearts of my opponents. All the grand families were suddenly faced with the happy acceptance of their loss of privilege, by all their usual supporters! They were beside themselves with rage. But what were they to do? They could hardly go round to the men of cavalry class, and say, 'Look, if you vote for this, the sons of great families won't be able to carve out a privileged career.' Nor can one hope to gain much by telling a man that it will be the ruin of the state if he has a chance of office! No wonder I reaped hatred. Not just the dislike, the contempt, the opposition that I had always attracted, but real hot hatred, that burned men's eyes when they looked at me, and dried up their voices when they had to talk to me. I enjoyed it; it made me feel really dangerous, and therefore really great. To be hated by an Alkmeonid, or by a Philaid, is a crown of olive to a man like me. How many times, by now, I've worn that crown! It takes longer to fade than the crown of an athlete, too.

They made an attempt to get rid of me. They persuaded the Assembly to vote for holding an ostracism that year. The law on ostracism was so dusty that Alkmeon, who proposed it, had to remind the people how it worked, or was supposed to work. Kleisthenes had given it to the people. They were allowed to vote for its use, every year. If they did, then six weeks later they could cast votes against any citizen, and on the man who got most votes, providing six thousand votes or more had been cast, a sentence of exile for ten years was imposed. Xanthippos hastened to point out that this isn't a punishment; oh, no! It is merely a device for making the city safe from potential tyrants. The victim doesn't lose his citizenship, or his property, and has the right to return when he has served his term of exile. And it was not to be administered in a vicious spirit; Kleisthenes expressly stipulated there was to be no debate at either stage of the process; just a vote. Well, I can't think what the Assembly was after, except the sheer fun of the thing, when they voted to hold an ostracism that year; but I know very well what the Alkmeonids were after, and Xanthippos too, presumably; they were after me.

As soon as you think about it you can see that the only way to escape being the victim of an ostracism is to see to it that someone else gets more votes than yourself. Since one isn't allowed to debate the question when the votes are cast, that means campaigning against someone in the streets of the city for weeks beforehand. Well, at least I had my cronies, my partisans, my following to rely on. I chose Hipparchos as the target. Not that he'd done anything blameworthy, as far as I knew, but that with his family connections, and because he had been made archon just before Marathon – all in vain as far as placating the King went – I thought he was vulnerable. One could easily present him as a danger to freedom, the more easily because it was being said that the law on ostracism had been invented especially with him in mind. Kleisthenes knew that he was an upright character, which made it unlikely that there could ever be criminal charges against him, and feared him as a possible tyrant. As to that, I don't know; but as long as other citizens do know what was in Kleisthenes' mind I don't hesitate to make use of it. Anyway, Hipparchos was easy; one had only to remind everyone of his connections with Hippias, and if someone remarked pointedly that Hippias was, after all, dead at last, one could talk darkly about that shield, flashed from Pentelicos, by somebody seeking to bring aid to Datis the Mede. Everybody was very patriotic in the years after Marathon.

Other people, of course were busy campaigning against me. The first of many plagues of scandals broke out against me. My mother's foreign birth was transformed into the tale that I was the son of a flute-girl, born out of wedlock. Luckily my mother, being dead, could not be distressed by it. Further, everyone in the city seemed to know of foul deeds done by me in my youth, for it was well known that I had been unruly and uncontrollable. These stories, I imagine, were supposed to show that I was neither respectable nor reliable. Maybe they cast doubt on me in the minds of some ancient greybeards, but the effect on the ordinary citizens was different. Every day some fellow would ask me, grinning, whether I had really slept with so-and-so's wife, or blacked the eye of a dignitary, or seduced a priestess. I made answer depending on the tone of voice – if it seemed admiring I owned up to the rascality at once, adding that it was the wildest colts which made the best horses.

I suffered greatly, Lord Artaxerxes, during the counting of votes in the ostracism. It seemed to hold us in suspense for a cruelly drawn-out time. The votes are scratched on potsherds and cast into great jars, standing in the agora. First they are counted unread, to make sure there are six thousand at the least; then they are sorted and counted, and a tally is made. It was a near thing, that first time, but Hipparchos won, or lost rather, by a lead of a hundred votes. In my relief, surrounded by my exultant supporters, I wandered along the piles of sherds, shuddering inwardly at the size of the heaped 'Themistokles' fragments, and saw with astonishment the number of citizens who had attracted a vote or two – several dozen of them – from a depth of obscurity so great that I hadn't even heard of them – I who as everyone knows, never forgot a name! Poor Hipparchos! Still, I thought, his fate will teach our bold blue-bloods a lesson. We won't have them flourishing potsherds again in a hurry! So thought I, but, Lord Artaxerxes, even I can be wrong.

Since I had just won a trial of strength with my enemies, the ostracism brought me a new wave of power; everyone knew it was because of the archon reform I was proposing that I had been attacked, so my victory in the jars was taken to mean that the city supported my plan. Riding high on the wave while it lasted, I formally proposed the change in the Assembly, and the Assembly obligingly voted it through. The larger the wave, of course, the stronger the backlash; my success alarmed people. There was another ostracism the very next year.

That year my youngest son, Cleophantes, was born, the fifth son to grace my house. But the gods, like the Athenians are jealous of too much good fortune; that year too, my eldest child, Neokles, was savaged by a horse as he went to mount it. My slaves rushed to hold the beast, but the boy died. May you never know, Lord Artaxerxes, the private grief that overshadows the affairs of whole cities, whole empires! In that same year, made kindly by sorrow, my wife and I took pity on the grief of my father-in-law, Lysander, who was without a son, and, being an old man now was haunted by the fear that his name would be lost, and his household gods neglected, and his fields tilled by a stranger. So we let him take Diokles, our second son, and adopt him as his heir. I have often wondered if we did the right thing – a man may well wonder, when he gives away his son. You won't find Diokles, son of Lysander, figuring prominently in accounts of Athenian life; but he's wealthy enough to raise horses, and contented enough, I think. He'll be in the ranks of hoplites fighting against you when you march into Hellas. I can't claim he'd have cut a grander figure if I'd kept him at home with me, for none of his three brothers have done any better. None of them takes after me. They're a throwback; how they'd have pleased their grandfather! Honourable men, seemly in private life, willingly serving the state, and without ambition.

'Well, look where ambition has brought you, father,' Archeptolis said to me, the last time he came here to see me.

'But look what it did for Hellas!' I reply.

'You said that too often at home, you know, father,' he said. He's right, of course. But, I think, if any of my sons had half Kimon's fire and force, would I be still in exile? I'm wandering. I was telling you about the ostracisms.

In the first year, we exiled Hipparchos, son of Charmos, the last powerful Peisistratid in Athens. In the next year, Kallixenos son of Aristonymos, and after him Megakles, the head of the mighty Alkmeonids. And then Xanthippos. Well, I was running out of likely targets, and it served him right for procuring the fall of Miltiades. You may well wonder what was happening, when a stream of noble and capable Athenians, the pride of the city, are cast out of it, year after year. What was happening was that the aristocrats were trying to get rid of me. It never seemed a hopeless attempt. Huge numbers of votes were cast against me. When the votes had been counted, they were carted away, and used to fill potholes in the city streets; they make a good dry, durable road-metal. It got to the point where if I stumbled in the agora I kicked up a sherd saying dustily, 'Out with Themistokles!'

But, however many votes had been cast against me, I always managed to get a greater number cast against somebody else. The casual support of the humble citizen who voted for me because I spoke in his interest was no longer enough – I had to get organised. I developed a body of partisans, who would walk the streets for me, soliciting votes, and pass round an agreed target-name to concentrate on when the ostracism came round. The core of my partisans were my family. My brother, for example. He, like my sons, was a private man at heart, but he was loyal to me all my life, and at that time, although he was racked with worry for Phrasikles, his son, whom the Aiginetans held hostage, he worked hard in my cause. So did my father-in-law, who cajoled and persuaded his friends, older men, against me by instinct. Then there were certain friends, chief among them Epikrates of Acharnai, who had a passion for intrigue, faction and the political life, but lacked the weight to become a leader in his own right. He hitched his fortunes to mine, and worked for me, and most loyally remained my friend when all our luck ran out, even bringing my family to me here, though it cost him his life. There was Aeschylus, too, and Phrynichos, both willing to give their talents, and Simonides, a greater poet than either. I had come by Simonides' allegiance in a curious way; he asked me to find in his favour in a dispute in which I thought him to be in the wrong. 'You'd be a poor poet, my friend, if you sang out of tune,' I told him, 'and I a poor magistrate if I did people favours against the law!' And he, magnanimous and fair-minded almost always in his long life, respected my decision, and liked my way of putting it. So we grew to be friends. He had been a firm friend of Hippias, in his early life – and he finished his life as a firm friend of mine; all the long distance between tyranny and freedom and he had travelled in his own heart. Around me also were innumerable friends of a more distant sort, and around them many plain Athenians who had no reason to support me, except that they saw I was right. Through all these people, I was able to triumph in the struggle for power.

Of course, it was not only the archon-reform that sustained the heat of battle year after year. A violent controversy rocked the city. And the nub of the argument was simply this – that Themistokles, son of Neokles, urged the city to build itself more ships; we needed more ships. 'How are we to overcome the menace from

Aigina?' I asked in the Assembly. But in the back of my mind, I thought of Persia, and the struggle that would surely come. No good telling the Assembly about it, for now that Darius was dead they thought the whole danger too remote to trouble with. And to hear them talk about Marathon you'd think we had annihilated the whole army of the King, whereas it was clear, at least to me, that for the King that horde under Datis was no great matter. I only asked for ships, yet men opposed me as though I had proposed the ruin of the state. There were two reasons for this. One is the natural laziness of men who would always rather avoid exertion and expense if it can be avoided. It was true that I was trying to run the city into great expense, and natural that men should oppose me for that. But at a deeper level I frightened men because what I wanted would bring change, and men always fear change, even for the better. And ships alarmed the Athenians, Great King, simply because ships need oarsmen.

Now a hoplite must have bronze armour, and good weapons. Only a man of a certain wealth can afford to be one. But to row a ship a man needs a strong back, and a willing pair of hands – the poorest man in the city would be as well fitted for it as the richest. In practice we would recruit thetes – that is, our poorest citizens – to row the ships; and then we would have to train them, and pay them, and then they would play a part in defending the city, and so would win a share in the dignity and power that till then had belonged only to the men of bronze, the hoplite class. Naturally, I myself had no objection to increasing the power of my supporters; but men suspected my good faith in urging the need for ships. They began to call me the new Peisistratos, for he had ridden to power on the backs of the poor. We had heard that the new King, Xerxes, your father, was having trouble in Egypt; that would detain him for a year or two. After that, I reckoned, we had best be ready for him. What I learned of his character from talking with Sikinnos my slave made me doubly sure. I think I must like living dangerously, for I remember being happy at that time. I kept on asking for more ships.

I got tired of attacks on me which harped on scornful accounts of my low ancestry. After all, though my father was not in the mainstream of it, I was one of the Lycomid family, and now the head, for what it was worth, of that ancient clan, burdened with family cults more elaborate than most, as befitted a priestly line. I decided to remind people, by restoring the family shrine which had fallen into disrepair. That meant commissioning a good

He asks for more ships

sculptor, and a good painter, and buying marble and fine pigments, and finding a mason who could inscribe well-made letters in stone. I invited Simonides to write an ode for the occasion. The shrine was at Phlya, in the countryside, near a spring of mildly sacred fresh water. I invited any citizen who wished to come for the sacrifice to consecrate the new altar, and we slaughtered ten oxen to feed everyone, and had singing and dancing and roast meat, and garlands of flowers for the guests at my table. The stories died away a bit after that.

One of those I invited to this party was a boy called Antiphates. I had seen him stripped, running in the Kynosarges, and admired him. He had a lithe, thin, body, and a grave and thoughtful face. He was beautiful. Liking him, I assumed his company was mine for the asking; he would be proud to be seen around with the greatest man in Athens, and if that lovely serious face did not belie him I could make use of whatever talent he most possessed, and start him in public life. I sent him a gift of silver dice, and an invitation to ride out to Phlya on the day of my festival. Of all those whom I invited, I saw at once that two had not come – Aristeides and Antiphates. I hadn't really expected Aristeides, but I kept looking round for the boy, noticing his empty place, and the flowers made ready for him wilting in the sun. Beside me Phrynichos talked about his latest play, and I hardly heard him.

'I have to reap glory while I can,' Phrynichos was saying, 'before Aesychylus here outclasses me for good!' Then a slave unknown to me came up, and touched my shoulder, and put a small box on the table in front of me, saying that his master told him to deliver it. In it lay my silver dice, and an insolent scrawl with them, 'That was a losing throw'. No more. Phrynichos tactfully went on talking beside me while I shut the box, and put it away. 'You can't win them all,' he said ironically, 'but as long as you win the ostracisms you've no complaint to the gods.' I drowned Antiphates in wine, called myself an old fool, and forgot about him.

'Didn't you invite Aristeides?' asked Aeschylus. Aristeides was speaking against me in the Assembly nearly every day at that time, objecting to my request for ships – objecting chiefly, I think, because I made it, and he felt I should not always get my way. 'Yes I did,' I told Aeschylus, 'but being Aristeides he can't keep his private life and his politics apart – as soon as he disagrees, he disapproves. He probably thinks I'm a moral danger!' Gods, I think, gulping more wine, perhaps he even suspects I've invited him here to bribe him! Oh, well, a free man is free to decline invitations. Now I come to think of it, that young puppy Kimon isn't here either – he whom I invited not because I like to see him, with his daddy's face and scornfully tilted chin, but because in the goodness of my heart I imagined he might be grateful for a little expensive fun.

We returned late to Athens that night, swaying on our feet, arms round each other's shoulders, still escorted by the flute-girls and dancers, and classy tarts I had hired to join the feast at the evening and dance for us under the trees, by the smoky light of tarred torches. We didn't rise early next day, either: and so I was the last man in Athens to hear the news, with which the whole city had been entertaining itself the day before. Kallias was married; Kallias the richest man in the city, and as if that was not gossip enough he had chosen as his bride Elpinike, Kimon's sister, daughter of Miltiades.

No wonder Kimon had been busy yesterday! That would confound all the idle tongues who had made disparaging remarks about the girl's chances! Kallias was of noble family as well as disgustingly rich. He was the most eligible man in Athens. The very next day young Kimon went to the Treasury, and paid off the debt of forty talents still outstanding against Miltiades' name. Soon he had bought a fine house, and owned horses, and went round the city surrounded by a gang of companions, all of ultramarine descent. I noticed with distaste that he still wore the starkest possible attire; only a short mantle round his naked body, as though he were a Spartan boy. I wondered if Kallias was up to something, and since Aristeides was his cousin I asked Aristeides when next I met him in the Assembly.

'My cousin has been able to remedy the cruelty of the city,' he said dryly.

'I am of one mind with you about that aspect of it, Son of Lysimachos,' I said. 'But Kimon with money just might be in a mood for revenge on the city. The aristocrats are leaderless just now, after all.'

He was a democrat, too, in his way, and he could see what I was getting at. 'I doubt if Kallias had anything more in mind than the beauty of Elpinike,' he said. 'Of course, he'll back Kimon, now he's in the family. But Kimon's young yet. No need to worry about him.' Well, Aristeides never had much gift of foresight.

But I, I was tortured by it. What was it Phrynichos once said to me. 'You and I must bear the pains of Cassandra' – something like that. In the seventh year after Marathon, having quelled the disorders in Egypt, your father Xerxes began to prepare his great attack. I heard of a bridge over the mouth of the river Strymon; rumours of activities on the Hellespont; most sinister of all, hard news, brought to us by a deserting party of Miltiades' Dolonkoi from the Chersonese, that the Persians were cutting a canal across the neck of the Athos peninsular to bring their ships safely past the cape where Mardonios had come to grief years before, leading an abortive expedition in the years before Marathon. These fugitives, who had been labourers on the canal, had been driven to escape from fear of a grim death, for the sides of the trench, they said, kept slipping, and burying parties of men underneath. They came, naturally enough, to Kimon; and he, having fed them and clothed them, brought them before the generals. The college of generals had been greatly improved by my archon-reform, for now the polemarch was chosen by lot he was little more than a courtesy chairman at meetings. The generals could pull their full weight.

Kimon's protégés told us all about the canal, and added a good deal more. All through Thrace, they said, great dumps of grain and other supplies were being made at regularly spaced intervals. What was happening at the Hellespont, they added, was the making of a bridge, by lashing ships together, side by side, and laying a roadway across them, over which men and horses could walk dry shod. They babbled about special cables of hemp or papyrus, brought from Egypt, as long as the Hellespont was wide, and sections that could be floated away to let ships pass up and down, and then brought back into place again. Only when they had been talking for some time did we gather that they were saying there were not one but two bridges. We didn't believe them. Even I was incredulous about the bridges made of ships; the others were refusing to believe any of the story, because of the fabulous sound of the last bit. But the rest of the tale was only too credible. When the Dolonkoi had retired to go and drink more of Kimon's wine, we sat together, and I tried to convince the others. Obviously, the Persian King had returned to the strategy that Mardonios had tried, and that a storm, not we, had defeated. Since they couldn't land a large enough army in one direct sea-borne strike – Marathon had proved that – they would march their army round the Aegean, through Thrace and Macedonia, and coming that way bring immense numbers, more than the cities of Hellas could dream of.

'What I don't see,' said Aristeides, 'is how they can hope to feed so vast an army so far from home.'

'That's what those grain dumps are for, doubtless,' I said. 'The task would be beyond the Hellenes, surely, but may be within the power of the King.'

'If he isn't using ships this time, what's the canal for?' asked someone.

'He's got to have ships as well,' I said. 'Otherwise we could sail in behind the army, and cut his supply-lines. The ships will sail along the coast, holding the flank of the enemy like another unit of infantry.' And inwardly I groaned at the need for such instruction from me. In the end the meeting broke up without anything decided on – most of them thinking, I suppose, that, whatever was going to happen, at least it wouldn't happen quickly. As you know, Xerxes, your father, took three years to complete his preparations. Fortune was kind to us – I needed three years to complete mine.

At least I was undisputed leader of the Athenians, in those days, my rivals having gone, all except Aristeides. I did not imagine he would continue to oppose me now, for was he not always in favour of the right? That year we had no ostracism; the Assembly, having tired of throwing other men out of the city in order to keep me, merely voted against holding one.

But how desperately certain people wanted to be rid of me! Since there was no ostracism they tried an even more unlikely and preposterous weapon – they persuaded Epykides, son of Euphemides, to stand against me in the election for the generalship of my tribe. I heard of various people having been asked to stand. But who wants to be general when the whole might of the King is about to descend? Epykides, however, was thinking of Persian gold. He had never fought a battle in his life, but he was a good speaker – a comic, able to make men laugh and like him. Since he never uttered a serious thought he made all his listeners feel equally clever; such are the dangers of democracy. I went to see him. I said, 'Listen, Epykides, perhaps the Persians will not come. Not everybody, you know, believes those stories about their canal, and their bridges. Anyway, they aren't very likely to get here during your term of office, and you might not be re-elected. So you may never get offered bribes by Xerxes. On the other hand, you have a chance now of accepting a handsome bribe from me, at this very moment.' I undid a leather purse, and poured out before him on the table flocks and flocks of shining silver owls.

'Themistokles,' he said, grinning, and gathering them up, 'your strategy is so good it would be a shame not to let it succeed.' So much for Epykides, thus persuaded not to stand. What a brave soul he had!

Soon after that I first learned the news that was to save us. Surely the gods love Attica; they gave us gifts in our time of need. I remember sitting at home, alone, drinking a little wine, and meditating on the fate of Athens. So greatly did I fear your father's strength, that I was idling my evening away with thoughts of taking all the citizens to Italy, and making a new city there, for by that means at least we might save our lives. I wondered if the people could be prevailed upon to go; but it seemed certain to me that they could not be prevailed upon to arm themselves and fight. Had they not suffered the Aiginetans to harass and defeat us all these years for lack of a few ships? To save the expense of ships they shut their ears to me. Marathon had gone to their heads, and they thought of the Great King as though he were a defeated athlete, from an Olympiad long ago, beaten in a single fall.

Sikinnos my slave came to me, and said there was a stranger at the door, very well wrapped up in his cloak, wanting to speak with me. 'Bring him in,' I said, 'and stay with me while he speaks. Keep your hand on your dagger.' For I had heard murmurs that a sudden death might be easier to arrange than an ostracism. The stranger was a young man. He uncovered his head as soon as he came in, facing me with a steady enough glance.

'I have something to tell you, Son of Neokles, that may be of use to you,' he said.

'Tell me your name first,' I said.

'Eurymachos, son of Eurykleides,' he said.

'Eurykleides the corn merchant? I know him well enough,' I said.

'The same. I work for the city treasury, Themistokles. Not an elected office; a paid one – just as a money-counter. I keep the accounts relating to the leases of the silver mines. I am not supposed to speak about them till the accounts are completed and published at the end of the year.'

'But you have chosen to wrap up your face in a cloak and come out after dark to talk to me about them?' I imagined some scandal – talk of embezzlement, or such like. 'Be very sure that I shall want to hear you!'

'I believe you will, sir,' he said steadily.

'Very well, then, you have my attention. Sikinnos, pour him some wine.'

'The accounts are not ready yet,' he said, sipping from the rim of his cup. 'They have not yet been cast up. As you know the leaseholders keep a proportion of their profits, and pay the surplus into the Treasury. Well, most of this year's payments have come in, and they are huge!'

'Huge?' I asked.

'They have been keeping it dark as much as they can, but they have struck a new vein of ore, below the old workings, and the smeltings from it are many times richer. Every day now they pay their profits into my coffers. The part due to the state will be, as I said, huge.' He gulped his wine now, and looked at me. 'I just thought you might be able to use that information.'

'I might indeed,' I said. 'Tell your father his son has a good head on his shoulders, and that I say so, who have the best head in Athens!'

It took a day or two to confirm his story. Then my following gave a helping shove to the rumours that were already in the air, and as soon as the rumours were widespread I began to campaign in earnest. 'Athenians,' I told the Assembly, 'if what I hear is true, the gods have been good to us. They have given us the silver we need to pay for the ships; all we need to do is to forgo sharing out the money, and we can have ships without raising an obol in extra taxes. We can have ships enough to crush Aigina for ever, to get her safely out of the way before any greater danger threatens us. And the ships will help in a greater danger, too.' Of course it would be a long time yet before the accounts were presented to us, and the choice would be made, but I wanted to soften them up; after all, one needs a good argument to make men vote money out of their pockets.

But as soon as I began to speak about the silver Aristeides began to oppose me. 'Themistokles has no regard for seemliness,' he said, 'no respect for tradition. He asks you to sacrifice a distribution of money which is your immemorial right, and has always been made in our time. Usually he does not bother about it – now, on the one occasion when it is worth something, he wants to take it from you. What will it buy if you give it to him? Power for Themistokles....'

The light is dying, Great King. I cannot see the letters any more, and I must call the little Lydian slave to bring a lamp, and some supper. I could not win, with Aristeides pitched against me. That's

better; a warm pool of light, and the shutters put up to stop the
moths coming to die in it. I could not win while Aristeides opposed
me. He had a shining reputation, he could win people's hearts. I pit-
ted my oratory against his. 'How does the Just Aristeides think that
the Athenians will defend themselves against the Persians if they
do not build ships?' He answered, 'What the spears of Marathon
did once they can do again. The strength of Athens and her hope
of victory lie where they have always lain, in the strong arms of
her hoplites. Let us give the money where it is due, and let those
who need buy armour with it, in case the Persians come.'

'Oh yes,' I answered him, bitterly, 'let us float across to Aigina
on shields of bronze, and master our enemies that way!'

I was getting nowhere with him against me, and the time was
coming round again for voting whether to hold an ostracism the
following spring. In the meanwhile I was not the only man in
Hellas to be alarmed by all that digging at Athos; a man called
Chilios from Tegea was patching up everyone's quarrels with
Sparta, and there was talk of an alliance, a league of Greeks pledged
to fight together against the King. Naturally we supported that.
It was our only hope of not being left to fight alone, as had happened at Marathon. And we had no doubt at all, after Marathon,
that Athens would be the first target. It was revenge that inspired
Xerxes; and the fires of Sardis would come home to us, at last.

I was driven in the end to seek out Aristeides. Like me, he was
never to be seen about the city alone, but went everywhere with
a band of followers. I did not like to present myself at his door,
and risk being turned away. My chance came when one day I
met him with his friends as I went up the Acropolis, wearing
flowers, going to sacrifice to Athene. Bent on the same errand
himself, he too was holding garlands.

'Will you make your offering along with mine, Aristeides?' I
asked him.

He considered it. 'As you will, Themistokles,' he said. Each of
us with a gesture bade our companions wait outside. We stepped
from the bright sunlight of the noon into the dark heart of the
temple. At first our eyes made out nothing except the fiery lamp
burning upon the altar; then we could see the white robes of the
priestess, and her mask-like face, eyes full of darkness. Last in
the flickering golden firelight, we made out each other, the white
flowers splashed with scarlet light in our hands. From the shadows
came virgins, handmaids of the gods, who took our wreaths, and
crowned us, and brought sacred water to sprinkle us. Upon the

altar we laid our gifts; his a honeycomb, mine a newborn kid.

'What do you ask of the goddess?' said the priestess. I waited for him to answer.

'Wisdom for the city in time of need,' he said at last.

'Amen to that!' said I.

'Your gifts are acceptable,' said the priestess, and handing me a knife she stretched the neck of the kid beneath my hand. We watched it bleed upon the flowers, the warmth of the pulsing flow melt the wax on the honeycomb, till the blood and honey mingled and ran thick upon the altar. 'Your prayer will be granted,' said the priestess.

We withdrew towards the doors. On the threshold I stopped, turned towards him, and said, 'Aristeides, let me speak with you.'

'I'm listening,' he said.

'This question of the silver from Laurion. By the gods I beg you, do not oppose me on this.'

'Why not?' he said, with snow in his voice, like a torrent in spring.

'Because I am in the right; I must have my way. The safety of the city depends on it. I know, Son of Lysimachos, that you do not love the city less than I.'

'Because I'm less clever than you, Themistokles,' he said, speaking rapidly, 'you seem to think I'm a fool. Don't underestimate my grasp! I can see perfectly well what you're up to! You will never have enough power for you in Athens till the balance of the city is upset, and all men's rights and duties changed about. The farmers won't heed you, but the city rabble will, and because of that you are ready to have everyone chained on the rowing-bench like a slave, willing to consign the defence of the state to the lowest class of men, who have never been trusted before, and indeed can be trusted for nothing except to support Themistokles!'

I could have flared into anger on behalf of the plain men whom he so grossly misjudged, but I restrained myself, and said only, 'Believe me, no. I am thinking only of the need for ships to save us from the King.'

'When did Themistokles ever before speak plain?' he said. 'Always snake-tongued, whatever you're after, you feign to intend something else. You will use any means that will serve to get your way. Nobody can trust what you say.'

'Since you think so, leave my motives on one side. Consider your country, with the sea all around her, attacked by sea and land, and since you are so straight and honest you will openly admit we need ships.'

'If I thought so, I would be asking for them myself.'

'You are right in this at least, Aristeides,' I said, 'that I will use any means to get those ships. Therefore, I warn you, though you oppose all else I do, in this do not oppose me. You will force me into acts I shall be sorry for.'

'I will not be threatened, Themistokles,' he said, and walked out into the sun. Threaten him? I had meant to plead. Honest Aristeides! What a pity the gods who made him virtuous also made him blind. Standing between the columns of Athene I watched him go, wrapped in his dark cloak, still brisk and lithe enough in his walk, though his head was greying a little. As always when he grieved me, he angered me; or perhaps when he made me angry he grieved me – I made speeches to myself about his stupidity as I stumped down the rocky path to the agora. But after that I gathered my following, and began to organise support for another ostracism.

Athens was surprised at me. 'Themistokles wants an ostracism!' Well, that weapon was one that better suited my enemies. I hadn't used it before. Now I needed it. It was voted in the Assembly easily enough. So there we were, with news of great Xerxes coming in with every ship, with alarm in Hellas from end to end, and an ostracism promised for the spring, which would take place some few days before the silver royalties came up for distribution. If politics made me happy I was in for a good time.

I had no idea whether the ostracism would work for me. After all, it had never been used against a democrat, never before against a man who was dear to the people, who had that intangible power over men's hearts. And Aristeides had that; by the gods he had it! He is the only man I have ever seen who had an air of dignity that was not assuming. His manner of looking men straight in the face, with bland, unfrowning forehead and clear eyes, won instant trust. And he was, so everyone believed, incorruptible. He lived quietly in a small house, spent modestly, even for his dinner parties, drank little wine, paid no flute-girls, and wore a plain Spartan garment every day of his life. 'Just Aristeides,' his supporters said, 'how could he be a danger to you? Why, he lives like one of you. The danger is rather from people whose way of living reminds you of kings!'

'Aristeides the Just!' rang round the streets of Athens as though he had been a commodity for sale. 'When has he ever done anything wrong? With what can you reproach him? Do you not seek him out to judge your cause when any dispute needs settling?' So on interminably. My brother, and Epikrates, who were my right-hand men, were worried by it.

'There really isn't any answer to it, Themistokles,' said Epikrates.

'Don't answer it,' I said. 'I think they're rather overdoing it. In this place men very easily hear enough praise of other men. Start attacking him for it – say he is setting himself up as a judge, by-passing the courts, as though he were a tyrant. Call him the uncrowned king of Athens.'

Well, that's what he was calling me, so I might as well return the compliment. But all the time I knew he had the money on his side. After all, he was telling the Athenians to pocket their profits, and they would be all right; I was telling them that a fearful struggle lay ahead, and they must sacrifice the money, and a good deal else besides, to have any hope of saving their skins. There's not much doubt which is the more popular message. And when it came to attacking Aristeides I wasn't at my best. When I spoke savagely about him, I felt as though I would choke my-self. If only he would see sense, on this one thing! After a while I left the mud-slinging to my willing helpers, and stuck to the politics myself. Because in all this I did have one thing on my side – one weighty ally – and that was the Great King.

I remember, for example, an Ionian sea-captain, putting in at Peiraieus with news. He had been trading a cargo of rope out of Egypt, and peddling it up the Ionian coast. It had all been bought from him at once, and he had heard gossip, and used his eyes. About the size of the Persian army he babbled incoherently of myriad hordes innumerable, but about the fleet he was clear enough; not less than a thousand ships. At the thought of them a winter chill fell over the Athenians. I saw the captain myself, and probed a bit further. Asking question after question, and piecing together hazy answers with oddments of news from other sources, I came to my own conclusions. If Xerxes needed, as I heard he did, old ships, hulks without masts and without gear, then the story about the bridges on the Hellespont made of war-ships roped together might be true. Heaven knows how many ships it takes tied side by side to cross the Hellespont, but the numbers in Xerxes' fleet could be docked by that many. Even so it was bad enough. But the gods have a fine sense of irony, Great King. The huge numbers of ships which your father prepared, without any attempt at concealment, were supposed to scare us –

to ease his path to victory. In fact, by defeating Aristeides, his rumoured ships laid the corner-stone of his defeat.

At first I didn't realise that the news had defeated Aristeides. The day of the ostracism was nearly upon us, and I was discovering a new truth about politics; when one is very deeply involved, it becomes difficult to feel the mood of the city. No one openly says, 'I'll vote against you.' Instead everyone protests loyalty; their words are useless, don't tell which way the wind is blowing.

A day in spring. The grey and gentle light of skies full of rain clouds, and the sunlight in between. On the crest of the Acropolis poppies break scarlet from the craggy rock, and the wild iris stands upright like a soldier. From up there, looking across the clustered roofs of the city houses, over towards Hymettos, one can still see snow on the mountain peaks, but most of the snow is running loudly down the river courses, and in the city fountains a clear and icy draught is drawn in every dipping-cup. A wind blows from the sea, and turns the olive leaves, so that they shimmer palely; the wind tugs men's cloaks as they walk, as they talk, as they stand to speak to their fellows on the rostrum in the Assembly. Across their raised voices, birds call. The wind wraps Aristeides' cloak tightly round his lean body as he stands facing it, facing the Athenians, to appeal to them on this day, the last day that he had.

I had just finished speaking, on the subject of defence. I had recommended that we co-operate fully with the League the Spartans were forming, and that we build ourselves ships. Then Aristeides stood up to answer me.

'Athenians,' he said, 'our friend Themistokles has lived in Attica all his life, without seeing that it is not an island.' They laughed. 'No,' he said, 'it is no laughing matter. Themistokles' ignorance of geography will lead you all into slavery if you attend to him. In a time of peril, such as we stand in now, it is my opinion that a city should rely on its known strength, rather than attempt at the last minute to remedy its weakness. It should use well-tried, rather than untried, means to protect itself. We have defeated the Persians once before, standing with our feet squarely on our own dear soil, firmly on dry land, meeting the enemy's onslaught with the strength of our arms. On an earlier occasion, when we were persuaded to launch ships, and cross the water, and go to the aid of Aristagoras the Milesian, we were not so lucky. Therefore, my advice to the city is unchanged. We must prepare for war. But the handful of silver owing to us from the mines at Laurion is neither here nor there. Spend it how we will, it will not keep the enemy from our farms. Only our spears, and our courageous hearts can do that, and the Spartans, if they will.

'And now I have something to say to you which is of even greater importance. In a time of peril men ought to stand together. This is the last time at which the city can afford to be divided. The laws of the Athenians, given to us by Solon, and by Kleisthenes, define our rights and our duties to the city which we love. In Athens power, and the duty to fight for the city, are given to ordinary men, especially to those whose property is enough to allow them to buy armour, and to take leisure to perform their duties as citizens. Because these people have most at stake, because they largely own Attica, they are the best people to defend it. We do not need to burden the poor with such a duty, or ask help from the metics and foreigners who live among us. Yet, I warn you, that is what we shall be doing, if we try to man a large fleet in addition to an army. For what free-born Athenian would stoop to the rowing-bench, unless poverty bore him down? What brave man wishes to go into battle, with his back to the enemy, pulling on an oar? A soldier stands straight, and looks forwards. What Themistokles proposes will change Athens, just at the time when change in the city is least desirable. Really it is surprising that he has the impudence to propose such madcap schemes; he tells you that we will defeat the Persians with new and untried ships, and in the same breath he tells you that we have been unable to defeat the Aiginetans these twenty years. That hardly suggests we have a natural talent for sea-faring! But Themistokles, I warn you, is a dangerous man. He is clever at thinking up new ideas, but he lacks the sense to sort out the good ideas from the bad ones. He is so vain that he thinks merely the fact that he thought of something is a guarantee that it will work. And, although he is an Athenian, he has no respect for Athens. He does not love her as she is, with filial reverence. If it would serve some whim of his, some new theory that has just clouded his brain, he would throw away anything Athenian. Have we not all heard him speak lightly of many most sacred things? Was he not choregos for Phrynichos' blasphemous play? Themistokles loves change as a child loves a new toy. But I love Athens as she has been, and as she is. Therefore I will oppose him with all my strength. Athenians, above all things the city now needs to be united; and I say to you, there will never be peace in Athens until you cast out either me, or Themistokles!' As he finished the shifting clouds rolled away towards the agora, leaving him standing in a patch of sunlight. I had never heard him speak with such passion before.

I was stung by his scorn, and afraid, too, that his rhetoric would sway the people. But it was too late to answer him; that day's debate was cut short at noon, for the ostracism that followed, and people in the Assembly were already dispersing, making their way down to the agora in crowds to cast their votes. For a while I sat in my place. Fear tightened round my heart. I looked up at the Acropolis, rising above us on my right, and down at the rostrum, where the great men stand and speak, and thought that perhaps I might not look on them again for ten years. At once a worse fear overtook the thought; if the Athenians banish me for ten years, there will be no Athens to come home to. Or long before that I shall be free to return to a heap of ashes and broken marble, and there will be none to prevent me left alive. I rose, and walked down to the agora myself, with a great crowd of my supporters around me.

In the agora a wide area had been roped off, and kept empty, and crowds seethed in the whole remaining space. The stall-keepers had all withdrawn, to the outer edges of the agora, and jammed up the side streets with their wares and their cries. Just outside the entrances of the roped-off enclosure were rows of baskets, full of broken fragments of pottery to use as votes; just inside were rows of huge jars, the great pithoi used for storing grain, into which the votes were thrown. Ten jars, at ten entrances, one for each tribe. Already the citizens were beginning to file into the enclosure, casting their votes, and then standing around within the ropes till the whole business was done.

My companions dispersed, as each man went to join the pressing mass of his own tribe, flocking to the voting-jars. I went, with a few, who were also Leontids, around me, through the crowd. As I said, the city provided baskets of potsherds to be used for the voting, but some enterprising citizens had been even more helpful and were pressing through the throng hawking ready-made votes against me. 'Roll up, roll up, votes against Themistokles!' we heard someone calling. I went towards him to see what he was up to. He had a basket slung round his neck, full of sherds. 'Here, get me one of those, will you?' I said to my brother, for the man backed away sharply when he saw me. My brother and friends brought him back by the scruff of the neck, and we took a look at what he had to offer, while he squirmed, and whimpered, and tried to free his arms from my brother's pinioning grasp. They

were really classy potsherds, those! They were all made of spoilers
from a good pottery – all nice round pieces broken from the foot
of a wine-cup or a jar, and most of them with a fine quality black
glaze on them too. Carefully scratched on each one was a fine
topical slogan: 'Out with Themisthokles!'

'Gods!' I said, 'I knew my enemies were an ugly lot, but I didn't
know they lisped!' That raised laughter from the crowd. 'How's
trade this morning?' I inquired of my victim. 'Not good, perhaps,
since you seem to have plenty left? Anyone want a vote against
me?' I asked, grasping a handful, and offering them round the onlookers. 'What, nobody?' Such clowning makes a man popular.
There's no room for dignity, if one wants to lead the Athenians.

'I'll have one, Themistokles,' somebody said. I looked at him;
not somebody I knew. He held out his hand, and I rummaged the
basketful. 'A round one? Or do you find an irregular shape more
picturesque?'

'Oh, a round one, I think,' he said, grinning. 'I only want it
for a keepsake!' Laughing, I tossed him one.

'Give me one, too, Themistokles!' called another man. For a
second I hesitated. 'It'll be safe with me, Themistokles,' he said. I
gave him one.

'Come friends!' I shouted. 'Who else wants a keepsake? Step
up, step up, votes against Themistokles, looking for a safe home!'
Then I turned to my brother, and said loudly, 'Well, if we leave
them here, just *anybody* might get hold of them, and you never
know *what* they might use them for!' Great roars of laughter
answered me, and for several minutes I handed out votes to the
crowd, till the basket was empty. Then at last I could let the smile
slip, and think for a moment. I supposed not many of those sherds
would find their way into the jars, but how many other basketfuls
were being hawked around? And, damn it, it was a good idea, just
the thing for all those farming folk, in from the country just to
vote, who could hardly write their own name, let alone another
man's. Why the hell didn't I think of that myself?

'They'll get their six thousand votes, and more,' said my brother,
looking round, 'with all these men in from the farms.'

By this time we had moved up to the voting-jars. My brother
wrote, 'Aristeides, son of Lysimachos' on a sherd, and handed me
a blank one. 'Aristeides', I wrote on it, 'the Just'. Then I threw it
into the jar, and heard it chink upon the pile, and rattle down
among the others.

The crowds waiting within the ropes at an ostracism are always particularly cheerful. All, that is, save those who might be filling the jars. It takes a long time for all who wish to vote to file through, and the waiting adds to the excitement. Until the votes have been tallied nobody is allowed to leave, so everyone remains packed together, talking, waiting, laying bets on the result. People elbow their way through the crowd to speak with their friends, and round the ropes the traders' little boys scramble, selling honey cakes and figs to those within. The wind had blown the clouds away by the afternoon, and a chill sunlight shone.

Very soon they had counted to six thousand, and so we knew there would be a valid ostracism. Now they were sorting the votes. My brother went to the edge of the crowd to see how it was going, and came back with a long face. 'There's a big pile building up against us,' he said.

'Us?' I snapped at him. 'You mean, if they kick me out, you'll come too?' He winced just faintly.

'If you want me, brother,' he said. I regretted my sharpness with him, but could not find words to say so, with a press of men around us who would hear. Even in a crowd of ten thousand, a man can be alone. I was racked with anxiety.

But, as the count drew to an end, it wasn't my name that began to be muttered, a hiss of excitement and rumour, passing from one man to the next, moving across the crowd like a wave on water. It was his. Xerxes' rumoured ships had done it. No peace till you cast out one or the other, he said: and the Athenians had cast out him.

The official sentence of banishment began to be read out over our heads; the ropes that confined us were removed. 'Aristeides, son of Lysimachos, by the sentence of his fellow citizens, being considered a danger to the city, shall within the space of ten days remove himself from the land of Attica, and dwell afar from us. . . .' But where was Aristeides? I looked for him. Thrusting aside the congratulations, ignoring the cheers men offered me, I elbowed through the crowd looking for him. I don't know what I imagined I would have said, if I had found him, but I couldn't find him.

Then someone said to me, 'Now for those ships, eh, Themistokles?' And the meaning of my victory swept over me. At last there would be ships, a great fleet, great power! I closed my eyes, and saw below Sounion the sea dark with ships, all triremes and all ours! Then I rushed off to find men to drink with, to rejoice with, to reward for their support, their faith in me, with feasting and music, and lavishly provided wine. But, however drunk one returns home, sobriety returns in the end; in the first light of morning it overtook me. I raised my aching head from my pillow, and remembered the day before.

I rose, and called a slave to bring me my writing-tablets. I wrote, 'Themistokles, son of Neokles, asks Aristeides to remember that in this one thing he begged you not to oppose him.' I sat and looked at this message for a long time. He had said, 'I won't be threatened.' He always put the worst possible construction on my words. Now he would only think I meant to gloat over him. Taking the lamp I held it beneath the tablet, and watched the wax glisten, the words blur, and run into smooth nothingness in the heat of the flame.

The profits from the silver mines came to one hundred talents, enough to pay for an entire fleet of warships; but also enough to make a nice little sum for every man among us, a most desirable little nest of owls. The speech that I made in the silver debate was one of the most crucial of my life; I put heart into it.

'Athenians,' I said to the Assembly, standing on the speaker's rostrum, looking at their innumerable faces on the slopes above me, and blinking a little, for the sun, illuminating the speaker's face, dazzles him, and casts his hearers into haloed shadow. 'Athenians, give me this sum of money, and I will make you great.' Someone called out, 'Miltiades said the same!' 'With this money,' I continued, 'I will build for the city two hundred ships of war. Within a month of the keels being laid, I promise you, the Aiginetans will come to heel like the hounds they are. For what is Aigina? Since the death of Ajax, who has heard of a great deed or a noble spirit coming from them? Only because of one thing have they been able to humiliate us – because they have more ships. Give me the silver, and we shall have more ships, we shall have more than any other city in Hellas. You all know that we are threatened by the King; he is on his way to us. Give me the silver, and I promise you that when the great trial comes we shall not be deserted by the Lakedaimonians nor by any other city. Instead they will sue anxiously for our support, and in the defence of Hellas the crown of glory will be ours. You have heard it said that Attica is not an island; but let me teach you what geography I do know. We Hellenes do not live, as the Persians do, in a rich land, full of corn. Our land is rocky, precipitous and harsh. Our land is unkind to strangers. Can the King bring enough men against us to defeat us in our own land? They cannot eat by foraging on the way, among our barren stones. The King can bring men enough against us only if he can feed them from his ships – only if he is master of the sea. Athenians, let us be masters of the sea! The most powerful city in Hellas is Sparta, and yet what does she command? She is mistress of the Peloponnese, a rocky peninsula, with some rich plains, but still more snow-capped mountains. If Athens will build ships, she will outshine the Spartans, for she will command not one small stretch of land but the whole sea, all the islands and ports and shores, all the trade routes in all the world. You have heard it said that my proposals involve relying on an untried class of men. I say to you, have confidence! Where is the Athenian so poor that he does not love his city? Which man among you, however mixed his blood, is unwilling to serve his city? Athenians, I can remember Marathon; and at that time it was not the humble citizen, nor the metics, nor the trading folk who were unreliable, or who were in favour of making treaties with the King. To all of you I say, you are all Athenians; in peril you will not fail. Come, my friends, the gods have given us silver; shall we not say, "At the time of our greatest need, the gods gave us ships!"'

I expected some counter-attack to be ready. But when it came it was too clever by half. Alkmeon was on his feet, saying, 'Themistokles asks for the money out of our purses, and says he wants it to build ships. But he knows perfectly well, all the time, that we can't build ships now, it's too late. We might manage one or two, I grant you, but two hundred? Where could timber be found for even twenty? The truth is that the barbarians are already in control of the places where timber can be got; of the Ionian coasts, of Thrace, of Macedonia. What will really happen is that Themistokles will tell us he is sorry, but timber could be found for only a few ships; and in the meanwhile most of the money will have disappeared into his voracious maw. We all know how money is only too likely to disappear when he's around. I advise you to take it, and keep it safe – in your own pockets!'

I was almost laughing as I rose to answer. 'I propose to get timber from Italy. We have not got timber from there in the past only because we could get it nearer home. Are there good timbers to be had there? I have been there myself, and I can tell you. The land is green; even as you approach it from the sea, it is green upon blue that strikes the eye. And I have walked in wide forests there, and seen pine trees tall enough to cut two masts from one trunk, birch trees enough for oars without number, and beech trees so huge that one trunk would make a keel, cut in a single piece. I shall not keep the money, if you give it to me. I shall divide it between a hundred substantial citizens, of whom I will make but one, and each man shall supervise the building of two ships. Should my two look as though the least thing has been skimped on them, I invite you to prosecute me. I shall certainly prosecute the others if there is anything lacking to theirs. Athenians, shall we not build ships?'

And Athens, being mine, all mine, like a bride with her husband or a boy with his lover, smiling, agreed. We voted for ships.

It was only just in time, for they were to take us two years more to build. The last of them raced towards Artemision, with the pitch on their sides still soft, and dragged into dark ripples by the speeding water, while the first were already engaging the enemy. The Peiraieus rang from morning till night with the knocking of the adze, the blows of the hammer. The fragrance of newly cut timbers drifting on the offshore breeze greeted one on the road; the gear shed was full of new ropes, new canvas; pans of hot pitch were carried smoking to the ships in hundreds. We made all our new ships to the same design; there's an advantage in tactics to be got from having them all the same length and speed. No pleasure could be more acute for eye, for ear, for nose, and for swelling pride, and the stinging undertow of hope and fear, than to walk in the roadways of the Peiraieus, walk among the slipways, and watch the ships grow. They grew from curved bones of wood, slowly fleshed out with planks, with rope, tar and bronze, till, finished, they could be pushed out to float on the calm water of the harbours, each with its own image wavering upside down beneath it. When you see a ship in the slips you see its strength, as never in the water; from the high stern the outline sweeps down in a long curve, and runs forwards, straight as a spear, all the great length of the hull, to finish in a savage bronze-clad ram. When you see that you see them for what they really are; not travelling platforms for hoplite fighting, but weapons themselves; bolts for Poseidon to throw in his strong hand.

But I had little enough of the pleasure of watching the ships, for the Athenians sent me away, to join the great conference called by the Lakedaimonians at the Isthmus, and to represent them there. I chose my companions, thinking that I could not choose the man I would first have thought of for such a job. Still, there were other men in the city. The city voted us horses, and tents of scarlet canvas to live in when we got there, and money enough to make a good showing, and not shame the Athenians.

The Corinthians had found the required neutral ground: a green meadow full of flowers, on the borders of their land and Megara's. Delegates of one city after another were arriving, and pitching tents, but I made sure that ours were near the Spartans'. A gang of carpenters were busy, making wooden benches that could be set round in a circle, on the little slope the field afforded, to make an amphitheatre for debates. This place which was called 'the League at the Isthmus', or just the League, and from which the war against your father was conducted, changed overnight from a field of grass and flowers to the most important place in Hellas, and when the war was over vanished without trace, being returned to the plough, and thus back to meadow.

Not every city sent delegates. Of the important places, not Thebes, or her Boiotian allies, or anyone from Thessaly, nearest the King's advance. In the Peloponnese not Argos, Sparta's bitterest enemy. And many smaller places also held back, for as before men were everywhere in two minds about whether to fight the King. Some who did not wish to fight were those in whom despair of victory had sapped manhood; others were that snake-like and bestial kind who hope to flourish under tyranny.

The man who had done more than any other to assemble all Hellas in a single field was Chilios of Tegea, a white-haired man who dreamed of unity among us all, as other men dream of the Elysian fields, and in pursuit of it had talked away enough bitterness for several wars. He invited me to dine with him, at the tents of the Tegeans; and when I arrived I found not a party but a modest meal set on three tables only, with three couches; the other guest was Pausanias.

'It's Themistokles!' he said, and I was puzzled, not recognising him. 'If it's you I'm to dine with, I must ask my host's permission to send for a flute-boy!'

'At Olympia, listening to the boy from Kos,' I said, remembering. 'I'd no idea who it was I had met there.'

'Pausanias the Spartan,' said Chilios, 'grows in importance like a tree. It is good you two should know each other.'

I agreed, but it took a lot of flute-playing to break the ice. Like many Spartans, Pausanias had a stern and haughty demeanor. He was so unused to conversation outside a military mess that one wouldn't have thought he was intelligent at first, if his face hadn't insisted on it. He had a sharp face, all over acute angles, like a sketch for a sculpture. Had he been an Athenian, a face like that would have been athletic, very mobile, but being Spartan had frozen him. He had pale eyes; they were lit by a certain shifting sardonic gleam. I have heard it said that he went mad; certainly he did hand the Athenians a rich gift of power by being intolerably haughty to his allies, and making himself insufferable as a commander, and since that is not like the man I knew perhaps it was madness in him. Of course, what the Spartans say of those whom they have killed is, to say the least, open to doubt. Kleomenes, too, they said, went mad. Yet there is a weakness in their manner of living which holds them to virtue and temperance with a vice of iron while they are at home, and does not hold them at all when they leave, so that merely going abroad has been the downfall of many of their leaders.

But Pausanias had something which I never met in any other Spartan; he had charm. He loved ideas. He loved to hear me talk. It was like showing a child a game of dice. He lit up, frowned slightly, to indicate that he was thinking and found it slightly painful, and leaned forward, hanging on one's every word. Then he would break out in surprise and pleasure as one finished, asking incredulous and delighted questions. That evening I was talking about strategy.

'It all depends on the fleets,' I said. 'Their fleet, and ours. They won't be able to let their army march far ahead of their fleet, in case we slip in behind, and land a force to cut off their supply lines. So they'll come, left foot right foot, fleet and army advancing in step. As for us, we won't be able to hold them anywhere on land unless we can also hold their fleet, otherwise they'll play leap-frog with us, and turn the position by landing a force behind it.'

'You mean,' Pausanias exclaimed, 'that we couldn't hold even the Isthmus without ships?'

'Of course not. They would simply land troops, say in the Argolid, and that would be that.'

'But if you're right,' he said, getting excited, 'the Spartans would need ships as much as anyone else!'

'If they want to defend the Isthmus, yes they do. I hope we'll defend ourselves further north.' So it went on. He was delighted with the possibilities of ships and armies in concert, acting as one. So first we played with strategy, and then I showed him Kottabos – a frivolous game, not played in Sparta – and laughing, and delighted with that too, he played and won. I let him win.

Anyway, I had drunk rather more than he. He demonstrated the remarkable moderation of the Spartans in drinking wine, by pouring only a few drops into his cup to fling at the target, while I played like a good Athenian, filling the cup and drinking to the dregs each time. The solemn Chilios had gone early to bed, leaving us together. At last we rose to leave, sending messages of thanks to our host, through his sleepy slave-boy, and going out to steady up in the cold moonlight. Then he towards the black tents, I towards the red. I was well content with my evening. Pausanias had been the guardian of Leonidas, the young king; he was important in Sparta still, and it seemed I could dazzle him.

The next morning all the delegates assembled to talk. Great King, such a thing had never happened before, and may well never happen again. In a way, though not as he intended, your father did bring unity and good government to the Greeks. For us, to whom such unity was a new, an awesome thing, the spectacle of men from so many cities sitting all together was moving enough to weep over. We coined a new word to describe so remarkable an assembly: it was 'panhellenic'. The day opened with a sacrifice, a holocaust of a kid. Then Chilios spoke on the need for unity.

I'm not the man to miss an opportunity, and I saw a chance to secure peace with Aigina without loss or damage to even one of our precious ships. I rose and offered the Aiginetans an end to the war, in return for the release of our hostages, lacing it with a good deal of flattery about how all Hellas needed their splendid fleet – not that it wasn't true. Speaking to the Athenians, I might call the Aiginetans dogs; but I knew enough to respect their courage and skill. A fight between us and them if it had damaged many ships on either side, would from then on have been a disaster for all Hellas. They knew they were being out-built, they knew we would have more ships than they could hope for, and so they were ready for peace, and asked only for guarantees of support from the other cities there assembled, and punishment for either side breaking the truce, and for the return of their own hostages, whom we had now kept for upwards of ten years. So the first morning of the work of the League at the Isthmus was crowned with success, and a private satisfaction for me, in that by the way I had secured the safe release of Phrasikles, my nephew, into his father's arms.

After that we resolved several other quarrels, until no city present had failed to make peace with its neighbours except for Corinth, which was scrapping with Corcyra, from whom no delegation had been sent. We resolved to send a peace-maker to Corcyra. We resolved to send spies to Sardis, to get accurate estimates of the force being prepared against us, and we sent messages to every city in Hellas which had not joined us, asking for their help, in conciliating terms. We sent also to Gelon in Sicily, asking for help, and with high hopes, for the tyrant of Syracuse was the master of a great fleet, and wealthy, and he was a lover of the homeland, having sent chariots to race at Olympia and gifts to Delphi. The messenger chosen to pacify the Corcyreans was me.

Then we came at last to the question of who should command us in battle. It is one thing to get everybody camping in the same field, another to get a free city willingly to put its troops at the disposal of another. About the supreme command there could be no doubt – willingly we offered it to the Spartans. Sparta after all was the ally and leader of most of the cities there assembled, and had incomparably the finest soldiers. But the lists of ships available from various cities showed that ours, when completed, would outnumber all the others put together. The Athenian delegation, therefore, confidently asked for command of the allied fleet. I expected trouble from the Aiginetan delegation; it was, after all, rather much to expect them to serve willingly under an Athenian commander. But they did not protest; the Spartans did it for them. The Spartans demanded command of the fleet themselves, saying that if we had it we would arrange for the brunt of the attack to fall on others and save our own vessels. At this even their own allies spoke against them; the Corinthians reminded them that they had hardly any ships, almost the smallest contribution of all. They behaved like a sulky host, who when worsted in discussion reminds everybody that it is his dinner party – they angrily told us all that it was *their* alliance. Chilios anxiously called a break in the debate to allow tempers to cool, and the delegations trooped down the slope towards their tents, talking and gesticulating while the Athenians stood and looked at each other and at me in open dismay.

I took a loaf from the bread-basket brought by a slave, and a sip of wine from his bottle, and asked the others to leave me alone to think. I turned my back on them all, and walked out alone to climb the little slope beyond the meadow. From even that small height one could see blue water to east and west. How Poseidon loves Hellas, that he embraces it so closely in so winding a caress! The great assembly beneath me were blotches of colour on a field of grass. I could see men sitting to eat, massed in groups, moving around, as though I were watching an ants' nest. Do the ants fight among themselves? Are not the men of Hellas capable of more than ants? But, indeed, my Lord Artaxerxes, I was in great agony of mind. The command that the Athenians had asked for would, of course, have been mine. And yet I had no doubt what must be done. I resolved to do it in such a way as to shame the Spartans, for they deserved ill-will. And I consoled myself with the thought that, since they had no generals with the slightest knowledge of warfare at sea, their commander would perhaps take advice from his colleagues. Slowly I went back to the conference, with my handful of bread untasted in my hand.

'The Athenians,' I announced, 'are grieved that the Spartans, even while they ask for our friendship, will not trust us with command of the ships. We deserve to command, because we have more ships than all the rest of you put together. You have heard the Spartans say that we would arrange things to endanger their ships and save our own. But the danger comes upon us all alike, and from a more terrible source than the partiality of a commander. Against this common danger we are resolved to stand, side by side with any other city here, even at great sacrifice to ourselves. It shall never be said of us that our pride, or our claims to leadership, were the cause of divisions in Hellas when the enemy was at the gate; it shall never be said of us that we took advantage of the common danger to extend our sway over our neighbours, or that we would not make sacrifices in the cause of freedom. Rather than hear any of this said about us, we will accept second place. We agree to put our ships under command of the Spartans.'

The Spartans are unaccustomed to humiliation. Their spokesmen visibly coloured, and hung their heads while I spoke. Later, Great King, for a short while, I enjoyed at Sparta boundless fame and glory; in those days then yet to come, I learned not the least of my shining actions in Spartan eyes was my selfless nobility on that occasion – admired in Sparta more than anywhere, because of all I had achieved that single thing was the one least likely to have been done by a Spartan!

At the time, though, my nobility of soul was very little consolation. I didn't doubt I had saved the unity of Hellas; but I wanted to save our skins as well as our unity. The ships of your father's armada outnumbered ours very greatly; and they were faster, by all reports. It was therefore going to take a good deal of low cunning, indeed strategic brilliance, to win battles against them. I knew I was the only man in Hellas who could provide it, and time was to prove me right. So the loss of command left me with a sickening increment of fear. The last thing we needed was further weighting of the odds against us.

For the moment there was work to be done. We agreed to disperse, each city leaving a representative and a small staff, and expecting to return quickly when summoned to hear what answers our messengers had brought. I myself went back to Athens briefly.

The ships were doing well. I'll give the Athenians this, when they once decide on something they throw themselves into it wholeheartedly. Even though I hadn't been there to see to it, nothing had gone wrong, nothing had been slowed up. I reported to the Assembly what had happened at the Isthmus; then, allowing a few days to assemble crews, I set off with all the completed ships to sail to Corcyra, to settle their quarrel with Corinth, and glad of the chance to train oarsmen and drill the fleet. I was glad to go; Athens seemed empty. The only new thing in the city, apart from the ships, was a story about Aristeides on the day of his ostracism. Some illiterate peasant had handed him a sherd, and asked him to write, 'Aristeides' on it.

'Why, what harm has Aristeides done you?' he asked the fellow.

'Oh, none,' came the answer. 'I've never clapped eyes on him. But I'm sick of hearing him called "the Just" all over the place!' And Aristeides, so the tale went, scratched his name on the sherd, and handed it back. Of course, the Athenians manufacture almost as many good stories as they do good pots, but that one had a ring to it. I could so easily imagine the sardonic expression on his face as he wrote. The only cheerful thing that happened before I left, was that Kleinias, son of Alkibiades, came to see me. He was a young Alkmeonid, filthy rich, and usually to be seen on horseback, riding round with young Kimon and his bully-boys. He wanted to know whether, if he built a ship and fitted it out at his own expense, he could serve with it in the fleet.

'Any willing man will be welcome to serve in the fleet,' I told him. 'You don't have to pay for your own ship to do it.'

'Yes, but ...' he glanced rapidly at me and away again, and his cheeks reddened slightly.

'But buying your own ship is your only chance of getting command of one?'

He gave a sheepish smile. 'Exactly,' he said.

'The city will be grateful to get an extra ship,' I told him, 'if, and only if, that ship serves on the same terms as all the others. If you join the fleet, young Kleinias, you'll take orders, and obey them. Who paid for the ship will make no difference. Understood?'

'Thank-you, Themistokles,' he said. 'I understand.' Off he went, vastly pleased with himself. I felt doubtful about what use he'd be. (Well, one can't foresee everything!) But just the fact that he wanted to do it represented a change at last in Athens. A small straw for hope to cling to.

At Corcyra things went well. The quarrel was over a colony that had been founded by Corinth and Corcyra jointly. I cast longing eyes at the fine harbours full of ships owned by the Corcyreans. I arranged to find in their favour on many, but not all, points in dispute. Both sides accepted, and called me just. I too could be called that, you notice, Lord Artaxerxes. Then we set out to tackle a nest of pirates who preyed on the western trade-routes. I thought privately that if they had much taste for sea-fighting the Corcyreans ought to be able to manage that themselves, but I needed the exercise. I couldn't get my captains to see what I wanted. They were happy enough to row up to an enemy ship, and back water. That would leave a crazy, almost single combat going on between the hoplites on each ship. Ramming old hulks didn't convince them, so I had those pirates in mind instead. They only had to try it to get the point. After all, compare the situation of the oarsmen in a grappling battle – sitting barebacked, exposed to the enemy while armed men wrangle above them, with those in a ship that's just rammed, backing water gently to disengage, and then sitting safely watching the enemy go down in one piece. After some weeks of this operation, sailing round sinking Illyrian pirates, when I could see the discipline beginning to work, the lines growing less ragged, answering more swiftly to signals of command, I detached a small squadron, and sailed down the coast to Italy, to visit Sybaris and Siris. These cities were colonies of ours and had been destroyed in some local war a long time ago. I wanted to see what state they were in, and how much land was untenanted there. I found them rebuilt, and underpopulated. If the worst came to the worst, that knowledge might come in useful. Having spent as long as I dared away from home, I returned.

I was back in time to rejoin the delegates of the League at the Isthmus. There was plenty of news, and all of it bad. First the

Argives. They said they would join only if they could share the command with the Spartans. When our messengers replied that making such a condition was tantamount to refusing help, they said that Apollo at Delphi, whom they had already consulted, had told them to keep themselves safely at home. Therefore they had given earth and water to the King. No help from them. Worse: the possibility of a stab in the back as soon as the Spartans moved up to the Isthmus, or beyond, and that boded ill for Attica. It was also a sinister sign of the sort of advice Apollo would be giving to inquirers – Delphi was on the side of the King.

Next Gelon. He had troubles of his own, your father having concerted efforts with the Carthaginians, who were threatening to attack Sicily. But he did offer help – many ships, provided he could himself hold supreme command. The envoys refused him, and so he sent ironical messages instead. The spies we had sent to Sardis had also returned to us. They had been caught by the Persians, they said, and taken before Xerxes. They told us he was a handsome man, of strong physique, richly clad, and sitting on a throne of gold. And Xerxes, they said, had told his men to strike off the chains from their wrists, and escort them round the encampments of his army, and round the harbours where his ships were being made ready. When they had seen all they wanted to see, and been given accurate reports of the size and strength of the Persian force, they were to be set safely on the fastest ship that could be found to bring them home again. 'For Xerxes says,' they reported, 'that he considers the truth about his forces is better calculated to bring about our surrender than the death of our spies would have been.' I can't tell which struck us with more dismay, the information they brought, or the cunning of our enemy thus strikingly demonstrated to us. Xerxes had twelve hundred ships.

In this welter of bad tidings what could we do? Little enough. Grimly, we swore oaths. We swore that when we were victorious we would tithe every city which had helped the King, and pay the tithe to the god at Delphi. Perhaps some would hesitate before Medising; perhaps the priests at Delphi could be moved by greed to temper their oracles somewhat. Idle threats, idle promises, serving only the feelings of those who swore, for the chance of their fulfilment looked slight. I was the only man, it seemed, in whom a flicker of hope burnt steadily. Over and over again I repeated to this man and that how victory does not always go to the strongest and the land was on our side.

The Greeks conspire to resist the King

While the League was still gathered at the Isthmus, after the tithing oath had been sworn by all, before all, there came messengers from Thessaly, galloping on sweating horses. They told a plausible story, and they asked for our help. They sketched a map showing that through Tempe in their country there was only one pass, by which the King must come. They wanted us to march there, and hold it. Something about them made me suspicious – perhaps that they were all young men. However, there were no reasons I could give for the feeling, and the allies voted to give help. I argued fiercely against the suggested position, for the whole coast of Hellas there is like a wall of mountains falling into a dangerous sea, racked by north-east winds, with no shelter for ships, as your father's admirals were to find to their cost. Because of this we could not take the fleet, and so the most effective strategy was not open to us. I argued for a line further south, but the Thessalians prevailed, and an expedition was arranged. The Athenians were to contribute a force of hoplites, with me in command.

I rode back into Athens to assemble a body of men and march at once. The Spartans, who could always act quickly, having men under military discipline all the time, were already on their way. I clattered on horseback through the familiar streets, round the corner to my own front door, and saw, with a lurch of apprehension, a jar of water standing outside my house. The Athenians bring water to a house of death, Great King, because that within the house is defiled; a custom which you, with your reverence for pure water, will readily understand. My heart was full of fear for my sons. I pushed the door open, and saw lying inside the portals my wife, wrapped in white upon a bier, feet towards me, a honey cake in her right hand, and a silver coin wedged between her lips. My son Cleophantes was leaning against a pillar, head drooping, fast asleep, with the fan of branches hanging in his hand; and the flies had settled undisturbed upon her face. I cried out, and Sikinnos came running; the boy woke up, raised eyes swollen with crying, and brushed away the flies. My brother came to meet me from the inner house.

'You got my message, then, Themistokles,' he said. 'Thank God you are here in time.'

'Message?' I said vaguely. I had left my wife with child, and near her time; I was just at that moment realising that there was no small white bundle beside her on the bier.

'I imagine you'll want to have them exposed,' Timoleon was saying, 'but I hesitated to get it done till you indicated agreement.'

'Exposed?' I said, staring at him like an idiot.

'Dear brother,' he said, grasping my hands in his, 'Archippe died giving birth. Two girls. It is three days since, and they must be put out at once, or found a wet nurse.'

'Find them a nurse,' I said, dully.

'This is no time to raise girls, brother,' he said to me, gently.

'It's the only time, for these girls,' I said. 'Let me see them.'

Two ugly wretches. I did not love my wife; but she was dutiful and fruitful, and for these two she gave her life. I did not for one moment consider exposing them. I called them Sybaris and Italia, thinking that they might find new lives in the west, little thinking they would find homes in the east instead, my two golden-skinned twins, whose beauty has drawn many gifts from you, Lord Artaxerxes, and won for the one an honourable Athenian, for the other a dark Persian husband; my two girls, who have been like sons to me.

I sat by my wife all night. Two hours before dawn we carried her out to burial, in darkness, lest the sight of death should offend the sun itself. I poured out wine and oil for her, and then having barely seen her into the ground I embraced my weeping children and walked away. At the edge of the burial ground a soldier waited with my armour and my horse, and I mounted and rode to join the phalanx and march into Thessaly.

That was a misbegotten expedition. When we got there we found at once that there were at least three passes through the mountains, and that nearly all the local people were hostile, having given earth and water to the King. The young men who had brought us there were leaders of a faction only, who were trying to promote a revolution, and all the more powerful families were against them. We had no fleet to extricate ourselves if things went wrong – the whole situation was hopeless. Just to add to it all, there was that snake Alexander the Macedonian nearly frantic with anxiety at the thought that we might hold up the Persians in his territory – naturally that was the last thing he wanted – claiming to be our friend, and as a friend advising us to beat it back home as fast as our legs would carry us. He had a sister married to some Persian big-wig, and he even had a plausible story to account for that; it seems it was the result of his enmity to Persia! Frankly, I was only too glad to take his friendly advice; I couldn't get out of his range fast enough, and Evanitos the Spartan agreed with me. We withdrew; and I was back in Athens in time to join in the thirtieth-day ceremonies for my wife, and purify my house with sea-water and hyssop. Swiftly following after us came news of Persian hordes pouring into Macedon and Thessaly, advancing towards us like the waters of a river in flood.

Panic is ugly. After Marathon we had made a shrine to Pan in a cave in the Acropolis, for poor exhausted Philippides, running like a madman in the dry hills on his vain errand to Sparta, had seen Pan, and Pan had called himself our friend. True, he had driven the Persians from their senses in the route that followed their defeat. Much good a shrine to him did us, since he now infected us! It was all the cooler heads among us could do to stop hotheads running screaming disaster in the streets. Not that the fear was groundless, for unless the allies would advance north of the Isthmus Attica could not be defended. I went in person to the Isthmus, to plead and persuade, and beg for Attica. While I was gone the Assembly sent an appeal for advice to Delphi, choosing as envoys two well-respected pious citizens. They turned out to be patriots as well, and possessed of a modicum of courage – for which we had cause to be grateful.

At the Isthmus things went hard. That was the time when I first took the measure of the task the gods had laid on me. If only there had been nothing but the Persians to contend with! But the Spartans were in a state of obstinacy, brought on, I think, by fear. We had friends enough in Thessaly to have received accurate estimates of your father's strength, especially in the two forms of armament, archers and cavalry, that we lacked, and that could defeat us. For the first time the Spartans, accustomed to thinking of themselves as invincible, were facing the fact that there was simply no hope at all of victory in a pitched battle. Failing that, their thoughts turned naturally to their other fixed idea – defending the Isthmus. And we lay helpless beyond it. I made for Pausanias. To him at least one could talk without meeting the barrier of stubbornness and a closed mind. Once more I expounded; the enemy have to keep fleet and army in step, so we should choose a position flanking the line of advance of their ships – they cannot sail past us, so sooner or later they must attack us in a position chosen by us to minimise their advantages. At the same time, there is a place where an attempt could be made to hold the army on land; the place I had in mind was Thermopylai. There is a narrow pass there, and it lies roughly on the same line as the northernmost tip of Euboia, where I suggested the fleet should lie in wait. That would block the sheltered passage between Euboia and the mainland, offering instead to the enemy the long, windy, rocky, harbourless outer shore of Euboia, notorious among sailors. And while we lay in wait there they could not supply the army on the mainland. I convinced Pausanias, but I could not make him see the need for haste. 'It will do if we get there before they do,' he said. But I knew that the Karneian moon was approaching. Once it began we had good cause to know how lightly the fate of the Athenians would weigh against the possible displeasure of the Spartan gods. And just to make matters worse it was an Olympic year, and the time of the games was approaching. That and the Karneian moon together might even cost Hellas her liberty. Pausanias promised to do what he could to persuade his fellow Spartans, but I still did not know what the outcome would be when I left to return to Athens.

I got back only just in time. The men sent to Delphi had returned bringing terrible answers, and the Assembly was gathering to consider them. The envoy who stood before us to report to us was pale; his face was worn, sagging with stress. I remembered seeing such a look upon the faces of men waiting and waiting before Marathon.

'When we had performed the customary rites,' he told us, 'we entered the sanctuary. But no sooner had we crossed the threshold, while we were still walking towards the seats set ready for us, and before we had presented our questions, the Pythian priestess cried out to us, addressing us in these words:

> "Why so inactive, you wretches?
> Escape to the ends of the earth.
> Leave the peaks and proud emblems
> Of the wheel-shaped town of your birth.
> For neither head nor body, nor hand
> Nor foot shall be found;
> The Syrian armies of Ares
> Will plough them into the ground.
> Not only your fair city
> But many a city shall fall;
> Many temples of gods will be ransacked
> And blood run black in the halls
> Where those who foretell the future
> Now tremble and sweat with fear.
> Go, and go while you can.
> Disaster and death are near." '

148

For several minutes he could not continue against the voices of grief and dismay ringing round the Assembly from a hundred voices. 'We were dismayed,' he said at last. 'We withdrew, and stood consulting upon the outer steps of the temple. Then Timon, son of Androboulos came to us, and advised us to take boughs of olive in our hands, like suppliants, and this we did, entering the shrine again, saying "Lord Apollo, have pity on these boughs, and grant us some better oracle about our country." And, having decided together that we would rather die than return to you with no better words than those we had already heard, we added that if we were not granted a better answer we would not leave the shrine, but would starve ourselves to death within the doors, and thus defile the holy place. Then we were given another answer – this one:

> "Goddess Pallas Athene
> To Zeus' will must bend;
> Not even her wisdom or cunning
> Can stay his mighty hand.
> And yet a cool word of comfort
> Would sustain her hopes:
> When the plains of Athens are taken
> From the sea to Cithaeron's slopes,
> Far-seeing Zeus to Athene
> A wall of wood will give;
> Wood that will protect her
> And her people while they live.
> Do not wait for cavalry charges
> Or hoplites with spears and shields
> Marching from Asia to Europe,
> But turn, and leave the field.
> Holy Salamis, Holy Salamis,
> Thousands of men were born
> For you to scatter and destroy
> In the season for sowing, or reaping, of corn."

Thinking that this answer was gentler than the first, we wrote it down, and have brought it before you now.'

The second oracle we heard in silence. In silence we listened while the president of the Assembly thanked the messengers for their courage in the face of Apollo's anger, and dismissed them, their task being fulfilled. Then he turned to the people and asked if any man could help us fathom the dark words of the god.

First we listened to the experts, the learned, who made a life's work of reading oracles. They were all of the opinion that the god told us to flee. We should, they were saying, without striking a single blow, retire to the west and begin a new city there. There was nothing to be argued against that except each man's stubborn love of his own land; and indeed one old man, getting shakily to his feet, declared that if the Athenians left Attica they would leave him behind, and many like him, for he would sooner die at home than survive in an alien place. Many of us felt the same.

Another opinion came from an ancient fellow who declared he could still remember a time when the Acropolis had nothing but a wattle wall around it – just a wooden wall to keep people from slipping over the precipitous sides. Surely, he said, the god meant the Acropolis would not fall. We should shut ourselves up there, and make ready to stand a siege.

'If the god thinks one can hold out on the Acropolis,' I muttered to Epikrates beside me, 'he's got a shorter memory than I have.'

Someone leapt to his feet and reminded us that there was no water on the Acropolis, except the well of salt water sacred to Poseidon. 'Besides which, even if we could supply ourselves with water, we could not all crush into the space on the Acropolis.'

'Then some of us should hold the Acropolis, since the god has promised it will be safe, and the others should go up into the hills, the high and lonely places, and conceal themselves there.'

'I don't see a wooden wall round the Acropolis!' cried a younger voice. 'Where is it?'

'Perhaps the god means we should replace the wooden wall; that's doubtless what he means.'

A priest said yet again that he thought the oracle was open to no doubt; it advised us to flee at once. And all the while faces were turned anxiously towards me. At each speech men looked around, their eyes ask for me, draw me, and as I sat silent, at last somebody said, 'What does Themistokles think?'

'Athens has not one wooden wall, but two hundred,' I said. 'The god warns us that the whole of Attica will be ravaged. I believe nothing can prevent that, if the King is not stopped in the pass of Thermopylai. But our wooden wall is our fleet, which the god says will be safe for us. Therefore my opinion is that as soon as the King's march threatens us we should send away our old men, and our women and children, and our slaves and property, and we should enlist every man of military age in the fleet, and give battle at sea, for to my mind this is what the oracle has advised us to do.'

Then I sat down, and listened in despair, as pandemonium broke out. There were voices enough agreeing with me, seizing on the ships as desperate men seize at straws. But more voices were raised against me. And even some of those who in a calm frame of mind would have supported me were terrified into stupidity. The oracle spoke of Salamis destroying the offspring of women, and everyone seemed to think that meant we would be defeated at sea.

Whatever gods there are, I face them now; I hope that indeed on the other side of death I shall find only Ahura Mazda, the One and Mighty, as you believe, Great King. For if there were indeed an Apollo how could he have spoken as he did? When we were in utmost peril he forgot the burnt offerings and the images, and the songs, and the love the Athenians have lavished on him year by year, and he let the craven cowardice of his priests, their crawling Medism, their desire to save themselves though all else perished, answer us with an attack on our courage, infecting us with their own vile weakness. Was it not enough to have half the city against me, and the Spartans dragging their feet in the common cause, and no voice but mine urging the right course of action, without having Apollo to face as well? And how in Hades did his lackeys know we were thinking of fighting at Salamis? Oh, well, I suppose they know that island is our natural retreat.

For a long while I let the debate rage on. I knew that I had to steady the Athenians, and bring them to a determined state of mind. If I did not get them aboard their ships, then there would be no battle at sea, and without a victory at sea there was no stopping Xerxes on land. And I held back, therefore, from making my appeal to them, as a man holds back from casting his last throw at dice, for until he throws it he has not lost the game. Also, to sway the Assembly it is best to delay; if one speaks early one's words are overlaid by a torrent of other men's voices, and lose their force. Better to speak late. Further, if one wins in the Assembly by carrying a matter to the vote before all men have had their say, they leave muttering to each other, voicing all round the city the opinion they did not have a chance to deliver, and so undermining support for the decision that has been made. Never before had the Athenians needed to believe in what they decided as much as they did then.

So I sat, watching the light, calculating how much time remained before darkness forced us to vote a decision. When at last I took the speaker's place again the sun was already burning as it sank down the westward sky. Behind me the Acropolis was shining against the tender shadow of Hymettos stretched across the sky. And in front of me, in the centre of the front row of the people, I saw with distress, was the lovely curly head of young Kimon, sitting surrounded by his friends. He didn't go quite as far as to wear hoplite gear in the Assembly, but he was wearing a short black riding-cloak, and holding, as he lounged back, arms crossed, spurred sandals stretched out before him, a little whip decorated with silver wire.

I could not look straight at the main body of the people without seeing him all the time. Gods, how I hated him! I had no doubt he was scorning my advice, and was ready to ride out gladly with his companions to face the enemy in the foothills of Kithairon, and die there foolishly with a brave epitaph, like another Leipsydrion.

'Athenians,' I said, 'I do not think that those who threaten us with defeat at sea have read the oracle carefully enough. Surely, if we were the offspring of women whom the god says will be destroyed, the oracle would read, "Cursed Salamis, or Luckless Salamis, or Dreadful Salamis", anything but "Holy Salamis". Let us take heart, for in calling Salamis Holy the god is promising us victory.' Thus I spoke to them, knowing their faith in oracles, knowing that I must appeal first to their piety, and then to their sense. 'You can see that I must be right, by considering what we would be likely to do if the god had not spoken to us. If we are to have a victory at sea, and yet Attica is to be sacked, then we should send away those who cannot defend themselves. By doing so we shall in effect be turning our backs on the enemy, as the god advises us to do. Athenians, what the god, and the situation, ask of us is terrible enough already, without making it worse by imagining that we ought to flee for ever, or that we ought not to fight for our country at all. Was it for nothing, then, that we fought at Marathon? Is our dear Attica so poor a land, so unrewarding to plough and sow, so shadowed from the sun, so little loved by the Athenians, that it is not worth fighting for? I am not the man to tell you that we can by ourselves keep the King out of our land, for that is not possible. But with the help of our allies, we may yet hope to defeat him. Can we expect the help of our allies if we ourselves think only of running away? And without us, Athenians, what will become of Hellas? Hold up your heads; we may be weak compared to the King, but in Hellas we are mighty. The Spartans are stronger indeed on land, but at sea we are now the greatest among the cities. Come now, what will the Spartans do without us? We can't desert them, can we?' I raised the ghost of a laugh, saw a wry smile on Kimon's face. 'Athenians, let us take courage, for like a new sword shining in the scabbard our silver ships lie at Peiraieus and we are not without means to fight for our freedom, if we can only find the courage for the fight!'

Then suddenly, briefly, but with feeling, they cheered me. Kleinias was on his feet (how he wanted a chance with that ship of his!) to propose that the Assembly should ask Themistokles son of Neokles to draw up the necessary decree, and present it to the people the next day. Then it could be voted, and be put into effect when the danger required it. This they approved, and this I agreed to do.

When I reached my house, I threw myself onto my couch, weary like a man who has marched all day. My son came to me, bringing a jar of wine, a bowl of figs. 'They say you have decided it, single-handed, father,' he said.

'Yes,' I said, 'I am single-handed. And I hate it. Too much depends on only me. I am alone.'

'Shall I stay with you, father? Or shall I bring you food?' he said, offering his services as though he were a slave.

'I need sleep first,' I said, 'my head spins. But wake me within the hour. I have work to do.' The boy brought me my cloak, and spread it over me where I lay, and left me.

How if I tried to get the others recalled, I wondered, would they let me? Today they would have done anything for me; will they still be with me tomorrow? I slept. A light, brief sleep, such as men seize on battlefields, or watching at the pallets of the dying. I could sleep such a sleep at this moment, if I did not now see the rising moon, pouring a finer silver than that from Laurion over my shadowy lands, and, with the best things yet to tell, I know I must count the time. Besides, what's sleep for? To get courage for the following day, I think. And for my tomorrow memory will brace me better than sleep could do.

Sounds in the street woke me. Laughter, running footsteps, and voices. I lifted my head. The footsteps had almost a marching pattern to them. The voices were young. I rose and went to the window, and could see nothing in the little street at the side of the house. I took up my cloak, and went to the door. When everything depends on the mood of the citizens, I cannot afford not to know what is going on. At the foot of the street, where it crossed another, I saw a small cluster of people standing. They were looking towards the noise. Then suddenly Kimon came by, swaggering, leading a little group, all of them stamping, and one of them, bringing up the rear, playing a march on the flute. I raced to the street corner, suspicion seizing me. What in Hades was that young idiot up to? What did a dozen young bucks think they could do alone? As I reached the corner, and strode after them, several other citizens falling into step beside me, I saw that they were swinging bridles in their hands. Across the agora we followed them, stared at by citizens on their way home, and up the approach to the Acropolis. Are they going to start remaking the wattle walls? We mounted from the deep evening shadow in which the city lay, into the shining indigo haze that haloed the Acropolis. Everything was tinted and misty, even Kimon's golden head. Piped by their flute, they marched into Athene's temple, and the onlookers they had drawn with them crowded the doors, looking in. They gave their bridles to the priestess, and asked her to dedicate them to the goddess; and, as it penetrated my unbelieving head what they were doing, I laughed, from joy and surprise. The white-robed girls took their black leather, jingling with bronze fittings, and hung them upon the walls, above the rows of dolls given by young girls on their wedding-eve, and ploughshares given by old men who handed their land on to their sons to till.

Then Kimon, without asking, took down from the wall a shield his father hung there after Marathon, and stood trying the strap for size, while his companions also armed themselves with trophies. Coming out into the evening, they found themselves face to face with the little crowd. Kimon smiled.

'Who'll offer wine with me tonight?' he said, giving his libation cup to the nearest onlooker. 'Tomorrow I'm enlisting on a ship!' He threw his arms round the shoulders of the young men who stood on either side of him, and down the path they went, three and three, still laughing, and then, as the flute-player broke into a love tune, singing, as their voices died down into the darkness below.

The crowd dispersed, talking excitedly, but I stood in the deepening shadows, alone until the torches were lit at the temple gates, and the stars at the gates of heaven. A great relief had swept over me. We would get the Athenians afloat, for almost anyone in

Athens who would not follow me would follow Kimon's sort. I was grateful to him, and I should have been so still, even if I had known the future. Whatever you say about Kimon you have to admit his magnificence, his mastery of the splendid gesture, his power to win men's hearts; that evening, even mine.

'How this would have pleased Aristeides!' I thought, and shivered again with loneliness. 'It's worse for Aristeides,' I mused. 'What must it be like not to be here at such a time!' I thought about that as I walked home, wrapped tightly in my cloak. A bitter fore-taste of exile possessed me, and I saw clearly that powerlessness was the brunt of it. What pity I felt for him!

Going in, I calmed my anxious family, ate and drank a little, and took up tablets to write. I made the decree to lay before the Assembly the next day. I can remember it every word: 'Themis-tokles, son of Neokles, proposes:

'To deliver the city in trust to Athene, the mistress of Athens, and all the other gods, to guard her and ward off the barbarian from the land; and that the Athenians themselves, and the foreigners who dwell in Athens shall deposit their children and wives in Troizen, and old people and goods in Salamis; that the treasurers and priestesses in the Acropolis remain, guarding the things of the gods, and the other Athenians all, and the foreigners of military age, embark on the two hundred ships which have been made ready, and defend against the barbarian their freedom, and that of the other Hellenes, with the Lakedaimonians, and Corinthians, and Aiginetans, and the others who choose to share the danger. He proposes that there be appointed trierarchs two hundred, one for each ship, by the generals, beginning tomorrow, from among those who have land and house in Athens, and sons born in wedlock, and are not over fifty years old, and that they assign the ships to them by lot. And when the ships are fully manned, he proposes with one hundred of them to meet the enemy at the Artemision in Euboia, and with the other hundred off Salamis and the rest of Attica to lie and guard the land. And, that all Athenians may be of one mind in the defence against the barbarian, those banished for ten years shall go to Salamis and remain there until the people come to a decision about them....'

This decree, including the recall of the ostracised, was voted the following day. And I asked, and received, authority to order the enactment of this decree at what time I thought best. I ordered that the people should not depart from the land until the King had got as far as Thebes, so that we might gather as much of the harvest as possible. But the manning of the fleet was to begin that very day. And the first man to offer himself to the generals drawing up lists was Kimon, son of Miltiades.

I sent messages to the Isthmus, that the Athenian fleet was sailing for Artemision, 'and will hold the enemy fleet there, with or without help from others, if the Lakedaimonians will hold the pass at Thermopylai. If they will not, then nothing can be gained by our fleet, for the enemy will be able to pass on, and cross to Euboia to land men behind our beaches. Therefore, come!' When I learned that they were indeed on the march, bringing four thousand, a small number but surely enough in that narrow place, I ordered half our fleet to sail north, as the decree gave me power to do, there to face the enemy.

There was a good station at the Artemision; a shallow bay, on the north coast of Euboia, in which the fleet could line up with either flank protected by the curve of the shore – a necessary protection, for that we might be surrounded by superior numbers was our great danger. In this position we commanded the flank of the line of advance for your father's fleet, should it attempt to move down the channel to rejoin his army on the coast road. We were well placed there, though there were thirty miles of water between us and the pass of Thermopylai. I chose Habronichos, son of Lysikles, a good citizen and a friend of mine, to take a fast thirty-oared cutter to the pass and keep communication open between our two forces. Then we busied ourselves posting lookouts, organising supplies, making beacons, agreeing signals, and suchlike.

The day after we took up position off Artemision we were joined there by a hundred ships from the Peloponnesian allies, for they had approved our strategy and decided to match us, ship for ship. Like us, they had left reserves in the south, for we feared that your admirals might strike directly at Attica or the Peloponnesian coast. They brought with them Eurybiades, the Spartan, from whom I had agreed to take commands. I was heartily glad to see his ships, and a good deal less pleased to see him. However, he approved the station I had chosen, pitched a black tent on the shore to hold conferences in, and slaughtered a quantity of swine which he had brought with him for meat. All in all I found my colleagues sufficiently businesslike.

The next day a man called Polyas arrived and delivered a message to us that the Spartan force was in position at Thermopylai, under the command of no less a man than Leonidas, one of the kings. There they could hold the only road south where it was narrowest.

It ran through a precipitous place, mountain one side, sea the other, where a great number of men could not be brought to bear. For, faced by the vast horde of the Persians, on sea or on land, we had only this simple stratagem to aid us; that we should lie in wait in narrow places. I was satisfied with the news. With a king in command it was clear that the Spartans were serious. Polyas spoke also of reinforcements which the Spartans would send when the games were over at Olympia.

Having no news of either army or fleet of the enemy, we posted three ships to Skiathos, to keep a look-out. But the only news we ever got of them was a beacon fire telling us they had been captured. I was angry at their stupidity; it seemed likely that with our largely untrained crews we would suffer only too many avoidable reverses. But one man aboard the Aiginetan scout ship fought so bravely that when at last he fell he had won the admiration of the Persians who bound up his wounds and saved his life, so that later he could tell his tale at home. The Athenian ship escaped to the north, ran aground in Thessaly, and under Phormio, its captain, the crew walked back to Attica. I would rather have lost the men and saved the ship.

When news of the beacons on Skiathos was brought to us we were in fact in conference together, because the wind was getting up, and we thought that we should have to run for shelter, for the storms on that coast are terrible. A gleam of hope cheered us, for, as I said, 'If the Persians have just reached Skiathos, with a few ships which have captured our three, then perhaps those few are the vanguard of their advance. If so then all their ships are strung out along the coast beneath Mount Pelion, and the wind is rising!'

So going out from our tent at once, we seized some sheep which were grazing near by, and sacrificed them to Boreas, god of the winds, and then gave orders to withdraw the ships into the lee of Euboia, out of the way of the storm. The Athenians withdrew last, and I was walking along the shore, making certain that everything went smoothly and that the men understood what was happening, and why, when a farcical incident occurred. A party of eminent Euboians, rich cloaks flapping round them in the wind, came running after me along the shore. As they caught up with me, one of them threw himself at my feet, and embraced me round the knees like a suppliant. I had difficulty restraining myself from kicking him away, for I was in a hurry, alone now on the beach, my companions already climbing aboard the ship.

'Themistokles, have pity on us, help us!' said the fellow who was gripping me.

'What's the matter?' I asked him.

'Don't leave us!' he said. 'You are going away, leaving us exposed to the enemy. We beg you, we implore you, stay for a few days, so that we may take our women and children to safety!' And with this he brought a bulging purse from under his cloak, and jingled it at me.

'My friend, you are mistaken,' I said, really meaning to tell him that we would return when the storm blew itself out.

'We know that Eurybiades is the commander,' he said, interrupting me – a pricey piece of rudeness that proved to be – 'but we have tried to speak with him all day, and he will not see us, but sends a message that he cannot hold his ground, because it is too dangerous. Look, we have brought money for you. Take it, Themistokles, and persuade the Spartan to stay!'

I'm not the man to resist that sort of thing. 'Very well,' I said, laying hands on the purse, which was of most pleasing weight. 'I will follow after him now – as soon as you will release my knees – and persuade him to return.' Then they were in such haste to let me board my ship that they practically carried me to it! When I got on board, and looked at the purse at leisure, it turned out to contain thirty talents. Thirty talents! They'd have done better far to buy themselves a ship or two of their own, and a little courage. It wouldn't have been fair to keep it all; I gave five talents to Eurybiades, telling him where it came from. Later, when Adiemantos, the Corinthian commander, ran out of money to pay his crews, and was having trouble with them, I gave him three talents from the same purse, hidden under a dish of meat, with a message that he should eat first and see to his crew afterwards. Well, there's always a use for money!

The storm blew for three days. A mighty storm; for which in gratitude we poured out nearly all Eurybiades' unpalatable Spartan wine into the sea, watching with satisfaction the red stain spread and fade into the water, and praying to Poseidon the Saviour, and to the winds. When at last the winds abated, and the waters smoothed a little, we could see the slopes of Pelion, clear in the rain-washed light, ablaze with beacon fires, and soon small boats came over to us, struggling on the choppy seas, confirming the news. They said that catastrophe had overtaken the enemy. For fifty miles the coast was strewn with their wreckage; they were beached in every cove, trying to ward off attacks from the land by building palisades out of their broken vessels, and from the drowned men's golden ornaments there was enough money in the coastal villages (the messenger grinned) to buy off poverty for many years. Counting one estimate upon another, we thought that not less than four hundred ships had been lost – a welcome shortening of the odds. A few ships were even now rounding Cape Sepias, running for shelter, and with them the current was thick with flotsam and the drowned.

In haste, we made back up the channel ourselves, to take up our station again. We could see them then, beached in groups, for no beach was great enough for all of them, over five miles of the northern coast of the channel, facing us. As we came up to the Artemision, the last of them to round the Cape, a squadron of fifteen, mistook us for some of their own, and sailed right into the midst of us. So we captured them and their crews, including a man of note, Sandokes, governor of Aiolis. Our prisoners cheered the men a good deal, but hardly cheered the generals, for we learned from them that we had still a vast armada to face. From them we learned also that Damaratos the Spartan was with your father, the King. That meant Xerxes would have good local knowledge. We cursed Damaratos; since he chose Hippias' role, let Hippias' fate await him! Having questioned our prisoners, we despatched them to the Isthmus.

That night, the first night the two fleets spent beached on opposite shores, within sight of each others' fires, with incredible daring, Skyllias the diver came over to us, deserting the Medes. He had slipped over the side of a ship, and swum underwater for a way, and so had escaped unseen, and swimming steadily under the stars, keeping his eyes on our camp-fires, had crossed the straights. He brought us confirmation of enemy losses, and the news that the Persians had detached a fleet to sail round Euboia, and take us in the rear. We were dismayed. Such a movement might also allow them to join Xerxes, and thus imperil Leonidas. We lit beacons down the land the very night Skyllias came, calling into action fifty-three of the Athenian reserves that were lying at Sounion, bidding them sail in haste to the narrows of the Euboian channel, and intercept the Persians there.

We spent an anxious and dejected morning. I think my fellow commanders, on hearing of the losses the enemy had suffered, had hoped that we would have hardly anything left to face; now that we could see the numbers of hostile ships on the opposite shore, we were downcast. However, as the day wore on, the enemy seemed to have no intention of attacking us. Since courage would drain away if we stood idle, counting the enemy, we put to sea, very late in the day, to attack them ourselves, and try out what their tactics were like. When they saw us coming, they put to sea with a considerable number of ships, and advanced, their line much longer than ours on either side. As we closed, their left and right wings turned and sailed behind us, wrapping us round. I had a counter-move ready for that; at the first signal our ships brought their sterns round to form a circle; the Persians found themselves sailing round, not a ragged line with exposed ships ready to be rammed, but a tight hedgehog of ships, prows facing the enemy. Since they were rowing round and round us, it was their sides which were exposed to our rams. At a second signal we launched outwards in all directions at once, and attacked them. We took thirty ships, and holed a good many more. This was well done, considering the rawness of our crews, but we could not have maintained the advantage long, against superior numbers, and with the centre of the battle drifting dangerously closer to the enemy shore. But, as I had planned we were saved from long danger by darkness, which broke off the fighting and allowed us to withdraw.

Eurybiades congratulated himself. He really seemed to think that, however clever a plan of mine may be, it was cleverer still of him to accept it. He was best pleased with the capture of ships and prisoners, but I was better satisfied with having put a little heart into the men. It was during that first engagement that a ship deserted from your side, simply coming away with us under cover of dusk, as we disengaged, and made for our home beaches. Its captain was Antidoros of Lemnos, who claimed he had been forced to join Xerxes' fleet. I was glad to see him, and glad later to vote him his farm on Salamis, but I had hoped for more like him.

As darkness fell that night on our return, thunder began to rumble on the mountains of the north. The air was heavy with the weary heat of summer, and caught fire, like dry leaves, in flashes of tongued flame. Then rain began to fall, and the thunder roared over our heads, and so continued for half the night till at last it rumbled away southwards, and died down. In the morning the channel was rocked with a slow and heavy swell, and so we were content to make ready in case we were attacked, rather than starting an engagement ourselves. I considered that we would be at even more disadvantage than usual in a swell. For, although my Persian friends decline to believe this, knowing the ultimate outcome, we were not as good seamen as the men of your father's fleet. Many of our crews were unused to the sea, whereas yours had been drawn from islands and coastal towns, from the Phoenicians, and Egyptians, and the Ionians who have long been masters of the water. Further, the ships of your fleet not only outnumbered ours but were able to move much faster in the water, being made of seasoned timber and well dried out, whereas ours were full of sap still; and since we could not risk, with our small number, beaching them to dry them out they always had bilges awash. At midday, however, we were joined by the fifty-three from Sounion. They came to us unscathed, bringing with them the news that the squadron sent round Euboia by the Persians had been caught on a dangerous stretch of coast, the hollows of Euboia, by the thunderstorm, and destroyed. 'Indeed,' said Eurybiades, 'the gods are with us!'

'And Themistokles,' muttered the Corinthian Adeimantos.

I was glad to see more of my fellow Athenians, more of our fine ships, *my* ships. Now that all of them were in action we had needed to find more men than the city had ever before put into combat: some forty thousand Athenians. We had enlisted many men who had scarcely seen the sea all their lives, coming from the inland farms, and the hilly sheep-runs. When I went to inspect the ships I found we had also roped in a contingent of Plataians, who had offered themselves from their shoreless stronghold. Though they could not have been more ignorant of water, yet they could not be readier to our need. Indeed, Great King, it is impossible not to smile at the Plataians. The Athenians going to war are like a hunter with a very small but very stout-hearted dog running at his heels! What could I say to them? I embraced their leader, and told him to watch what the Athenian captains did, and do the same. How's that for a battle order?

On the evening of the day on which they joined us, reinforced also as we were by ships from other cities' reserves, we sallied out again, and attacked the Cilician contingent, the swell having abated a good deal. By my advice orders had been given to ram, and then immediately disengage, and chase another ship; to damage rather than kill in fact. We caused a thoroughly enjoyable havoc, and then ran for safety as the darkness fell, getting away with it. By this time we were more cheerful, beginning to rejoice at the long separation we were imposing on Xerxes' army and his ships, gleefully imagining the army's rations running out, and all those myriads of hungry men held up in the lean land beyond the pass. We had news of fierce fighting there, but no cause for concern.

I dare say a Persian admiral is as quick to imagine the discomfort of the King as any Greek, even me; it was to be expected that they would seek battle in full force, trying to get past us. On the next day we saw them all, moving out from their base, and marshalling for an advance down the channel. We put to sea to meet them, confronting their vast crescent with forward-pointing wings like the horns of a bull with our own formation – a much smaller crescent, curving backwards, so that we might have a chance of wriggling into our defensive circle again if we were surrounded. Of that third engagement at Artemision I do not like to think. Once one of our ships, with ten hoplites and four archers on board got tangled with one of yours, with thirty or forty armed men swarming all over it, there wasn't much chance for us, least of all for the rowers, packed so tightly, in stepped ranks one above the other, perched on their seats inside the curving hull, unarmed and naked, and with no deck to protect them from blows raining down from above. Worst of all was the fate of those brave inlanders, who could not swim, and more of whom died from water than from wounds. Lykos, among countless others, whose face I saw as my ship went on to ram an Egyptian vessel. Lykos, who had a lovely voice, and whose dying face, under the water rises before me so clearly that I cannot call back the living face beyond.

Our tactics were to compress our line, so that trying to engage us your ships drew too close together, and fouled each other, giving each other no oar-room. Those of us who could backed water, and then moved in to ram, jerking forwards on the sweat and groans of our rowers. To be honest, it was a shambles, but we wrecked more ships than we lost and, fighting all the day till nightfall, we thwarted your fleet from moving down channel. That far at least it was a victory.

I thought it was a pretty marginal one. I dreaded the outcome of the same ordeal repeated on the following day, for some half of our ships were damaged. We cheered our exhausted men by telling them to help themselves to Euboian sheep, since those stout-hearted people hadn't seen fit to remove them, and so at least everyone had roast meat in his belly with which to find courage for the following day.

And indeed we were to need our courage, especially we Athenians, for while the men were still eating, round their camp-fires, Habronichos came to us, bringing his triaconter to the shore in the darkness, and asking to see the generals. When we hastily assembled in Eurybiades' tent we found Habronichos steadying himself with a gulp of wine, and even so speaking to us in a shaking voice. The pass at Thermopylai had been turned, he said, and Leonidas was cut off from help, and surrounded, and although the sound of fighting had not ceased entirely as he had pulled away from the shore he thought there was no chance for any man there. So tomorrow the King's road would lie open to the south, and there was no chance of saving Attica.

Eurybiades didn't need help arranging a retreat. We left our fires burning along the shore, so that over the water they might think we still held our position. And manning every ship that would still float, including captured vessels (fortunately for us most of our ships, even the damaged ones, would float after a fashion), we rowed away down the sheltered landward channel, with the Corinthians leading, and the Athenians in the rear. Of course, I knew as well as any man, and better than most, that we could not continue at the Artemision once the pass was turned, and the enemy could contrive to cut us off. But I was as downcast to see the shadowy ships pass away into the night as ever I have been in a long life, for I wondered whether they would ever again assemble in one place, and whether each ship would make for its own city and desert the Athenians.

Even so, I myself stayed till the last, and taking a fast, undamaged ship I sailed to all the landing-points down the channel where ships put in to take on fresh water and set my men working to scratch words into the rocks there: 'Ionians, remember that it was fighting for your sake that Athens first provoked the anger of the King.' Or 'Ionians, remember we are your kith and kin.' Perhaps some would be moved to desert to our side; or at least fear of desertions would sow suspicion, and with luck, dissension among them. When we had left messages in many different places, at last we raised our sails, and sped away after the others, for all we knew the enemy might have been close behind. I sat, head on knees at the helmsman's feet, drowsing with fatigue in the soft morning light, now and then looking at the watery golden sunrise behind Euboia, in which the sea looked molten and the land looked black. And I thought of Leonidas with great bitterness. Justifiably, for that fool by his defeat had thrown away my victory.

He's a hero now. To hear the Greeks tell of it, you'd think that Thermopylai was a victory, and Artemision a defeat! The plain fact, Great King, is that Leonidas was a fool. He had a strong position, and he lost only through bad generalship. Perhaps the Spartans should have abandoned the games at Olympia, and afforded him more men, or brought up reinforcements more hastily, but five times the number of men could not have kept him from the disaster into which he fell. For he neglected, from sheer incompetence, to set a sufficient guard on the hill path. It isn't hard to reconstruct what happened. The Phokians with him were anxious, because they thought that finding the main path blocked the Persians might take the path over the mountain, into the heart of Phokis. They told Leonidas about the path and offered to guard it, and that boneheaded Herakles neglected to ask even the simplest questions, any of which would have revealed at once that the path forked in the mountains, one branch leading to Phokis, the other back to the main road in his rear. Then the public-spirited Phokians guarded the path that led to Phokis, and the Persian immortals walked past them, and took the eastern track, the really dangerous one. As soon as they got past the Phokians in the dark Leonidas was done for. But once having thrown away other men's victories, and imperilled every man in Hellas, Leonidas behaved magnificently; he and his Spartans – and a few wretched Thebans who insisted on staying with him, having no choice, since their city had Medised – they fought and died to a man. Hellas has remembered and rewarded the magnificence; where he fell there is a marble lion, and words by Simonides, who can write lines that a man need read only once to remember for ever:

> 'Tell them in Lakedaimon, passer-by,
> Obedient to their orders, here we lie.'

Hellas has not remembered the criminal folly. As for Artemision, however much it has been overshadowed, it made victory possible, both by cutting down the numbers against us – though Poseidon and the winds must have much of the credit for that – and by teaching me two things about the ships; about yours that they were top heavy, with all those fighting men on deck, and very vulnerable to crowding; about ours that more could be expected from them than I had dared to think. We could manoeuvre on signals as long as there were only a few signals, only a few manoeuvres. In a battle one manoeuvre might be enough, as long as it was a good one.

Do I seem ungenerous, abusing Leonidas, whom all others agree

164

to admire? One might admit that he had redeemed his mistake, in his own blood. Yet as far as I am concerned, had he paid with every drop of Spartan blood in Hellas, he would not have redeemed the harm to which he exposed Attica. Much later I heard, Great King, that your father had crucified Leonidas' corpse, and summoned the captains to gaze on it. I ought to tell you, lest perhaps the body of a conquered Hellene is ever yours to dispose of, that such barbarity does not impress, or frighten the Greeks. Only their contempt could be gained by it. Much more effective was the action of those Persian captains who bound up and salved the wounds of the Aiginetan sailor, out of admiration for his courage. What Xerxes should have done with Leonidas was to bury him with honour, and thus demonstrate to the Hellenes that they were fighting a man like themselves; they respect none other.

At that time, anyway, Xerxes didn't need to make gestures to frighten us. The fall of Leonidas was a moral disaster, such that I hardly know how to explain to you. That a Spartan force should have been defeated on Greek soil; that a Spartan king should have lost his life on the battlefield; such a thing had never happened before, and till it happened seemed unimaginable. More than anything else it brought home to the Greeks the vastness of the danger, so that many despaired, and became enemies of their country. With what boot-licking haste did the Thebans rush to congratulate the King, and offer their services! As for us we had some five days now, and perhaps less, to effect the rest of the decree, and to get the people away to safety.

Sailing down towards Sounion, my ship at first lagged far behind the others, because of the time I had taken leaving messages for the Ionians, but being undamaged, and among the fastest, she caught up with the rest before half of them had rounded the cape, and rowing hard in the lee of the land came up with Eurybiades' ship. I went on board to speak to him, and begged him – as I do not remember begging any other man before or since, not even you, Great King, when I spoke for my very life, but for my own life only – begged him to bring the whole fleet into the straits of Salamis and help us ferry our wives and children to safety. I told him there was a good anchorage, promised to make the timber reserves from the Peiraieus available to all for repairs, and when he doubted that I could be serious in proposing that the whole of Attica would be evacuated I showed him the decree of the Assembly in which that had been resolved. The decree that is always called the 'Decree of Themistokles'. Eurybiades was a difficult man to serve under – indeed I never recall serving under any man who carried off the task well – but he could be persuaded, though he didn't like it. In fact his chief limitation as a commander was that he didn't like being persuaded. He was very aware of his dignity as a Spartan, and truly he looked a Spartan every inch, all muscle, and stiff as a ramrod, and eternally funeral-faced. But his view of Spartan superiority led him to think that his own ideas must always be better than anyone else's, even when in fact he hadn't any idea what to do. Since he seldom thought of anything himself, he usually finished up accepting my proposals, but he never quite got over the feeling that he had been persuaded against his better judgement. This time his better judgement was that we should all go to the Isthmus, but he was not without pity, and he enjoyed I think the feeling of power that seeing me pleading with him produced. He agreed at least to take the ships to Salamis, and call a war council there.

That much gained, I sped for home. The Athenian ships were all ahead of me in the Peiraieus, not in bad order at all, considering their battered state, and the likely despair of those who manned them. But the jetties were in chaos, crowded with immense piles of baggage, and howling and crying women and children, and people clambering into boats, and offering huge sums to be ferried over to Salamis, all pressing so close to the planks and ladders that one had to fight one's way ashore. And all rich; not a poor man in sight. And those boats that were skulling out into the harbour were loaded nearly to sinking-point with bundles, and leaving the people behind. My anger and contempt were unbounded. I had thought I was tired, but the clear need to rush to give better orders, and conduct the withdrawal with some dignity, banished tiredness and spurred me on.

I saw horses among the crowds, fine beasts many of them, used as pack animals for the first time in their lives. I tried to borrow one, to ride to the city, calling the owners 'friends', and saying that I needed to join the other generals in the city, in haste. I met only with craven refusal. Then, behind me, a young voice.

'Have my horse, Themistokles.' I looked round. A boy had made the offer, and was holding out to me the bridle of a handsome enough horse, from which a slave had just unloaded a bundle. The boy was supporting the veiled figure of his mother, who trembled, and leaned on his left arm, head cast down, suffering like many of her sisters from the unnatural ordeal of being abroad in the streets. He reminded me ineluctably of a lion, smooth-chinned though he was; something about him ... perhaps that his head was too big for his body. At his feet there fawned and whimpered a brindled hound, frightened, poor beast, by the smell of fear in the air.

I took the bridle, and seized the horse's mane to pull myself up by. Then, hesitating, 'Have you no more need of him?' I asked.

'Kleinias is coming to take us across,' he said.

'Whom do I thank, then?'

'The son of Xanthippos,' he said.

'Have you word of your father? Does he come home to us?' I could use a man like Xanthippos, I thought, to tongue-whip a little public spirit into some of these fine folk around me.

'He is here already,' said the boy.

I got astride the horse, and said, 'Tell him, if you see him again, to come to me,' and then kicking my heels into the beast's flanks I made off towards Athens with all the speed I could coax out of him.

The generals were all in the Bouleuterion, with the Council. They had already issued a single order, 'Let him save himself who can', which had led to the confusion on the shore from which I had come. I broke in on them, asking for this and that instruction to be given, so that the confusion should be set right, and found myself talking out of turn, for the order had been given as soon as the first ships of the fleet came in with the news of Thermopylai, and all except me were agonising over the slowness of the flight rather than its speed. It seemed there was no hope that the mass of the people would budge. A small band of lunatics were busily erecting round the Acropolis a highly inflammable wooden fence, and dragging their provisions up there, but most people were stunned, and dazedly walking round, telling each other liberty was not worth the loss of their homes, or asking if the Spartans would not come and fight the King in the Kithairon passes. And, as if the reluctance of the people was not problem enough, having never before had so many people under arms, the city had run out of money altogether, and was incapable of paying the men in the fleet even what money they would need to buy enough food for themselves, to embark in the ships again. So desperate was the Council that I, smiling grimly, was unsure which was worse, the quays, or the Council room. First things first. Money first. I suggested we should ask for some. Agreed instantly. While they all cried, 'but whom shall we ask, and who will do the asking,' I had shot outside to fix it, and waiting outside found Xanthippos, saying, 'You commanded me to come to you.'

Oh, had he been Aristeides, the fittest for the job! But, failing Aristeides, Xanthippos would do. 'My friend, welcome,' I said hypocritically. 'I have a job for you. Will you go to the Areopagus, and tell them the Treasury has no money with which to pay the men in the fleet. Just tell them, and then stand there; don't come away till they answer.'

'Why, Themistokles,' he said, eyes shining, but mouth twisted sardonically, 'I thought you of all men could call up a mob at the flick of a finger to do errands for you!'

'None so fit for this task,' I said, allowing him his jibe. To do him justice it was the only reference I ever heard him make to his ostracism. 'And the need is very great.'

'I'm on my way,' he said.

Now, to shift the people, we needed something dramatic. A portent. I returned briefly to the Council, to hear orders going out to send a Council member at once, on horseback, to ride to each district, assess the situation and argue with the people the need for flight. That seemed so sensible I didn't even need to break in and agree. Running into the agora, I gathered a few of my old following, who joined me as they saw me. I seized a honey-cake from a stall, and up the Acropolis we went, at a run. The place was a madhouse, but I pushed my way through to the temple. The oldest priestess was standing in the sanctuary, hands held high to the gods.

I slipped the cake under my cloak, and approached her. I ought to explain, Great King, that the Athenians believe that a great snake goddess guards the holy places of the Acropolis, living in the heart of the rock; and each day food is left for the snake, which is each day, somehow, consumed.

'Madam,' I said to the priestess, 'if the oracle should be read as I have read it, and the gods have told us to leave Attica, then it seems to me that the most holy snake will have left her dwelling here; and, if I am right, then the food offered to her this morning will be still untouched.' I spoke with emphasis, eyes holding hers, to make sure she understood. So haggard a face, such a long life, so worn with mysteries; I feared she might be like the mob outside, disposed to cling to the rock of the past.

'I am sorry for it, Themistokles,' she said, as though apologising for not having thought of it herself. 'The food is eaten.' Then she drew back the veil over the hollow where it was laid, to show me, but turned her face away just long enough so that I had time to slip the cake I had brought onto the empty dish. 'Behold!' I said solemnly, 'it has not been touched. What can this mean?'

She let out so ear-piercing a shriek that my head buzzed. I was really startled. And before my astonished eyes she scratched her cheeks, viciously, so that I winced, and had all but reached out to stop her. Then with bloody fingers she ripped her robe, and staggered, still screaming loudly enough to shake the walls down, towards the doors, and out onto the steps. We had gathered quite an audience by then, I assure you.

'Aaaaaah, Aaaaaah!' she shrieked. 'She has gone, she has gone, she has gone! Woe, woe, woe, woe!' and a lot more like it. Her attendant virgins ran pell-mell out of the temple to raise her.

'The food of the goddess is untouched!' she yelled, sagging, apparently grief-stricken, in their arms. 'The goddess has left her holy place!' I slunk away between the columns. I was struck dumb with admiration. May the gods bless their handmaiden, that wrinkled old hag! She did the city proud. Within the hour she had led her virgins down to the shore, telling all and sundry that the goddess had left the Acropolis, and that they must seek her elsewhere if they were to continue to serve her. A dream, they said, had told them to seek her in Salamis. And these theatricals certainly shifted people. The road to Peiraieus was crowded with citizens.

At that point, I went to my own house. My brother and his family, and my children and slaves were waiting for me there.

'We are going to Salamis,' I told them. 'And from there, if a chance arises, to Troizen for all you children. We are going to set an example, going quietly, and as if unafraid. We will take nothing more than provision for our barest needs in food and clothing, and, because of their youth, a single plaything for each of the children. Choose carefully, for you will never again see anything that we leave behind. Brother, I must trust you to see to this for me, and pack food and garments for my needs also.' Then I caught sight of Sikinnos, with a suffering face. 'Master!' he said, suddenly with an eastern gesture throwing himself at my feet. 'You will not mistrust my loyalty? You will not send me away? How long may I stay at your side?'

'Till Xerxes is defeated, man,' I said to him, prodding him with my toe. 'Get up at once, and follow me.' When I said, 'Till Xerxes is defeated,' I saw my son smile.

Then I left them, and returned to the Council. The news was better. It seemed that many of the country people were driving their flocks and their cattle into the mountains, carting their harvests away, taking to the high and rocky places that they knew well. I didn't think the Persians would catch many of them. Old men were hard to move, but most of the others would come away, except the poorest, men who could not even buy the bag of meal each one would need to live on.

The Areopagus had answered Xanthippos by finding sixty talents. That would give every fighting man a month's pay, at any rate enough at least to buy them food. It must have emptied many rich men's hoards. Let it be remembered. It was not enough. I turned my attention again to the conduct of those people who were filling the boats, trying to ferry away the last of their goods and chattels, while their fellow citizens were still without a passage. I sent Sikinnos on an errand. 'You must do this for me,' I told him, 'because I don't know an Athenian with a stout enough heart for it. Go to the temple of Athene. You'll see the shield on her statue has a boss of gold, made like a gorgon's head. Wrench it off, and bring it to me. The priestesses have gone; but, should anyone see you, you must run like a common thief and not get caught.'

As soon as he had gone, I went and told the Council that the golden boss had been stolen, and got orders to search the baggage of the people embarking for Salamis. For this job I rounded up as many of my old following as I could, but in the confusion I could not find enough, and I had to get Xanthippos' help enlisting more. He found me the crew of the indomitable Kleinias' ship, together with Kleinias. My instructions were that every party of citizens on the road was to be stopped, and their baggage searched, looking for the gorgon's head. 'You won't actually find it,' I added, 'so there's no need to rifle the small belongings of the poor. But look through every bulging sack. Allow everyone a generous sufficiency, and some well-loved things. Understand, I don't want a girl's only earrings, or anyone's wedding-pledge, though it be made of gold; but whenever you find anyone with a disproportionate excess, greedy with food, or with money, or valuing their tables and chairs more than a man's place in a boat, you are to impound the surplus, letting them take only what is reasonable. Keep the rest, and guard it. It's earmarked for the city. You'll need to be tough — you're acting in excess of your authority.'

'But Themistokles,' said Kleinias, grinning from ear to ear, 'what if we actually *do* find the gorgon's head?'

'Get on with it!' I growled.

'Just as a matter of interest,' said Xanthippos, 'where is it?'

'Now, how would I know that?' I said, indignantly.

'Somewhere safe, I dare say,' he said. 'What are you going to do with the confiscated stuff?' Was that my old reputation for sticky fingers cropping up again? But he was smiling.

'I was going to ask some monument of respectability to get it made up into small parcels of food and money, and offer them to everyone we can find who is staying behind for want of means,' I said.

'Am I respectable enough for that job?' he asked.

'None better,' I said, and added inwardly, 'save one.'

It took us five days to clear the city. Towards the end we let men return to bring away more property, especially grain, provided they put it into the common store. The last day was terrible. The old and the sick were left, and many of the poor, for although we shared out all we had plundered while searching the baggage there was not enough for all. Some of the Euboians' futile bribe to me went the same way, but in the end we had to tell people to go inland and hide in the hills. We had not been able to prevent many from blockading themselves in the Acropolis. Some who held that stronghold were merely old fools; some few knew very well what fate they confronted, but preferred it to the life ahead, having no hope of victory. But there were also some brave hearts among them; sons who would not leave obstinate fathers, or men who hoped to die striking a blow on their own ground, for the holiest things in Attica. And also there was the priestess; Sikinnos had seen her there when he stole the Gorgon. She had taken ship at the Peiraieus for all to see, but although she had sent her maidens to Salamis she herself had been put ashore in some lonely place, and returned to her temple. I have often wondered about that woman. Having lived in the temple all her life, she must have known exactly how the gods are served. She must have known who takes the food set before the snake; and she certainly knew what I was up to. One would not think it could seem worth dying for such things. And yet perhaps, sometime, once in all her days there, there was something, some sign, some seeming answer to prayer, which had shown her the goddess, so that even when she tricked the people into thinking the goddess had gone she knew something stayed. I would like to believe that she had seen the goddess.

At last everything had been seen to. The streets were empty, save of those whom we could not help. I myself had made sure that every single piece of usable ship-gear had been taken from the sheds, with all the rope and timber, and pitch barrels. An appalling quiet had descended on the city. One ship rode beside the jetty, waiting to take me off, with the other generals, and Xanthippos, who had remained till the end. Some hours were left before dark, and I prowled the streets, gazing, for the last time.

I walked silently through the empty streets, towards my own house. I remember that the doors of the house were swinging open, unregarded. I went first into my garden, and remembering how my wife had loved it I scratched up a root of herb, and took it to carry away. Then, going into my room, I saw that my brother had left hanging in its usual place the wine cup Exekias made, my father's 'freedom cup'. 'Not even I, brother,' I murmured to myself, wondering at him, 'meant anyone to leave such a thing as that! But of course,' I remembered, 'my brother is too young to remember. He knows nothing about it except that it is a cup painted in the old fashion, only a cup of clay. Thou'lt not reach the lands of the King in one piece, if I can help it,' I said gently to the cup, taking it down. I found in a box somewhere a woollen ribbon, to thread through the handles, and so slung it from my shoulder, and let it hang by my side. Then I went from my house, closing the door behind me.

I met the others in the agora. Down to the shore we went, towards the last ship. I fell in with Xanthippos on the way. 'Do you know, Son of Ariphon,' I asked him, 'which of the other men we ostracised will come home to us?'

'Megakles won't,' he said. 'He told me himself he'd done with Athens. Well, you have to remember he doesn't know what welcome awaits him. Hipparchos won't either. He's with Xerxes, I've heard tell. It's only a rumour, but maybe he is. I haven't heard anything about Aristeides.' After this we walked in silence for a mile or so. Then, as we entered Peiraieus, he said to me, 'Themistokles, when will it be, do you think, that the people will come to a decision about me?'

I looked at him vaguely, for a moment.

'The decree that brought me home,' he said. 'We were to go to Salamis till the people decided about us.'

'Oh, yes. And you didn't go to Salamis!'

'I would have, as soon as I'd got my family out. Then you sent for me.'

'Well, just now, Xanthippos, I'm the people, more or less; and I've decided to offer you command of a trireme; we lost one or two captains at Artemision. Will that do?'

'I was hoping for it. I am no longer a danger to the city, then?'

'Oh, compared to the Persians, I rather think not!'

On the shore was a litter of abandoned chattels, and a pitiful crowd of small beasts, household pets and dogs, whining, and running aimlessly beside the water, sniffing the tracks of some-one's footfall till the water washed over them. They came round us, barking, and howling and creeping and fawning to us. From among them one dog leapt, tail wagging, overjoyed to see Xan-thippos.

'Down, old boy, down,' he said, pushing the dog's muzzle away. But the dog fell in smartly at his heels, as though he had been walking it to the hunt.

We embarked, not looking back, none speaking a word, with the frantic barking of dogs ringing in our ears, and as the ship pulled away an old woman ran down the jetty after us, screaming, and holding out her hands to us. We looked towards Salamis, grey island over blue water. But, when we were already half-way over, we heard a desperate yapping in the distance, and looking back saw Xanthippos' dog, swimming after us, far behind. Xan-thippos suddenly covered his face with his cloak.

When we landed on Salamis, he said, not turning his head, 'Is he still coming behind?'

'I can't see it,' I said.

'He belonged to my son,' said Xanthippos, walking away.

So there we all were on Salamis, with night falling.

Once there, we had time to take stock of the situation. Salamis wasn't an ideal refuge for a whole population. It is a rocky island, with commanding heights of its own, Great King, lying near inshore across the mouth of the bay of Eleusis, with only a narrow chan-nel between its each end and the shore. At almost every point it overlooks the coast of Attica, and from many places on it Athens herself can be distinguished, whenever the light is clear. So the Athenians could see smoke rolling off the land when the Persians began burning their farms; could smell the burning from the opposite shore, drifting across the still water in between. We could see the ships, streaming up the coast from Cape Sounion, and coming to beach or anchor in such numbers that we could not see the shore for ships over towards Mounychia and Phaleron.

There wasn't, of course, shelter for everyone. Mostly, men slept in the open, and made camp-fires to warm themselves, though by good fortune we didn't have sharp cold in the bright summer nights. The women and children shouldn't have been there at all, they were supposed to go to Troizen, where the citizens had built wattle huts for them, given money to support them, and even voted that the children be allowed to pick the ripe fruit from the vines and trees. Many, however, had not managed the longer journey, including the children of my own household, and had no choice now but to live and camp like an army, and endure the hardship as best they could. I gave orders that the men were not to mix with their families; nor the families to cook or sleep on the beaches; we couldn't do with an agony of last farewells hampering the embarkation if we had to put to sea suddenly.

Such reserves as we had came in from Poros; and many of the allies, faced with the losses at Artemision, had scraped up a few more ships from somewhere and sent them to us. Six ships from Naxos deserted to us, raising hopes that the Ionians and the islanders might really turn against Xerxes, but no more followed the Naxians. The Corcyreans brought sixty ships into the Lakonian gulf, and waited there, rousing slow anger as the hope of their arrival each day disappointed, until we realised they were waiting to see who won. Meanwhile the allies had gathered a large army at the Isthmus and, we learned, were building a wall across it from side to side, and at the same time were working to remove the road there, the road cut on the cliffs, made by Skiron of Megara long ago, and which they were now busy hacking off the face of the rock. So narrow a place could have been held, I would have thought; but doubtless Thermopylai, which put no heart into anybody, put least of all into men who were asked to hold passes. The news from the Isthmus meant trouble for me.

On the first evening on Salamis, the commanders of all the allies gathered together in Eurybiades' black tent. With men of so many cities serving together on the island, and men of so many cities fighting for Xerxes so short a width of water away, it seemed to us likely that every word we spoke would take flight to the ears of the King, so we ordered a fence to be made around the tent, to keep men back, out of earshot from the canvas, and we set guards at the entrance. Eurybiades asked each man to speak in turn, giving his advice as to what waters still under Greek control would be best for giving battle. One after another the generals counselled going to the Isthmus. There the ships could attempt to stop the Persian fleet from turning the flank of the Isthmus defences. Alone, I gave my voice for fighting where we were, at Salamis. Eurybiades put the matter to the vote without further discussion, as though he thought he were passing some unimportant bill in an assembly, and then dismissed the meeting. My angry protests were unheeded.

I followed Eurybiades to his ship, therefore, and went on board to talk with him. I persuaded him to call another meeting; we had till dawn before the captains would sail away, and it was then just nightfall, the hour when the evening meal is eaten. He did not willingly agree. I told him two things to change his mind. First that, in my opinion, if the Spartans and Corinthians went to the Isthmus wall, and seemed intent thereby on defending their own territory, they could expect all the smaller allies also to look for beaches near their own cities, and the fleet would fragment hopelessly. And whether he thought that opinion well founded or no, I added, the whole Athenian people, and all the property that remained to them, being now on Salamis, he need not think that we would abandon them, and take our ships away to the south, leaving the island to the enemy. 'If you go,' I told him, 'you will take not a single Athenian ship with you.'

'The ships of the Athenians are under my command, just like all the rest,' he said.

'Just try to command them to abandon their people!' I said. 'Abandoning Attica is the least likeable trick the Spartans know!'

He coloured, and jumped to his feet, fists clenched, as though he would have liked to strike me. I remained sitting. Raising my unprotected face to him, I said quietly, 'Hit me if you must, *but listen to me*!'

'What exactly is it you suggest I should do?' he said at last, collecting himself.

'Call another meeting, and this time let the question be fully discussed before any vote is taken. Let me present my case for wanting to stay.'

'At first light, then,' he said.

He sent a Spartan to carry a torch before me along the shore, back to the Athenian encampment. On the way we passed close by the fireside of a group of old men, nodding in the warmth, while it lasted. One of them recognised me, clambered to his feet, leaning on his stick, and called me by name, laying a hand on my cloak to detain me. Mnesiphilos. The Spartan held the torch to light his face. His companions pressed round me, grotesque in the flickering shadows, old lined faces, creased with worry, like the masks from the tragedy. Sudden affection for them swept over me. Mnesiphilos didn't speak, so that for a minute I wondered what he wanted, till I realised that he wanted to show that he knew me, could stop me, and I would speak to him. Times have changed, old man, since you said you'd not talk with me again till I made some mark on the world! But that was a harmless vanity; I humoured it.

'Mnesiphilos, old friend,' I said, laying a hand on his arm, and noticing the limp, shrunken feel of him, bone and loose skin, 'tell me, what do you think of the situation?' I put inches on his height at once, for he straightened proudly and said, 'They say the commanders are sailing away at dawn. Is that true, Themistokles?'

'Not if I can help it,' I said. 'You think it would be a mistake?'

'If once they take themselves off, they'll not be got together again!' he said with sudden spirit. 'They'll run like foxes, each to his own earth, and neither Eurybiades nor anyone else will be able to stop them!'

'Do you believe in the gods, Mnesiphilos?' I asked him. I knew he did not, for hadn't he mocked me out of my boyhood faith? It was as though I wanted to say to him, Give me back the gods, I need them now. 'Let any who believes pray now,' I said. 'Goodnight to all of you.' I am glad I was kindly to Mnesiphilos that night, for I never saw him again. He died on Salamis; the night air killed him.

I went back to my ship. The narrow decks were crowded with men rolled in their cloaks, sleeping under the stars. I could not reach the small shelter under the helmsman's stool, where the captain's pallet was, without waking a dozen men, so I rolled a sleeper over, and eased myself into the narrow space beside him, and gratefully slept till dawn.

I was the first man to reach the general's tent the next morning. Eurybiades must have overslept. Adiemantos the Corinthian came next, with some of the others close behind him. As soon as he came I went up to him, and began urging him to agree with me. 'Themistokles,' he said, 'at the games those who start before the signal get a thrashing!'

'True,' I said, 'but they don't crown those who are left at the post!' Everyone laughed, and at that moment Eurybiades arrived, frowning with disapproval at so frivolous a sound as mirth, and striking the ground with his staff called us to order, and began the conference, merely saying that it had been called to hear what I had to say. A golden dawn was coming up behind Kynosoura point in the east, but within the tent it was shadowy, and we had lit a row of lamps. By their light I set out to win the others, so that they would agree with me in their hearts; grudging acceptance of tactics one doesn't believe in won't do to win battles with.

'These are the reasons I have against going to the Isthmus,' I said. 'If we withdraw we shall certainly lose Salamis, Megara and Aigina, as we have already lost Attica. We shall give them sea-room to supply their army by ship all the way to the Isthmus, and so facilitate their advance. And there, when at last we do give battle, we shall fight in open waters, which will be greatly to our disadvantage, because of their greater numbers, and because they have had a chance to dry out their vessels, and caulk them a few at a time, which we cannot afford to do, and so they are swifter moving than ours. Whereas here, we can fight in a narrow space, and we can surely contrive a plan between us that will prevent them from bringing their numbers to bear. Fighting here will protect the Isthmus as much as fighting there; and it will protect much else besides.'

Then Eurybiades protested, 'But what if they don't attack us here? What is to stop them sailing past the southern shore of Salamis, and reaching the Peloponnese, while we lie here useless in our backwater?'

'If only they would!' I said. 'They would confront a hostile and often stormy coast, with an undefeated armada in their rear. Should they take leave of their senses, and do as you suggest, our watchers on the hills of Salamis will give us good warning. We could sally out, and take them in the rear. They won't risk that, have no doubt. But just because they can't risk it, and the army cannot get much farther forward without supplies, they will be stuck until they fight us. Sooner or later they will have to give battle in waters of our choosing. Anyway, though Xerxes has taken Attica, he has not as yet taken the Athenians. He has only a poor revenge for Sardis and for Marathon. And he knows we are here. I think he is as likely to attack Salamis next as the Isthmus. Therefore we should be resolved to stay here; all you generals should walk the shore till you know every feature of the coast on either side of the channel like your own palms. Then we should agree a battle line, and get the ships beached in good order all along the shore. All this needs doing, besides anything we can contrive that will tempt the Persians to attack us within the straits.'

So I carried the day. Adiemantos said, 'I'll have trouble convincing my men.'

'But you'll try, my friend,' I said.

'Come Themistokles,' he said rather sharply, 'you don't have to teach us everything.' But it had seemed to me that I did.

Soon after daybreak we were called down to the shore, to see on the opposite side men bringing cart loads of stone down and throwing it into the sea. Xerxes was beginning to make a mole, to bridge the channel to Salamis. At least that confirmed to the others my theory that he would attack Salamis first. We watched the mole-building with some interest, knowing how deep the water was in mid-channel. At either side, towards the shore when the sun shines on the water, it seems turquoise and green; at mid-channel the water is blue, almost indigo. We brought up such archers as we had, and waited.

The one thing wrong with my plans was that they made waiting necessary. Each day we waited eroded men's patience, gave more time for disagreement and mistrust to grow. Adeimantos was right to expect difficulty in holding the Corinthians; we all had to spend a good deal of energy making speeches to raise morale; we all had to carry a cheerful and confident public face, whatever misgivings lay within.

After a week we saw fire on the Acropolis; at least, we saw a tower of smoke rising above it. I had known that would happen, but to know it and to see it are two different things. I wept with all the others. We were crowded on a hillock, watching the distance, and some of the women keening as for a funeral, and men of other cities staring at us curiously; then a murmur ran round the crowd, whispering, then rising, that I was also in tears, and such was the dismay at it, the sheer terror it provoked, that I was compelled to stop it. 'The King has burned away the tyrant's crown of temples on the brow of Athens,' I said, putting on my public face like a grimace, 'a token that the city will be free.' Then I made my escape, bowed down by the burdens they laid on me.

It was as much as I could do to carry my responsibilities in those days. Men had come to rely on me, on my confidence of victory, on my indomitable cheerfulness, and so I had to keep it up interminably. I had to keep walking among the Athenians, showing a firmly confident demeanour, and at the same time I had to present to my fellow generals every day the same unwavering belief in my own words. They had nobody else to look to. Among the Athenians Xanthippos did his best; but people weren't easily inspired by Xanthippos. He wasn't exactly a lovable man.

One day, seeking to be alone, dismissing even Sikinnos, I walked up a hill-path that led away from the sea. I climbed on and on, letting the loneliness of the dry hills refresh my flagging spirits. When I had gone some way I heard a little spring tinkling in a ravine a short way below me, and I left the path to go and drink at it. It sprang from a cleft in the rock, and fell into a small pool. In the pool, back towards me, knelt a naked girl, washing her hair in the fall of bright water. At another time, Great King, I might have behaved like a man of honour and, covering my eyes, have hastened away. I might have. What I did then was to stare, to let my eyes feed a sudden overpowering greed for looking. She spread out her arms, and steadying herself with her hands against the rock, leaned away from me, holding her brown head directly in the main force of the fall. The water combed out her hair into sleek straightness, over her shoulders, and a river of it ran down her back, rippling over the gleaming undulations of her spine. A dull pain I did not recognise lay on my heart, and I stared on, and took no care to hide myself, or to withdraw, so that when she suddenly stood up and turned round she found me face to face.

She screamed, long and loud. When at last her cry died away from lack of breath, it came bouncing back at us from this hillside and that, and rang faintly about our heads. Dying, the echoes raised no answer, but only a sweet silence as before. I followed her desperate eyes to the ground at my feet, and saw lying there her chiton and her cloak. I picked up the chiton and held it out to her but still she stood, frozen, flinching beneath my debauching gaze, knee deep in the pool. At last I stepped into the water, and slipped the chiton over her head with my own hands, letting it fall to cover her. Then she said,

'Tell me your name, that my brother may find you, and kill you!'

'Why, then,' I said, smiling a little, 'tell him to kill Themistokles!'

Her eyes opened wider, and she began to cry, noiselessly, tears running freely down her cheeks. I picked up her cloak, and laid it over her shoulders, and taking her hand led her out of the pool onto dry ground. I said, 'You would surely do best to say nothing about this to anyone. If you don't tell anyone it can do you no harm.'

She said, 'Why did you stare? You should have gone away.'

'Lady, your beauty confused me. I took you for a naiad.'

'I prefer the truth!' she said angrily. 'Do you take me for a fool? What were you thinking of, standing there?'

'I was thinking that I wished you had been a hetaira,' I said, injudiciously.

At this she covered her face with her hands, and the tears trickled through her fingers and ran down her palms.

'You haven't much stomach for the truth, for one who prefers it,' I said brutally. But I did feel sorry for her. I turned away, and thought over the situation as rapidly as I could. Then I turned to her again.

'I have meant you no harm,' I said to her. 'I advise you to keep our encounter a secret. But if you can't do that, and your family are angry, I accept responsibility, I will take you into my household. Go back to the other women now, and I will follow later.' There was, after all, only one path. She raised her tear-stained face to me, and stared, in her turn. I remembered that I was nearly fifty, that my hair turned grey, that I had gone without sleep, without exercise and without oil for many days.

'No,' she said. 'If I tell my family and they make a fuss, there will be talk about you in every boat. It's no time now for shame to hang over the commander of the Greeks. But you have wronged me; you must put it right. You'll have to ask for me. As soon as you ask I will tell my brother what happened, since he will wonder however such a request came to be made; then he'll have no choice but to hand me over, and there'll be no open scandal.'

I was half-impressed, half-amused. She doesn't *want* to get out of it, damn it! I thought to myself, trying not to smile. 'Suppose I don't ask?' I said. 'Don't you realise that a bawdy reputation would increase my popularity? The men like to think their leader is the devil of a fellow.'

'You will,' she said. 'I saw you look at me,' and triumph glowed through the shame, taking my breath away. Then she turned and ran, lightly, jumping over the thyme and the stones of the mountain, till she gained the path, then running steadily down it. I watched her out of sight, round a turn of the hillside. Only when she had gone did I realise that I couldn't ask for her; she hadn't told me who she was. There was no concealing from myself the feeling of loss that thought brought with it. But half-way down to the shore, where the path was still high and lonely, I found a kerchief, laid out quite flat, upon the path, each corner weighted by a stone. I lifted it, and found in the dust beneath it, neatly written, 'Cleis, sister of Thoas.' She could write, too!

I sent a message, using Sikinnos, to any Thoas who would admit to having a sister, that I wanted to speak to him about her. Then I let my mind return to the subject of ships.

Thoas came to see me the next day. He turned out to be a young man, scarcely more than an ephebe, flushed deeply with anger, and speaking to me with a laughable combination of servility and indignation. He took not the most simple precautions to keep it all quiet, just marching up to me, as I stood eating from a pannikin of broth warmed on the fire near my beached ship, with my brother, and some of my crew standing round me.

'I gather I am to give my only sister to you in concubinage!' he said, between clenched teeth. Really, he astonished me. All round the cooking-pot men froze, soup pots half-way to their lips, and looked at each other very cautiously, as though merely moving the eyes might do some irrecoverable damage. My brother gaped.

'Haven't you got a father?' I demanded, reeling with the lack of tact with which it seemed things were to be conducted.

'He's on the Acropolis,' said the boy. 'Was. And I don't care who you are, you're not going to trifle with me! I was told you had promised to take her in, and you're damn well going to!'

'I have said not a word about concubines....' I began.

'Will somebody tell me what in Hades is going on?' said my brother, exploding into speech and spilling his soup.

'This ... this.... He,' said Thoas, 'has ruined my sister, and now he's trying to get out of doing anything about it, and if he weren't the bloody general I'd ... I'd....'

'I don't believe it,' said my brother, looking at me.

'Thoas,' I said, 'I am not asking for your sister as a concubine, I am asking for her as a wife.'

'Impossible!' he cried, almost in a wail.

'Why so?'

'We are plain folk,' he said, 'and our whole wealth was in olive trees.' We both glanced across the water to Attica, remembering the smoking farms. 'She'll have no dowry.'

No wonder she didn't want to get out of it, I thought wryly. I can see myself supporting this brother of hers for a lifetime. Aloud I said, 'I'll marry her without one.' I had forgotten how fiery and proud the young can be; but seeing his face I added, 'Or, if you prefer, we'll agree on a sum to be paid, in some ten years time.' For a new-planted olive-tree, Great King, takes ten years to yield a good crop. 'And listen, boy,' I went on aggressively, 'think well before you refuse. If you carry on like this you'll find that I'm the only man in Attica who will believe in your sister's virtue.'

'Themistokles, you can't be serious,' said my brother. 'Who are this family, anyway?'

'Brother, I have already got sons, well connected and legitimate. This time I'll marry whom I please. Listen now, Thoas. By nightfall we may either or both be dead. Bring witnesses quickly, and we'll swear a betrothal at once.'

He was calmer, but still very suspicious. As soon as he left my brother demanded to know what I had been up to, and I refused to tell him.

Anyway, we swore a betrothal contract, standing at the stempost of my ship, that very day. Timoleon remained bitterly unhappy about it. 'It's all completely unsuitable,' he complained. 'They are nobodies, and poverty-stricken nobodies at that. I just don't see what you get out of it.'

'I get the girl,' I said, with a certain pleasure audible in my voice. I could see from my brother's face that he thought it was disgraceful, at my age. Well, so it was.

We had drawn up a battle order. Corinth not too near Megara, Aigina not too near Athens. We had not been cut off from daily news from the Isthmus; indeed a flurry of small boats raced to and fro. But the wait had been a terrible strain. I had misjudged how long it would last; I had calculated that with the season well advanced the King would be in a hurry. He couldn't winter in Hellas without defeating the fleet. He seemed to have abandoned the attempt at mole-building. I supposed we were waiting for the enemy to become sated with plundering and destroying Attica.

All through the days of waiting the first fingers of morning light found us sleeping on the shore. The ships were drawn up, half in half out of the water, and each ship had some of her crew sleeping aboard her, and some on the beaches, and the shorewards slopes of the hills. The fires had all burned out long before dawn; waking men stretched their limbs, stamped their cold feet, took breakfast from pans of cold milk or cold wine, and cakes of bread burned hard in the ashes the night before. The captains slept and ate as their men did, and, although Athens had provided her generals with a pitched tent, I preferred not to sleep there – I preferred to share with my men. And each daybreak, sitting on the shore, eating, shivering a little, hearing the talk in sleepy voices, I had noticed something. When the sun has risen a little way, a wind comes off the land; it blows across the channel to Salamis, tugging the glassy surface of the water into small waves that reach the island shore and rebound. Disturbed by the wind the water rocks in the channel like water slopping from side to side in a jug being carried, so that soon waves from one shore are meeting waves from the other, and the whole channel is choppy with wash and backwash from side to side. After a little while the offshore breeze drops; the prevailing wind of the day's weather begins to blow, or no wind blows, and the water settles down again. Each morning I watched this happen, looking at it with attention, noting the time after dawn.

Then one morning there was something else to see. Over the bay towards Eleusis, a great cloud of dust was rising, as though many thousands of feet were beating the road along the shore there. The dust cloud rose high into the warm air, and then the offshore breeze carried it towards us, till the prickling dust and the familiar smell of a dry road in the sun reached us as clearly as if we had ourselves been marching. Some men even swore that they could hear singing, coming to them with the dust. Now it was the very day when the holy mysteries at Eleusis were usually celebrated; so that in time of peace a great procession of garlanded Athenians, singing loudly, would have been on that road, and remembering this the common Athenians became very excited, and talked of a divine force coming from Eleusis to our aid.

But everyone else knew that the road to Eleusis was also the road to Megara and the Isthmus, and had no doubt that the dust was raised by Xerxes' vanguard on the move. A terrible panic ran across the island. Adeimantos tried in vain to address the Corinthians, and steady them, but backed up by the men of other cities they gathered together and began to make speeches and hold a vast assembly, bitterly attacking Eurybiades for holding them there, and talking of going to the Isthmus whether they had orders or no. But, of course, the Athenians and Megarans and Aiginetans were then alarmed and angry, and began to dispute with the others, and while all this was going on Eurybiades called a meeting of the generals, so that the men were left to continue their debate without their leaders.

I don't know that the generals' debate was any more orderly than that of the men. As soon as I arrived Eurybiades asked for my advice; indeed he needed it, since I commanded half his ships. I said that if their army was on the move their fleet would have to move too; therefore they would attack, and we should make ready for it. Eurybiades asked for a vote of confidence in that; and then Adeimantos, distraught, leapt up and began to shout: 'Shall we listen to this man – without a city? And you Eurybiades, before you take votes at the instance of Themistokles, let him say of what state he is envoy, before he stands giving his opinion with the rest of us!' A long silence answered him. Everyone in the place cast eyes downwards; he had uttered many unspoken thoughts. As for me; well, so terrible an insult is like a wound in battle – you feel the blood draining, but for some moments do not believe that anything has happened. While I still stood there, stunned, he said in a quieter voice that it was better for the Greeks to fight for their own cities rather than to give battle at Salamis for a land that had already fallen to the enemy. I was still standing.

'Adeimantos,' I said to him quietly, 'I have a city, and a country as good as yours. I have two hundred ships, and all their crews. Where is the city in Hellas that can match us? Which of your cities could resist us, if we chose to take it for our own?' Nobody answered me. I turned to Eurybiades, and raised my voice. 'Sir,' I said to him, 'you are our leader. At this moment you are master of the fate of Hellas, for the whole outcome of this war depends on our ships. If you will stay here, and like a brave man give battle to the enemy, all will yet be well. Listen to me; for if you withdraw, and leave us, we will take our families on board, and go just as we are to Siris in Italy, which is ours from of old, and which our oracles have declared we will colonise some time or other. And when you try to hold the Persian ships at the Isthmus without us you will remember with bitterness what I have said!'

Eurybiades was shaken, as well he might be. 'I am of your mind in this, Themistokles,' he said. 'We will vote, as I suggested before.' And fewer than half the generals voted for me. They are not listed in glory, like the great list at Delphi honouring all who fought, but I have remembered who they were. Myself, Eurybiades, the delegate for Megara, the delegate for Aigina; none other. As soon as the vote was taken voices were raised to propose that the whole fleet, or the loyal fleet – with poisonous glances at me – should retire under cover of darkness.... I slipped away, leaving them to it. If they noticed I was not there they must have thought I was going to set up an embarkation for Siris. By the gods, I would have done, before I had spilt Athenian blood for them, who would not fight for us! Before I had led my people to certain defeat in defence of those who throw away the victory I could yet contrive for them! And yet, Great King, proudly though I call myself 'The Athenian' before your throne, I am a Hellene too. I am as good a Hellene as any of that stiff-necked crowd. I determined to try one last throw.

It wasn't something I thought up on the spur of the moment. I had been wondering for days whether there was anything I could do to bring the King to battle, and I had decided it was a desperate chance. Now I was desperate.

Leaving the tent I walked away through the barricade, and at once Sikinnos fell into step behind me; patient Sikinnos, whom my orders bound to my side. I walked down to the shore, where the Athenian ships were drawn up, and climbed to the prow of one of them.

'Sikinnos,' I said to him, 'if you look across the water from here you can see your own people.'

He said, 'I do not look that way.'

'A time of battle is coming,' I said, 'and either my people or yours must lose.'

'Master,' he said, 'though the King were my flesh and blood, I should win or lose on your side.'

'Then do something for me,' I said.

'Anything you command.'

'I won't command. I ask. It will probably cost you your life.'

His eyes lit up. They had a bronze glint in the dark iris, as though he reflected gold. 'For you, and for your sons?'

'For us all. Take a message for me to the King.' He did not even blink. 'Listen, you must get it by heart, and you must go at once. I cannot make the allies stay here, so the King must make them. Tell him you come from a well-wisher, Themistokles the Athenian. Tell him the Greeks are terrified, and divided among themselves. Tell him they are resolved to flee under cover of darkness, and are waiting only for nightfall tonight to make their escape, through the western channel to Megara, and through the eastern to Troizen. Tell him half of them have hearts of jelly when they contemplate his might – use your own words here, call him what he likes to be called – and repent of their rashness in opposing him, and that half of them plan to save themselves from his revenge by turning against their allies as soon as battle is joined. Make it sound as good as you can. Answer questions so that the answers fit the message. If they ask about numbers tell the truth; they know already, and it will make you sound reliable. Then, if you get a chance, save your skin by making yourself scarce. Go and hide in the ruins of a house somewhere, or make for the hills. Can you do all this?'

'Master,' he said, 'answer me a single question.'

'Anything.'

'You do believe, if you bring the King to battle, you will win?'

'There is a chance of it. Not a good chance, but the only one we have.' He deserved a truthful answer.

'How shall I go?' he said.

We found him a fisherman's boat, and a few men I could trust to row him across and put him ashore somewhere on the Sounion road. We had to take the boatmen into our confidence, in case they were caught and questioned too. Sikinnos asked only that he might go to the children and bid them farewell, and I refused him, because we were short of time. I wanted Xerxes to hear him, make a plan, and have time to effect it before nightfall. But as Sikinnos stepped into his boat I said to him, 'My friend, if you live, and if I have my freedom still, you shall have yours. By our hope of victory.' He hesitated, sitting in the stern of the little craft, and then extended a hand to me. I reached out to grasp it in farewell, just as my men put their shoulders to the oar and heaved the boat forwards. Our hands just brushed and parted.

I watched the boat away; then I returned to the congress of the generals. They were still in debate, still divided. Most were for sailing, but they could not convince the stubborn few. And they could not face the prospect of losing the Athenian ships. It is this more than anything that I mean when I say the Greeks owe their freedom to me; had I not secured the extra ships out of the silver revenues from Laurion, had the Athenian contingent been smaller, and less than indispensable, the allies would not have listened to me, and so would have been defeated.

'Surely Themistokles is right about the advantage of these waters,' Eurybiades was saying.

'He would be right,' said Adeimantos, 'if the Persians would give battle here. But they have not. They have marched, and we shall be cut off here, and starved out on this miserable island, unable to help our own cities. Even now, if they would come....'

'They will come now,' I said.

'How does he know?' someone cried.

'They must move with the army. They cannot risk passing us, and the storms have trimmed their numbers, so they are unlikely to risk dividing,' said Eurybiades, who by now knew his Themistokles by heart. 'Hellenes, all these arguments have been put before you so many times before....'

That did not mean, it seemed, that they need not be presented again. We spent the whole day arguing, in deadlock. The delegates from states north of the Isthmus would not agree to go, those south of it would not agree to stay. I stood firmly by my threat:

either fight here or fight without the Athenians. I wondered how much news was filtering across to Xerxes, and for the first time hoped he had good intelligence, for the truth about us would give weight to Sikinnos' tale. But now that I had circumvented this debate, and knew that it was not important, I found it insufferably boring, my head felt heavy on my shoulders, and knowing the ordeal was soon to come I felt the need for sleep. I crept to the back of the tent, behind the delegates' chairs, and rolling up my cloak for a pallet lay down there, within call of the other Athenians should they need me. To the drone of voices I let my thoughts wander towards sleep. The bright daylight pricked needle points through the canvas roof above me, and fell in a long bar between the drapes across the door. Each time we are tested by waiting, as before Marathon, I thought. The waiting should be over now. And yet it didn't feel so. I was still waiting, for something, and the feeling was still with me when it was overtaken by sleep.

I woke at sunset. My youngest son had entered the tent, and was shaking me. A buzz of voices reminded me where I was. Servants were bringing food to the generals, and my son had crept in among the servants. I looked at the light first; darkness, but not thick yet. Then I saw my son's face was wet with tears.

'Father, father!' he was saying, 'Sikinnos promised to come and he hasn't come!'

'You should not be here,' I said, sitting up. 'You know that the citizens have been ordered to keep away from the camp. The order applies not less, but more, to the son of Themistokles.'

'They are saying Sikinnos is a traitor; that he was seen going over to the Persians. Oh, I can't bear them saying it! It isn't true, father, is it? Say it isn't true, and I'll go back to the others at once.'

I thought, I have been so occupied with great affairs that my slave has become a father to my sons. More gently I said to the boy, 'It isn't true.'

'You know where he is?'

'I can't tell you. Go back to your brothers now.'

'He is coming back, father?'

'I don't know.' Then the boy cried again, and so I took him by the hand, and led him back along the shore towards the place where the citizens were encamped. Half-way I met one of my domestic slaves, coming to look for him. So I gave the boy to him, and returned to my place. The men were eating at their camp-fires as I passed among them, and from each fire drifted a murmur of voices, a scatter of smoky light, and the good smell of cooking.

Looking at the last smouldering glow of the sinking sun I thought, 'The waiting is over now. Why am I still waiting, every nerve in my body taut with it? I know tomorrow is the day.' I told myself reasonably enough what I was waiting for – some news, some lookout to come saying he had seen their ships. Over towards Megara in the western channel we had lookouts posted, and nearer, on every promontory towards Attica. If Xerxes believed me, he would surely send out his ships to hold the channels and cut off our lines of flight, and when the moon rose his ships would be seen and the news would be brought to the generals, and then at last they would agree to act.

I lingered, standing on the shore, before going back to the debate. I watched an enormous moon, like a fine silver coin, sail from beneath the horizon, making a shimmering roadway across the sea. Then, all too soon, the clouds blew across her face. Cursing, I prayed for good light. Would they believe me, if I just told them what I had done? May the moon shine, may the news come swiftly!

It was late before it came. The moon had been up perhaps two, perhaps three hours. The generals were still in session. Men were tired, tempers were frayed, voices rising; again and again the general debate broke up into a dozen local arguments. Into the middle of one of these noisy outbursts came another sound – a voice from outside the tent, crying, 'Themistokles! Themistokles!' The cry was cut short abruptly as though someone had clapped a hand over mouth, and then there was a scuffle, and shouting, and footfalls, and then a yell of 'Themistokles, come out!' I went out into the night. A dark banner of black cloud trailed across the face of the moon, so that I could not see.

'Who is calling me?' I asked the guards.

'This man,' they said, 'we cannot silence him.' And they thrust a burning torch at the stranger's face. He had come.

He was held by each arm, till I gestured the guards to release him. He was greyer than I remembered, his eyebrows particularly, though they still drew the same stern line above the eyes. The torchlight threw an exaggerated shadow into the hollow of his cheeks.

'I thought you would never come!' I said.

'I was far off. I came as soon as news of the recall was brought to me. But now, Themistokles, for the gods' sake, let us put enmity aside; believe what I have to say. We are surrounded. I have come this night from Aigina, with difficulty. My ship found the western channel full of Persian ships, moving in silence in the darkness; we escaped by the skin of our teeth. Then we found ships in the eastern channel also, and at last we slipped through and landed. Believe me; we cannot set sail for the Isthmus; we are surrounded!'

'The gods be thanked for it!' I exclaimed.

He looked so startled I could have laughed. Instead I said, 'Aristeides, dear friend, come in with me now to the others, and tell them what you have seen,' and putting an arm round his shoulders I began to draw him with me.

He said, holding back, 'Themistokles, is this *good* news?' Somehow I'd expected him to know, though indeed he never was quick at such things.

'It is my doing,' I said. 'I got a message to Xerxes, telling him we were about to escape. He has taken the bait; now we shall have him hooked. Come, speak to the others yourself – you will carry more weight than I can.'

In the light of the lamps in the tent I saw him better. He had grown thinner, and so had that old black cloak of his; he spoke firmly, with admirable conviction. He said nothing but what he had seen and, having said it, made to leave, but I held him back and brought him to sit with the Athenians.

I had expected uproar at the news. But there was none. The dispute was decided for them; and in the face of death or slavery men's anger and pride were stilled, and they bent themselves to the task. A plan of battle had been ready for days; my plan, ready and agreed upon. I had made a painted drawing on a piece of wood, showing the straits and the places of embarkation, and each man looked at this again, memorising the part he was to play. It was a damn good plan already, the plan for Salamis, but that night we put finishing touches to it. Someone had to make sure we were not taken in the rear by the Persian squadron that had entered the western channel. Racking his brain to remember something useful, Aristeides at last came up with an uncertainly remembered Egyptian emblem on one of those ships, and we remembered the skill of the Egyptians with bitterness from Artemision.

At that Adeimantos, whose men were beached furthest west, offered to deal with that danger, and we accepted his offer gladly. Stationed furthest east were Aigina and Megara, and after some thought we gave them, too, special orders; they were to wait till the Persian fleet came past them and then attack in the flank. When all this was settled we sent out orders for the men to make ready an extra meal, and then extinguish their fires, one by one. And to get that last order executed, I had to explain that Xerxes thought we were slipping away under cover of night, and why he thought so. I had to confess my trickery. But before indignation had sprouted wings, I added, 'Since this is all my doing, Hellenes, you will surely execute me for treason if we lose the battle. I accept that; but I expect to be given a crown if we win!' And at that they laughed.

At last the generals dispersed, going to their ships to seize a few hours' sleep before dawn. I, well prepared, and well rested, offered to keep watch, receiving any news that came, and waking the others if necessary. And that I did.

When the moon had set, the captain of a Tenian vessel came to me, having brought his ship over from the Persians. He confirmed our earlier reports. The Persians had been at sea since nightfall, expecting to spring an ambush on a disorderly retreating and demoralised enemy. He added two new details. First, that Xerxes had set up a throne and a canopy somewhere on a height of the Attic shore, to watch his ships and his victory, with scribes all round him to write the names of his captains, with good marks or black marks against them, as they conducted themselves. And second that Persian infantry had been put across onto Psyttaleia, a little island in the mouth of the strait, to rescue friends and kill enemies.

I thanked the Tenian captain, and gave him a place in the line for the following day. He fought well, and earned for Tenos her place on the list of victors at Delphi.

When he had gone I went outside, to walk up and down in the darkness. There were fantastic stars that night, or so I seem to remember. Were they really thus bright, or were my eyes sharpened by danger? I said to myself, 'The immeasurable heavens break open to their highest ...' and coming up quietly behind me Aristeides said, '... and all the stars shine.' Words of Homer that we learned together, long ago.

'You never liked Homer,' he said. 'And now you are telling him to the stars.'

'I am watching for the star of morning, and the first flush of the dawn,' I said.

'Themistokles ...' he began.

'And I am thinking of our men, who lie sleeping, and of the enemy who have rowed all night beneath the moon, labouring at the oar, and waiting in vain for the escaping Greeks.'

'Themistokles ...

'Reason enough for Homer? After all it's only two lines!'

'Themistokles, I beg you, give me something to do. Must I stand tomorrow on the shore, and watch, among the women? If it's only an oar to pull on, still give me something to do!'

I smiled at him. 'I thought you were averse to rowing,' I said. 'I'll find you better than an oar. You must wait till the battle turns our way, then you may take the reserves, and some of the supply boats, and get across to Psyttaleia; the enemy have garrisoned it. Cut them to bits. But don't try it till it's clear we shall be in control of the waters around it at the end of the day. Will that keep you from boredom?'

'Splendid!' he said. 'I thank you. I'll need a written authority, I take it?'

'I haven't the official seal here,' I said. 'Come to me at dawn and I'll have it ready for you.' He was about to go. 'Aristeides....'

'Yes?'

'How are you? Does all go well with you?'

'Abroad didn't suit me. I'm well enough now. I thought ... for a time I thought ... I would never see Athens again.'

'You won't. Neither will I or any man. Not as she was.'

'Oh, the buildings; well the city is in the ships now. I see her clear enough.' He couldn't have come nearer to admitting I had been right. 'And you, Themistokles? You have been well? Working hard, by all I hear! And your wife? How is she?'

'She is dead,' I said. 'I am about to marry again.'

'Look,' he said, 'there is your morning star. I must leave you.'

'Aristeides....'

'Yes?' I hesitated. 'Nothing,' I said, failing at the last minute to get my tongue round what I wanted to say. He left me, and I watched alone for the grey light of dawn. The darkness faded, and the stars were overwhelmed with light, and slowly the eastern sky flushed pink, and brightened to limpid gold. I watched for it; but I was waiting no longer.

Muffled trumpets met the dawn with muted notes of war. There was a clattering of oars, and splashing as ships were launched along the shore, but men were moving softly, with lowered voices, so that we might not be heard. While the ships were launched, the hoplites who would man the decks were gathering to hear the generals. We used neither lamps nor torches, lest we should be seen from the opposite shore. By now, of course, the Persian captains afloat must have feared they had been tricked; but it would be disaster should Xerxes or his officers see that we were still there, and realising that something was amiss give orders to bring their ships ashore. Without light the assembled men were like a sea of shadows. They stood on the slopes of the shore like an audience of ghosts, while we stood to address them at the stern post of the Athenian flagship, beneath the gilded owl, my emblem.

Each general spoke in his own way; the Spartan laconically, the Aiginetan defiantly, the Corinthian frenetically, and I, the Athenian, philosophically. I contrasted what was noble in life with what was base, having it that all things Greek were noble, all things Persian slavish and base. I told them that they were subject to fate in some things but not in all; some things were within man's range, governed by his choice. Wisdom, I told them, was within a man's range; and courage in a right cause. 'Wherever a choice is possible,' I exhorted them, 'let us unhesitatingly choose the better part.' And thus uplifted with cloudy sublimities I dismissed men to their ships.

As I stood waiting my turn to embark, Aristeides came to me, and I gave him a scrawled writing, with the general's seal upon it. We stood, watching the long line of ships moving quietly out to sea, with gently dipping oars plashing in the still water under the rising arc of the fast-brightening sky. This time I found my tongue.

'Farewell,' I said to him, taking his hand. 'May it be needlessly said. And I have this to say to you – I would never have done it for anything less than the ships!' He flashed that rare, brief smile of his. 'And never did silver shine more splendidly!' he said, and offering his hand to steady me he helped me climb on board.

My ship was the last to be launched. I steered into the end of the line, now forming up and down the channel, between a little island and the friendly shore. The leading ships, those of the Corinthians under Adeimantos, were to haul steadily northwards, until every ship of the main fleet had fallen into line astern behind them, like a necklace of spaced beads unwinding. So for a while we rowed like men asleep, leaving the dawn and the enemy astern. The shining water embraced each gently dipping oar with an encircling eddy, and released it beaded with jewels of water. So quiet was our progress that at the pause between strokes I could hear the tinkling water dripping from the balanced wings of oars. Can Xerxes see us, I wondered, in this soft and dreamy light? That depends where he sits. Does he think we are in flight? Or does the regularity of our movement trouble him? Then at last, following at the end of the string, my ship cleared the island, and I could see down the channel, and sure enough there they were;

they were, far off, thrown into black outline against the rising sun, sailing towards us on a sea-road of molten gold!

I cried out – a great lung-bursting cry that made my sides ache on the next few breaths. From the prow of my ship a trumpet answered me, and then another further off, and another, and all the ships began to turn. First sideways, to face the shore of Attica, then round again, to face back the way they had come, so that I was now at the head of the line. Looking back anxiously I saw far off white sails rising on masts; the morning wind had begun to blow that would presently bring the choppy swell, and Adeimantos was setting his sails to run before it into the bay of Eleusis, looking for the Egyptian squadron. All well so far.

Then we cried orders. Bending their lithe bodies in the great hollow of the hull, the rowers worked. And from somewhere far down the line behind my ship, a sound came, softly first, and patterned the formless air. The Greeks were singing, louder and louder, all together, in ancient music, calling, 'Oh Saving Lord!' So we all moved and sang as one, raising a paeon to the sky, and the song moved on the glassy water, the sound both diminished and enlarged by the vastness of the theatre in which it rang.

We moved swiftly down the channel, and closed the distance with them rapidly, our right wing leading, with me commanding the vanguard, Eurybiades a way back, leading the right centre, and the allies in due order behind him. And now the surface of the water rolled aside in great shining dolphins' backs, and boiled and foamed round the oars. The Persians came as I had known they would come, lagging on their left, towards the hostile shore of Salamis, and so much further advanced on their right that we could sail on, rapidly passing their front, till our line extended across their front from side to side of the channel. Then, to trumpets, we turned into line abreast, and faced them, just as they reached the narrows of the channel, and began to pass through. Some of their ships had to fall back here, for there was not space for all, but all their captains wanted to be the first to attack; competing for space they pressed forwards, and fell foul of each other, and I even saw one ship cripple its neighbour, shearing off a whole bank of oars. Struggling, and in poor order, they got a first line through. They were near us now, their ships like birds in the water, beating their sloping wings; we could hear the drum beats and the cries they rowed to, and see the hoplites glittering in the morning on their decks, tall decks, heavy with armed men. Now a second wave of ships had got through the narrows, and they were trying to restore the line.

And we were backing water. My end of the line was easing forwards, near the friendly shore, hoping to break through, with that famous tactic called in Greek 'Diekplous', and the main line was sagging gently, backing up, inviting the enemy to come on, waiting till enough of them should be drawn into the trap. Then, as they tried to line up, and more and more of them pressed through the narrows, striving to reach the enemy among the first, and taking the moving space the leaders needed, the swell struck them. Suddenly the water was knocking, heaving and rocking them, swinging them round broadside to our rams, smashing them against one another. Top heavy with all that bronze they swayed and lurched, while our undecked ships rose and fell lightly on the water, riding like babies in arms.

Eurybiades at last – it was nearly too late, and open water was appearing between my end of the line and the shore – gave the order to stop backing water. By then our sagging line lay like a noose round the head of the enemy column, and all was poised, so that by my cunning we had defeated their every advantage. Were they faster, better-moving in the water? But they had rowed all night. Were they a thousand, to some three hundred? But in the narrows their great numbers only crowded them. Were they untroubled by disunity, directed by a single mind? But I had mastered friends as well as an enemy, and brought them to battle here. Then suddenly the air was splintered with the rending noise of breaking timber, and the yells and screams of men, the noise of battle, booming in the hollow drums of ships. Looking across to see if the left wing had engaged at the same time, and seeing that they had, I saw also a bright patch of colours, a mosaic of scarlet and purple and gold, crowning the opposite hill. There was Xerxes, beneath a canopy of gold, sitting in glory to watch. I yelled, 'I'll give you sights to see, Great King!'

By now the sky was brilliant with light above us; on either side the sloping shores were crowded with spectators, like the banks of the amphitheatre, Athenians on one side, barbarians on the other, looking down at the drama. The chorus have entered and sung the opening hymn; now it's the time of the protagonists! And to Xerxes there, who sits to judge the play, I say I am choregos here, and dramatist, and you shall give the prize to me!

The Persian front line were in trouble as soon as we closed with them, tossed in the troubled water, and crowded together, they were helpless. We rammed them, and watched them sink. And the vast horde of others, coming up behind, would soon have troubles of their own; from the shore near the town of Salamis, coming out of the deep bay there, the Aiginetans and Megarans would soon strike the flank and rear of the following squadrons. For the moment it was enough to choose a ship, and ram it, and let the plan work itself out. A great judder runs through a ship as she crashes through the timbers of an enemy, and all the seams let water. The oarsmen are thrown off balance, and some are jerked from their benches to fall over the heads of their fellows into the bilges, and scramble back cursing. For a few minutes of disorder the ship would drift, with her great bronze beak sunk in her victim's bowels, and the fighting men on the enemy deck would try to scramble onto her, to seize her instead of their own. Then the rowers would recover, and back water, and release the wounded vessel, and the water would pour into her through the rammed hole, and her crew would struggle to swim, crying piti-fully. Not many of the Persians could swim, and bronze sinks like a stone. At one time I was riding high on my flagship, perched beside the helmsman, and we came up to a Phoenician ship just as she fell foul of another, which was trying to push past her into the front line. The other ship crashing through broke every oar along the far side of the Phoenician, and before it snapped each oar crushed its oarsman against the side, so that the whole tiered bank of men fell broken and screaming into the bottom, and the vessel was so lop-sided that she rolled over, very slowly at first, and then fast, towards us, and the water swallowed her. We had to be very nifty to get past her unscathed, and the suck of water round her as she went gave us a buffeting. We swept on, and looking back I saw her lying half-submerged, her wet curved side floating like a dying fish; and the water round her was stained with mistily floating red.

Quite soon the blue water of the channel disappeared, and we were fighting in a thick bobbing carpet of wreckage and corpses, and struggling shoals of living men. Your captains didn't have a chance, Great King. In any other battle, I think they'd have pulled out and saved their shipping, but with Xerxes watching them, and keeping score, nobody would pull out, and they fought like maniacs, like lions. They had their successes, for we took heavy losses. But their courage had a fearful price; time and again, as the front rank collapsed and turned to flee for safety, they found their path blocked by eager captains pressing up behind them in search of glory, and tangled with their friends they waited broadside on, helpless, while we rushed in to ram.

The day wound on. They came, and still they came, the wreckage impeded all alike. Then, as I hurtled through the water, my oarsmen shouting, my captain shouting, chasing a fleeing victim, I passed close by a rammed ship, being boarded by the victors. And a voice hailed me; 'Hi! Themistokles! Who says now the Aiginetans are friends of the Kings?' We had joined with the Aiginetans. Then I knew we had demolished the enemy right through to the rear, and there would be no more ships pressing up from behind.

'Who indeed?' I answered laughing. 'Not I, for one!' When I had seen my quarry to the bottom I turned, and we rowed back up the channel, and I saw here and there groups of ships locked in dog-fights, and many ships that had escaped by running aground on the enemy shore, and many of our ships rowing round, but no more of the enemy line. Then I came up with a Corinthian ship, and by shouted questions discovered that they had found the bay of Eleusis empty, and learning from a pinnace that the other Persian squadron had not moved from the mouth of the western channel they had turned back and joined the battle, and had been fighting with us all the day.

At last the noise and crashing died away, and we were left, afloat on the stained and laden water, through which our ships nosed slowly, staring, glutting their painted eyes. And then ships drifted, while their crews, who all day long had suffered danger with no chance to strike a blow, took broken oars and spars, and, like men gaffing tunnies, speared and smashed the living flotsam on the sea. Only darkness put an end to the slaughter. There's no doubt that Sikinnos earned his freedom: as your friend, I ought to advise you, Great King, never to trust messages from a Greek.

In the gathering dusk the assembly of the generals met. We met in the open, our chairs drawn up in front of a row of torches blazing on poles, so that we might hear reports from our captains in public, as our custom is. Of the tales we heard then I can still remember some details. Demokritos the Naxian, who had deserted to us with six ships, claimed to have sunk five of the enemy and rescued one of ours – a ship for a ship was his score. Polykritos, the Aiginetan, with a formidable list of triumphs to his credit, had rescued from a sinking enemy Pytheas his countryman, who had been healed of his wounds by the barbarian when they had cap-

tured our scout ships before Artemision. I remember he was
brought before us, his face crossed and crossed by still livid scars,
and he took up a handful of the ground and kissed it, saying, 'I
never thought to see the soil of Hellas free again while I lived.'

Ameinias, the Athenian, whose ship had been the first to be
engaged, had fought in the front line throughout the day, with
conspicuous bravery, but he was not eager to boast about it.
Instead he was fuming with explosive rage. It seems that he had
chased a ship, and had it cornered, for its escape was blocked by
another enemy vessel. Suddenly the ship turned a little, and rammed the enemy broadside on, and assuming that he had mistaken
it, and it was one of ours, Ameinias had urgently swung round,
backing water furiously, and somehow managed not to hit it; and
then it had resumed its flight, leaving its victim foundering, and
Ameinias' men had seen, too late, that it carried the emblems of
Artemisia, Queen of Caria, one of your father's captains. Ameinias'
grief at losing her was entirely understandable, as the allies had
offered a reward for her. 'That bitch!' he said. 'Pranging one of
her own side! Whoever heard of such a thing? A dog wouldn't
do it! Curse her! And she, doubtless, is telling Xerxes it was one of
ours, and adding it to her score. Gods! If ever in life I encounter
that monstrous Amazon again. . . .' One couldn't help hearing the
reluctant note of outraged admiration beneath the wrath.

'Thank the gods women don't usually fight, eh, Ameinias?' we
said, laughing. Poor man, he lost his Amazon, and the money on
her head, but we gave him the prize for personal valour, next after
Polykritos, and crowned him then and there.

Last of all, in a torn and blood-stained tunic, and with the plume
upon his helmet shorn away, came Aristeides. He stood before us
to report. He had taken the shore defences, the reserve troops, and
he had crossed to Psyttaleia, and slaughtered the Persians there,
with bitter fighting. He had lost fifty men, and they five hundred.
'Seeing their comrades fleeing across the water all around, and
none coming to their rescue, they had lost heart,' he said.

'They were fighting against a lion,' I said, and across the flickering torchlight we smiled at one another. How lightly he stepped,
how high he held his head! He was triumphant, and I, having made
him so, happy to see it. In front of all those who had witnessed
our struggle over the silver, we stood, and smiled like boys.

So, listening to one tale after another, the generals pieced
together what had happened. We saw we had won a great victory;
how great we did not comprehend at once. Our own losses were

forty ships, and a hundred with damage, great or slight. Your losses we could not number, and great as we thought they had been we prepared to fight the remnant the next day, if there should be need. Of all the Hellenes none had shamed us, none failed in courage. But the Aiginetans earned the crown for the bravest contingent. Starting at the rear, they had fought their way right across the channel, through the entire enemy line, closing the western sound between Psyttaleia and Salamis, and then still advancing to harry ships fleeing through the eastern sound to safety at Phaleron. The Athenians have spiteful tongues, and I have often heard men grudge the crown to Aigina, just as I have heard it said that when Adeimantos hoisted sail and moved off in the morning, he was in flight before battle was even joined. But the truth is that all did as they had been asked to do, and more.

In the morning we could see Persian soldiers still posted along the opposite shore, and so we put out to sea, and expected their ships. When they did not come, we sent scouts round the headland, and they found the bay of Phaleron empty. So we returned to Salamis and beached our ships and rested, and ate upon the shore, and watched the Persians across the water march away from their strong points, one by one.

Do you imagine, Great King, that I was frenzied with pride, and rejoiced over your father's defeat? Well, naturally I was pleased with myself. But it seemed to me that what I had accomplished was beyond what could have been hoped for; I was awestruck at it. And since it was beyond human possibilities there must have been gods with us. I remember walking along the shore, and it was laden with Persian dead. They lay like stranded fishes, thick as the shining bodies in a netted shoal, and the water washed round them, tarnishing the lapping scales of bronze upon their sides, clouding their open eyes. Many of them were brilliant with gold, jewelled armlets and rings, that caught my companions' eyes. I walked on. I'm not a crucifier of dead bodies, Great King, nor a robber of them; some of those dead were craven, but most were brave, and being slaves to their ruler they did not choose to come here to die.

'My family could eat for days for the value of one of those rings!' said one of my companions, when we had walked some way. 'Or plant a scorched glade with a hundred sapling trees,' another said.

'Help yourself,' I said dryly. 'You are not Themistokles!' and Aristeides, who was walking with me, smiled again.

At the end of the promontory, when we reached it, we found

roughly piled a little cairn of stones, just above the beach. We strolled over to it, in idle curiosity. It was topped with a stone bearing a scratched inscription. 'Xanthippos' dog, washed up here, drowned,' I read.

🏛🏛🏛

At noon that day we sailed away after our enemies, reaching Andros by nightfall. We demanded an indemnity from them, as a fine for Medising – that special word for treason involving the King. The Andrians were not very willing. I said two gods accompanied me, called Persuasion and Compulsion; and they answered two other gods dwelt with them, and would not go away, Poverty and Inability, who would prove stronger than the might of the Athenians. At this answer we set about ravaging the island and assembled the allied war council to consider what to do next.

The meeting on Andros turned out to be important to me, because of what was said of it later, though at the time it seemed unremarkable enough – a working meeting, coming to a sound conclusion. Giddy with triumph the men of the fleet were already talking of sweeping on to the Hellespont, especially the Athenians. We considered it. I said it would be a great strategic advantage to us to break down Xerxes' bridges, thus cutting off his line of retreat. But Eurybiades thought that, if we were going to the Hellespont, it should be to build another bridge, besides those already there, and so speed his retreat. For the aim was not to destroy Xerxes, but to be rid of him out of Greece as soon as possible. 'If we make him desperate, there's no knowing what damage he may do.' There was good sense in that opinion, and I accepted it, but I took advantage of it too, saying to my colleagues, 'Once more then, the cause of all the Hellenes requires a great sacrifice from the Athenians. For if the Hellespont remains closed we shall be hungry this winter, since much of our grain is brought to us through that strait, and we have lost our harvest. I agree that it would be wisest to rid ourselves of the Persians as fast as we can; but what will the rest of you do for Athens, that we may not starve?'

They said they would sell us grain out of their surplus, and I replied that we had no funds, having indeed been hard put to it even to find money to leave Attica and man the fleet. Then Eurybiades suggested that we collect reparation money from all the islands that had Medised, and that all the money we collected should be paid to Athens to keep her going till the spring. In spring we could think again about breaking Xerxes' bridges. I accepted the offer of money, and agreed. And then we all ate and drank together very amiably, and went to bed – I in the house of Timocreon the poet, of whom I will write in a moment.

The next day I addressed the whole Athenian fleet. I told them we would not advance any further. They were angry, and chanted 'Hellespont! Hellespont!' at me. I can remember exactly what I then said, with thousands of witnesses. I told them to beware of hubris. Not we alone, but the gods had struck down our enemies. We should give thanks. And, the season being late, we should go home and patch up our houses and get some corn into the ground. That's what I said. And in saying it, it's true, I was recommending the Athenians not to break Xerxes' bridges. But it has been said that I also wrote a letter to your father, claiming credit for having stopped the fleet from cutting him off in Europe. And I did this, it is said, to curry favour with him, that I might be free to Medise at my leisure. Great King, my ruling lord, I did not write to Xerxes, not at that time, or at any other. It is true, when I needed your protection, my Lord Artaxerxes, and all Greece was ringing with the tale of that letter, I let you believe I had written it, and so let the story recommend me to you. It is a lie. Why would I have wanted to do that, at the height of my triumph? Did they think I could foresee what they would do to me? Gods, had I foreseen it, I would have committed treason to more effect! See, I have written, 'I would have committed treason', and yet it seems that I would not. For now, after all, my chance of revenge has come, and I'm rather dramatically refusing to take it. Yet it still angers me that they could believe such a tale against me. To be precise, the tale is that I chose some servants whom not even torture could persuade to reveal my message, and sent them to Xerxes, with a moonshine message. Behind it lies the ugly truth – I am so hated that when I had been driven from the city they put my servants to the question, under torture, to make them say I had committed treason, and could get nothing out of them. I have been lucky at least in this; I have had faithful service even from slaves. Those nearest me have loved me.

Now I face death, Great King, I beg forgiveness from you for the deceit I practised on you over that letter story. I don't in the least mind cheating a King, but I'm sorry to deceive a friend. Or did I deceive you? You must have looked for that letter in your archives, when I turned up; you can't have found it. Was that another occasion when my insolent boldness amused you?

When I had not written the letter from Andros, and we had

done what we could there, we sailed to Paros, and levied contributions from thence, and from nearby islands. At this time, too, various men whom the war had caught away from home, or who had arranged to be out of Athens, came to me asking permission to return home. Most of them offered money to smooth their path. And at that time money was particularly useful. I would not help those whose complicity with the enemy had been too flagrant, and I didn't help Timocreon the poet, although he had lent me his house, not because I was bribed by one of his enemies as he alleges – and he gets believed, too, for he had more enemies than most men – but because he had once circulated a cruel little jingle about Simonides, a better poet than he and a friend of mine.

Having collected our indemnities we sailed back to Salamis. There I paid over all the money from the islands, faithfully into the Athenian treasury. What had been paid to me personally, of course, I kept.

And now once more the Salamis channel was packed with ships, ferrying the Athenians home to empty Attica. Riding through the country far inland went scouts, looking for the King, and among them a Spartan contingent who continued far beyond the frontiers of Attica, and kept going till they found him. Then they asked him for satisfaction, for killing a king of theirs; and he smiled, they said, and answered that Mardonios would pay the debt. Mardonios in fact was staying behind, and keeping with him in Thessaly the pick of that great army, ready for a new offensive in the spring.

I was in Athens among the first of those returning. The land was desolate. The olive groves were rows of charred stumps; they would not run with gold again for many years. The corn had been burnt where it stood, and even the thyme and bitter herbs of the mountain had been fired, and ripples of black banded the mountain side, where fire had tracked before the winds. The city lay in ruins. The nouses of the poor, built only of mud brick, had suffered worst; they had been crumbled into poor mounds of debris by fire and the ram. Rich men's houses, made of masonry, had lost their roofs but boasted some standing wall at least. The streets were choked with rubble, the statues were all gone. There was no sign of the little water-carrier that I had erected, Harmodios and Aristogeiton, made by Antenor in bronze, had gone from the agora. What Persian wants an image of tyrannicides? Most probably, we thought, some of the Peisistratid curs whom Xerxes brought with him pointed them out as enemies and had them melted down.

Packs of dogs roamed the streets, starving and savage. All the fountains and wells were fouled with muck piled into them. The walls had been razed to the ground. Fire and crowbar had sheared away the crowning glories of the Acropolis, leaving it flat and bare, a blackened stump, as of a ruined tree. Only a few columns of the temple of Athene, saved, one supposes, by a wind bending the flames, stood in a broken row, with most of their architrave down. Before the temple the sacred olive tree stood shrivelled and charred, with one small branch miraculously still green upon it. But all the kouroi and kourai, the shining marble boys and girls, who with their placid smiles had crowded the Acropolis, a serene throng, dreaming of the past – all these were thrown down and broken, even the newest and loveliest of all, the boy that Kritias made, so beautiful that he made all the others look stiff and frozen.

They looked now like the crippled and mutilated bodies of the slain. Because they had been offered to the gods, and were sacred, we made a trench, and buried the broken torsos, and the disfigured smiles, calling on the gods to witness the blasphemy. Then I left the Athenians making brushwood and canvas roofs for their houses, and setting about the autumn ploughing, and I returned to the allied fleet.

回回回

First the allied commanders made offerings to the gods, our gratitude for their saving help being sharpened by our knowledge of future need, for Mardonios like a cloud loomed over Thessaly, and was still to come. We dedicated three of the ships we had captured; most splendid vessels, with gilded poops, and three-pronged rams, looking very magnificent, but also too battered to be seaworthy, or I'd have grudged them to the gods till they promised to man them and sail with us. In any case I'm not sure about forked rams. They look ferocious enough, but they make it harder to disengage the ship after impact with the enemy, and that cuts two ways. One of these ships was offered at Sounion, one on Salamis, and one at the Isthmus.

At the Isthmus the field had grown green again, with the coming of autumn rain, and the absence of tramping feet during our long campaign. We gathered our plunder there, and divided it. Many of the captured ships had been carrying money, and treasure of various sorts. The ships were themselves valuable, and then there were the personal possessions of the captured and the dead. From the proceeds we made an offering to Delphi – a tall statue of Apollo, holding in his hand the prow of a ship. The men of Aigina made an offering of their own besides, to commemorate their prize for valour.

Then one last thing remained to be done; the assembly of generals had to give their own prize of valour, to the one of their number whose services had been of most worth in the campaign. The prize is only a crown of olive, that the day after it is given has wilted, and on the next day is shedding its leaves. I thirsted to have it nevertheless, and the wearer is chosen with great solemnity, the votes being laid on an altar, that the gods may bear witness. When at the Isthmus we sought an altar, not being in any city, we could find only a local sanctuary, a flat rock standing on the shore, that the people held sacred to Poseidon, worshipping him there. So confident was I that the crown would be mine, that I did not vote, but instead walked apart a little way, leaving other Athenians to vote for Athens. The Isthmus shore is beautiful to walk on, blue water, long distances and misty heights, capped, the eye cannot clearly tell, either with cloud or with snow. I walked, and nobody came to fetch me. At last I returned, and found everyone quarrelling, though shamefaced, they hushed when I appeared. I soon heard what had happened. Everyone had received one vote, presumably his own, for first place, and had voted second for me. Because of this they were quarrelling, and would not give the prize. Before evening they had all struck camp and sailed away, except the Spartans; and Eurybiades, who was deeply ashamed, came to see me, and made generous speeches, and asked me to go down to Sparta with him the next day. I suppose, though I had laughed and made light of the lost crown, I was hungry for recognition, so I went. But even at the time I thought that if I had served Xerxes as I have served the Hellenes I should have been better rewarded.

On the journey down to Lakedaimon I tried to persuade Eurybiades that the whole quarrel was funny, more than disgraceful, as indeed it was. And Eurybiades declined to laugh with me, but instead became more and more respectful at my contempt for glory. Of course, he was only a Spartan, and the Spartans are so simple that it would never occur to them that one might laugh and be wounded at the same time.

The valley of Lakedaimon is beautiful – wide, and level, green with olive trees all unburned, and ringed with hills. To the west the Taygetos mountain rises like a wall, bright with snow. Sparta, though, is a dreary sort of place. It has no walls, for, they tell you proudly, it has never needed them, and lacking walls it straggles across its plain. It grew from four villages, and having four centres seems to have none. The temples are old, lumpish and crude; the only buildings they seem to care for are the mess halls to which they all belong. They eat in these messes, and the main entertainment there is soldiers' talk, and soldiers' jokes, and the main dish a filthy black broth made of pig's blood, which the old men in particular lap up greedily, leaving what meat there is to younger men. I am glad to say that I suffered such entertainment as this once only, the first night of our stay there, when, having arrived a day earlier than expected, Eurybiades took me into his ordinary mess, to eat with his fifteen regular companions. After that, when it got round that I was in Sparta, I ate in the kings' mess, and in the ephors' mess, and every mess in Sparta competed to invite me, so that I had to refuse some, and those who had managed to entertain me boasted of it to others. They brought game and cheese and figs to table in my honour, and though they still carefully doled out the scant measure of wine that they each drank for themselves they poured it more freely for me. It seems that to give tone to the proceedings they have a custom of making speeches about the noble deeds, if any such there be, of anyone who is eating with them, or any of their own number who has something to his credit, and so I found my own praises ringing in my ears over and over again, an ordeal not without a certain interest.

Themistokles, it seems, was the only Hellene outside Sparta whose exploits were worthy of praise. It seemed that I was the wisest man in Hellas, the one who had known that battle should be given at Salamis rather than anywhere else, if Sparta was to be saved. Until then, Great King, I confess I had not really seen myself as the saviour of Sparta!

While I was there they held a great assembly to offer thanks to their gods for victory – hideous gods, very ancient, made of hacked wood, and standing upon altars crusted with dried-up blood. After the sacrifice they brought Eurybiades and me before their assembly, and gave him a crown for courage. I watched that not without a pang of jealousy, though indeed he had fought stoutly and deserved it well enough; and then taking me by surprise they brought another ring of olive, and crowned me with it, saying it was for wisdom. Then they all stamped and cheered me, till the glory made me weep. I was never to reap such honour in my own city.

While I was in Sparta, I met Pausanias in the street one day, and he asked me how I liked Spartan life.

'Well enough, my friend,' I told him, 'though it does have disadvantages.'

'What are those?' he inquired, smiling.

'One is always in a crowd here,' I said, 'or a guest at a crowded table. There is no chance to speak with any of you quietly, man to man.'

'And which of the Spartans is it, Themistokles,' he asked, 'in whose honour it might be said that Themistokles wished to know him, man to man?'

'Well,' I said, laughing, 'there is a certain Pausanias, among others!'

When I rose the next morning, there was a fine horse waiting outside my door, and beside it Pausanias, ready mounted, attending me. So we rode out of the town together, towards Taygetos. In a little while we left the plain, and began to climb a foothill of the mountain range – a foothill only, but nevertheless brutally steep, so that we took a path at a tangent, and our horses picked their way carefully. He was a much better rider than I, and at turns of the path he kept having to wait for me. At last we reached a small craggy outcrop which made a natural platform, and turning our horses free to crop the flowers of autumn we sat and gazed. We could see the roofs of Sparta as a blotch of earthen colour on a sea of green treetops. The hills surrounded her like the rim of a dish.

'Hollow Lakedaimon,' I murmured, out of Homer.

'A fair enough place,' he said, glancing round swiftly, 'but to an Athenian it must seem oppressive.'

'How?' I asked.

'There is no shore, no sea, no change,' he said, but I got the impression he had changed his mind, and the subject.

'Tell me,' he said after a pause. 'How did you come to be the greatest man in Athens?'

'I am not that,' I said. 'The Athenians are all my fellows. Anything I have achieved has been achieved by persuading men who all the time could have cast votes to stop me.'

'Could have, but did not,' he said. 'How strange the ways of the Athenians seem to us, who hold the common people so much our enemies that we live among them as in an armed camp, in hostile country.' At this I launched into praise of democracy, telling him how the high born in our city were capable of anything that benefited their faction, while the common people were sound, and, indeed, it was from the common people that I derived my power. Even Kleisthenes, I told him, who had shaped the democratic laws by which we lived, had apparently been ready to Medise to defend his settlement. Indeed, only the men of common stock could be

trusted with the conduct of the city. I didn't know what I was
doing, planting such ideas in his quicksilver head, sowing seeds of
his ruin, and of mine. I had no means of knowing, even though he
questioned me closely, especially about Kleisthenes. I was simply
enjoying myself. I have met few men so pleasant to talk to as
Pausanias was. He was so alert, so keen, so overjoyed and interested
by anything new, that the weariest commonplace came to life when
told to him. He would try to encompass things within the narrow
circuit of Spartan ideas, and realise at once it wouldn't do; and
instead of freezing, like his fellow Spartans, he would be delighted,
like a child, the first time you tell him that beyond the furthest
hill he can see lies more land, and beyond that still more. Possibilities were lands to Pausanias. So to spend time with him on his
flowery mountainside was as refreshing as the company of boys.
Like a boy he had a kind of foolish grandeur in his opinions, and
I did not see how little weight he would have, how little steadiness,
outside his own grim world. Sparta breeds fine men of unimpeach-
able virtue and courage, who are ruined when they go abroad; and
there was I breathing alien air to him.

When we had pleasantly idled away a morning, we rode back
to Sparta, and I announced that I would leave the next day, for I
had duties in Athens. On the ride back we were hungry, having
left without eating, and I grumbled a little. Pausanias saw a helot,
toiling in a field and, stopping, he demanded the man's midday
meal from him. I expostulated in vain. Pausanias brushed aside my
protest, and took a small loaf and a lump of cheese, and offered
them to me smiling, and saying he was not himself hungry, being
used to a manly life. Glory or no glory, there are things in Sparta
that made me glad to leave.

And what a leave-taking they gave me! I found the whole street
outside my door full of important men, and a gilt bronze chariot –
the finest in Sparta they said, standing waiting for me with a team
of matched horses yoked to it; a gift, they told me, for a friend of
Sparta. I was delighted, as well I might be, since I had never before
received so splendid a present. (You had not yet, Great King, had
occasion to give me three cities!) I got into the chariot, and made
a flamboyant speech of thanks, giving them just what they wanted
to hear – at least any Athenian statesman is an old hand at pleasing
an audience – then I flicked the gilded reins and drove away. And
at the outskirts of the city a detachment of three hundred young
men was waiting for me. They fell in behind as I drove past them
and, forming a guard of honour, marched with me all the way to

the frontiers of Lakedaimon, and there halted, and cheered me out of sight. Were it not for the day of Salamis, I'd be tempted to think leaving Sparta was the grandest thing I've ever done!

Getting home to Athens in winter brought me down from the clouds abruptly. Winter does not usually afflict the Athenians as it does folk further north, or east. The snow lies on Hymettos, and on Parnes, but does not lie in our streets. There is only a bitter ice-laden rain, coming on cutting winds from the north, and a cold sunlight of terrible clarity. But even these rigours are much to bear for men without houses. Most people had left their women and children still in safety, and were living in a rough and ready manner. We gave orders which made it possible for all the land to be ploughed and sown, even if only slaves remained on it and the owners had not returned. There was a certain dignity about it all – men going up a scorched path to lay the accustomed offerings on ruined altars – surely such a sight must be pleasing to the gods. But it was very uncomfortable, and spirits flagged. I remember making a speech to the Assembly, not wanting any particular decision from them, but just to cheer them up. 'Athenians,' I said, 'even for the Trojans the sack of their city was the end. But we, who have lost as much as they, are unchanged, and meet here in the same place as before, indomitable. The essential spirit of other cities, maybe, lies in some well-loved place, some shrine, or ancient stronghold. But though we love our places not less than other men, the spirit of Athens is not attached to hills, nor to marble monuments, nor even to the graves of our fathers; wherever as free men we meet to decide our actions, there Athens is, unconquered and unharmed. The ruin that we see around us does not harm us; for it affects only what is external; whereas we are fighting for an inward thing, our freedom; and pillage though he may the King shall not take that!'

Brave words; but behind them I knew, as all of us did, that our victory at sea had saved the Spartans, but only the Spartans could save us, when in the spring Mardonios came again. Your father, Lord Artaxerxes, whom we had driven home like a dog with his tail between his legs, was not a very good general; too proud for the job perhaps, too prone to believe in his own might. Truth to tell, Mardonios was a tougher prospect without him.

That winter I found time to cross to Salamis, and marry the girl I had betrothed. She was never to be meek and gentle, like my first wife; she was always proud and spirited. For her domestic failings I cared nothing, for by then I had companies of slaves who had served me for a long time, and were quite able to run a house without help or guidance from a mistress. But something about her has always been a trouble to me; something unbridled. Too spirited for a woman, perhaps, she often reminds me uncomfortably of myself. And the first night, with friends within earshot, playing and singing outside the door, as the usual custom is, she refused me, and struggled so that I had to use force; and when I had overpowered her she submitted swiftly, that it might be over. Yet she had contrived the marriage; she might have escaped me, by keeping her mouth shut. Though she behaves so badly, yet the truth is I rather like it. At least she never bores me. I was proud when I learned a little later that she was carrying a child.

Sikinnos turned up again that winter, coming down from the hills where he had been hiding with the country folk. I freed him at once, but he stayed with me, living in my household as a free man, teaching the boys, until a time came when the Thespians were enrolling new citizens; and I got him admitted there, and made him sufficiently wealthy.

The winter lingered into spring. At the spring elections the citizens elected Xanthippos and Aristeides to the college of ten generals. I welcomed them. And when it came to giving commands for active service Aristeides got the army, and Xanthippos the fleet. There's no doubt that was rash of me, I suppose. But it never occurred to me Aristeides was not my friend; indeed danger made us all act like blood-brothers to one another, for a time. And I had a reason, a good reason, for supporting their appointments. I wanted to be at the centre of things – at the Isthmus, at Sparta, in the Assembly, where the decisions were made. I wasn't going to repeat Miltiades' mistake, of sailing away after chancy victories, leaving enemies behind him. Besides, I'm not the man to worry who does things, as long as the right thing is done. I had stepped down to others before, and relied on my tongue to persuade them. So when spring came I was happy enough to let Aristeides march to victory, and Xanthippos sail there, as long as they did what I advised, and I stayed near the heart of power. It was as well if I wasn't the centrepiece again, for the Spartans had overdone things a bit, and men in Athens were jealous of my fame. A fellow from Seriphos, for example, who followed me around, saying it was not my own merit that had won me honour in Sparta, but the fame of Athens, my city. Once, twice, three times, I was glad to agree with him. But when he kept on and on, I answered him, 'It's quite true; *I* should not have been famous had I come from Seriphos; but neither would *you* though you had been an Athenian!'

Before the fine weather Alexander came, slippery Alexander, from Macedon, bearing, of course, messages from Mardonios. The way in which he was dealt with shows very well what sort of role I saw myself playing, though on this occasion I was foiled. We brought him first before the ten generals, and heard what he had to say. He was offering terms. Mardonios would have liked to detach us from the others, and use our ships to turn the Isthmus defences. He was prepared to bargain for such advantages. Now, although we had long since arranged to have one of our number in sole command of a fleet or army on active duty, we were still using the rotation of command laid down by Kleisthenes when no force was in the field; a system which still seemed safer in time of peace. And it happened that Alexander presented himself to us on my day. All the others were in favour of sending him packing at once, with a dusty answer, but I argued against that, and wielded my authority. It was a heaven-sent opportunity, as I saw it, to blackmail the Spartans. Let them think we might be wavering, and perhaps they would promise us some effective help. But Aristeides in particular was unhappy about it, even when I had carried the day, and got the others to agree. He said it showed Athens in a bad light; the slightest suspicion of entertaining Persian proposals, he thought, however unjustified, would attach a smear of Medism to one's reputation. I gathered that he was speaking not only of the city, but of me personally, and I thought the idea ridiculous; had we not, had not *I*, been the chief means of the Persians' defeat?

We gave Alexander a good house – one of the few with a watertight roof on it – and appointed a sufficiently distant day for him to speak to the whole Assembly; and, sure enough, before the appointed day an embassy came hot-foot from Sparta. I wanted to make sure that any offer we squeezed out of them was made before witnesses enough, so I contrived that we should hear them, after Alexander, in the full Assembly. Then I felt I had everything ready : Alexander would offer terms, the Spartans would be alarmed, and offer help; we could seem unconvinced till they bid their offers high enough, and promised to hold Mardonios in Boiotia, and so keep him out of Attica, and, as soon as we had that, we could tell Alexander to get out. It was a good diplomatic plan, but it overlooked the fact that it was Aristeides' day that the debate fell on; so it would be he, not I, who would speak in the Assembly on behalf of the college of generals, and so effectively be in charge.

Mardonios' offer was a good one, of course – it had to be that, but it was so good I almost wondered if it would tempt the people. It was good enough anyway to terrify the Spartans. Athens was to be taken into the King's friendship, all past offences forgotten, and no further vengeance taken. She could govern herself, keep her own lands, and take for herself any other lands in Hellas she desired. The King himself would pay to rebuild her temples, streets and squares; all this if Athens would befriend his cause. Having delivered this message, Alexander added words of his own. He had, he said, always been our firm friend. As our friend he advised us to accept the terms we were offered. We had no possible chance of winning against Persian infantry, and would suffer most from the coming storm if we were adamant.

As soon as we had heard him out, we heard the Spartans. They appealed to our loyalty, expressed their sympathy for our sufferings, and offered to support our women and children, and our old and sick, for as long as the war might last, since we had lost our harvest. Then was the time to have told them that nothing less than the Spartan army north of our frontier would keep us firm, to have used a little blackmail. But when Aristeides rose to move a reply he proposed an answer to Alexander first, and so threw the chance away. The answer he proposed for Alexander was as follows. 'We know very well the King is mightier than we, and yet we still cling to freedom enough to fight for it. No matter how much you urge it, you will never have our agreement to your proposals. Tell Xerxes that while the sun runs in its usual course across the sky he shall have no alliance with us; we shall oppose him, trusting in the gods whom he held lightly when he burned their temples down. And let not Alexander come to us again with words like these, urging unholy deeds on us. He is the guest of our city, and we would not like him to come to any harm while he is here.'

Naturally enough the Assembly voted happily to endorse this answer. But I sat grinding my teeth, and clenching my palms in frustration and dismay, so angry was I at the noble foolishness of what was being done.

When Alexander, receiving his answer, and seeing the vote, bowed himself out, a little stiff, a little flushed with anger, and withdrew, Aristeides rose to speak again. This time he presented for approval the answer he had made ready for the Spartans. I have heard him make many good speeches, but never a better than he made then. If a noble answer was all the occasion would yield for us, then certainly he did well enough. He told the Spartans it was ignoble in them, knowing, as they had cause to know, the temper of Athenian courage, to fear that we would make terms with the barbarian. 'Not all the gold in all the world, or the fairest and richest lands under the heavens would buy us to take sides with the Medes, and enslave our countrymen. How could we do so, even if we wished, when there are many things which make it impossible? First there is the burning and destruction of our holy places, and the images of our gods, which force us to pursue the destroyer with implacable resentment. Then there is our common brotherhood with the Greeks, our common language, the altars and sacrifices of which we all partake, the common character we all share. Should the Athenians betray all these, it would indeed be ill done. Know from us now what you should have known before, that while one Athenian remains alive we will not join with Xerxes. As for your promise of sustenance for our families, now that ruin has befallen us, we are ready to endure hardship as best we may; but what we do ask of you is that you march forth, and do battle with Mardonios before he again enters Attica!'

So that's the answer we voted to give the Spartans; an answer calculated to warm the hearts of the Athenians; a generous answer and a proud one. That's how Aristeides saved Athens from the least suspicion of Medism, and laid her open once more to the ravages of the Mede. For just how little all that sentiment about our common character amounted to in Sparta was shortly to appear. Mardonios began to march south, and the Peloponnesian allies began to beaver around at their Isthmus wall again. We sent entreaties, and they did not come.

They did not come; so once again we embarked, in every ship and boat we could find, and left the land empty behind us. Once again we stood on the Salamis shore, and watched smoke rising over Attica. This time the smoke did not last so long; when the new roofs had smouldered away there was little else to burn. Aristeides moved a solemn curse on all who Medised; I, in my heart voted a curse on any man who trusted the Spartans. Accepting a crown from them, and a gilt-bronze chariot was very well; trusting their panhellenism was quite another thing.

Aristeides was appalled at their callousness and, to do him justice, disposed to admit, in private, that my plan might have come off better; but underneath, however many second thoughts he had, we were again at odds. For this was the latest, and was to be the last, thing to divide us; he was a man for all the Greeks, and I was a man for Athens. This conflict showed clearly later; for the moment, meeting under canvas on Salamis, we agreed. We agreed to send delegates to Sparta, who were not to leave till they got what they had come for, and if all else failed were to threaten the Spartans that we would Medise, and our ships would turn the Isthmus defences. For this job we could not spare Aristeides, or so I said, secretly thinking that for this job we could not trust him; and the others declared they could not spare me. In the end we sent a carefully mixed delegation, led by Xanthippos, who as commander of the fleet would know how to play that last throw, and Kimon, then holding a public appointment for, I think, the first time, and with them Myronides. They went down into Lakedaimon, and we waited and wondered what we could do alone, if it came to that.

All over Hellas it is a well-known tale what happened to our embassy in Sparta. They delivered their reproachful message and asked that the Spartans should march. But the Ephors said they would answer on the day following, and the next day they postponed the meeting for another day, and so on for ten days. And all the while they were labouring to put battlements on the Isthmus defences. In the city of Sparta they were keeping the Hyakinthia, yet another festival. The Spartans can meet every crisis, it seems, with some imperative piety or other. At last on the tenth day our delegates were admitted to see the Ephors again, and they then delivered the second part of the message; if the Spartans would not do what was right, we would look to our own safety, and make what cause we could with the King. Then Chilios of Tegea, who was present, and whom the Spartans honoured as a friend, also spoke, and said that if the Athenians sided with the barbarian, then, however strong the Isthmus wall, there would be ways enough open into the Peloponnese.

Then the Ephors coolly replied that they could not understand what the fuss was about; the army of the Spartans under Pausanias was already at the frontier, marching north, at that very moment; to which Kimon in exasperation replied that it was a fine thing to trick your friends instead of your enemies. I notice that from the first Kimon thought of himself as a friend of the Spartans.

On the plain of Eleusis, the Athenian hoplites, eight thousand men in arms, met with the Spartans and their allies. We had half-expected to find Mardonios waiting there, but he had withdrawn, in haste, on hearing that the Spartans were marching, and had chosen his ground near Plataia, on the plains beyond Kithairon. As a result Delphi was wrong again – they had promised us victory, 'fighting in our own land' and we waited only to swear oaths before marching out of it. Delphi, at that time, was having a particularly bad patch; only a week or so earlier they had been threatening the Spartans with being driven from the Peloponnese 'by the Medes and the Athenians', apparently supposing, like Alexander, that Athens would change sides; but even after this débâcle Delphi was formidable, and the Plataians thought it worthwhile to pull up their boundary posts and present us with their territory, so that it might indeed be our own land we would fight in. Great is Apollo at Delphi, whose reputation survives even his own priests! As for the Plataians, never were there allies such as they; the Athenians might do well to consider that, and to remember that their loyalty was acquired by friendship, not by force. The conduct of the Plataians might well have shamed the Spartans, who, having idled while our land was ravaged, were not above taking advantage of us, even while they came to our aid.

At Eleusis, for example, when all the gathered armies were laying their shields on altars and swearing brave oaths of eternal friendship, the Spartans added an unheard-of clause to the oath. It was a fine oath otherwise, the oath for Plataia, full of ringing Hellenism, the brotherhood of all the Greeks. 'I will do whatever the generals order. I will bury the dead of those who have fought as my allies, on the field, and will not leave even one of them unburied. After defeating the barbarians in battle I will tithe the city of the Thebans. I will never destroy Sparta, or Athens, or Plataia, or any of the cities which have fought as our allies, nor will I consent to their being starved, or cut them off from running water, whether we be at peace or war....' Fine sentiments indeed. But in the midst of all this the Spartans were not above thinking how well it would suit them if Athens, their most powerful rival, were never to be rebuilt, and so we found ourselves being asked to swear also '... and I will never restore the temples which have been burned and cast down, but will leave them to remain as a memorial to men hereafter of the impiety of the barbarians'. A somewhat obvious trick, since none of their temples had been touched.

Myronides, in particular, still smarting from his long wait in Sparta, was angry, and wished to refuse to put the oath to the Athenians. Aristeides and I were both ready to accept it – Aristeides in cold anger, but knowing that at all costs unity must be preserved, and ready for that reason to give in, as I had done, over the command of the fleet, when I was myself in such a dilemma. I accepted it for that and another reason; I could see, in my mind's eye, a dream furthered by it – a dream of the Athenians living in glory, in a mint-new city, built beside their ships, at Peiraieus, leaving the old city, high and dry, a garden of ruins and flowers, as a memorial to the land-locked past.

I dare say I was the only Athenian to swear the temples clause of that oath with a light heart.

We marched through the passes of Kithairon, and encamped north of the mountains, on the foothills, looking down at the enemy on the plains. Once more there was a wait to be endured – a long one. And a very uncomfortable one, too, for Mardonios cut us off from our best source of water, and we were thirsty. It was during the parched days of waiting that a crisis blew up. We might have expected it, I suppose, but we did not. All the makings of a very nasty situation for the Athenians were there, however. Assembled together for the first time in years were all the young aristocrats, in arms. The common people, and the new men, most of the democratic faction, were away, manning the fleet, with Xanthippos commanding them. Victory was uncertain, and defeat would bring a swifter and a worse disaster upon the Athenians than upon the others. And the well-born were bound at that time to be discontented. They had lost power and status under the democracy, and now had lost, many of them, the fruit of their lands, and most of their wealth, at Persian hands. And now they sat idle on the sloping ground at Plataia, and talked. Well, there was always talk. Always anti-democratic talk among the younger men – hard to say just where it tipped over into treason, but turn to treason it certainly did. There was a conspiracy to take command and offer to betray the allies in battle. We were brought details, and a list of names. The list was already very long before someone made a mistake, and tried to recruit a loyal man, who told us of it. There was no knowing how far the disaffection had spread.

Aristeides gave orders for the arrest of some eight of the men on the list – the ones we guessed might have been ringleaders. My advice was to execute them immediately, but Aristeides would not hear of it. They might, he said, have friends enough to save them or avenge them if that were tried. Instead he proposed to let two of them escape, and then use that as a reason for releasing the others.

I said, 'You must be out of your mind, Aristeides. We can't possibly let treason in the face of the enemy go unpunished.'

He said, 'They are young, hot-headed. It's true they have lost their property. They do have grievances. We have given them, and any who think like them, a fright by making arrests – a chance to change their minds.'

'You speak very mildly about the public enemies,' I said, angrily.

'The Athenians who in their hearts agree with these,' he said, 'could easily number eight thousand. They could be all of a like mind whom I am to lead in battle. I dare not inquire how many they are, nor challenge them, by punishing their leaders.'

'I suppose you may even be right,' I said. 'But gods! How it stinks! These men will sell their city only because other men share in running it – will Medise because in Athens all men's voices may be heard.'

'You are forgetting Lykides,' he said.

I was; I have even forgotten to tell you about him in the right place, Great King. He was a citizen who had proposed, when we reached Salamis the second time and were discussing what steps to take, that we should after all accept Mardonios' terms, since the Spartans had not yet marched; and the Assembly had been so enraged that they had stoned him to death on the spot, while the women inflicted a similar outrage on his family. 'The opinion we have now to contend with is one that was violently denied a hearing, Themistokles,' Aristeides said.

So I allowed myself to be sent away, starting immediately not even waiting for dawn, to ride back to the Athenians, on Salamis, and discover if the disaffection had spread among the citizens. If it had, I was to rally the people. 'You must go, Themistokles,' Aristeides said, 'because you are the only man who can do it if the rot has spread far.' Off I went, leaving him to deal with rot in the army in his own way. He faked the escape of two of the leaders, and then released the others, hoping thus to steady those who did not know they, too, were suspected. He made a good speech when he set them free, saying that the coming battle was a great tribunal, in which they could clear themselves of any taint of disloyalty to their city. It was all well judged; the plot came to nothing – but looking back it marks in my mind the beginning of that undue sympathy with the undying oligarchic faction among the Athenians that marked Aristeides' later career. It made him a friend of Kimon's, and therefore not of mine.

Before the battle was fought, therefore, I rode away, and I found the Athenians on Salamis unswerving and of good heart. Then I started back again, but too late for the fun. While I was gone

Pausanias and Aristeides fought their battle, the greatest land battle Hellas has ever seen. They swept the myriad hordes of the barbarian quite away, so that of that overwhelming and uncountable number of Persians not three thousand escaped. By the time I rode down from Kithairon they were already burying the dead and dividing the spoil, and the war was over.

Pausanias on the field of triumph played the true Spartan with magnificence. Among the spoils was Mardonios' dinner service, all of gold – so splendid that the Greeks could not believe it was his, but thought it must be Xerxes' own, left behind when he decamped after Salamis. I have one now just like it. Pausanias had the purple cloths spread, and the dishes set out by Persian slaves, and then had a Spartan dinner put on the dishes, and invited his fellow generals to dine. When there was a move to hack up Mardonios' body in revenge for Leonidas, Pausanias had it buried secretly in the night, with due respect. Such was his sense of honour at that time. And later, when Thebes submitted to us and agreed to hand over her Medising leaders and one of them escaped, Pausanias was given the man's wife and children instead, and he at once set them free, though the others he took down to the Isthmus and executed without trial. And yet within a month or two, all Hellas was ringing with the scandal about the serpent column. Really, one couldn't tell what Pausanias might do.

Aristeides, too, made grand gestures; he proposed to use the oath we had sworn for the battle as the foundation of a league in perpetuity of all the Hellenes, a proposal that came to nothing. How shaky a basis there was for unity, after all our marching and sailing together, and all our common danger, appeared as soon as the question of the crown for valour was raised. The Athenians refused to offer it to the Spartans, to whom in truth it did belong; Aristeides with much argument got the question put to a meeting of all the allies. Then Theogeiton, the Megaran, said that if Aristeides' panhellenic league was not to be strangled at birth by this dispute the crown must go to some third city. Kleokritos, the Corinthian, rose to speak and proposed, not Corinth, as everyone had expected, but Plataia, and this both Athenians and Spartans gladly accepted. Slightly less disgraceful, therefore, than the fuss over my crown for Salamis, but showing clearly nonetheless how Greek unity is of Persian making. Still in apparent harmony we all went home; home to poor ruined Attica, in time to plough and sow, and with a good hope of reaping where we sowed this time. In Athens news was waiting; the fleet under Xanthippos had won a victory at Mykale, and the seas were open for us again. They said later that Mykale had been fought on the same day as Plataia.

回回回

The war was over. How hard that was to believe! A long aftermath began, which even now preoccupies the Greeks. Like a boxer skipping and feinting, fists clenched at the ready over his fallen and unconscious opponent, unable to believe that the man is not going to jump up and swing another blow, so have the Greeks, ever since Plataia, dressed up to an imaginary King, to a phantom threat of barbarians marching in armies, declaring at the same time that the danger has not ceased, and that it must never be forgotten, at the same time that the threat to our safety comes always out of Persia, and that there is no risk in driving eastwards, looking for victories, for the King is easy to defeat.

Even when they triumphed over the King, your father, Lord Artaxerxes, the Greeks had no clear idea of what they had done, no idea how vast is the dominion of the Kings, the Great Kings, the Achaemenids. For them Hellas was the centre of the earth – was not the very navel of the earth at Delphi? They did not imagine that having failed to subdue a troublesome border-people the King would cut his losses, and turn his attention to other matters; they could not see that our great victory might not be his great defeat – that he would change his plans, and therefore there was, from the moment the last man turned and fled from the field of Plataia, no more danger to us from Xerxes.

I lost interest in the Persians at once, though we did have mopping-up operations still to perform. I got myself sent with Latychidas, the Spartan king, to reoccupy northern Greece – a necessary job. I wanted to do it myself, because I wanted to keep a sharp eye on the Spartans. When the armed man is down, beware the scorpion on the ground behind you! Pausanias was commanding the allied fleet, with Aristeides as the Athenian commander, and Aristeides had Kimon with him, Kimon having been newly elected to a generalship. The allied fleet was to free the islands, and any cities of the Ionian coast who would allow themselves to be liberated. As you know to your cost, many of them were willing enough; I have cause to be glad now not all of them were! Good luck favoured the Athenians that spring, for Pausanias got a bad attack of Spartans-abroad disease, and gave himself airs, and insulted the allied commanders. I suppose one has to remember that the Spartans still have kings, and are not familiar with democratic manners. Naturally enough, Aristeides was treating everyone with faultless courtesy, and Kimon was showing that repulsive charm which he has always at his disposal, that lordly manner with which he treats men as his equals and yet gives the impression that to be the equal of Kimon is a privilege. Anyway, the upshot was that the allies all came in a delegation to Aristeides, and asked him to command them, for they would serve under the Spartans no longer. Aristeides, who after all loves Athens well enough and who has panhellenic associations on the brain, leapt at the chance, and so set up a new league, 'the Athenians and their allies' with a treasury in the temple of the Delian Apollo. After all, why should the Peloponnesians be the only ones to gang up together!

And what did I think? I thought it one of the most agreeable ironies I had ever witnessed, that the seapower of Athens, for which I had planned and struggled all my life, was now made safe and established by the very man who had grudged me the money for the fleet! Sweetest of all victor's crowns, to see one's opponent carrying out one's own policy with a will! I was never one to mind who carried it out – him or me, as long as the right thing is being done by somebody. And when Kimon with the fleet supported by the new league went patrolling the whole Aegean, pin-pricking the Asian satraps, and winning his easy victories, I wasn't the man to resent that either. Of course he got to be ridiculously popular in the city; but I knew that his triumphs were babies riding on the shoulders of other men's giant victories. I could never bring myself to take Kimon seriously enough.

While Aristeides was establishing his league, Pausanias went home in a huff. People in Sparta were saying that they ought to have known better than to trust him, after the affair of the Serpent Column. For he had made a monument at Delphi, from a tithe of the spoils of Plataia, a splendid tripod of gold standing on a brazen column made of three snakes intertwined. Nobody objected to that, but the inscription read 'Pausanias, Captain-general of the Hellenes, having destroyed the host of the Medes, set up to Phoibos this memorial.' And that made people furious. The Spartans sent a smith to erase the words, and write instead, 'These fought in the war: Lakedaimon, Athens, Corinth, Megara, Tegea, Sicyon, Aigina ...' so on and so on, the names of one-and-thirty cities. Perhaps Pausanias' victory had gone to his head; if so, well, it's a fault I find easy to forgive – as well I might, for men were always telling me my Salamis had gone to mine.

Meanwhile, Latychidas and I were marching around. I was never much of an infantry commander, but I had other reasons than that for lack of enthusiasm for the job of tithing the cities which had Medised. It seemed fair enough that Thebes had been punished; after all she had always been an enemy of the Athenians, and a powerful one at that. There was some point in knocking Thebes. But the others; well it would have cost a lot of effort to bother all of them, and as for breaking their strength ... who but perhaps our noble Aristeides could believe that the Spartans were disinterested in seeking to keep that oath? Extraordinary as is the capacity of the Spartan party in Athens for believing in the superior virtue of those military bullies, nobody objected at the time to letting the Medisers off lightly. Only later, when they wanted my blood, did they find that slackness in punishing collaborators smelt of treason.

As for me, I knew perfectly well what I was doing; I was conducting the opening rounds in the struggle with Sparta. That struggle is inevitable. For the power of Athens cannot grow without overshadowing the power of Sparta, and Sparta will not sink to second place without a fight. Sooner or later, therefore, the Athenians will have to fight the Spartans, in one way or another. To my mind the struggle began almost at once, while the wretched remnants of your army were still in flight through Macedon and Thrace, when the Athenians came home to their city and started to rebuild the walls; but the other Athenians cannot see it, or have let themselves be duped. They have pursued a course of friendship with Sparta, foolishly postponing the showdown, throwing chances away. In a flood of sentiment about the unity of the Greeks they have let themselves be hoodwinked, and for the sake of the Spartans have even punished me for serving them, hounding me out of the land like a criminal, making accusations against me which are, I must admit it to you now, completely false. And yet after the crisis which arose over the rebuilding of the Athenian walls it is incredible to me that anyone with a head on his shoulders could fail to see the Spartans for what they are.

The walls are not where I would have liked them to be. I asked the people to rebuild the city at Peiraieus, making some play as I spoke with the oath we had sworn. Since we could not rebuild our city as she had been, we might as well build her on a new site. But the people were not ready for it. We resolved, therefore, to begin at once to rebuild the walls of the old city, enclosing a wider circuit than before.

While the masons were still marking blocks of stone in the quarries, an embassy came to us from Sparta. They requested us not to rebuild our walls. Instead we were to join with them in flattening the fortifications of any other walled city north of the Isthmus, so that the barbarian, if he came again, might not have the use of any strongholds. The Peloponnese, they assured us, was fortress enough for all Greece. And they added, just in case we had missed the threatening tone, that for the job of dismantling walls they had men on their frontiers, ready to march.

I'm the only man for a crisis such as that; the Athenians looked to me. The first thing to do, I thought, was to get rid of the envoys, and as fast as possible. So we answered we would send an embassy of our own to Sparta, to discuss it with them there. Then I acted fast. I got the Assembly to agree to leave the matter to the generals, on the grounds that it was a question of defence. I got the generals to send me down to Sparta, appointing Aristeides and Habronichos to go with me, but not sending them for the moment. For once I had ungrudging support, for they were all as angry as I was at the dirty trick the Spartans were playing on us, so soon after we had been comrades-in-arms with them. So we were all agreed; I would go down into Lakedaimon alone, and every man, woman and child in the city, every soul who could carry so much as a pebble, would set about building those walls. Aristeides and Habronichos would come later, as soon as the walls were high enough to defend. And for stone every usable block was to be seized, if need be every house wall in Athens, new-made along with old, was to be demolished – anything that would serve for a wall.

Leaving these orders behind me, off I went, riding in my Spartan bronze chariot, just to remind them of the last time I was there. Sparta again; riding under olive trees, and towards the rugged mountains, eating in messes. I liked the black broth a little better, and the men a little worse than the last time. They certainly made me welcome. I began to see that they really thought I had made the Athenians fight at Salamis for their sakes, not our own; that I was a friend of Sparta in the sense that I would put Spartan interests before those of my own city. They had the wrong man there – they needed Kimon for that. However, they seemed to think that it was a good sign that I was the man who had come to answer them.

But I didn't answer them. First I asked for a few days' grace to recover from my journey there. Days passed, and I made no request to see them officially. Soon I was being approached every day by some greybeard or other, asking why I delayed.

'The Athenians appointed three ambassadors for this important mission,' I told them. 'I am waiting for my two colleagues who seem to have been delayed. Without them I am not empowered to negotiate.' So great was my prestige with them that they believed me, and yet all the time messages were reaching them from Aigina, and from Corinth, afraid of us now that we had grown into a sea-power, telling the Spartans that we were at work on our walls. At last they confronted me with some of all this. 'We know for certain,' they said, 'that you are building walls even now.'

'That is quite untrue,' I told them. 'Am I not here to discuss the matter with you? I dare say there is a lot of building going on in Athens – remember that we have not one house left standing in the ruin left by the barbarian, save one or two in which they housed their officers. I expect some of this rebuilding has given rise to mistaken reports.' But naturally I began to be anxious, to wonder how long I could stall them, and if it would be long enough to raise the walls. Pausanias already had murmured to me that he knew I was up to something. He didn't give the game away. I wondered why at the time, but it turned out he was no friend of the Spartan establishment, the stiff-necked Ephors. In time to come they murdered him. I had gained another day's grace, and then they were at me again.

'If you cannot believe me,' I said to them, 'why don't you choose some of your most eminent men, whose word is beyond all question, and send them to Athens to see for themselves.' I suppose that sounded as if I had nothing to hide. Anyway they fell for it, got together a party of dignitaries, and sent them off to Athens carrying in their train a servant of mine, with a message for the generals that they were to be detained with as little fuss as possible until I got safely home.

The next day Aristeides and Habronichos turned up, having crossed on the road with the hostages I fixed for them. 'It's high enough,' they said. 'Just.'

'The gods be thanked!' I said. 'I have lied fit to crack the sky, and there has been no thunderbolt!'

'I am willing to believe you are the only man in Athens who could have done it, Themistokles!' said Aristeides.

I told the Spartans that now that my colleagues had arrived I would like to speak to them. 'Spartans,' I said to their assembly, 'Athens is now provided with sufficient walls, and can protect her citizens. If the Lakedaimonians and their allies wish to negotiate with us henceforward, they must deal with the Athenians as men who know well what is for their own, and the common good.

When we resolved to leave our city, and take to our ships, we did not first ask the advice of the Spartans; when our two cities met in the council of commanders, the advice of the Athenians as to what should be done was as good as anyone's. And now we have arrived at an independent judgement that it is better far, better for ourselves and the whole body of the Hellenes, that our city should have a wall, for when any member of a confederacy does not have equal strength his counsel does not have equal weight. As for your allies, who have complained about us to you – let them pull down their own walls, or admit that we have a right to ours!'

In a stunned silence we withdrew, and hastened to pack up our things to leave, expecting that if we lingered they might try to stop us, and punish us. But before we got away they had summoned us before them again. And to our astonishment they met us with smiles – a little forced to be sure, but smiles all the same – and said that they had not intended to question our independence, but only to offer a suggestion for the public good. And then a lot more empty courtesy about the bonds between us that our mutual help in the war had made. . . .

We laughed most of the way home, to think how they must have been biting back their rage. However, the walls were up, and there was no open quarrel between us. When we got home again we found that Kimon had entertained the Spartan embassy in his house, pouring out very strong wine, and being so absolutely charming that they weren't even absolutely sure they had been prevented from leaving.

Aristeides took me on a triumphal ride around the walls, incredible walls, solid, and high enough, but not exactly beautiful. They were made of a huddle of irregular stones. White marble shone in the fabric here and there, and broken grave-stones, and statue plinths. Half an inscription here, another half there; the round column drums from the temple standing jammed together between great rough-hewn blocks from the quarry, the stone hacked out, not dressed, and the chip marks of the mason's adze still pock-marking them.

'Heavens, Aristeides,' I said at one point, for the benefit of a crowd of proud citizens, who were thronging along with us, 'I thought we were trying to put this up in a hurry – and here someone took time off to decorate it in relief!' And I pointed to a marble block with a wrestling match carved on it, built into the wall above my head. The people laughed.

'I assure you, we were working fast!' said Aristeides. 'Any

citizen here will show you a calloused palm to prove it. And look, over here some poor fellow got caught, and the wall went up on top of him so fast, that he can't get out!' And he pointed to the feet of a statue, poking its toes grotesquely from under a vast slab of rock.

That disgraceful rubble-heap is known to the Athenians as 'Themistokles' Wall' to this very day, Great King, though I was fond of telling them that, far from the wall being mine, I was the only Athenian, man, woman or child, who had laid not a single pebble in it! I'll say this for them all – it stands up steadily and solidly enough. It had a good effect on the city too, for Athens had been transformed from a sea of broken stones to a place swept clean of every loose pebble. One could walk in the streets again without scraping one's shins and twisting one's ankles, and everything was ready to be made new.

But what I was saying, Great King, was that you would think that all this would have opened the eyes of the Athenians once for all about the value of friendship with Sparta, even for those who could not remember the struggle with Kleomenes. And yet it was soon forgotten. Men were soon talking again as though Athens were deep in the Spartans' debt.

I supposed that my crown for wisdom must have been a bitter joke by now in Sparta, but they continued to treat me as their friend, sending gifts at festival times, and making courtesy visits to me when they had an embassy in the city, so I still had some goodwill left to lose. I lost it over the Amphictyonic League. The Amphictyonic League, Great King, is an ancient alliance, a league of states that once went to war to defend the freedom of Delphi. The Spartans proposed at the usual meeting of the league that all the cities which had not fought against Persia should be expelled. And I spoke strongly against that, saying openly that the thirty-one states which had fought were mostly quite small and could not claim to represent all Hellas. In fact, of course, had the Medisers been expelled that would have left a vast majority of the votes belonging to Sparta and her allies, who would then have controlled Delphi. Once again Sparta was using the war as an excuse to extend her power, and once again the best interests of Athens lay in checking the Spartans. On this occasion I succeeded, and the membership of the league remained unchanged. It was remembered against me later in Athens that I had spoken up for the friends of the King, but remembered in my favour in Argos, which was a Medising city, that I had befriended her. When I was in need she sheltered me.

The day of my need was still far ahead of me then. After the war I lived peacefully for nine years in Athens, giving, as I thought, good service still, and not suspecting what was to come. From the time of the Amphictyonic debate, the Spartans treated me no more as their friend, but looked for a supporter of Sparta elsewhere, and lighted upon Kimon, making him 'Proxenos of the Lakedaimonians', loading him with honours and gifts, and getting better value for their money out of him than they would ever have got from me!

The Athenians were pleased with me about the walls. There's no doubt the tricks I played made better street talk for the common man than the high-minded nobility in which the aristocrats traded. They, Great King, were disdainful about it all, sneering at the dishonourable means as though that could undo the achievement. Just so, my Lord, are you shocked by my talent for lying, and will be shocked now by what I confess to you, because I have deceived you grossly. I admit that you have cause for complaint, my King, because you have been deceived to your disadvantage, in that I am now deserting your service, and fobbing you off instead with a cloud of words and a theatrical exit. But the Athenians had profited by my every deceit. Which of the Athenians had the effrontery, while he built him a new house behind safe and solid walls, to complain that it was dishonourable to tell lies to our generous allies the Spartans? Kimon, of course, and his cronies.

There's a kind of selfishness about Kimon so godlike that it takes some understanding. He doesn't care what happens to his city; he doesn't act to get the best possible result, he acts to have it seen that Kimon has acted nobly. He really would have left us defenceless sooner than tell a public lie. He is Achilles, playing at being splendid all day long, his armour always golden, his cloak scarlet, his tent of Tyrian hue. He keeps an open feast in his house, a banquet from which none are turned away, treating the citizens as a good king treats beggars. And they love him for it – selling their independence for a handout of spiced loaf and a dish of wine. I, on the other hand, am Odysseus, who is a trickster, and who invents the means of winning, because whereas *he* wants to live and die nobly, *I* want to win.

In the time after the war, I wanted the Athenians to face their destiny, to challenge the Spartans, to seize dominion over the sea, and with sea power to crush the cruel grip of the Spartans on their once impregnable lands. But the Athenians wanted to ride the crest of victory, chase the King out of the Aegean, seize the trade routes, and, remembering only half of what the Spartans did, treat them as our stout allies and friends. The time after the war was Kimon's time. About that I was perfectly good-humoured; the politics of the city have been my life, and I am a hardened debater, an old campaigner. I don't wound easily, and I know how victory goes in the long run to the man who is right in the long run. I knew I was right. I was content, if I could not get agreement yet on the main issue, to win on smaller things, to prepare the ground. But Kimon was not an Assembly man of the same kind at all; he hated me, with a direct and personal resentment, and with me all democrats, even, I thought, Aristeides, because we had condemned Miltiades his father, unjustly, when he was dying. To Kimon, I suppose, the perfect retaliation for the Athenians having condemned the victor of Marathon is to have them condemn the victor of Salamis also. Spiteful Achilles!

But the time when he found power to act against me was long in coming, for I was immensely popular. The young men hung about my house, to escort me in a deferential and admiring throng wherever I went, calling me Sir, pressing round me, eager to hear my talk. Old men told their sons, and their sons' friends that they knew me, or had served with me then and then, and among my contemporaries I had another reward; they believed me, if I said that from one thing another would follow, or that this plan would work better than that. Nobody now mocked my eagerness to run after wild ideas like hares, for the wildest ideas of all have sent the King of the Lands scuttling from our land of Hellas! You can imagine how I enjoyed myself. And yet almost at once I lost my footing again with Aristeides, and so did not enjoy friendship and admiration where I would most have desired it, but only the usual coldness.

There was a time when our walls were just built, when our ships were safe at Peiraieus, and the ships of all the other allies in the Persian war were lying across the Saronic Gulf, at Poros. I stood up in the Assembly and told them that I had a plan which would be of immeasurable benefit to them, but which would not work if it were once made public. Would they trust me with it? I think they might have done, if someone had not shouted, 'Remember Miltiades!' Whom was he warning – them or me? They told me to confide the plan to Aristeides. If he approved, I could have authority for it.

So he and I withdrew. We went to his house, which was nearer completion than mine, being less elaborate. He called for wine, and we sat together in a little white-walled room, looking on to a stony patch that would be a garden when the masons and tilers had finished. I caught sight of his son, wearing an ephebe's cloak, and carrying a halter, going out to ride, passing us by, and saluting his father, with easy grace. The sight of him rolled the years away, and I remembered in his likeness another lean youngster, walking out to Hippias' fort on Mounychia, or coming to ride one day at Sounion.

'You used to look like that,' I said to Aristeides, smiling.

'Surely not,' he said, frowning, deepening the invading lines on his brow.

'Yes,' I said, 'once. It's a while back.'

'You're snow-capped now yourself,' he said. 'Come, what's this scheme of yours?'

'The allied fleet at Poros,' I said. 'I propose we should attack it and burn it.'

His mouth set rigid, hardened into an iron line. His eyes froze, gazing at mine, into an unblinking stare. So still was he that I might not have taken his silence for anger, but for the light rattle against the table of the cup that he gripped in a fist clenched so tightly it trembled. His anger astonished and wrong-footed me; I had expected no worse than the rueful regret, the dry mockery, that had met my performance in Sparta.

At last he said, 'Why do you propose this?'

'To gain a great advantage. It would make us the most powerful state in Hellas. Once we had done it not even Sparta would be able to match us – her coasts would lie open.'

He said, 'But it would be vile; preposterous. What have they done to provoke us that would justify us in any assault, let alone so monstrous a one as that?'

'They haven't done anything to provoke us,' I said, impatiently, 'but they have been unwise enough to leave all their ships un-defended in one place. Now, just as they tried to take advantage of us, for their own gain, and to stop us building our walls; just as they have tried to take advantage of the war-oaths to crush all their enemies, I propose we should take advantage of them, to do ourselves a little good.'

'I can hardly believe what I hear,' he said, very quietly. 'Those whom you would injure are our allies, who fought beside us in our time of need.'

'Oh, remember what kind of allies they really are!' I cried, jumping to my feet. I wanted to pace fiercely around – I felt caged in his small room. 'Remember Kleomenes, trying to force oligarchy on us, till we kicked him out in a linen basket? Remember the Karneian moon, that keeps them safe till Marathon is fought and won! Haven't you heard how I sweated blood to keep them at Salamis, when they only wanted to abandon us, and sneak off to look after their own? Didn't I have to trick them to make them fight there? Was it easy to make them march to Plataia? Didn't we have to threaten to change sides before they budged? Indeed, indeed, they aren't such allies as to leave us in their debt!'

'Perhaps you would have found them more satisfactory,' he said, 'if you had fought beside them in a battle won by courage, instead of one won by foxy tricks!'

A disbelieving numbness caught my breath, as it had done when Adeimantos before Salamis called me a man without a city. And before I had come round from it, he said, in an altered tone, 'That was unjust, and I retract it. Forgive me, Themistokles, but ... *you* Themistokles, you grieve and anger me so that I am driven to speak unfairly!'

'*Grieve* you?' I said, startled.

'Yes,' he said. 'You, Themistokles, with all your dazzling powers of mind, your wit, your forcefulness! To hear you talk of what will happen and why, to hear you explain yourself, and follow your clear-sighted gaze, is like keeping the company of a god! You make a man see the reasons for things as a sculptor makes one see the bones beneath the flesh. Can there ever have been a man like you? Such gifts! I could almost have loved you, once, if only you were straight. But you are rotten through and through! You will cheat, and lie, and take bribes, and posture before the people, you will sink to anything, you will do anything that serves! You have no core, no moral core. So there is no wickedness you will recoil from to gain an advantage, nothing you won't do if it's slick and clever! You are vile; you are a dangerous man.'

The outburst seemed to leave him exhausted. He sat with his wine cup before him, head bowed, hands clasped on each curved handle.

'Time was,' I said to him, 'when I would have done anything to please you. So if you had loved me, Aristeides the Just – if I had ever had anything from you but chill disapproval for my every fault, self-righteousness directed at me, while you doted on that decorative pea-brained boy of yours – if, *if* you had, then

I might have been what you call straight. I dare say I'd have thought it worthwhile. For you I'd have thrown away the money, all freely offered, that you so begrudge me, to share your dignified poverty; for you I'd have forsworn the tricks, even those that made the Salamis victory; for you I'd have disdained to lie, even to build Athens her walls! Think about it, *Just* Aristeides! What state would this city now be in, if you had loved me? Think about it hard and long, before you ride another high horse, and reject another scheme of mine to do the city good!'

'You would have us turn traitors and fratricides, and you call that doing the city good,' he said. 'It can never be good for Athens that Athens should act unworthily.'

'Oh, have done with the high-minded tripe, and see sense, Aristeides,' I said, brutally, leaning down over him, and thrusting my face into his line of sight. 'Can you point to any harm that has ever come to the city from following me? Even from following me through the mire? But suppose they had listened to you instead – where would they be now? Won't you answer? I'll tell you where they'd be – led away like cattle by the King, to be slaves in Persia, without so much as a fight, all perfectly in the right, and each with his own small share of the Laurian silver to choke on! Do you think they'd thank you for it? As for your clean hands – they are clean because I'm around to do the dirty work for them. I'm the one who gets the ships, and plays tricks to force a battle; but you are happy enough to come home in time for a share in the glory, or to go sailing off in those same bloody ships afterwards! I'm the one who twists his tongue in Sparta, but you don't exactly object to having walls! For myself, if I am wicked, I can't see that anyone is any better who willingly enjoys the advantages I gain for him – not even you, Just man!'

He listened absolutely rigid, unmoving. He did not stir when I had finished. 'I ask you to think hard of what I have said, before you decide to oppose me,' I said, and with that I left him, still rooted to the spot.

No sooner had I left his house than Aristeides went down to the Assembly and told them that nothing could be more advantageous to the city than Themistokles' proposal, and nothing more iniquitous; and the Assembly ordered me to abandon the idea. So I was denied my clever short cut, and the friendship of that one man.

The Assembly, however, let me work towards the same end in other ways. I was voted money to rebuild, and extend, and improve the Peiraieus, and fortify it with a landward wall, and I spent a good deal of time over that. The walls in particular interested me. I made sure they were wide enough for two chariots to pass one another on the circuit along the top. I made them of large blocks, braced with iron clamps. I wanted to make them so high that an enemy would take one look at them and give up an attack as hopeless, but the citizens thought that was extravagant. Still, I got them high enough. I liked to tell the Athenians in those days that if ever they were threatened on land again, they should remove themselves and their property to the Peiraieus, and take to the ships, leaving a few men to guard the walls; and a few would suffice to guard walls such as I had made. The Peiraieus could never be starved out while we held the sea. And the sea was ours. So I talked. Sometimes in the Assembly, sometimes walking with companions, in the city, or in the country round about, or taking the road to Peiraieus. The land with swift mercy grew green again, and forgot its scars, and though we were short of shade then, and yearned for the dappled deeps of shadow under cool olive trees, yet the silvery grey of the tender young saplings gave a watery shimmer to the land new-planted, that promised shade and wealth to come. And I never lacked company, and talk.

Everyone in Athens, save one, wanted to know me. That impudent puppy of a boy, even, who had sent back my gift of dice and refused my invitation, turned up again, smiling and mincing at me. 'Well, my boy,' I said to him, 'time has taught us both a lesson, though we left it late.' I saw no more of him! But there were others I was glad to see. One day, I rode to a meeting of the Council, and dismounted, and gave the bridle to a slave to hold, and there was a crowd of youngsters at the foot of the steps, murmuring and pushing one of their number to the front, and whispering behind their hands. I took no notice till a young voice cried out, 'Themistokles! Lend me your horse.' I looked round, and saw a young man holding out his hand for the bridle, and all his friends awe-struck, staring, their eyes saying clearly they had thought he was bluffing, they didn't think he'd really do it. I stared at him. I'd seen him somewhere before. He'd be handsome if his head were not too big for his body.

'You *owe* me the loan of a horse, Themistokles,' he said, with a shaky smile.

That's it – young lion-head from the quay, waiting to cross to Salamis. I remembered. 'So I do,' I said, handing him the bridle, smiling a little at the way his eyes lit up. He jumped astride, and rode off; but he looked back over his shoulder, to make sure his friends were sufficiently impressed. 'Young show-off!' I muttered, as I went in to my meeting. I had resigned myself to walking home, but he kept the horse for three days, riding it everywhere, which I thought was going rather far. Then he brought it back himself, with a new gilded bridle upon it, and thanked me very gracefully.

'Since all the world now thinks I'm his closest friend,' I said, drily, 'will the boy remind me what his name is?'

'Son of Xanthippos,' he said. 'Pericles.'

'Oh, yes,' I said, 'I know your father. Well, Pericles, will you walk with me this morning?' From then on he walked with me often. There are many good things in the life of an elder states-man in Athens, and the loving admiration of the city's young men is one of them. Listen to Pericles, for example, answering the ques-tion 'who is the most powerful man in Hellas?' with a confident, 'Why, Themistokles!'

'No,' I said, laughing, 'my son is. For the Athenians rule the Greeks, I rule the Athenians, he rules his mother, and his mother rules me!' There was wishful thinking in that jest; the sons of my first wife are all upright, competent young men, but none of them will ever rule anyone, none of them takes after me; how my father would have approved of them! If any son of mine had been likely to make a ruler, it would have had to be the last born, then a babe. But a swift fever killed him in a single night; and my wife bore me only girls after that. Only girls, but pretty ones. I'm glad I reared them all.

It is a good life, that of a famous man in Athens. One morning I'd go and see how my temple was coming on, for I was building a new one – a new one since we couldn't rebuild the old – dedica-ted to 'Artemis Giver of Good Counsel', a dedication which annoyed some people almost as much as Pausanias laying claim to the Serpent Column, but which gave me satisfaction. I had ordered rather an austere temple, with a severe plain colonnade, but all the statuary gilded. It was near my new house, at Melite, where the road to Peiraieus leaves the city. There is a small hill there, and the garden of my house looked across to the Acropolis in the north, and overlooked the new temple to the west. I made myself comfortable there, as much as by Persian standards Athe-nians ever do.

Another morning I would go to the Kynosarges, and watch the young boys wrestle and run. I would sit in the sun, among the other old men, and look my fill at the smooth silken bodies of the young, glowing with oil. Perhaps I would meet Xanthippos there, or Ameinias, whom we still chaffed about missing Artemisia, or Aeschylus, my schoolfriend, whom many thought now outshone even Phrynichos in the theatre. 'That boy of mine talks nothing but your stuff about ships all day long, Themistokles,' grumbles Xanthippos. 'I keep telling him I know something about them myself, but it seems you always know better.'

'I'll talk to him about flute-girls instead, then, shall I?' I ask.

'What d'ye make of him, my dear fellow?'

'Oh, he'll make much of himself, I'd say.'

'Ah, glad you think so. Glad to hear it....' Xanthippos was looking older these days, and thinner. There was less of him, somehow. The viper had turned into a harmless old man. But I was the same as ever, I told myself. I'm as strong as ever. My time to be harmless hasn't come yet, I swear it.

But a time did come when I wasn't re-elected a general. That hurt, but when friends came flocking round to ask how I felt about it I had a ready answer. 'The Athenians treat me like a plane tree. When it rains they flock to me for shelter, but when the sun shines they lop my branches. Wait till it rains again.' I was sure it would. I was busy all the time making ready, holding my party together. To do that I had to keep in the public eye, to keep talking, and being talked about – never a hard task for me. We put up a new statue in the agora, to Harmodios and Aristogeiton, calling it 'The Tyrannicides' – that sort of thing. So I spent my time inside the city trying to manoeuvre them into a strong position against Sparta, and further afield, looking out for Sparta's enemies in any city.

There were moments of glory in those years too. I was chosen choregos again. I asked Aeschylus for a play this time, but he said I should ask Phyrnichos. 'For he has one written, and if he doesn't see it performed this year he will never see it. Besides, you'll like it.' I did. It was a gloating celebration of the discomfiture of the Phoenicians at Salamis. It opened with slaves setting golden thrones for the sea-captains before the fight, and ended with Xerxes executing them upon the shore, in rage at his defeat. It won the prize; and the crown was still green on Phrynichos' grizzled head when we laid him to rest beside his father in the Kerameikos, among the broken remnants of monuments to those who died before Xerxes came. Then I set up a monument to the play's victory.

And then when I went to Olympia; I had the time of my life. I went splendidly equipped, and set up a pavilion of gilded pine and white linen, and took all my sons, and good horses, and a great congress of servants so that I could give feasts and invite hordes of guests. Not even Kimon did better, though he too put on an extravagant show. It's a great meeting-place, the games. Every important man in Hellas is there. From Argos, for example, both the top men in the democracy, which then ruled the Argives, and the disgruntled displaced oligarchs, who had been kicked out when Kleomenes' victory at Sepeia had decimated them, long ago. These last still talked of a come-back, calling the democrats 'slaves' and themselves 'the sons of the slain'. Naturally enough it was the 'slaves' grateful for my help over the Amphictyonic League who visited my table, not the sons of the slain. There were oligarchs enough for *them* to hobnob with, and that golden-tongued bum-sucker Pindar hanging around them all, offering to immortalise beauty or victories. When *he* calls Athens 'city of god-like men' he means men like Kimon. Thank the gods for poets like Simonides, whom a man can invite to his table without shame! The place was nearly as full of poets as of athletes that year, including that rogue Timocreon, whom I had refused to take home with me from Andros, circulating scurrilous verses about me:

> 'We know that Leto,
> Who loves the truth, detests Themistokles,
> That liar, cheat and traitor....'

So he said. But when I went into the stadion, and took my place, the great crowd of people took no notice of the competitions, but spent the whole day pointing me out to each other, those who knew me by sight directing the gaze of those who didn't, praising and applauding me as they pointed and stared. My brother, sitting beside me, grumbled that it took his mind off the pentathlon to be surrounded by so much fuss; and my raw sons blushed, and disliked it, but I was delighted and told them so. 'I have laboured all my life for the good of Hellas,' I said, 'and I am now reaping my reward.'

I have never seen another man enjoy fame such as that. And like a boy given a new sword, who must have it out of its scabbard and decapitate a swathe of grasses just to give the blade a try, I could not resist giving all that glory just a try; I picked on the tyrant of Syracuse, who had brought horses to enter in the chariot races, and set up a very fine pavilion. I made a speech saying to the Greeks that it was an outrage for a tyrant to show his face among us when we had just repulsed the tyranny of the King – and I persuaded them easily, and with a feeble argument such as that, to pull down his purple tents, and refuse to let his horses run. Now it's perfectly true that I had heard that the horses of Epikrates of Acharnae, who was an Athenian and a close friend of mine, had a good chance of winning if Hieron's were out of the way. I regretted having offended Hieron later.

A good life while it lasted; moments of glory and moments of calm. Athens was a strange city to live in, and will be till men forget your father, Great King, and the oath they swore. Not a house in the place but is new, walls straight and clean, everything crisp as a newly minted drachma. The rich all made themselves fine houses, with a tree and a pool in the courtyard, and even the poor men, though their houses were made of mud-wall, and had been hideously tumble-down before, made themselves streets of dwellings with a self-respecting air about them. Palaestra and gymnasium and theatre, and speaker's rostrum on the Areopagus hill, were all new made, all cut from marble that sparkles in the sun, and the magistrates have straightened and widened the streets, and improved the lay-out of the markets; and in the midst of it all rises the Acropolis, girded with a new wall of broken stones, and within the wall bare craggy rock, and broken things. A blackened wall hung with old fetters, partly melted away, and a gap-toothed row of columns, standing broken at different heights. The sacred olive still grows – a single straight green shoot caged in a tangle of blackened branches. Yet how soon the agony faded with which we saw this desolation first! Soon it came to seem right, almost right like that. Athens, our fine new city, cradles and holds skywards towards the gods these broken relics of her past. Looking upwards at the city's shattered crown, when we had time to muse and remember what had once been there, we would find ourselves completing the line of columns with the eye; replacing the fallen capitals, the broken architraves, the smiling serpentine gods poised on the pediments, and making thus out of ruin an intellectual temple, a temple of the mind, beautiful as doubtless the temple of marble never was, being a substantial thing. The rock herself put out flowers to cover her nakedness. From the dry stony debris grew scarlet swaying poppies, and the stiff military iris, saluting the spring. The Athenians still climb the hill, and still make sacrifice there; and every evening the gods, too, honour our shorn sanctuary as they always did, with a shining crown of violet, an immortal brightness in the air.

If I had been content simply to live in quiet, I might be living there still. Yet how could I have changed so greatly, at such a time of life? And how could I have ignored the people, for whom I was the great leader? For the whole of Hellas I was a great leader – had I not seen the wrestlers struggle and fall without an audience, because all eyes were turned on me? And I had all I needed for power. Besides status I had money, having amassed, to be truthful, quite a lot in one way or another. I spent a good deal, of course; rather ostentatiously building my temple to Artemis, and putting up bronzes like the Tyrannicides. And I would have spent a fortune at Delphi, but after the stoa – a long colonnade against the great wall of the temple foundations, which we built overlooking the sacred way, and filled with the prows of your ships – the priests would accept no more from me, but sent my offerings away, and took only those of Kimon. They say now that they knew I would Medise; in fact it was because they are always in the pockets of the Alkmeonids, and the Alkmeonids hate me. Still, it saved my money. And besides money I had time. I wasn't fighting, or sitting in meetings of the generals, and my three sons were old enough now to manage farms, buy and sell horses, and lift from my brother's ageing shoulders some of the tasks which all his life he had done for me. Soon I had a son-in-law too, a man of impeccable honesty, who had fought very bravely at Salamis. He had no money, but I preferred him to the others who offered themselves, saying I'd rather have a man without money than money without a man. I think the girl's kindly treated, and he makes himself useful to me.

So I had the money and the time to stir things up. When I knew the Peiraieus could be defended, and the ships were in good order, I began to manoeuvre against the Spartans. Not with the permission of the Athenians, but on my own, and by invitation from other cities. For so impressive was the might of Athens, and so corruptible were the Spartans in any city other than their own, that many cities began to wonder if democracy wouldn't suit them better than oligarchy, and meek allegiance to Sparta. Mantineia, for instance, and Elis, and the scattered towns of mountainous Arkadia came to me for advice. In Argos there was already a democracy, eager for allies. I travelled round, invited here and there as an honoured guest, doing for the cities of the Peloponnese what Theseus, they say, did for Athens when he made Attica one place. I helped them to draw up their laws, always giving every town and village, every homestead, in their whole territory equal rights with the men of the city, carefully establishing a democracy based on demes, so that one faction, or one interest, as of town against country, agriculture against trade, should have no possibility of unfairly outvoting another. Inspired by my model constitutions the Argives drew in Tiryns, and united with her. It was harder to unite the Arkadians, scattered in their harsh and spectacular landscape, with many small towns and no cities, but I managed it. And the new democracies of all these cities joined in alliance with Argos, an alliance which stretched in unbroken line across the northern Peloponnese, between Sparta and her precious Isthmus; between Sparta and my beloved Athens.

The Spartans were thoroughly alarmed; they appealed to Kimon to stop me. But not even Kimon could get anywhere in Athens attacking me for making democracies in other cities. He called it 'troublemaking' and I would stand up blandly smiling, and say that I had been asked for advice, and had recommended laws just like our own. Which particular aspect of Athenian law did Kimon find troublesome, or object to the Mantineians having, or the Elians, or the Argives. So for a long while I kept him at bay.

It was while I was working on the Argive alliance that my agents ran into other agents, coming out of Sparta. For a long while I regarded them with suspicion, thinking they were playing a double game. Then I was riding through the mountains one day, coming down from Arkadia to Tegea, with an escort of Tegeans to bring me there, when my path was blocked in a lonely place by a small party of Spartans lying in wait for me, and Pausanias among them. He had set up a tent by the road, with a dinner laid out in it, and couches, and he invited me to rest and eat.

'Only if these friends of mine are welcome too,' I said. I couldn't afford to be seen hobnobbing in secret with a Spartan.

'Welcome indeed,' he said, 'and all I have to say is for their ears also.' So we all went in to eat with him.

'It's clever, what you're up to, Themistokles,' he said, 'but I can improve on it, if you'll let me. You cement your anti-Spartan league, and then I'll raise the helots, and with luck the Messenians as well. Between us we'll wipe Sparta off the map, and then you can come down into Lakedaimon, and make a democracy there!'

'Steady on, steady on, Pausanias!' I said. 'One thing at a time. You must tell us clearly what you are doing.' It seemed from his talk he was already conspiring with helots and Messenians and making some progress. He said that it was easy, for there were always grievances from such iron rule as the Spartans practised, and he was confident he could set the land aflame. So before we went on our way we had agreed with him. He said he wanted to set his country free. 'It is a fortress,' he said, 'not a city. Both are trapped, those we hold down, and we ourselves, for fear makes us soldiers all our lives.' I don't doubt he thought he would rule Sparta, if he could bring off his revolution; perhaps he could have done. Anyway, between us all, we had a nice pot on the boil in which to cook the Spartan goose.

One last stone needed to be in place before we could move. I proposed to the Athenians that Athens should join in alliance with Argos and her friends. And that, to safeguard the fruits of our victories in the Aegean, we should now make peace with the King. I promised the Athenians that, if they would take my advice, they would be safe from the danger from Sparta, now and for ever. But Kimon said there was no danger from Sparta; the Spartans were our allies and the King our enemy. He proposed to reject offers of friendship from Argos and mount an expedition against the southern coasts of Asia Minor, or even to raise revolt in Egypt.

I had loyal adherents, and so had he, and many Athenians were undecided. So they set about choosing between us in the old way, by voting to hold an ostracism.

The attacks on me were very bitter. In the Assembly, of course, the ostracism itself could not be debated, while the question of the alliances which gave rise to it could. And on every street corner, and in every barber's shop, and at every market stall the ostracism was chewed over, till hatred rose over the city like a heat-haze. Kimon had plenty of tongues to wag for him; the Athenians, have this weakness – that they are jealous, that they hate to see a man excel. It was treachery they accused me of – I had deserted, so it went, to the side of the Medisers, to cities like Argos which had supported the King in the war, while Kimon remained faithful to the grand old cause.

I said it was common sense to have done with fighting the Persians when the Persian war was won. I said I was not supporting Argos because she had Medised, but because she would make common cause with us against Sparta. 'Can you not see the danger? Do you not know that the Spartans, being jealous of any power but their own will crush us if they can?' They could not see it. 'Athenians! my fellow citizens, my friends, surely you will not believe that *I* am a Mediser? For when there was really a danger from the King, who did more to avert it than I? And what's all this talk about how often I take bribes? Don't look for instances when I have taken money, of which I admit there have been many;

look for an instance when a bribe has moved me to act against your interests in the smallest particular – you will not find a single one.' So it went on, Athenian politics, undamaged by the war, back to the usual bitter, invigorating brew.

'Don't listen to Themistokles! Aristeides did as much as he to send the Persians packing!'

And I answered, 'The-day-after-the-Festival once taunted the Festival Day, and said, "You bring nothing but anxiety and trouble, but when I come along people can enjoy at their leisure everything they have been getting ready beforehand." The Festival Day replied, "True. But if I had not come first, you would not have come at all!" My friends, it's the same with us. If I had not been there on the day of Salamis, where would you all be now?'

I thought I was keeping my end up. I had plenty of friends standing by me. Xanthippos being dead a little while, young Pericles had his fortune. Pericles was choregos that year, and he put on a new play by Aeschylus, a play called *The Persians*, a play of the despair in Susa after the victory at Salamis. Aeschylus won the prize for it, too – it should have reminded the Athenians what I had done for them. I think I'd have scraped through somehow if it hadn't been for Aristeides. But when the day for the ostracism drew near it happened that I went to the Assembly, and found Aeschylus and Pericles and a few others barring my way. 'Don't go to your seat yet, Themistokles,' they said. 'A speech is being made against you. Wait here a little while.' I saw concern on their faces.

'I'm not afraid to hear what anyone has to say!' I said, and pushed past them. The speaker was Aristeides. Lean, black-mantled figure, like a crow, he stood before them, the wind flapping in his cloak like wings. 'It isn't as though it were a small thing,' he was saying. 'It's a great matter he puts before you. He'd have you unite with men who turned their backs on our danger, in order to protect yourselves against those who came to our aid. If you follow him there'll be a great upheaval, perhaps even war in Hellas. No wonder he wants peace with the King; but suppose we don't get it? Shall we fight both the Persians and Sparta? Shall we make peace with our enemies in order to be free to fight our fellow Greeks? Athenians, I don't deny Themistokles has reasons for proposing an alliance with Argos. His reasons sound good – he knows how to talk. Themistokles has always known how to talk, Athenians, has always had clever plans. But some of those plans are wicked, ignoble. It may be you will reject an alliance with Argos; but while Themistokles is among us you will never be safe from his tricks. He is a man who recommends wise and wrongful actions with equal forcefulness, and there is never a blush on his face, for he is without a conscience himself. While he is here there is always a chance he will sway you, will lead you astray. He is a dangerous man....'

Listening to all this I felt not anger, nor even grief, but only a great weariness of spirit. I am tired; tired of trying to convince people, tired with the effort of moving this vast concourse, persuading them, leading them. And they are ungrateful, and will not remember anything to my credit, though they can dredge up from my remotest youth even the slightest accusation my enemies ever made. Out it has all come again: I am a Metic, only a half-blood Athenian, I am a bastard, I take bribes, I write letters to Xerxes, I drag my feet punishing the Medisers ... a slimy conglomeration of half-truths, lies and misinterpretations. It's all enough, perhaps, to mislead mean minds, and the stupid throng of Kimon's hangers-on, and those who hate me because by setting the people free I have undermined their privileges – but how could all that mislead Aristeides? Aristeides, who knows me, has known me all his life? Aristeides who has worked with me, fought with me, talked with me, and when he has disagreed with me has lived to see me proved right? How *can* he believe I am a danger to the city? No, it must be he just wants revenge for his own ostracism. But he could not.... He is Aristeides the Just who never stoops to pettiness. I did not, could not, do not understand. But he took the heart out of me.

Nevertheless, I told my family that I would speak in reply the next day. 'You will speak well, father,' said Archeptolis, my eldest son. 'But the truth is it will do no good. They are just sick of the sound of your voice.' So I did not speak. And, with Aristeides' help, I was the man they ostracised.

🏛🏛🏛

'They used to use sherds with my name on to fill up the holes in the streets,' I said. 'And tough-wearing sherds they were, too, I've heard. I suppose they'd run out of them!' And the glum-faced crowd gathered round me laughed, glad to see that I still looked indestructible.

To my wife I said, 'No, you must stay here, and so must the children. My brother will befriend you at need, or Epikrates.'

'You are cruel!' she said, holding her head high. 'Do you think I am asking to go with you because I am afraid of going friendless? You may have regretted many times the first way you looked at me, but you married me, and it is my right to serve you, to go with you, and be of use to you.'

'Have courage,' I said to her. 'I do make use of you in leaving you here. I must have it known that this is a setback, a temporary setback, and that I expect to return.'

Pericles said to me, 'One day, one day, I will smash Kimon!'

'His turn will come,' I said to him, 'and so, in the long run, will yours. But don't write off anyone too soon!'

I kept my dignity for the whole of my ten days' grace; packed up my goods, chose a slave or two to accompany me, received my distressed friends, and bade them farewell. Archeptolis wanted to come with me, and I let him come, indulging myself with the thought of his company to stave off loneliness.

When everything was ready for my departure, I went down to my house at Peiraieus, to sleep the night there, and take ship at first light. I could not sleep; and a bright moon kept off the comforting darkness, lighting my room like a ghost of the day. And a great foreboding came over me, and I knew two things that were to be true, though I cannot say how I knew them – that I would never return to Athens the place I loved, and that in all the world else there was no other place in which I would long prefer life to death.

Other men have talents that they can take with them; they are good soldiers perhaps, or good potters. Megakles can take his blue blood and his talent for horse-racing and his gold to Delphi, and still be Megakles there, and Aristeides, I am very sure, took his virtue wherever he went; but I have excelled at leading the Athenians, and without the Athenians what am I?

But when the moon set I slept, and with the morning had recovered my sense of proportion. My ship was ready at the jetty, and beside it a small crowd of people, most of them weeping, waited to see me off. Even Simonides, poor, withered, frail old man, had had himself carried down in a litter to embrace me for the last time.

'My friends,' I said to them, 'do not weep. I have been ostracised, not condemned to death. For a while the Athenians will turn their back on the policies I have recommended to them, but the wind will change. In a while they will see sense and recall me. Look at it this way; I have only to win one victory in the Peloponnese, and the Athenians will see the value of what I was offering them; while Kimon, who trades on his victories, has only to bring one defeat, and he will go the way his father went. I need good hope from you all, not tears. This is a brief farewell.' In the bright light of morning I really believed my own brave words. And it was not an idle but a reasonable hope I laid before them. It was a reasonable hope, though the fulfilment has been longer in coming than I thought possible, and now has come too late. So the ship put out to sea; and I stood a long while in the stern, looking at the Acropolis fading and diminishing into a blue haze, and the land fell away behind us. And I went to Argos, where they received me gladly, and gave me a house, and made me an adviser to their generals, and where I hoped to achieve great things for Athens, whether she would or no.

I have been walking in the shadowy garden a little, my Lord Artaxerxes, to rest my fingers that are aching from holding the stylus. I watched the moon sink, and the fixed stars begin their setting, one by one. I have only the dregs of the night left, and the end of a tale to tell you. Coming in I filled and trimmed the lamp myself, since the little boy is asleep. He is only a slave, it's true, but then, what more am I? I did not want to wake him.

My alliance in the Peloponnese did well enough. Better than one could have expected, without the help of Athens. Almost at once we captured Mycenae, and drove the Spartans off the Argive plain. I rode through Mycenae's strange and ancient gate, over which a pair of lions rear, pawing a pillar of stone, like Agamemnon coming home. Then there was a battle at Tegea, for the Spartans were very alarmed, and they counter-attacked. We sent messages to Pausanias, to make a diversion, by letting loose his helots, and then we waited for the invincible enemy, with a plan of battle drawn up by me. I worked out that a division of hoplites was like a ship being rammed – the thing to do was to take evasive action.

The Spartans seemed long in coming – I hoped that was Pausanias' doing – and every day more young men came in to us, young Athenians, who came each of his own accord to volunteer. They came because of me. I remember one group of twenty who arrived the day before the battle and offered their services.

'It amazes me,' I said smiling, 'that so many men who unlike me could be in Athens this spring choose not to be.'

'I speak for us all, sir,' said one of them, 'when I say that for us Athens is where you are.'

At least I have been able to inspire love as well as hatred.

When the Spartans came up to Tegea, we would not meet them with all our forces in the field. Instead we sent skirmishing parties against them, and ambushed every defile, every turn of the hills.

As soon as they wheeled, and brought a phalanx to bear, we broke and ran. They claimed a victory, having put us to flight, but in fact our losses were small, and we withdrew in good order within the walls of Tegea, and they could not take the city. They laid siege to it for a while. Anxiously we waited for Pausanias to stir up trouble that would force them to draw off their forces. Nothing happened. But reinforcements were on the way to us from Arkadia, where the men are always slow to muster, and from other cities in our league, and before they reached us the Spartans proclaimed a victory, and left. It was a poor sort of victory that left Tegea undamaged, her green fields unscorched, still free to make what treaties, and with whom, she pleased. A Spartan victory to cheer Sparta's every enemy!

But when they withdrew news reached us again, and we learned what had happened to Pausanias. He had trusted a man who had betrayed him. He had, we were told, sent some fellow with a letter to Xerxes, and he had taken it to the Ephors instead. I don't know how much truth there is in it; I suppose Pausanias could have been writing to the King. He was rash enough. Anyway, they accused him of treason, and he took refuge in a temple – the temple of Athene of the brazen house – flinging himself at the foot of the altar, and demanding the protection of the gods. Then they bricked up the doorway, and, climbing up, took off the roof tiles, leaving the temple open to the sky, and left him there to die. They say he lived for five days and five nights, slowly starving. Then at the last minute, they opened a way in, and brought him out, so that his death might not defile their temple. He died in their hands, as they carried him down the steps.

He was my friend. To this day I wake sometimes, at night, hearing hands bricking up the doors, hearing hands taking off the roof, seeing a starved man crawling endlessly at the angle of the wall and floor. This is the fate that waits for men who lead the Greeks to victory. Kleomenes dies in prison from the knife; Miltiades lies helplessly rotting away alive, while lesser men pass judgement; Pausanias dies slowly like an unwanted dog; that leaves me. What would they do to me? I still had hopes; if only Kimon were defeated; if he lost a battle now, just now, while we still hold Tegea, all would yet be well. I prayed to the gods he would lose; just this once. But he came home in triumph from Eurymedon, with a shining victory to his credit. And that was the end for me.

The Athenians might not notice the significance of our success at Tegea, but the Spartans had noticed all right. They attacked

Argos, and crushed the democracy, bringing back the old oligarchs from exile, by force of arms, and setting up a tyrannical, pro-Spartan government there. By the grace of the gods I was in Arkadia, training men when it happened, or I should have fallen into their hands. And Kimon, from the dizzy height of his glory with the Athenians, offered to bring Athens down into the Peloponnese at last – but to fight on the Spartan side! Indeed he is worth every rich present the Spartans ever lavished on him! Mantineia deserted to Sparta at once, and a few other cities with her, but even that didn't extinguish the fires of freedom altogether. Tiryns, which had been happy under my constitution, revolted at once from the new government of Argos, and the Arkadians helped her. In vain; they were defeated. Pausanias' long-awaited helot-revolt broke out too late, to be crushed in a sea of blood. But before either of these last disasters I was in headlong flight.

The Spartans claimed that they had found certain letters of Pausanias, which implicated me in his plot with the King. That cannot have been true; wild enough though Pausanias' lack of judgement sometimes was, he had not been fool enough to tell me what he was up to there. If, indeed, the whole thing was not a lie, and he had been up to anything. But the Spartans sent an embassy to Athens, demanding that since I, too, had committed treason I should receive the same punishment as Pausanias. Then Leobotes, son of Alkmeon, one of Kimon's jackals, brought a prosecution against me, which I could not return to answer because of the ostracism. I sent letters in answer, but I knew they would do no good. Kimon and the Spartans sent men to find me, and bring me, they said, before the panhellenic council – that cloudy hope that Aristeides made after Plataia. If they had caught me, they would have made a murder their first and last action together. I didn't wait to be caught.

The Elians shipped me over to Corcyra, where I was respected as a friend, because years before I had not unfairly favoured Corinth in settling a dispute. They were kindly. They said they did not believe the charges against me, but they dared not harbour me. For who could resist the combined might of Athens and Sparta? And the arresting party was close on my heels. They offered to take me westwards, but I had to refuse, because I had gratuitously offended Hieron of Syracuse, when I stopped his horses from competing in the games. In the west his arm would be long, and I felt sure he would hand me over as soon as he was asked for me. I requested instead a passage to Epirus, thinking I might find refuge, or even a place as an adviser among the mixed people there. But the agents of the Greeks were there before me, seeking everywhere, offering gold in handfuls, so that I was in mortal danger, and fled into the hills, taking goat paths over the mountains, into the land of the Molossians.

I have told you this story many times, Great King, making light of it, making jokes over my narrow escapes. I did not tell you that I was cold, and weary, and hungry, that my clothes were in rags, and my wealth reduced to one leather bag carried on my own shoulders, for I had sent all my companions and my son away, from a wish that they should escape my danger if they could. Only one slave remained with me, and he could not carry the load all the time, on such steep paths as we took. I have not told you that I was terrified, sick and trembling with fear of death. Even death, my lord, has many faces. How I recoiled from the long humiliation, the fetters, the abuse of my enemies, and then the long slow hunger; or the kick in the back, and the fall, and the twitching death on the rocks in the pit that the Athenians would have inflicted instead! I recoiled, I, who have outstared death fearlessly when it glared over battlefields. I who go now to meet it gladly, and find it wearing the face of a longed-for friend. But the death of a criminal made a coward out of me; and I fled friendless from one place to another, with only bitterness against the Athenians and hatred of Kimon to keep me warm.

The kingdom of the Molossians, too, was full of men looking for me. And Admetos, the king there, was helping in the search, declaring that I had snubbed him once in my great days, and he would enjoy revenge. What had I done to him? I could scarcely remember. Some embassy or other. But I saw I would never get out of his land, for his men were holding the passes into Macedon, and on the watch for me. So I went to his house of my own accord. Athene, who guided Odysseus on his journeys, and who loves me also, I would swear, although you tell me she is only a phantom of a greater god, must have guided my steps. For when I reached Admetos' house, he was hunting, and his servants brought me into the presence of his wife, Phthia, the queen.

I said to her, 'Have pity, Lady.'

'Who are you?' she said, and her voice was not unkind.

'I am Themistokles,' I said to her, 'who was once a great captain, and now is hunted through your kingdom like a wolf. Help me if you can.'

She said, 'My husband will not refuse a suppliant, if he is asked in the old way, the way that must not be refused. You must sit in the ashes of the hearth, and hold his son in your arms. If he denies you then, the gods will punish him through the child.' Hardship makes a man swifter to think of others. 'Lady,' I said, 'do you believe this, too?'

'Yes,' she said quietly.

'And, believing it, you will give your babe into my arms?'

'Trust me,' she said, 'he will come to no harm.'

She brought tears to my eyes, and I let them fall, hoping to touch her heart. I called her Queen Arete, after the story of Odysseus, who also was forced to ask help from strangers, and received it. And later I sent her a necklace of Persian gold. But for the moment I did what she said, sitting in the grime of his fireside, and holding his baby to my heart. 'Admetos,' I said to him, 'when I injured you in the past, it was not a matter of life and death; but if you revenge yourself now, it is to death you will consign me.'

Then he held out his hands to me, and raised me up, and said, 'You are safe.' And at that moment there came a commotion at the doors of his palace, and the Spartans and Athenians were outside, saying they had tracked me to his very doors, and asking him to hand me over. Admetos brought them in to where I was standing, and showed them the child in my arms, and declared he could not refuse to protect me, for fear of the gods. Then there was a fierce dispute, and threats were flying around, and my head was spinning from hunger, and from the heat of the fire, burning so near beside me, and also I think from shame at being seen by those Greek curs in such a woeful state, so that in a while I pitched forwards onto the floor, swooning. And when I woke it was to find myself washed and laid in a clean bed, with slaves hovering ready to bring me food.

I knew then what I must do. There is only one place in the world that is safe from the Athenians and the Spartans both; and that is your land, Great King. 'If I go to the King,' a part of me protested, 'it will be forever believed against me that the charge of treason was true.' But a stronger voice answered, 'They shall not have my death, as well as my victory.' And so Admetos put me on my way, sending me to the sea at Pydna, crossing the land on foot, with a party of goat-footed mountain-folk to guide me on obscure paths, in case I was followed and taken. And at Pydna I found a merchant vessel, bound for Ionia, and took a passage on her, keeping myself unknown. Or so I hoped; there were several men on board who stared, and kept asking if they had seen me before somewhere. 'Very likely,' I answered, uneasily, 'I've travelled.'

Then we were driven before a storm, and the captain ran for cover to Thasos; and there was a great multitude of ships, besieging the harbour. I knew those ships; every familiar line of them, every spar, every painted prow and gilded owl. The grace of sea-birds, and the power of armies, beauty to break the heart, and death to the man who made them! I had no idea what the Athenians were doing, investing an island that was supposed to be an ally. I went to the captain, and declared myself, and told him he must not draw inshore, or let anyone on the ship disembark, for if he did not save my life I would say he had been bribed to carry me, or anything else that would incriminate him. So much I have told you before; did I also tell you that he laid a hand on my arm, and said, 'There's no need to threaten me, Themistokles. I'm not one of your great men. Just a plain seafaring man, trading out of Pydna for the best terms I can get. I'm not the man to sell Themistokles.'

So for my sake he rode at anchor for a seasick day and a night, lying in the lee of the land, but standing well off the Athenian station, and at length he arrived off Ephesos. I did not wish to disembark among all the other passengers, in the midst of a city, where there might well be agents already on the watch for me, so he put me ashore in a lonely place, landing me on the beach, me and my slave, and my bundle.

For a long time I sat upon the shore, in abject misery. The Great Kings had been the enemy against whom I had spent the greater part of my life in struggle. It is no small thing to throw oneself into the arms of such an enemy, and I had heard much of the tyranny of the Kings, and little good of them, not of your father, Xerxes, nor of your grandfather Darius, and less than nothing about you, my Lord Artaxerxes, then newly made Great King. I had no means of knowing that you would be more to me than merciful, that you would be a friend. Indeed, who could dream of finding friendship on a throne? When I had sat dejectedly for a long while, and the sun was past its highest in the sky, I was thirsty, and told my slave to bring me water from a little stream that trickled from the rocks a small way off.

'How shall I bring it, sir?' he asked.

'There's a cup in my baggage, somewhere,' I said, and delved in my leather sack. And bringing out my drinking-cup I found that somehow on the way it had been broken. Then I sat with a piece in either hand, and wept till my head ached, and my eyes burned, and my throat was stinging with salt. It was the cup I had brought with me from Argos, and before that from Athens. The cup I had carried over to Salamis, and in triumph brought back again; the one thing I had always had, that had come with me unbroken all the way. It was my father's cup, that Exekias made. What was it my father said? He showed me an old hulk abandoned on the shore, and said, 'This is how the people treat their leaders, when they have no further use for them.'

No master could be worse to serve than the Athenian people, not even the Great King. So I turned my back on the shore, and the sun setting in the west, my Lord, and came to seek you, to serve you if I could.

From the first moment I reached your court, Lord Artaxerxes, I have met with ceaseless jealousy and suspicion from the princes and nobles who serve you – some of them would be vicious enough to survive in a democracy! – and ceaseless generosity from you. Thus, on the first day on which I came to you, Artabanos your servant tried to prevent me from getting an audience, on the grounds that being a Greek I would insult you by refusing to make the usual obeisance. That caused me a certain bitter mirth – as if a man who has grovelled in ashes at the feet of the petty chieftain of the Molossians would hesitate to bow before the Great King! He was right, of course, when he said Greeks find the ways of the Persians overpoweringly strange. Being a Greek, I was dazzled by your magnificence; your encrusted throne, your shining garments stiff with gold and silver thread, by the number and glittering splendour of your attendants, and the great diamond in the head of your staff of office. Dazzled, my lord, and repelled. I expected only brutality to exist in such terrible glory. I gave you my name in fear, in fear of death. The web of speech I had prepared seemed threadbare enough. The heart of it, the only part that had the merit of truth to it was the last bit, for the help I claimed to have given your father, consisted of two messages, the one which had lured his fleet to destruction, and the other, on the subject of the retreat across the Hellespont bridges, which I had in reality never sent. Only the last of it was true: 'I am persecuted by the Hellenes for your sake.'

And you were generous with me from the first, granting me at once the year's grace I asked for in which to learn your language, and then telling your treasurer to pay me the two hundred talents you 'owed' me, since that sum had been promised to anyone who brought me alive before your throne! I was very startled to be thus joked with; looking up boldly at you for the first time, I gazed not into the blood-lusting, vengeful eyes of a gold-gorged monster, but into the level gaze of a young man, triumphant, and amused.

I did well to learn Persian. So jealous are men of your favour, my Lord, that a man who has you for friend has all the world else for enemy, and I should certainly have been done to death by mistranslation long ago had I not been able to speak for myself. As I say, I have been surrounded by suspicion, and have had to take care of my reputation in your lands. To be truthful, not all the suspicion has been groundless. I gave grounds to the satrap of Lydia, for instance, when travelling in his district I visited the temple of the Great Goddess at Sardis, and saw in it the little water-girl, holding a jar, that I had had made for Athens, long ago. I was overwhelmed with emotion, seeing her there, and the exile of that lovely lifeless green-eyed girl seemed so much harder to bear than my own, that I asked the satrap to take money for her ransom, and send her home. He thought I was merely trying to make gestures to the Athenians. He threatened to report me to you, for having a heart still Greek, although I professed to serve you. I had to bribe half his harem to make him change his mind. Then Epixyes, the satrap of Phrygia, has it in for me, too. His grounds are that he got hold of some of the money I coined in the mint at Magnesia. Half of them are silver, and the other half plated copper, and they all have my name on them. Well, I meant the plated ones only for trading with Athens, and I owed the Athenians a bad turn. I grant you it was very unfortunate that some found their way to Phrygia. But Epixyes took his vengeance rather far; for it was he, I am almost sure, who ambushed me on that journey, and tried to murder me. I told you at the time I did not know who had done it; I didn't want you to get to hear of the coins.

I know that your pleasure in my coming was real enough, Great King, for your mother, who has made me her friend and adviser has often told me how you prayed to Ahriman the dark god to make your enemies always of the same mind, that they chased away their ablest men. It seems to me Ahriman manages Athens for you very well! Amestris your mother says also that the night I came you were heard crying out in your sleep three times for joy, 'I have Themistokles the Athenian!'

For all that you have given me, Great King, I am grateful, I give you thanks. Perhaps you will say, 'He had three cities, Magnesia for his house, and for his governing, and Lampsakos to yield him wine, and Myous to yield him meat, and this was not enough?' My Lord, it is more than enough. My house is wide, and beautiful, rich within with carpets and hangings embroidered with flowers, furnished with couches and chairs of cedarwood and boxwood, floored with marble in many colours, and full of obedient slaves, and affectionate friends. And around it is a planted paradise, a small copy of yours, full of flowers and choice trees, and green places in which to walk, and breathe air sweetened with musk and pine. There had been some delight or other all day long to keep me content. Have I not had dozens of wine-cups set upon my table — goblets of fluted gold, each upright on the back of a crouching golden beast with jewels for eyes, all to console me for the loss of one cup of painted clay?

In truth I have much to be thankful for. And I have many debts to you which go deeper than thanks for gifts of wealth. You have made me a great man as well as a wealthy one. Have I not been admitted to your family, invited to walk within the last doors, and talk to you as a friend? I have sat at your table, and ridden on your hunting parties, like a well-loved brother. You make much of me, and though I have many enemies none dare treat me openly other than with respect. And Persians of high rank come to me, consulting me, asking my advice on how to win your favours. I have turned into a Persian of high rank.

After my first astonishment, for instance, at meeting women familiar with the world, and intelligent about affairs of state, and through my affectionate respect for your mother, I brought myself after a while to allow my own womenfolk freedom to live in the Persian fashion. I am a man with many daughters, and this life has made them as much a joy to me as sons, for they will walk and ride with me now, or sit and talk politics quite sensibly, and with seeming pleasure, as though behind their delicate lovely faces and bright eyes they had after all souls like the souls of men. The Magi whom you graciously sent me, to instruct me in the true religion, would have me believe it so. I was not disappointed when the last of my children, the only one to be born in your kingdom, was also a girl. I named her Asia.

There are other things, seeming smaller, which have bound me more closely to you, which have made the decision I make now harder to come to. That out of three cities you gave me, you chose two which look upon the sea. And then, like a dog that comes fawning and begging at the mere smell of meat, I have come to you inwardly yearning for the merest sniff of power; and with that abstracted, slightly amused gaze of yours, you have filled my dish and fed me, giving me commissions to carry out for you, hearing my advice on Persian affairs, hearing it and taking it, and when it proved good rewarding me, with gold, and with an ever more willing attention to my words. It has been more profitable to persuade you, Great King, than to persuade the Assembly of the Athenians to their own advantage. It is true my advice has been good, has been well worth your taking; but in your taking it I have felt your pity, your compassion for me. Never more than when once Damaratos, your Spartan dog-in-exile, offended you. He is a fool; he always was. He wanted, you remember, to be allowed to ride through Sardis, wearing a crown on his head. And I pleaded forgiveness for him. You were very angry. You raged at his insolence.

'He is homesick,' I told you. 'It is homesickness that has gone to his head. It isn't to challenge your power that he asks for his crown, it's just to feel the weight of it on his brows again. Oh, King, Great King, the Hellenes at your court are far from the land they love. You give them all the heart could desire, all that a King can give. But not even you, Great King, King of the Lands, can make the flowers bloom here as freely as they do on the other shore. Not even you can make a man forget his earliest home. Because he was a king in Sparta, it is a crown Damaratos misses most; but it is kingship in Sparta he is dreaming of, not kingship here.'

'You speak eloquently today,' you said to me. 'And you were never a king. What loss of yours, is it, Themistokles, which gives you such feeling for his?'

'I did have power — power to persuade and influence affairs, when I had freedom,' I said. It took courage to say as much. But your anger faded from your eyes, and you let my plea succeed, and spared Damaratos.

Your mercy, Great King, has enslaved me, because I have loved you for it, as a dog loves the master who feeds it, and of whom it is yet afraid. As Sikinnos my slave loved me once because I did not beat him, a thing for which I had no cause, and which it never crossed my mind to do. Even so, you have never crushed me; never made me feel powerless, and thus you have bound me to you.

Yet for a long while, in my heart I hoped to go home. A time would come, I always knew it would one day come, when Kimon would fall from favour, and the Athenians would see clearly again, and when that happened they would recall me. I have always intended to go. I knew just how the journey would be arranged; I would ride to Lampsakos, giving this or that business matter as a reason, to all my friends. Lampsakos, where every day one sees the corn ships for Athens sailing down, swiftly born homewards on the current in the Hellespont. There I would take ship, myself, for home. But not till they kicked Kimon out – if I have to be tried for treason I want a fair trial. I could not go home while he runs the city like his bean-patch. It doesn't take much imagining what he would do to me if he could; in small things and in great he is vindictive and cruel. That story that goes around, that sending letters to your father I chose servants 'from whom not even torture would drag out the truth' – the ugly truth behind that is that torture was used, in an attempt to make them lie to incriminate me. Kimon ordered the use of torture, a thing that has not been done in Athens since Hippias used it on Aristogeiton, extracting names. But Kimon did it.

Then Kimon, judging the Dionysia, put Aeschylus, with nine victories in a row to his credit, second to some obscure youth called Sophocles; that was to spite Aeschylus for writing *The Persians*. Worst of all he prosecuted Epikrates, my friend, who in friendship had smuggled my family out of Athens, and brought them to me, and Epikrates was put to death. For all that Kimon can't stop news and gifts from reaching me; even Epikrates' death has not extinguished affection for me at home. I have had news from home, and visitors, for it's easy enough to slip over the hills from Ephesos, and arrive at my door. Plenty of gossip has reached me. Timocreon, for instance, has been writing gloating lyrics on my downfall:

> 'Timocreon was not the only Greek,
> To make a deal with the Persians; many more
> Were no less guilty, other foxes too
> Have lost their tails!'

That came in a letter from Simonides. 'You will hear this sometime, from someone,' he wrote, 'so I send it with this other, as balm for its sting.' 'This other' was a mock epitaph for Timocreon, that made me laugh:

He comes out of an alien land

'Your tippling over, your guzzling done,
You're lying still, Timocreon!'

Simonides is dead now; no more elegant words from him. But
other men bring me news. And, however dark the news is, however
savagely Kimon triumphs, I have never doubted that he would fall;
the facts are against him. I was right. His time has come now.

My latest letters from home bring news that he took an army
out of Athens, to help the Spartans put down a helot revolt – there's
a brave cause in which to enlist Athenians! – and the Spartans, it
seems, didn't feel they could trust a democratic ally, so they sent
him packing, and he came home looking a fool. Now, I am told, the
streets buzz with indignation. 'However loyal we are to Sparta,
they treat us with contempt and suspicion ... perhaps Argos would
have been the better friend after all....' Aeschylus writes that his
latest play was in praise of the Argives, for sheltering a suppliant,
and that it was warmly received.... It will be all over for Kimon
now. Give them a month or two, or three, and the Athenians will
vote for my recall. A ship will come full of gifts, and old friends
overflowing with joy, and old enemies speaking uneasy flattery. It
will come; but it has been long in coming, and comes now too late.
For now that the chance is before me, I know that I will not go.

I remember bare, draughty houses, and a life of walking the
streets. For that I would have to leave this house, pleasant with
scarlet and gold, and my horses, and my chariots. These last few
nights I have not dreamed of Pausanias' death, and have dreamed
instead of home. I dream I am addressing the Assembly, a wall, a
sea of faces, from which a great murmur of voices rises continu-
ously. Every face is turned upon me; they are blank faces in which
I can distinguish the features, or recognise the countenance of
none. I am speaking to them, but my voice has grown feeble with
all that whispering in the King's ear, and it blows away on the
buffeting sharp spring wind. I lose my way in my speech, falter,
fall silent.... When I wake this dream makes me afraid. I give
myself other reasons for shrinking. 'Shall I take my wife and
daughters away from this open life, and lock them in small bare
rooms?' I ask myself. 'Shall I leave my dear Persian friends?' But
the truth is I have been corrupted by wealth and ease, Great King.
Your gifts have softened me. When we had to take ship for Salamis,
long ago, my Lord, and the people had to sleep on a windy island,
without shelter from the open air, the young were glowing and
invigorated, but the old men caught agues and died. I am an old

man now; an open life will chill old bones, cloud an old mind. I had much better stay indoors. Let them send for me when they like. I have longed for it. But I will not go home.

Yet if I stay, Great King, I must face the promises I made, the lies I told you. All this while those promises have been moonshine, no nearer to fulfilment than the chance of my being called home, and now like that chance, they loom over me, for your last letter speaks of preparing a move against Athens. If I stay I must keep my promises.

I swore I would enslave the Hellenes to you. I am terrified by what I swore. For comfort I tell myself, 'You could not do it. You are mad, Themistokles, you have promised what you could not perform. Remember what happened to Hippias, who doubtless made the same oath to Darius; remember what happened to him, crawling away into a ship with failure all around him, and dying on the return journey. That is where Hippias' example leads.' But I know that I am not he; I am infinitely more capable, more cunning. And I know that the Greeks would have lost their freedom last time, had I not been there, and that, old man though I am, I might yet do much. If I set myself to this task, I might yet do much. What possessed me to promise to do it? Nothing, I know, seems more vile to Persians than tricks and false oaths, yet do not think me vile, Lord Artaxerxes, for when I swore I meant to keep faith with you. I was in danger, and in need of your protection, and I wanted to seem useful to you; but also I was full of hatred and bitterness against my enemies, and fresh from my sufferings on my flight, and in bitterness I meant to do what I swore.

But the bitterness did not last. It has drained away from me like water poured on to sand. How long, indeed, could I hate the men who drove me here, where I have been prosperous, influential and content? You yourself swiftly healed my bitterness. It is true I have cause for revenge. I gave them their freedom, and they have repaid me by robbing me of mine. But now the dice are thrown I will not take my revenge. In all my long life I have never done anything yet that harmed my native city, and I will not do it now. Forgive me, O Great King, but I will not Medise. That accusation was false, and false it shall remain. False also was that other reproach, that there was nothing, however iniquitous, that I would shrink from if it served my purpose. For at last I do shrink from a practical wickedness and, rather than hurt the Athenians, choose death. Aristeides will get to hear of it. May he see at last that, though I

252

was not always honest, I was always right, and acknowledge that I loved Athens as truly as he.

A grey dawn creeps up now from the eastern hills. I cannot yet see that the land is green, but I can see the pale winding ribbon of the Maeander, with a faint shimmer of light upon it, and on the hill behind the garden the pale asphodel shows forth dimly in the darkness. I go to my death with only one burden on my mind – the deceit I have practised on you, Lord Artaxerxes. I made two claims when first I came to you – that I would help you in the future, and that I had helped you in the past, and the one, it turns out, was as little use as the other. And yet ... were you indeed deceived, my Lord? It has often struck me that you were unusually credulous about it. You had only to ask in the archives for the letters I claimed to have sent, and you would have unmasked the fraud. When I was amused to use all the slanders and lies that followed me to Persia, and turn them to my advantage, can it be that you knew all the time, and that you too were amused? Perhaps, after all, you did not expect anything from me. I never dared to ask, and now will never know.

A bright disc of gold rises above the hills across the valley now. They expect me in the temple at dawn, to sacrifice a bull to Poseidon, petitioning for the welfare of the citizens. I have been told that poison taken in bull's blood brings death swiftly and without disfigurement, so that is the path I shall take. Do not fear for me, lest Ahura Mazda, your great truthful god, is angry with me for the lies I have told; I am not afraid, having learned that a better welcome in the courts of the mighty waits for those who present themselves of their own accord.

Farewell, Great King.

THUS SAITH ARTAXERXES, THE KING, THE GREAT KING, THE ACHAEMENID: THE LETTER WHICH YOU HAVE SENT TO ME, I HAVE HEARD. GREAT IS MY AFFECTION FOR THEMI-STOKLES, MY SERVANT. LET HIS FAMILY INHERIT HIS LAND. LET THEM BE CONSIDERED THE FRIENDS OF THE KING.

AUTHOR'S NOTE

This is a work not of scholarship, but of imagination, and as such does not require a bibliography. My debt to A. R. Burn's *Persia and the Greeks* (Edward Arnold, 1962) is, however, exceptional. I gratefully acknowledge that I have almost everywhere followed his reconstruction of events, and that I owe to his fine book also a constant renewal of enthusiasm for the subject. The general reader who wonders how much of my book is history could not do better than to read Mr Burn; such a reader will also enjoy Plutarch's Lives of Themistokles and Aristeides, which are readily available under the title *The Rise and Fall of Athens* as a Penguin Classic (1960).

Herodotus was the father of historical fiction, as well as of history; in several cruces I have allowed myself to ignore the most reasonable grounds for doubting him advanced by modern scholars, because I like his version better. On naval tactics I have consulted J. S. Morrison and R. T. Williams, *Greek Oared Ships* (Cambridge University Press, 1968), and William Ledyard Rogers, *Naval Warfare Under Oars* (United States Naval Institute, Md. 1970). My account of Themistokles' activities in Argos is based on an article by W. G. Forrest in the *Classical Quarterly* (1960). The transcription of Greek proper names has presented difficulties; I have written 'Themistokles', 'Kleisthenes', etc., without taking consistency so far as to write 'Korinth' or 'Kassandra', for obvious reasons. Naturally enough, all the mistakes and wild guesses there may be in my book are entirely my own, and owe nothing to the above authorities.

I am grateful to the following authors and publishers for permission to quote from their translations of classical texts: to Mr Gilbert Highet and Oxford University Press for the lyric by Solon on p. 27; to Mr A. R. Burn and Edward Arnold Ltd for the Troizen decree on p. 155 and the Plataian Oath on p. 213; to Oxford University Press for Simonides' Thermopylai Epitaph on p. 164; to Ian Scott-Kilvert and Penguin Books Ltd for the lyric by Timocreon on p. 250; to J. M. Edmonds and William Heinemann Ltd for the lyric by Simonides on p. 251. I have also made extensive paraphrases of speeches from the Everyman Library edition of

255

Author's note

Herodotus (1910) and from Benjamin Jowett's translation of Thucydides (1881).

I would also like to thank Mr Stephen Corcoran and Mr Kevin Crossley-Holland for help in rendering the Delphic Oracle and the fragments of Phrynichos' lost play; Commander R. G. Moore, U.S.C.G., for lending me *Naval Warfare under Oars*; Miss Hester Dekker, whose help has made time available for me to write, and above all my husband, whose admiration for Themistokles was the original source of mine.

J.P.W.